OLYMPIAD

By Tom Holt

THE WALLED ORCHARD
ALEXANDER AT THE WORLD'S END
OLYMPIAD

EXPECTING SOMEONE TALLER
WHO'S AFRAID OF BEOWULF?
FLYING DUTCH
YE GODS!
OVERTIME
HERE COMES THE SUN
GRAILBLAZERS
FAUST AMONG EQUALS
ODDS AND GODS
DJINN RUMMY
MY HERO
PAINT YOUR DRAGON
OPEN SESAME
WISH YOU WERE HERE
ONLY HUMAN
SNOW WHITE AND THE SEVEN SAMURAI
VALHALLA

I, MARGARET

LUCIA TRIUMPHANT
LUCIA IN WARTIME

OLYMPIAD

AN HISTORICAL NOVEL

TOM HOLT

LITTLE, BROWN AND COMPANY

A *Little, Brown* Book

First published in Great Britain by Little, Brown and Company 2000

Map by Neil Hyslop

A CIP catalogue record for this book
is available from the British Library.

ISBN 0 316 85390 9

Typeset in Plantin by M Rules
Printed and bound in Great Britain by CPD Wales

Little, Brown and Company (UK)
Brettenham House
Lancaster Place
London WC2E 7EN

For Natalie, who'll have to make do with what's left of history;

And for Calle, who sings the glories of heroes.

'Men die, cattle die; only the glory of heroes lives for ever'

VIKING PROVERB

'So they found Achilles taking his pleasure of a loud lyre, fair, of curious work, with a silver crossbar upon it; one he had taken from the spoils when he laid Eetion's city waste. Therein he was delighting his soul, and singing the glories of heroes'

ILIAD, BOOK IX

'Achilles replied, "Don't try to kid me about death, Odysseus;
I'd rather be alive, and slave to some pauper,
Some landless man, making a piss-poor living,
Than be king and kaiser of all the glorious dead"'

ODYSSEY, BOOK XI

'History is hard to know, because of the hired bullshit'

THE GREAT SHARK HUNT, HUNTER S. THOMPSON

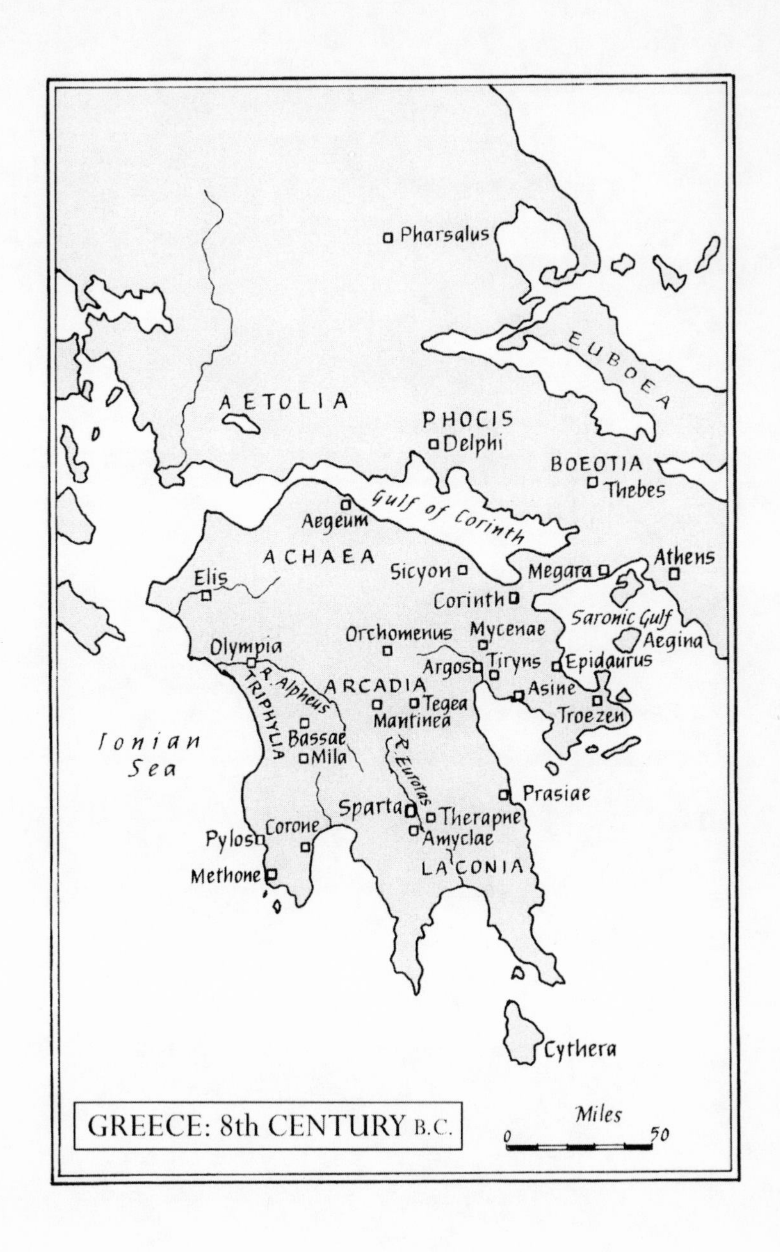

GREECE: 8th CENTURY B.C.

PROLOGUE: ABOUT HISTORY

(OR WHY TODAY'S DATE IS A MATTER OF OPINION)

History as we know it began in 776BC, near the Greek city of Elis, when some men we know next to nothing about ran from one pile of stones to another.

Anywhere you look, you'll see the date: day, month and year. Our days of the week are named after Norse gods; the names of the months are Roman; the third part of the formula tells us how many years have passed since a man called Jesus Bar-Joseph was reckoned to have been born, at Bethlehem in the Roman province of Judaea. We know the date of his birth because the Romans were good at dates and figures; they carried out a regular census, and they used a system of chronology based on the date of the foundation of the city of Rome (753BC, by our reckoning). If asked how they knew when their city was founded, the Romans would have put it into the context of the Olympiads – the tradition of holding athletic competitions every four years at Olympia, near Elis, on which the Greeks based their chronology.

So, if we trace it through (like film of a relay race run through the projector backwards), we know what year it is because the Christian church kept records based on the records kept by the Romans, who in turn integrated their chronology into the Greek tradition, which assumed as an article of faith that on a certain day in July or August (the second or third full moon after the summer solstice) some men ran 192 metres between two piles of stones in the one and only event of the First Olympiad, and that this event was reckoned to be so important by the people of Elis that they remembered it, held another games four years later, and carried on doing so at four-year intervals until humanity was sufficiently grown-up to find more scientific ways of calculating its place in time.

All we know about those first games (and for 'know', read 'take on trust') is that a man called Coroebus won a foot-race. At that time, of course, the Olympics weren't called the Olympics, nor was the place where they were held called Olympia. Later, as the games became an established part of Greek life, other events were added, the site was adorned with great and wonderful buildings, all wars stopped while the games were on and people came from all over the Greek world to watch them, until the first Christian emperor of Rome banned them as being too pagan for his taste, some 1,148 years later. There were no written records in those days (writing probably started in Greece at some point between 750BC and 650BC; the Greeks believed that the art was learned from the Phoenicians, or invented by a man called Palamedes, or both, or neither). This wasn't the Ancient Greece we know, the era of philosophers, dramatists, artists and politicians; in the eighth century BC, Greece was still in the Dark Ages that followed the total collapse of the civilisation we call Mycenean (what they called it is anybody's guess), materially poor and decidedly primitive in comparison with the great kingdoms of Egypt and the Middle East with their complex systems of government and neatly written state archives which recorded in great detail their many centuries of history.

But the great kingdoms were conquered and either destroyed or subsumed; the archives lay buried until the nineteenth century, when antiquarians dug them up and worked out how to read them – and, incidentally, revived the Olympic Games. Their records failed as works of history, the process by which what happened in the past is recorded and passed on to the future. History had to rely on the memory of Coroebus running between two piles of stones.

(The word 'history', of course, means different things in different languages. In Greek, 'historia' meant a question. It was the Romans, uncharacteristically slapdash with the phrase book, who gave it the meaning we've inherited. In French, 'histoire' means a story; colloquially, a lie. The Germans, typically, have no truck with such Romance ambiguities; their word for history is 'Geschichte' – onomatopoeia, I've always assumed, derived from generations of scholars sneezing over dusty old manuscripts.)

A neat analogy for history would be the Olympic flame, kept perpetually alive and transmitted across the world and down the years by the Olympic torch, from that first kindling over 2,750 years ago right down to tomorrow. The analogy would be neater still if the games hadn't lapsed for fifteen centuries, and if the flame and the torch weren't a masterly touch of Victorian showmanship, only dating back to the first modern Olympiad in 1896.

We have no idea what made that first foot-race so devastatingly memorable. The Greeks had been playing games for a long time before 776BC, traditionally as part of the funeral ceremonies of important men – as well as running, they jumped, boxed, wrestled, threw things and raced chariots, and prowess in the games was almost as important to them as prowess in battle. Whether Coroebus' victory stuck in their minds because it was Coroebus who won (whoever he might have been) or because the race marked some other important event long since forgotten, or just because it was a really exciting race and everybody enjoyed it so much they decided to do it again, is something we'll never know.

Appropriately, nearly all of what follows is pure fiction, though some of it is probably true, parts of it are possibly true, and much of it could conceivably be true for all we know.

Scholars, who are sceptical people not given to accepting anything without hard evidence, will tell you that the first Olympic foot-race was won by Coroebus of Elis. Their authority for this statement is a guidebook written nine hundred years after the first Games by one Pausanias. Pausanias is a credible witness because his book has survived where countless others haven't; it's *a* criterion of reliability, though perhaps not the best. Ancient manuscripts survived in many different ways; some were copied out over and over again by professional scribes, later by monks, a new copy being made when the old one fell to bits, so that the earliest manuscript of an ancient text may date from the Middle Ages. Some texts are represented by several copies (invariably slightly different); some only survived because they were cut up and used to bind other books. Quite a few pages of original papyrus manuscript have been found, mostly in Egypt; they range from substantial chunks of the *Iliad* to private letters and shopping lists. Very occasionally we find a list of dates, a genuine chronicle; but since every Greek state had a different calendar, with different names and lengths for the months and their own idea of when the year started and ended, even these aren't quite as rock solid as at first they seem to be. From these bits and pieces, together with a name scratched on the neck of a jar or the remains of an inscription on the base of a statue, generations of serious-minded men have built an artefact we call history. Very little of it would stand up as evidence in a court of law, where the burdens of proof are more stringent, and every ten years or so a new scrap of papyrus or scratched potsherd turns up that disproves the theories, scatters the pieces of the jigsaw and leaves them lying for the next generation of historians.

Pausanias never mentioned a King Leon, or two brothers called Cleander and Cratus, or their sister and uncle, or a Corinthian dynasty usurping power in Aegina; these are *genuine* fictions, reliably false. There is a certain amount of evidence, drawn from literature and archaeology, for how people lived and thought in the eighth century BC: their material poverty, their way of regarding emotions as the effects of external forces acting on them, the shape of their houses and sword-blades, some idea of what they ate and what they wore on their feet. There is a considerable amount of literary evidence that we know is almost certainly *not* true, such as the story, widely believed in antiquity, that the Olympic Games were founded by Hercules.

The sad fact is, we have no *proof* that Coroebus ever existed, or that the first Olympiad was held in 776BC, or that it was ever held at all – only fragments of records of stories of memories, a slovenly, unintentional relay race run by men who didn't know where they were going and who were in no hurry to get there. On that depends our knowledge of history, and on history depends our knowledge and understanding of who we are and how we got that way.

If Coroebus hadn't existed, of course, it would have been necessary to invent him. So I have.

Tom Holt
(?) 6th February, 1999

CHAPTER ONE

'No, no, that's completely wrong,' said the guest, shaking his head. 'Give it here, let me show you again.' He pulled the wax-covered board out of his host's hand, smeared the marks away and took back the little pointed stick. 'Like *this*,' he said. 'There, you see? The first part – well, it's like an arrowhead, or a man's elbow. And the other part's just a straight line coming down, like *this*.' He drew the point of the stick smartly through the wax, cutting a furrow. 'Now, try again.'

'All right,' his host replied tolerantly. 'But my heart tells me I'm not going to get the hang of this.'

The guest pulled a face. 'If you'd listen to me occasionally instead of your confounded heart, we might actually get somewhere. Come on. Have another go.'

The old man was, of course, holding the stick all wrong, but his guest had the common sense not to point this out, for fear of exhausting his fairly limited supply of patience and enthusiasm. In the event, it wasn't bad. At least, it was recognisable. If you knew what you were looking at. More or less.

'Excellent,' said the guest. 'You see, it's easy when you concentrate.'

The old man sat gazing at the waxed board and the scratches, while his family and household looked on in speechless wonder (except for one small boy in the shadows near the door, who repeated an earlier observation to his mother about the size of the foreigner's nose). 'And you're telling me,' the old man said after a while, 'that anybody in your country looking at that squiggle will know at once what it means?'

'Of course,' replied the guest. 'Well, not everybody. Most people. Most people of the better sort, anyhow.'

The old man shook his head. 'Remarkable,' he said, as if he'd just been shown a talking chicken. 'People can look at that scratch and know it means *aaah*.' He smiled. 'What does *aaah* mean?' he added.

His guest frowned. 'I explained all that,' he said. 'Each different letter – each design of scratch, if you like – means a different sound. Put them all together, and you sound out a word. For instance –' He gripped the pointed stick between his thumb and first two fingers and quickly drew some more scratches. 'There,' he said. 'That's your name. Look: *pe*, *aleph*, *lamedh*, *aleph* again, *mem*, *he*, *daleth*—'

'What's that stuff you're chanting?' asked the host suspiciously. 'It's not magic, is it?'

'It's the names of the letters. I mean, the scratches.'

'They've got *names*?' The old man chuckled. 'You people really do pay attention to detail.'

The guest sighed. 'All right,' he said. '*Pee*, *ah*, *luh*, *ah*, *mu*, *eh*, *duh*, *eh*, *suh*. Palamedes. Your name.'

The old man sat up. 'Those scratches mean my name?' he said. 'Really?'

'Really.'

'And if you took that bit of wood home with you and gave it to someone else, they'd look at it and know my name?'

The guest nodded. 'Any of my neighbours in Tyre could read that,' he said.

The old man sat back against the wall and blinked. 'Well,' he said, 'isn't that something? And if you kept that bit of wood safely, like in a box or on a shelf in the wall, it'd keep on saying my name even after I'm dead? For ever, even.'

The guest smiled. 'Well, maybe not for ever. To be honest with you, I don't know how long wax lasts before it goes bad and crumbles away. But suppose when that happens my son were to copy it on to a fresh tablet, and then his son after him, and his son after that – yes, it's possible your name could live for a very long time. Who knows, maybe for ever.'

'Without me ever having done anything to deserve it? Just because of a few scratches?'

'Of course.'

The old man scowled. 'You know,' he said, 'my heart reckons that's not right. I mean to say, suppose you're telling the truth. My name could still be remembered long after other people have been forgotten – better men than me, people who've done great things, heroes. Where'd be the sense in that?'

'I see your point,' the guest said politely. 'But we could write their names down too.'

'Yes, but then who'd be able to tell the difference? Between the real heroes, I mean, and the people whose names just happened to be scratched in wax? If that's possible, what'd be the point of being a great hero or a wise king or anything like that?' He shook his head disapprovingly. 'Sorry,' he said, 'but Wisdom isn't in that.'

'We've been doing it for hundreds of years in Phoenicia,' the guest said gently. 'And it doesn't seem to have done us any harm.'

The old man wasn't impressed. 'Maybe,' he said. 'But we see things different here. And besides,' he went on, 'how do you know?'

'I beg your pardon?'

'How do you know,' the old man said, 'that you've been using scratches for hundreds of years? Nobody can remember that far back.'

'Ah,' the guest said, smiling. 'But we have the writing to tell us. We call it –' He said some word in Phoenician that the old man didn't know. 'It means that every year we write down all the important things that happened that year, so that in years to come—'

'But how do you know they're telling the truth?'

It wasn't the first time the Phoenician had stayed at Palamedes' house; far from it. He'd made his first trip to Greece when his father was still alive, working the old route by way of Cyprus and Crete, and his father had introduced him to Palamedes' father over thirty years ago. He'd come back this way once every five years or so, but this was only the third time he'd bothered going as far north as Elis; usually he'd got everything he wanted by Calchis or Sparta. This year, though, he particularly wanted hides – good-quality untanned oxhides, to sell to the Sidonians, who sold them to the Assyrians, Lords of All Creation, to make into shields. Unfortunately, he wasn't the only trader with the same idea, which meant he'd had to go further to get what he wanted. And much further than Elis, he felt sure, there was no conceivable reason ever to go.

Elis had changed a bit since he'd first seen it, of course. For one thing, it was bigger – like it or not, there were more Greeks in the world now than there had been then, and the rate of increase showed no sign of slowing down. Why the gods were apparently stockpiling Greeks, he had no idea; presumably they had some use for them, now or in the future, but as usual they felt no obligation to share their plans with mortals.

As a result of the increase in numbers, Elis was starting to overflow its walls, like an overfilled jug; there were houses all round the outside of the old walls, the usual single-room, flat-roof Greek pattern with an open porch, though a few were two-storeyed, with brick walls carefully faced with meticulously cut stone. Inside the city proper, new buildings had sprung up where old ones had fallen or burned down, while others seemed to have oozed out of the cracks between the older structures, like sap from a cut tree. There was no trace of order or planning in the way the place was laid out; rather, it was as if some giant child had spilt a jarful of houses and run away without clearing up the mess. Only the big old places stood out of the general confusion, country houses stranded in a town, like high places turned into islands by floodwater; their arched, thatched roofs and rounded back ends stood proud so that their eaves were level with their neighbours' rooftops. A few of them still had their own back orchards and kitchen gardens; there was some superstition about building on these, since they'd originally been set aside for the householders' ancestors as a part of the social contract, whereby the better sort fought in the front rank of the battle and in return got the best of everything. Those ways were getting a little tight under the arms and across the shoulders these days, as the numbers increased and land was starting to be something you owned (rather than the other way round); nevertheless, even a great man of the better sort would think twice before building a granary or a shit-house on his honour, let alone allowing ordinary people to live there.

Mostly, though, the old ways were still reckoned to be the best ways, usually because they *were* the best ways, and nobody had been able to come up with worthwhile improvements. People still lived in the city because they'd be safe there behind the walls, or at least under their shadow, and they still walked to their fields every morning and trudged back at night because they had no choice in the matter. Now and again a brave soul would build a place for himself out in the open, where he reckoned he could scrape a little hitherto-undisturbed dirt together and grow something in it, but that was usually an act of desperation, where by bad luck or folly a man had no land of his own; if the bandits or the bears didn't get him, the bad seasons soon chased him out, and his silly little house would slowly fall apart, a landmark and a warning to all right-thinking people. All Greeks were, of course, right thinking; in their own estimation, at least.

By and large, he liked Greeks – mainlanders, of course, as opposed to islanders, who tended to indulge in piracy when the harvests were poor, and sometimes when they weren't; Greeks were, in fact, almost his favourite savages. He liked their strange, rather long-winded language with its enormous words and sweetly balanced sentences (if ever they find something to say, he'd often thought, they've got a fine language to say it in). He liked their idiotic notions of hospitality, their absurd pride in the few trashy possessions they managed to acquire, their often bizarre way of expressing themselves. He liked their habit of attributing their own stray thoughts and observations to 'the god' – unspecified, because they were realistic enough to admit that they didn't know which god to attribute their moments of intuition and insight to, and cautious enough not to appear blasphemously disrespectful by saying 'some god or other' out loud. Best of all, in his opinion, was the way they seemed to believe that the feelings and emotions they experienced weren't part of them at all, but acts of intervention by unpredictable and irresponsible gods – who else but a Greek could yell at you and threaten you with a knife, and a moment later inform you with a disarming smile that Anger had stolen his heart for a moment there, but it was all right now, she'd gone? And there was that ludicrous habit they had of thinking aloud, in public, debating with their 'beloved heart', as if holding a rational conversation with their own internal organs. At first he'd assumed it was all a pantomime they put on for the benefit of gullible foreigners; but no, he'd watched them when they hadn't known he was there, and they did it for real. Crazy. But crazy in a good sort of way, at least on the mainland.

Trade, though – that was something else, a quaint but ultimately frustrating ritual that a businessman could get tired of in an awful hurry. It wasn't like some of the aggravating trade practices he'd come across in other countries, an artful way of weighting the proceedings in favour of the home side. That he could understand and, with practice, cope with. But Greeks – well, they insisted they couldn't understand the very idea of trade. All they could get their heads, or their beloved hearts, around was giving and receiving presents. So, when he called on a Greek, the drill was—

'I've brought you a present,' the guest said.

'That's nice,' Palamedes replied. 'Let's see it, then.'

'Here we are.' The guest reached into his bag and produced a small mirror, heavily burnished bronze, backed with ivory tastefully carved in the image of the Goddess. Really rather attractive, and he could get as many of them as he wanted for a few ingots of pure copper in the market at Tyre.

'That's lovely,' Palamedes said, without excessive enthusiasm. 'Though it's a pity I've already got a mirror.'

The guest braced his smile slightly. 'Yes,' he said, 'but you could swap – you could give it to someone as a present. Someone who might give you a nice present too, something you haven't got and could use.'

Palamedes shrugged. 'What I could really use right now would be five handspan bars of fairly clean yellow bronze,' he said. 'I need to make a new ploughshare, not to mention a couple of new scythe-blades.'

'Oddly enough,' said the guest, 'I happen to have four handspan bars of absolutely pure yellow bronze. Would you rather have those instead of the mirror?'

Palamedes nodded happily. 'That's extremely kind of you,' he said. 'Happiness—'

'Bronze,' the guest went on, before Palamedes could tell him about Happiness lodging in his heart, 'is something I can always get hold of, no problem at all. If only I could get premium untanned oxhides as easily as I could get bronze—'

'Oxhides?'

The Phoenician lifted his head. 'Enough to make a comfortable load for five mules,' he said. 'That'd solve a lot of problems for me.'

The old man looked thoughtful for a moment. 'How many hides, would you say, could a mule carry comfortably? Twenty?'

'Pretty feeble mules you must have in these parts. Double that, where I come from.'

'I think,' said Palamedes, 'that a good mule could carry thirty hides quite easily. What do you think?'

'Thirty sounds reasonable to me,' said his guest.

Palamedes smiled. 'That's good,' he said, 'because it'd give my heart great pleasure to give you five times thirty hides, as my present to you. You did say untanned, didn't you?'

'For choice,' the Phoenician replied.

The Greek grinned at him. 'My pleasure,' he said. 'And,' he went on, 'it really is a very nice mirror. Quite like the one I've already got, but better.'

'Really? Then you hang on to it,' the Phoenician said, keeping his smile going. 'Another present.'

Palamedes nodded. 'I'll say this for you Phoenicians,' he went on, picking up the mirror and putting it down again at the other end of the room, 'you're a very generous people. Generosity must lodge in your hearts all the time.'

His guest sighed. 'Absolutely,' he said. 'In fact, she's got her own cup and plate and everything.'

Inevitably, there was a great deal of eating and drinking to be done. Mercifully, he'd managed to time his arrival so that the first meal he was obliged to eat was nothing more than a slice of bread the size of his head and half a cold roast sheep. He had the feeling, however, that now the deal was done he wasn't going to get off so lightly.

Sure enough, around late afternoon the preparations began. Two of Palamedes' sons burst into the hall, lugged out a huge trestle table and started putting it together noisily. Then someone else, another of the tall, slim young men that clustered round big houses like flies in these parts, lugged in an enormous block of wood, dragging it into the circle of firelight so that he'd be able to see what he was doing. Other young men, more or less identical, appeared carrying parts of animals (a sheep; the headless trunk of a goat; the front forequarter of a pig, white with fat), which they proceeded to chop up over the log with a great deal of enthusiasm and gratuitous flourish.

(Meat for dinner, the Phoenician thought. What a surprise.)

Then they impaled the slices on long spikes, while still more young men poked the fire awake. As the Phoenician stared at the rather stunning quantity of meat and tried to decide which he disliked more, the sizzle or the smell of burning, they hauled the spits down, scattered a few handfuls of salt at random and pulled out the spits as if yanking spears from the bodies of their foes. Finally, Palamedes' eldest son chose the choicest, least-burned chunk of flesh and threw it on the fire, for the gods.

'Pitch in,' the old man said. 'There's plenty to go round.'

In Phoenicia, he'd once tried to explain, what we mostly eat is bread with vegetables, herbs, spices; some meat, of course, but not a great deal . . . At which Palamedes had shaken his head and replied that in that case he needed feeding up, because bread and plants – well, you could live on that stuff, but it wasn't proper *food.* After that, the Phoenician had resolved in future to eat what was put in front of him and never raise the subject again.

The food he could probably have coped with, given time and the stomachs of two cows. But there was also wine – harsh, coarse stuff like the edge of a shoemaker's rasp, served without water and sprinkled with oatmeal, honey and grated cheese. Every time he got rid of it, some fool grabbed his cup and topped it up again, giving him the impression that he was trying to drink the sea—

'That cup,' mumbled the old man beside him, 'been in my family for generations. Belonged to Hercules once, they reckon.'

The Phoenician squinted at the object in question, trying to make his eyes focus. 'Really?' he said. 'Doesn't look that old. How long ago would that be, then?'

'What? Oh, hundreds of years. Hundreds and hundreds.'

'That's odd,' the Phoenician began to say; then he thought better of it. He'd been about to remark that it looked very much like the sort of cup they made on Cyprus, and wasn't that writing on the side there? But then he read the writing (peculiar patterns of strokes and flicks, easy enough to mistake for random decoration), naming the prince of the city of Qartikhadast it had been made for, and who was still alive . . . 'So when did Hercules die, then, do you know?'

The old man frowned. 'Now you're asking me something,' he said. 'Forgetfulness has emptied my mind. Here, Cleander, when did Hercules die? Was it before or after your great-great-great-grandfather was born?'

The man Cleander, a complete stranger, shook his head. 'More recent than that,' he said. 'My heart tells me my grandfather met him once. At least, I think it was my grandfather.'

'I thought he was still alive,' someone else put in.

'No, he's dead for sure,' someone else replied. 'It was after the war with the Achaeans but before the battle where my father lost his foot. Closer than that . . .'

Cleander frowned. 'Was that the second war with the Achaeans,' he asked, 'or the third?'

'What third? There were only two, unless you're counting Iphicles' raid.'

It wouldn't have made an awful lot of sense even without the wine; with the wine, it was like a horrible tangled ball of rope, where you tease open one knot only to find another, even worse. The cup, however, was fifty years old at most.

The Phoenician was just starting to nod off to sleep when Palamedes nudged him. 'There, you see,' he said, 'proves that point I was making earlier. If a man's done great things, made a name for himself, he'll never be forgotten. So who needs those scratches of yours, eh?'

'Absolutely,' the Phoenician said rather desperately. 'I can see that now.'

'Of course,' Palamedes went on, 'Hercules was the greatest of all the heroes, no question about that. He'll *never* be forgotten, no matter what. Others – well, I suppose it's touch and go, depending on what they've done. The greater the achievement, the better your chances of living for ever.'

Someone down the other end of the table sniggered. Palamedes looked up, annoyed. 'Did I say something funny?' he asked.

'Sorry,' the other man replied. 'I was just thinking of Coroebus.'

There was a moment of deep silence; then quite a few of the men round the table started to laugh, at roughly the same time. Palamedes was one of them.

'Shame on you,' he said nevertheless, trying to look serious and thereby making things worse. 'No, dammit, credit where it's due, he did – Oh well, anyway. By and large, what I was saying is true, though there's exceptions. Doesn't mean to say—'

'Who's Coroebus?' the Phoenician asked.

Another pause, rather sooner interrupted. 'Of course,' the old man said, 'I don't suppose you know that story, you weren't around then. Funny story, in a way, though I've got to say it. Sadness pulls down my heart sometimes when I think of some of those people, because really, none of it was right. But it didn't do any harm, and Leon was a good king, so—'

The Phoenician nodded appreciatively, hoping he could change the subject before anybody had a chance to launch into a narrative. He was about to ask how the olives were shaping up this year when—

'If you like,' Palamedes said, 'I'll tell you the story of Coroebus. Would your heart like that?'

'Well,' the Phoenician said, 'is it a long story?'

Palamedes shook his head. 'Not really,' he replied. 'By rights, though, it's Cleander here who should be telling it, not me. After all, Cleander was there at the time, weren't you?'

The man called Cleander lifted his head. 'I certainly was,' he said.

'All right,' said Palamedes, 'you tell it, then. Just don't spin it out like you usually do. Our friend here's only staying five days.'

As the Phoenician blinked and offered up a silent prayer to his gods that that was what passed in Elis for a joke, the man called Cleander leaned back against the wall and felt for his cup (the Phoenician hadn't noticed he was blind), then coughed. 'It all started,' he said—

It all started a long while ago (said Cleander), back in King Leon's time.

Any of you remember King Leon? Well, you do, Palamedes, goes without saying, but any of the rest of you? Too young, of course. Suits me; it means I can say what I like and nobody'll know different.

Well now, we're going back thirty-five, maybe even forty years, before most of you were born. Now you ask people, they'll tell you, Yes, they were great days, men were lions then. But it's not true, you know. They weren't. People like you and me, our hearts tend to see the way things go as an upside-down triangle; once, the world was wonderful, then it shrank down a bit into just good, and soon it'll dwindle away into really bad. I suppose it's because we all respect our fathers and reckon they were better than us, and we're better than our children – goes without saying, doesn't it? Except for your people, I believe, honoured Phoenician guest; don't your people say that the triangle's the other way up, and people just keep on getting better and better? Makes no difference either way. It's not true, whichever way up it is, and when you get to my age you'll know it's true and tell everybody the exact opposite. Well, isn't that what old people do?

All right, yes; King Leon. He was a good king. He was one of those good kings who make you wish you had a bad king instead. Oh, come on, you know perfectly well what I mean. All right, what makes for a good king? Brave, just, true; agreed? Well, Leon was brave all right – stick him up on a chariot with a couple of spears in his fist, he'd be off like a dog after hares; and the rest of us, well, we had no choice but to follow after. That's good most of the time, but there's a few good men's ghosts on the wrong side of the River because King Leon always fought in the front of the battle, and they were the ones who had to go and get him out again when he'd gone just a bit too far forward.

And just – oh, King Leon loved justice. Couldn't get enough of justice. That's a good thing, too. Many a time I've seen King Leon sitting in the market square, and there's been some small man, someone with not much land and not many cows, weeping tears of joy because King Leon found for him against his rich, greedy neighbour. And I've seen those same rich, greedy men hanging about the fountain-head later that very day with frowns like summer thunder on their faces, and you didn't need to be able to hear their hearts to know what was in them – which isn't a disaster when you've got a strong king, a man with the heart of a lion, who'll smack down the wolves and the bears when they come down to the treeline where the flock's settled. When you've got a king who's true, sticks to his furrow with his eyes on the far headland, you don't need to worry about men like that – let them make trouble; the sooner they act up, the sooner they can be smacked down. So that was all well and good. He was a good king.

But he was a bad king too; because his son – his legitimate son, who'd be the king when Leon crossed the River – was . . . Well, no hard words about the lad, many times in many places he'd have been a good man, but he was shaping up to be a bad king. Not his fault. He tried so hard, didn't he ever – he tried to be brave, tried four times where anyone with a place for Wisdom in his heart would've given it best after one. Two good friends of mine died pulling him out of trying to be brave the third time, and he was so ashamed afterwards that he tried to be brave a fourth time, and thank the gods I was the other side of the battle that day. So he stopped trying to be brave and tried to be just instead. He tried many, many times, until Anger stole so many hearts among the better sort that they'd have cut off his head and thrown him in the sea if they'd had a clear chance; and Leon couldn't rightly blame them for it – though he had to, of course, and lost good men that way, just because the boy's heart couldn't seem to understand that the little man with not much isn't always, always right (two times in ten he's a thief and a liar and no good, and three more he's just plain wrong). But no, he'd always find for the sparrow against the hawk and the mouse against the bear, and where's Justice in that? And as for true – his heart was always telling him what he'd just done was wrong (even when it wasn't) so the next day he'd do the opposite, and nobody had a clue where they were with him. The more he tried to be a good prince, the less chance he stood of being anything but a truly awful king. It's like they say: push one way and the tree'll fall the other.

Leon saw all this, of course; and his heart told him, one day this boy will be king and everything you've done well will turn out badly on him. All the enemies you've crushed and humbled will take it back from him, with an extra measure for the loan. All your justice is making him unjust. As for being true – well, a man must be true to his own son, but if you do that you'll be false to the whole of Elis.

'There's no hope in this,' he told me one day – we were watching them get in the apples, it should have been a happy day, but Sorrow had him. 'Everything I do makes it worse. It's enough to make a man give up and go live in a cave.'

I tried to sound cheerful. 'He's a good lad,' I told him, 'and he's still young.'

'He's seventeen,' Leon said. 'When I was his age—'

'All right,' I said. 'But he's younger than you were at his age. Most people are. What he needs is to get something right.'

King Leon smiled. 'That's no lie,' he said.

'No, that's not what I mean,' I said. 'He needs to do one thing – one big, splendid thing – and get it right. It's like when you're liming birds. You set out your snares and you wait, and the first five or ten birds fly over. They see the snares and sheer off, and all the other birds in the trees see them and they fly away too, and you think you'll never catch a single one if you stay there all year. Then Folly takes one bird and it drops in, puts its feet in the lime, it's stuck. So it perches there on the branch, pulling to get its feet free and flapping its wings. The other birds see it pitch in and stay there, so they guess it must be safe and they drop in too. Each one that pitches and gets stuck draws in another one, until the branch is full.

It's the same way with Success. Until you've done one big thing right, Success sees the snare and keeps flinching away. Once you've limed one Success, though, another'll drop in, until you find it hard to do a thing wrong if you try – even the things you do badly seem to go well – until the branch is full of Successes flapping their wings at you. Trust me on this: find one thing he can do well, keep him away from everything else until he's done it, and your problems will be over.'

He never poured half measures, King Leon. Either he was all happy or all sad – I've noticed, it's often the way with these big men. I suppose their hearts are big and they can fit more in. Anyhow, when I'd put this to him he went from all sad to all happy, quick as a fire catching. The problem, though, was finding a big thing the boy could do. We all tried to think, but either our hearts didn't know or they weren't telling. It had to be the right sort of thing, proper for a king's son to do – but the boy had tried all those and made a muck of them. Someone said, Let's try to find out what he *is* good at, everybody's good at something. But that wasn't any help. Sure, he was good at digging a ditch or minding goats, he could weave a basket tolerably well, he could jump over a chair with both feet together. None of that was going to help us much.

And then we had to put it out of our minds for a while, because that was when the Triphylians – you can ask me the name of their king but I can't remember it – the Triphylians came up the coast and crossed the river, and we had no choice but to do something about it.

Usually, King Leon wouldn't have waited so long. He'd have pushed them back before they reached the Alpheus, or at the very least held it against them; but here's what I mean about him being a bad king because he was a good one. He was being good keeping away from fighting, because his heart knew the boy wasn't up to playing the part a crown prince should play in a war like that. Because of it, we waited till those Triphylians were like floodwater lapping round our houses, which was very much the wrong thing to do. It's not just Successes that come to the lime, you see.

I remember explaining all this to my wife, when she asked me what the war was about. I told her there wasn't going to be a war, it was just a matter of taking a stand, letting them know we were prepared to draw the line somewhere.

'Letting them know how?' she asked.

I was in a hurry, it was late and I had to get the goats in. 'We'll send a small army,' I said.

'Why not send a big one?'

I was pulling on my boots; they'd got wet and tight. 'No need,' I said. 'Small one'll do.'

'Doesn't sound very clever to me,' she said. 'If I was invading a country and all that turned up to fight me was a small army—'

'They aren't invading,' I interrupted.

'Oh. Then why send an army at all?'

Obviously I wasn't explaining very clearly. 'To make sure they don't invade,' I said.

'Well, wouldn't a big army do that just as well? Better, even. And then, if they do decide to invade after all, you'll be ready for them.'

'It doesn't work like that,' I said. 'Where's my hat?'

'Where you left it. If you send a small army and they decide they want to invade, they'll defeat you.'

'It was on the hook here last time I saw it.'

'And if they defeat you, they'll get all full of themselves and brave, so when you send the big army you should have sent in the first place—'

'I don't think I'll bother with a hat,' I said. 'It's a cool evening.'

'Are you going on this war, then?'

I frowned. 'You make it sound like a festival picnic,' I said.

'Well, it can't be all bad or you wouldn't be so keen to go.'

'Who said I was keen to go?'

'If it's not an invasion but you're sending an army anyway, sounds to me like it's an excuse for something else. Getting drunk, probably, and having chariot races.'

I was starting to feel as if I'd put my head in a beehive; her words were buzzing round me in all directions. 'We only have chariot races when somebody dies,' I said. 'Or is that why you think we have wars, so people can die and we've got an excuse for a chariot race?'

She looked at me. 'With men,' she said, 'I could believe it.'

'That's a stupid thing to say,' I replied.

'Really? So what do you go to war for? And don't say it's to stop the enemy deciding to invade; I'm talking about the *real* reason. It's to win glory and get famous, isn't it? And you can get just as glorious winning a chariot race as you can getting killed in some battle. It's all the same thing, after all.'

I took a deep breath. 'How did we get started talking about chariot races?' I asked her. 'Nobody except you even mentioned them.'

'That sort of thing,' she insisted. 'You men sit around feeling bored, and then you start thinking, it's not very glorious just sitting around all day, we'd better start a war or something. Like this idea of yours, for the prince.'

I hadn't seen that one coming, either. Talking to my wife, you suddenly found things charging at you round about ankle level from out of the bushes, like when you're hunting boar in dense undergrowth. 'You've got my heart confused now,' I said. 'How does the prince come into it?'

'Right up at the front end, I expect,' she said. 'You want the prince to get glorious, so you've found him a war to be glorious in. Don't you want your hat?'

'Oh, for – where was it?'

'Right there under your nose, except you couldn't see for looking. So when are you leaving?'

I sighed. 'I don't know, do I? I mean, nobody's even said there's going to be a war yet. Because nobody knows if there's even going to be an invasion. What I mean to say is, we're going to send a few men up there, just to let them know we know they're there. It's as simple as that.'

She looked at me again. 'You call that simple?' she said. 'No wonder things are how they are, if that's your idea of simple.'

My heart told me that if I didn't want to get completely tangled up in this argument, like a goat in a thorn hedge, I'd better get out of there quick; so I did. I don't know how things are in Phoenicia, but here it's always like that when you start talking to women. We say that the gods made women's minds separately from men's – like when a man makes one thing, then tries to make another just the same. They look the same, but if you go up close, you'll start seeing all the differences.

I went up on the hill, and as soon as I was out of sight of the house and had time to think, my heart told me exactly what I should have said – because I knew, really. It's just that when words start stampeding at you, all quick and snapping like a hunter's dogs, you don't get time to think.

Up on the hill, it was all straightforward enough; most things are, it's just us who complicate them. And she was plenty wrong about the war – now she had me calling it a war, and I suppose she was right, at that; we all knew in our hearts there was going to be a war, otherwise where was the point – it being an excuse for putting the prince where he could make a name for himself. Other way about, really, like I told you earlier; Leon didn't want a war because he didn't want the boy to have to get involved. But it set me thinking; my heart was asking me, Well, why not? If there was someone to stand over the boy, tell him what to do, there was no reason why he shouldn't look like he was leading the army. Furthermore, if we sent a big army, what could possibly go wrong? It wasn't like the Triphylians could match us for numbers. Chances were, if they saw us roll up in thousands, they'd take one look and get themselves back over Alpheus as fast as they could go – and then the boy would have won a great and bloodless victory, and everybody'd be happy. The more we thought about it, my heart and I, the better it lay. I knew the Triphylians well enough to know where they'd bend and where they'd break; driving another man's land, running off his cattle, that's one thing, but fighting a big battle is quite another. You don't start a battle you know you can't win – where'd be the point?

So; the next day I went to see King Leon. As I recall, he was sitting outside the house watching them fix the big wagon – there were the wheelwrights, and the smith heating up the big copper tyre for the bust wheel, and a gang of the young men just standing around watching, like they'd never seen a wheel mended before. That made my heart think a small war might not be a bad thing at all; find them something to do instead of hanging about the king's house all day. You know what young men are like. Mostly they weren't any trouble, but once something gets into them, they're like a pack of dogs that haven't been taken for a run – they get snappy and difficult. Stands to reason – at that age you want to be up and doing, not loafing round a courtyard till your beard turns grey.

'Are you trying to confuse me?' King Leon said, after I'd said my piece. 'First you tell me to keep the boy away from the wars, next you want me to start one just for him. You're like those big walking-boots that you can wear on either foot.'

I felt embarrassed, I'll admit; after all, I'd been confoundedly eloquent when I advised him against the idea, so my opponent in the debate was me. 'There's wars,' I told him, 'and there's wars. It all depends on who you're fighting. Truth is, if you aren't Achilles himself, you'd best be choosy about who you pick a fight with. But Triphylians, for Zeus' sake; with them it's just a dance, like at summer festival. Nobody in his right mind'd want to get himself killed in a cattle raid.'

King Leon smiled. 'It's true,' he said, 'they've got a pretty shrewd idea of when it's the right time to call it a day and run. I remember fighting them – well, when I was not much older than the boy is now. Wasn't my first war, not by a way, but the old man let me lead the army all by myself. I tell you, Cleander, I was Hercules and Achilles and the Seven against Thebes, all packed up tight under one helmet; I had all so many clever ideas about how to fight a battle and lead an army it's a miracle I'm still alive. But in spite of my clowning about with masked flank strikes and feints and pretend retreats and all, we still managed to beat them in a single morning. They weren't interested, see.'

'There you are, then,' I said. 'And I'll bet you that when you got home again you were so full of it they could have stuck a spigot in your toe and wheeled you up and down the vine rows in a cart.'

'That's no lie,' said Leon, smiling.

'You see?' I said. 'You'd got something right, it filled your heart. But at the same time I'll wager you never felt like trying all that clever stuff again.'

'That's true,' he said.

'Well, there you have it. You learned a few valuable lessons, and still won. Just what I'm suggesting here.'

You know, I wonder sometimes why the gods suddenly take away our wits and make us stupid the way they do. Sometimes I think it's because they're like children, playing games with us. Sometimes I get the feeling they're punishing us, like parents. Half the time I say to my heart, the gods are no better than the worst of us, the way they treat us; the rest of the time I figure it must be our fault, we're doing something wrong without even knowing it. Anyhow, that's what some god put it into my mind to say, and the same god or one just as mean put it into Leon's heart to listen to me. That's all it takes.

The old blind man called Cleander stopped talking and sat still for a while.

The Phoenician, who'd been fidgeting for some time, reckoned that (being a foreigner) it would be in order for him to misconstrue this silence as the end of the story, and crawl away somewhere dark where he could get some sleep. 'Well,' he said, 'that's quite a tale you've got to tell, thank you. I think I'll go to bed now if it's all the same—'

His host looked round sharply – he'd been sitting with his head slumped forward, communing with whatever shared sorrow was tweaking the blind man 'Don't be silly,' he said, 'the story's hardly begun yet. Sit down. Thrasyllus, our guest's cup is empty, what the hell do you think you're playing at? Come to think of it, why are we still drinking this girls' stuff? There should be a jar of the five-year-old in the back room somewhere, unless the women have got at it while I wasn't looking.'

Compared with the five-year-old, the ordinaire was positively innocuous. Cursing his bad tactical judgement, the Phoenician leaned back against the wall and tried his utmost to keep his eyelids from folding down.

'You'll have to bear with me,' the old blind man was saying. 'It's been a long time, but it still stings my heart to think about it. That was a cruel god, I reckon, the one who robbed us of our brains that day.'

'That's my brother for you,' someone else said, a way further down the table, where the Phoenician couldn't see him clearly for the forest of wagging beards. 'Very sensitive man, my brother. Why don't I tell you all what happened next?'

'You sit quiet, Cratus,' ordered Palamedes. 'Sounds to me like you've had enough for one night.'

But the blind man shook his head vigorously, and as his head moved the firelight glistened on his damp cheeks. 'No, let him tell it,' he said, 'better him than me. It was the god who took my wits, but I deserve to hear him tell it.'

Everyone was looking dreadfully solemn, and the Phoenician wished very much that he'd followed his original plan and gone to Argos for his oxhides. Even Palamedes seemed depressed. 'Come on,' he said, 'don't show me up in front of my guest here. We don't need to hear stuff like that, when we're all friends together.'

But Cleander, the old blind man, kept shaking his head and insisting, with the air of a man to whom guilt and anguish have given extraordinary stamina; so, to shut him up, Palamedes finally said, 'Go on then, Cratus, let's have your party piece. But try to keep it short, will you? There's some of us want to be up early in the morning.'

CHAPTER TWO

'Now then,' said the blind man's brother, 'where had we got to? Ah yes, Cleander was telling you how he persuaded the heart of King Leon, who'd made up his mind against the idea, to take out the army against a bunch of Triphylians who'd slipped across the river. All with me so far? That's fine, then.'

Well (Cratus continued), as soon as the word got around that we were going to war, everybody got so excited you'd think they'd all been sitting on an anthill.

It's as if one of those clever goldsmiths – like the ones in your country, friend Phoenician – was making a cup or a bowl, the ones with scenes from upper-class life all round the edge. Damn smart the way they do it, by the way, with a little anvil and a stake to support the metal from the inside, and tapping away on the outside with a little hammer. Well, if you opened me up you'd see scenes from that war beaten all round my heart.

Partly I remember it so well because it was the first war I was old enough to go on. I'm the kid brother, you see; there's fifteen years between Cleander and me, though they've always said that I've got Cleander's old heart in my body and he's got my young heart in his. Which figures, if you ask me, but that's another matter. The point is, I was as excited about the war as I could be without bursting like a sodden wineskin. All I'd ever heard was the wars. I could've sung you songs about Theseus and Diomedes, all the battle scenes, I'd have got the names right too – who killed who and how, just like those old men who sing for a living. Our father had promised me that when I was old enough, I could have grandfather's old shield and spear – only fair, I'd been burnishing the blasted things every day since I was six, which gave me as good a claim to them as anybody – and he'd give me an old helmet of his and a breastplate and pair of greaves he'd been given by a visitor that were never going to fit him again; and I already had a sword of my own, from my mother's father. As soon as the word went round, I fetched them all down out of the rafters and set to with a scrap of buckskin and the finest white sand I could find – it's a wonder I didn't polish a hole clean through that helmet (it was thin enough, Zeus knows; useless bloody thing). When I wasn't polishing I was out in the back orchard practising my spear-throw; I'd set up an apple on a stump at twenty paces, and if I didn't split five out of six apples, I'd be ashamed of myself. And when I wasn't polishing or smashing up perfectly good apples, I was hanging round the horse-pens with the other lads of my age, watching them break in the horses and talking about what big things we were going to do, and what the war would be like.

I reckoned I'd be in the front of the battle. After all, I was big and strong and quick; not a fighter of course, I assumed I'd be chariot-eering for Cleander here. I was a hell of a good driver in those days, and that's my heart talking. I'm out of practice now, of course, just hauling logs and olives in our little mule-cart. Back then I could manage four big horses and still have a hand free. Of course, it helped that I still had all my fingers.

(Being human, the Phoenician immediately craned his neck and tried to get a look at the man's hands; but he had them folded in his lap, hidden by the table. This time, though, he caught a glimpse of his face; or at least his nose and eyes, the rest being in shadow.

Nondescript, he noted; not one of those people you can recognise in a crowd a hundred paces away.)

But I'm getting ahead of myself (Cratus said). Like I was telling you, I had it all worked out, every last detail of the battle – my heart could only see a battle, not a war; I was too young then to know they're not the same thing – every spear-cast, every one-on-one combat, all the moves like we'd been taught. I could close my eyes, and my heart could see wonderful battles, every scene crisp and sharp, just like those magnificent Phoenician plates. You're grinning, my young friends. Probably you do the same; it's one of the secret and rather disgusting habits of young men, fighting battles with yourself in the dark.

We went to the war as a family, of course; me, Cleander here, our middle brother Meson, our cousins Leucas and Melas, their father (our uncle Eumachus), our mother's brother Thaumastes and his three boys (Callon, Doryclytus and – help me out, Cleander, what was the third one called? That's right, Mylon) and her kid brother Deistratus, who was the family's pride and joy, a genuine first-class hero. I can't remember now which war it was in, either the third war against the Arcadians or the second war against the Achaeans (who gives a damn, anyway?), but he'd done something or other extremely brave at some point, and when we were kids our hearts were full of it. Naturally, Uncle Deistratus was in charge of us, or at least he told us what to do, and since nobody else ever seemed particularly interested in what we got up to, I guess that made him our commanding officer. Things were rather more flexible back then than they are now, in any case; so long as you showed up on time and didn't attack your own side by mistake, you were mostly free to go about things in your own way.

One of the good things about being invaded is that you don't have so far to go to get to the battle. It takes the shine off the sense of occasion if you've got to walk or trundle along in a chariot all day just to get to where the fighting's going to be. Fortunately, the Triphylians were in a particularly daring mood, and had pushed along until they were no more than a morning's drive away. We set off just before dawn, figuring that if we got there early enough we could fight the battle in the morning, have a picnic lunch and be back home in time for dinner.

My mother packed me some cold roast beef, the thick end of a loaf and a fist-sized chunk of white cheese in a little wicker basket that fitted nicely inside the hollow of my shield. To my surprise and great joy, I wasn't driving for my brother Cleander after all. Uncle Deistratus had brought two chariots; one for himself, Callon and Mylon, and one spare. Doryclytus was driving it, but he needed a fighter. Of course, I volunteered straight away. Cleander kicked up a fuss because of course that left him short one driver, but I solved that by volunteering cousin Melas to take my place. Neither of them was happy about the situation, but by then it was too late; you couldn't have got me down off that platform without a block and tackle.

Thanks to the slight disagreement there we were a bit late setting off, so we cut short all the goodbyes and stuff and hammered off down the hill to the road, which was already pretty well clogged with chariots on their way to the muster, which was being held in front of the king's vineyard gate. Now that was a scene, I can tell you; it'd look a treat on one of those clever Phoenician plates, if you could find one big enough to get all the detail in. I was young; I'd never seen so many people in one place before, not even at festival or the summer fair. And if the numbers weren't enough to take your breath away, the sight of all that raw wealth was staggering, at least to a kid my age who'd never been more than a few miles from the farm in all his life. Everywhere you looked there were helmets, breastplates, shields; two- and four-horse chariots by the dozen, and two men in each one, all armoured from top to toe. I could hardly believe there was that much metal in the whole world. Of course, it also made me realise, pretty much for the first time, how relatively poor our family was compared with some of the others. There were boys my age wearing what were obviously brand-new, made-to-measure breastplates and helmets, not the rather antiquated hand-me-downs I was wearing. Now, it stands to reason: unless you've got an awful lot of sons to get at least a certain amount of use out of it over the years, having an armour made for a growing boy is a waste of time and resources. Anybody who could afford an extravagance like that had to be extremely well-off, and that meant they'd found favour with the gods; and as we all know, the favourites of the gods tend to last longer and do more in battles than lesser mortals do. This is, of course, why people go to war in the most valuable and magnificently decorated armour they can afford; and naturally, the enemy steer clear of such people and their divine patrons, which is why they say gold and silver will ward away a spear much better than the best shield or pair of greaves.

By those standards, of course, I was an easy mark in my ratty old collection of bits. This didn't bother me in the least, it meant I'd probably see more action than most (there are some people, I know, who deliberately arm down, go to war in any old junk, for that very reason). In fact, my heart was as happy as a dog who sees the master put his boots on. I was seeing new, strange, wonderful sights, but at the same time I was with my family and my friends, men I'd grown up with, and we were all going to the big adventure together. And it wasn't just some picnic or festival; there was glory to be won, a chance to make a name for myself, take a step on the road to immortality – which is why men fight, after all, isn't it?

Well, fairly soon everybody was there, the wine was going round and the party was just starting to get good; at which point the prince showed up, riding in King Leon's own chariot, flanked by King Leon's own household men, looking alarmingly like a helmet and a breastplate supported by three vine-props. He was young, of course, at the age where the muscles haven't caught up with the bones, and even then, before he was fully grown, he stood a head taller than most people there. But you could see that he'd had to pad out his greaves with three pairs of buskins just to keep them from sliding down his legs and jamming his feet; there wasn't enough meat on his bones to feed a small dog. Not that we were bothered. He was only there to look pretty and give us something to order the line by. Once the battle started – well, he'd have to make shift for himself, like the smallest piglet in the litter, if he wanted to get any of the action.

It was a hot day, I remember; I can feel the heat now in my heart as I think about it. There was a goatskin full of water hanging inside the chariot (I knew enough about battles to know that thirst is probably more of a danger to men in armour than all the weapons of the enemy put together) but I made an effort and left it there. You see, I had this nagging fear that if I drank a lot before the battle started, I'd be going through the fighting bursting for a piss – don't laugh, I was young, I didn't know that when the killing starts, even the best men pee down their legs and never notice it till the battle's over. Anyhow, my heart was too excited to notice how thirsty the rest of me was getting. You were probably just the same when it was your first time, so don't sit there grinning at me. I know you all too well.

Being a great hero and all, Uncle Deistratus wanted us to be up as close to the front as we could get. Needless to say, he wasn't the only one thinking that; so, the closer we got to the place where the battle was going to be, the more crowded and bunched up the front of the column became, with chariots jostling each other like a flock of sheep going through a narrow gateway. To begin with we at least tried to make a show of being polite about it; but the nearer we got, the more we bumped and shoved, and tempers started to get short. Come to think of it, probably it was just as well we got there when we did, or there might have been serious trouble.

And then, quite suddenly, the column came to a halt, like when you're not looking where you're going and suddenly walk into a tree. We were at the top of a rise overlooking a little valley – I can't tell you the name of the place, because I don't think it was important enough to have one. Perfect spot, of course. No trees or big rocks to get in the way (the scouts had been working like mad the previous two days to get it clear) and a nice easy gradient for the chariots to amble down without any risk of getting bounced out or breaking an axle.

They were on the other side of the valley, where the ground rose again. Now that's one sight my heart is never going to forget, that first view of the enemy. At first glance, they didn't look at all frightening; they were small and colourful, a good way away. Lots of them, for sure, but there were lots of us too, so that didn't really matter. No, it was when they started to move that Fear suddenly slipped in under the shutters of my heart; they were coming towards us, coming to get us, meaning to do us harm. I'd never thought of it that way before. Always in my heart the enemy had been the prey, the quarry, put there at our disposal for us to turn into glory and honour. If we'd gone first, maybe my heart wouldn't have taken it so hard. But up to that point, honestly, it hadn't occurred to me that anything *bad* might happen to me, to us. It was only seeing that slow, stalking advance that put it into my mind: that they were just like us, they were coming to play the same sort of game with us as we'd got planned for them. I don't know; it was as if you were practising archery behind the house; and after a few ends the target suddenly pulled itself up out of the ground, drew out the arrows, looked at you and said, *Right, my turn.*

Not that it ever crossed my mind to run away. Gods no, I don't think I'd have been physically capable of it. I've heard it said, you know, that when the two armies are closing in, it takes more courage to run away, push through your own ranks with all your family and friends staring at you, than it does to stand and face the enemy. I can believe that, and let me tell you, I've never been anything like that brave.

Just then, cousin Doryclytus nudged me. 'There's a lot of them,' he said.

'Enough to go round, you mean,' I answered. Nothing like knowing someone else is scared to help fill your own heart with Courage. So, of course, I made a big show of hefting my javelin, getting the centre of balance nicely into my hand. 'The more of them, the bigger the target.' Naturally, I wasn't going to let Doryclytus know I was scared; he was a whole month younger than me, which made him just a kid. It was what Uncle Deistratus called 'leading by example'.

For a while I thought we were just going to stand there like idiots and let them come to us; but eventually someone must have given the signal, and we started rolling forward.

Traditionally, the start of an advance is reckoned to be one of the most profound religious experiences of a man's life; it's when you roll your eyes upwards and say, Get me out of this in one piece, Lord Ares, and I'll sacrifice twenty white oxen – and you mean it, too, every word of it. Maybe that's why the gods stir up wars; I don't know, it must be a good time for them, just before a battle. Anyway,

I was no exception. I got my prayer in early, hoping the god would hear me and accept it before the other man, the one I'd be fighting, managed to say his prayer. Assuming, of course, that it works like that; first come, first served. No reason why it should. It's just as likely that the god's already made up his mind in advance who he's going to favour. After all, whoever wins the god'll still stand to collect his sacrifice, since both men will have made the same prayer.

We gradually picked up speed down the hill. Doryclytus was a good driver, probably better than me. But he was in two minds. He was trying to be sensible, keeping the speed down so as not to lose control. But he was also trying to keep up with the others, Uncle Deistratus and Cleander and the rest, and they weren't being very sensible at all. They were still dead set on getting in front and staying there, which meant that they were pulling ahead, going a bit too fast, and paying rather more attention to the Eleans on either side of them than the Triphylians in front. Not that they were the only ones, not by a long way. Half our army were doing it, so was half of theirs. That's the thing about the wars in those days, so little of it was to do with fighting the enemy. There were all sorts of other issues at stake, so no wonder it was difficult to keep your mind on so many different things at once.

Anyway, Doryclytus was doing his best to stay back and charge forward at the same time; and a pretty good fist he was making of it, too. Unfortunately, the better he managed it, the worse our position became. He was holding perfect station in the middle of a thick clump of five or six chariots all trying to do the same as he was. We were blind to the enemy and the rest of our own people, and we couldn't very well stop without piling up on top of each other. The short version is, our end of the line contrived to get well ahead of the other end and the middle; and when Uncle Deistratus at the front eventually made contact with the enemy and we had no choice but to pull up sharply or ride him down, we found we were surrounded on three sides, with the fourth side, directly behind us, filling up fast.

That was when the fighting started. My heart was telling me, Hold on, this isn't right, and I could certainly see its point. We'd rolled to a standstill; Deistratus had jumped down and was striding towards the nearest visible enemy, twirling his spear in an annoyingly showy way. Now, it was clear enough for any fool to see that he was a great hero; he was wearing the price of a good farm in sheet bronze, and the confident way he was bustling towards the enemy was enough to make any sensible man realise he was in trouble and get out of the way. The rest of us, however, weren't nearly as intimidating, and the enemy were coming in round us. It was like when you've got the deer backed up against the sheer mountainside and you're gradually walking in on him; too far away yet to take a shot, so you've got to make sure there's no gaps in your line he can dart through and get away.

The main thing I remember about the enemy is the way they looked so like us, but different. They were wearing the same clothes, the same armour, the same boots on their feet. There were tall ones, short ones, fat ones, skinny ones, same as any other group of people taken at random. Chances are they were bunching together by families and villages, same as we were. In a way it was like walking towards a river or a lake and seeing your own reflection coming at you. But my heart was telling me that these were the most dangerous animals I'd ever encountered in my whole life; lions and bears and wolves and boars are dangerous because they'll go for you if they can't get past you, and they're worrying enough. These animals were dead set on killing us, for no reason that I could see at that particular moment, even though they were just us facing the other way. Fear was definitely at home in my heart right then.

But I wasn't going anywhere. I stepped down from the chariot; and since the rest of my family seemed to be walking towards these dreadful creatures, I reckoned I might as well do the same.

Now then, my new friend from far away, have you ever seen Greeks fight? No? You haven't missed much. We do it like this. The idea is to get within spear-cast – thirty paces for an aimed throw, give or take a foot; then you throw your spear, but honestly, there's no earthly excuse for getting hurt by a thrown spear, or at least not a spear that's been thrown at you. There's all the time in the world to watch it through the air and either get out of the way or hold up your shield and push it away. Rather more dangerous are the spears that are either thrown wild or glance off someone else's shield and whizz off at random, because you aren't looking out for those. Assuming you and he haven't done any damage with the spear, then, it's time to close with the sword; that's the bit you've been training for all your life, the bit you see when you close your eyes at night, the bit you've been dreaming moves for ever since your father made you your first wooden sword and shield.

And, the first time, you turn to stone. I don't know who he was or why he'd chosen me. He was just under middling tall, the second fighter out of a four-horse chariot – anyway, he appeared to have taken a fancy to me, and chucked his spear at just about the edge of aiming range, say fifty paces. I watched it carefully, you can bet, as it lifted, hung up there for an instant the way they do and then came down. I knew from the moment it hung that the cast was pretty good. But did I move my feet? Of course not. I just stood there gawping, like an idiot; and, right at the last moment, I shut my eyes and shoved my shield out at the thing.

It hurt. Now, you all know, but maybe our guest doesn't. When you fend off a spear, it needn't be said, you angle the shield so the spear glances off and goes bothering some other poor fool. You don't hold your shield up at right angles, because if you do the spear's got a fair chance of going through and doing you an injury. If you've got no choice in the matter, at the very least you fend it away with the top, not the middle, because the middle's where the hand-grip is, with your delicate, fragile little fingers trapped hard against the leather.

It hurt, like I just said; but my heart wasn't really aware of what had happened because my brain was being my drill instructor, telling me that I'd just made a stupid beginner's mistake, taking the other man's spear in my shield. You know what that means, it said to me, now your shield's weighed down, six feet of spear sticking through it makes it a real cow to move. The drill is, of course, you drop it and do the best you can without, because it's more a hindrance than a help. I didn't, of course. I was staring into the eyes of my old tutor Aristomachus – in my imagination, of course – and he was shouting at me, telling me what to do, but it was as if I couldn't quite make out what he was saying. Meanwhile the other man, the enemy, was coming at me, sideways behind his shield like a crab, nervously – like Aristomachus used to say, there's his shield, he'll be along some time tomorrow – and I was still standing with my spear in my hand and gawping at the guard; that was so much second nature that I'd done it without any conscious thought at all. Didn't even know it was there.

Now, Aristomachus would have approved of the other man, insofar as he ever approved of anybody, rest his soul. He was doing all the right things: shield up, left foot toward the enemy, back foot at right angles, sword resting on his right shoulder ready to be launched for the neck cut; well, he was doing it all, like dance steps, but not really thinking about what they meant. I know the feeling. You learn the moves and once you know them and Aristomachus has told you, Yes, you've got the idea, then you feel as if you're somehow guaranteed to be safe, so long as you do them right. That's the basis for all drill, right?

On he came, the shining bronze killer crab; I could tell he was as nervous as I was, maybe even more so. Thinking back, I can see why. I wasn't doing anything right, you see; he must have looked at me and seen absolutely nothing familiar, no guard, no first position; must've been absolutely bewildering for the poor man. I suppose it must have happened this way: he waited for me to put up, then he waited some more, and then his instincts or his training took over and he launched into the first step of the side-cut, anticipating my stroke and raising his shield to parry it. Only I didn't make the stroke. I just stood there like a statue; and of course, my spear was sticking out of my hand, and as he closed in on me he walked straight on to it.

I promise you, if I live to be eighty years old I'll never make a more perfect neck-shot; right in the classic spot at the base of the throat where the little hollow is, above the two ends of the collarbone. Actually, as soon as I saw what was happening I instinctively tried to get my spear out of the way – *Look out, you clumsy idiot*, my heart yelled at me, but by then it was too late. The light went out in his eyes, he made a funny noise and flopped down like a suit of empty clothes – crash went his armour, like when something startles you and you drop a metal bowl or a helmet on the ground and it clangs. I jumped back; Horror and Disgust had taken over my heart. I wouldn't ever have run from him living, but now he was dead I nearly turned tail and scampered. Remarkable thing.

But there was a battle going on; I caught sight of it, out of the corner of my eye, and my heart told me to wake up before some bastard killed me. I tell you, it was that feeling of panic you have when you've fallen asleep in the hall, and suddenly you wake up and there's people crowded all round you, and for a moment you don't know what's going on. Then I caught sight of Uncle Deistratus; he was down on one knee with his shield held up, his other hand braced against the ground, just as the man standing over him stuck him through the face with a spear.

I shouted – don't ask me what – and bounded forwards like a happy dog; then I felt the dead man's spear dragging down my shield, and I let go of the handgrip; and when I did that, my middle and fourth fingers fell off. The spearhead had severed them, neat as you like, and I'd been so terrified I hadn't even noticed.

I didn't know what to do next; some god had taken away my wits, and I stood there like a big straw target, just asking to be thrown at. In a battle, that's not a good thing to do, and someone (don't know who) must have seen me for the opportunity I was; a spear hit me on the side of the head and knocked me down, and I was out of it then, for a while.

When I came to, all I could see was feet. It was like being in a forest. They were shuffling about all round me, and I could hear grunting and bashing noises, like a blacksmith's shop. At least I had the wit to keep absolutely still, even when somebody stubbed his toes in my face. It didn't help that I'd been lying in a badly folded heap, so both my right arm and my left leg had gone to sleep; if I'd somehow managed to get back on my feet I wouldn't have lasted more than a couple of heartbeats. So, for once in my life, I did the sensible thing and stayed put.

As if to make up for my numb right arm, my left hand was hurting like you wouldn't believe, and the only thought in my heart was terror that someone might stand on it or kick against it; the damn thing felt so tender and sore that just thinking about it made me feel weak. In other words, I was stuck, useless and helpless. I won't say it was the most miserable moment of my whole life, because I'm not dead yet and some god may be listening. All I can say is, if there's something worse lined up for me in the future, someone kill me now.

Just when I was beginning to despair of ever getting out of there, something happened; there was a kind of a surge overhead, something fell on me and the feet shuffled past. I lay there under the thing (all I could think was, Oh great joy, it didn't land on my bad arm) until it was quiet, then I sort of rolled awkwardly – can't describe it, really, but it was uncomfortable and not very dignified – pulled my head out and sat up.

The thing was my uncle Thaumastes, and he was as dead as they come. I found that very hard to believe. Not that I'd ever liked him much; he was one of those grown-ups who can't pass by a small child without ruffling its hair, something that annoyed the hell out of me when I was small. But he'd always been there; he was the sort of inoffensive, amiable man you never really notice, you assume he's there because he always is. He was no fighter, that's for sure; not much of anything really, being the great Deistratus' kid brother, father of the promising young Callon, Mylon and Doryclytus, husband of Prince Agis' younger daughter – the sort of man you define in terms of other people, not himself. Anyway, he was dead; his helmet was off and someone had crushed his skull with a rock.

Which reminded me: the battle. It was about fifteen yards away by now and moving fast in the wrong direction; Fear and Panic were driving us like sheep back the way we'd come, and I was getting left behind. Now, you've seen a new-born foal flolloping around on its bendy legs; that was me, pins and needles like death in my left leg, stumbling frantically to keep up with the battle – I was facing the backs of the enemy, who were driving us back; I suddenly realised that somehow or other I was going to have to get round them if I wanted to rejoin my family and get out of there. Awkward. I didn't know what to do, and I was standing still being a target again.

And then something wonderful happened. I can't describe how wonderful it was. Imagine a god swooping down out of the sky and whisking you clear of all your troubles. It wasn't a god, in fact, it was Doryclytus with the chariot; he came bouncing up out of nowhere right behind me, yelled, 'Get in!' at the top of his voice, and was cracking the whip on the horses' backs before I'd had a chance to grab the rail. But I scrambled up somehow, and he took me away from the battle. I've never been so grateful for anything in my whole life.

Well, Doryclytus put a lot of ground between us and the battle. Then he pulled up and leaned forward against the rail, looking like death.

'You're all right, then,' he said.

'Yes,' I replied, in the interests of keeping it simple. 'What happened?'

'It was after you killed Strymoneus,' he said. I was about to say, 'Who?' but he went on, 'They pushed forward, you went down; we went up to get you and there was a ruck right over where you were lying. That's about it, really. I'm glad you're safe, after all that.'

I felt like I'd fallen out of a tree. 'You mean all that was because of me?' I asked.

He looked at me. 'Well, we weren't just going to leave you there, were we? Father and Uncle Deistratus'll be relieved; when they drove us back like that, I was sure we'd lost you.'

He didn't know. Well, no reason why he should; he'd got more sense than to stand about sightseeing in the middle of a battle. 'That's all right, then,' I said. 'Thank you.'

He shrugged. 'I didn't do anything,' he said. 'I was just driving the chariot, trying to keep out of the way. What happened to your hand?'

'Nothing, really,' I said stupidly, really wishing he hadn't noticed. After all, his father and his uncle were lying dead out there, apparently because of me. The last thing I could face right then was his sympathy.

'Your fingers,' he persisted. 'Are you all right? Sorry, what a dumb question.' He was gawping at me like I was a hero or something; and right then, quite apart from the shame and the embarrassment, I was ready to kneel down and worship him like a god for getting me out of the battle. The whole thing was ridiculous.

Anyway (Cratus continued), that was the battle. As you've probably gathered by now, we lost; though it was a fairly close thing, because we won on other parts of the field, and the next day the Triphylians packed up and headed for home. I gather they'd more or less finished their raid anyway, and were only holding on for the battle.

Probably the worst part of it all was that I was now a hero. It seems that the clown who managed to stick himself on my spear, Strymoneus, was the Triphylian king's nephew, second in line to the throne after a five-month-old kid, and the king himself was in his seventies and not a well man. Killing him was about the only notable deed we did in the battle, which had cost us our own hero Deistratus and a dozen or so other big names, so naturally we – I mean us, the Eleans – played up Strymoneus, which made me a big man. Of course, I didn't dare say anything, for fear of being strung up from a tree; denying our one major achievement in an otherwise wretched affair would have been the next best thing to treason under the circumstances, which were gloomy enough to be going on with. The battle was supposed to be the prince's first great deed, remember? I can't say any of the blame for what happened was his any more than anybody else's, but the fact remained that the whole deal had gone very badly wrong and made things a whole lot worse. Which, dear brother—

'Don't start,' said the blind man angrily. 'You've been going on and on about this for nigh on forty years. If we'd won—'

'Yes, but we didn't.'

'But if we had—'

'Yes, but we didn't.'

Palamedes held up his hand. 'You two,' he said, 'shut up, or take it outside. What will our guest think of you, yelling at each other like a couple of neighbours over a boundary stone? I'm sorry,' he went on, turning to the Phoenician. 'You know how it is with brothers sometimes.'

'That's all right,' the Phoenician said. 'Actually, I was thinking of turning in now, if that's . . .'

'You're a very tolerant man, I can see that,' Palamedes said. 'Usually they aren't like this at all. Best of friends, really. It's just this one subject brings out the worst in them. What I always say is, anything that happened forty years ago can't possibly be worth shouting about now.'

Cratus smiled. 'Really?' he said. 'My heart seems to remember you getting pretty worked up when you fell out with Mnesilochus over that ditch on your boundary. And that was fifty years ago, if it was a day.'

'Different matter entirely,' Palamedes said irritably. 'I know for a fact my father dug that ditch, so legally it's mine. Mnesilochus had no right—'

The Phoenician's head was beginning to hurt. 'Really,' he said, 'I would rather like to go to bed now, if it's all the same to you. It's a very interesting story, I can tell; but it's been ever such a long day, and I want to be up bright and early in the—'

Palamedes frowned. 'Well,' he said, 'tell you what. We'll take the story up to the funeral, and then you can hear the rest tomorrow. How's that sound, Cleander?'

'It's a good place to pause,' the blind man agreed. 'Shall I just finish it off? No disrespect to my brother here, but I was closer to what was going on than he was.'

'Be my guest,' Cratus grumbled. 'Never let it be said I didn't give you a chance to tell your side of the story.'

As Cratus just said (the blind man continued), the war had turned out pretty badly, for our family and for King Leon. But just curling up and licking our wounds wasn't going to help anything. Like my father always used to say, there's precious little in this life that can't be made worse and can't be made better, depending on how you set about it.

The first thing we had to do, of course, was hold the funeral. Regardless of what impressions Cratus may have tried to give you, Uncle Deistratus was a great and famous man; he served his family and his city all his life, and he wouldn't have wanted to go out any other way. It was only right and proper we give him a decent send-off.

Building the pyre was a major undertaking in itself. We worked it out; the least we could get away with was twelve wagonloads of reasonably dry timber – use freshly cut green pine and even if you can get it to burn, it'll spit resin at you and muck up a solemn occasion – but twelve loads was more than we could get our hands on in a hurry just then. We sent runners out to beg timber from everyone we could think of, but they all came back with the same story – nobody could spare us any timber because they were patching up their barns for the harvest. Fair enough, I could see their point, but it wasn't helping us build our bonfire, and all the while Uncle Deistratus wasn't getting any fresher. Then someone mentioned that there was a wrecked ship down on the coast. We were dubious about that; driftwood spits like the devil when it's burned, almost as bad as pine, and the flame's a funny colour because of the salt. But we didn't really have a choice, so off the wagons went, and sure enough they came back laden with timber. One look at it was enough to convince us we'd been right to have our doubts. Damn stuff was still pretty well sodden in the middle; we'd have to douse the whole thing down with oil and lard to get it to take, and that meant putting up with the smell.

Come the day, though, we were lucky. Some god sent a stiff breeze, and although it was a noisy old fire, all hisses and crackles, that's actually not a bad thing for a funeral pyre; a bit of noise masks the fairly gruesome sounds a dead body tends to make when it's burned.

Once we were certain it wasn't going to go out on us with the job half done, so to speak, we unstoppered a jar of cheap drinking wine and poured the libations (well, you don't give the good stuff to the gods, do you?), making sure we left enough to damp down the embers once the fire had burned itself out. Then we picked out the bones, folded them up in the fat from the ox we'd slaughtered for the funeral feast and stowed them in a big jar – gilded bronze it was; Deistratus got it from a Northerner, and it had scenes of harvest and vintage embossed round the sides.

We dug the pit, closed up and piled a barrow (one thing we're never short of in these parts is stones, as anybody who's broken a newly shod plough will tell you), sprinkled the last of the wine and did the respectful standing-around bit, which I can never see the point of, personally. I mean, if someone's dead you're either beside yourself with grief or glad that he's gone to the Happy Islands, or delighted to be rid of an enemy; hanging about looking quietly miserable is almost never appropriate.

Well, that concluded the solemn part of the occasion. Now we could get on with the fun.

Let's face it, everybody enjoys funeral games. Some people, the types who are naturally good at running and jumping and all that stuff, spend hours and hours training. Then there are the people who've got first-class thoroughbred chariot horses, or red-hot keen archers, or crackerjack boxers and wrestlers; a funeral's the only real opportunity they get to show off, compete with like-minded folks, maybe even win a prize and some glory. And, by some unkind chance, nobody worth holding games for had died for a long, long while in our city, so all the frustrated games enthusiasts hadn't had a chance to play.

Oh yes, everybody benefits from the games. It's not just the people who take part, either. The family gets a chance to clear out some of the accumulated junk the dead man's acquired over the years; you know the sort of thing – unwanted gifts from unwelcome guests, family heirlooms that everyone's sick at the sight of, loot from primitive and poverty-stricken villages, small and ugly items of gold and silver. They're no use to anybody; it'd be insulting to give them as presents, they just sit in boxes or up in the rafters, taking up space. Offered as prizes, however, they bestow honour on the giver and the man who wins them. A good deal all round, really.

Deistratus had been a terror for piling up stuff eminently suitable for giving as prizes. He had a shed full of hideously ugly bronze tripods, silver-plated cauldrons with the silver peeling off, great big ugly two-handed cups that looked like the sort of thing the cutler's apprentice takes home for his mother after his first month in the shop, bent swords with moth-eaten baldricks, armour in excessively large or small sizes, two left greaves – you name it, he'd got it stashed away, as if for this very purpose. Obviously, unwanted metalwork wouldn't be enough for the two main prizes, chariot race and foot-race; but it so happened that a few months before his death he'd been given a couple of flute girls by some foreign friend of his. Gorgeous, they were, to look at, but you wouldn't want either one of them in the house, neither the filthy-tempered one nor the clumsy one. I think his family were at their wits' end trying to think of ways to get shot of them when the perfect opportunity presented itself.

Well, the best men won, naturally. Thersilochus won the chariot race, Buprasius won the boxing and the javelin. Mecisteus won the wrestling – he cheated, of course, but there'd have been so much trouble if he hadn't won that nobody said anything, and we made up for it by giving him a mouldy old helmet for first prize, and giving Lyces, the runner-up, a really rather tidy mixing-bowl that had belonged to Deistratus' grandfather. Shame on me, I can't remember who won the archery or throwing the weight; what I can tell you is that I lost in the second round of the weight, because just as I was swinging and pushing with my back leg, like you're supposed to, I slipped on a patch of horseshit left behind after the chariot race and went down flat on my nose. That was the sum total of honour and glory I got out of those games, and I suppose in a way it wasn't a bad thing. What're honour and glory, after all, but reasons for people to remember you after you're dead? Now, I can't remember who actually won the prize, but you ask anybody who was there and you'll find that the one spectacle that lodged in everybody's mind was the sight of me sprawled in a little pyramid of horse dung, so I suppose I came out best after all.

But the reason I'm telling you all this, apart from the fact that it's a good story and it's about famous people who should be remembered, is that the winner of the foot-race was none other than our beloved crown prince, the one who was the problem we'd made such a hash of fixing. Won it easily, too, and against better men. At the time there was a certain amount of muttering – only won because he's the king's son, and shouldn't be surprised he's good at running, not after what happened in the battle – the usual stuff. But anybody who actually saw the race knew in his heart that it was a true win, fair and square. Quite unexpectedly, without any help from us, the kid had done something right. Well, that's life.

Something big, too. People were talking (not the sore-heads, other people), saying what a good race it had been and how the prince had run it well. But, when all's said and done, winning a race in a local funeral games wasn't big enough, not to establish the kid as a good man in the hearts of the people. Which led my heart back to wondering: we need to find something properly big to do, and fast. I wasn't deaf. They were starting to blame the boy for the defeat. Nothing specific, of course, because there wasn't anything specific to blame him for. But that's almost worse, in a way. A man gets a reputation for bad luck, there's nothing he can do about it because it's not up to him. He can't make up his mind and harden his heart to go out and deliberately have good luck, the way he can go fight a battle or kill a bear or something.

Worse still, the enemy were getting sure of themselves – particularly Prince Oeleus, Leon's brother's son, who'd be king if the crown prince didn't measure up. Did I mention Oeleus won first prize in the long jump? Also, he'd made a fairly good show in the battle (better than the prince did, anyway) and he'd always been popular with the peers of the realm, the people Leon and the kid had antagonised over the years by the judgements they'd given at law. Don't get me wrong; Oeleus was a good man, in many ways better suited to be king than Leon or his son. He had the knack of carrying off his mistakes as though they were successes, which is pretty well essential if you want to rule a city, and he didn't make that many mistakes either. He was a good, brave fighter, he managed his land well, he had a lot of friends in other cities all over the country, and yes, he was a fair-minded man in matters that didn't concern him – he'd have made a good judge and handed down sound judgements in law. But he wasn't Leon's son, only his nephew; so even though he was a good man, he wasn't good enough, and never could be. Not unless he could force the issue and push the kid aside when Leon died. The difficulty was, that was looking more and more likely as time went on, and that in itself was unsettling for families that had always enjoyed Leon's favour, been his advisers, that sort of thing. Knowing that the rival heir to the throne doesn't like you does wonders for your loyalty, I can tell you.

I was debating these things with my heart, the evening after the games, when we were drinking after the big dinner in the long hall. It was a fairly boisterous gathering, as you can imagine. The good wine was going the rounds, some of the men were singing, some of them had tied up some poor fool to a pillar at the side of the hall and were chucking the bones off their plates at him, first one to draw blood wins. In the background, our nonentity of a harper was playing some trash and mumbling the words of the big battle-scene under his breath, as if he was burgling a house and was terrified anybody would hear him. The hall was unpleasantly smoky (we were burning up the last of that damned driftwood) and I'd had more than enough of the good wine. What I really wanted was to get home, sponge the vomit off my clothes (had the bad luck to get between one extremely thirsty reveller and the door) and go straight to bed.

I didn't do that, of course. Instead, I got up, marched down the hall and stood next to the king. At that moment there was a really quite respectable fight going on in the middle, so everybody was watching that. I told King Leon I had an idea.

'Another one,' he grunted, but that was just show. Really I could've told him anything at that moment so long as it sounded like good news. 'Go on, then,' he said. 'What's in your heart today?' He paused and scowled. 'If it's a punitive action against the Triphylians, you can forget about it right now. My heart tells me we're not going to get mixed up in any more of your brilliant schemes. Promise.'

'How'd it be,' I said, 'if I told you I'd thought of a way to boost the prince's standing so much that Oeleus won't stand a chance, and help make good after the war into the bargain. And it's doing something the boy really is good at.'

'He's good at something? News to me.'

'Ah.' I smiled. 'That's because you don't watch him close like I do, you've got other things on your mind. I reckon I probably know him rather better than you do. His heart's quite easy to learn, you know, if you set your mind to it. And basically he's a good man. He needs the one big thing we've been talking about. Well, maybe I've found it.'

'Carry on,' King Leon said.

'Games,' I said. 'Specifically, the foot-race.'

He scowled. 'That's not enough,' he said.

'It will be,' I said, 'if we cook up the best set of games anybody's ever seen. Games so good people will be talking about them for years to come. All the best athletes in the world – except for foot-racers, of course,' I added. 'The boy's good but not that good.'

Leon thought for a moment. 'Right,' he said. 'And I suppose somebody really important and famous is going to drop handily dead just so you can hold these extra-special games of yours. Like me, for instance. Dream on, Cleander. I'm a good father, but there's limits.'

I shook my head. 'No,' I said, 'that's the clever thing. Not funeral games. Just games.'

'Just games? With nobody dead?'

'That's right.'

He looked at me. 'What a bloody stupid idea,' he said.

CHAPTER THREE

'Just a moment,' the Phoenician interrupted. 'When you say *games*—'

'Yes?' Palamedes replied.

'I'm sorry,' the Phoenician said. 'I don't understand.'

Palamedes looked blank, as if his face had just fallen off. 'You mean you don't know about games?' he said. 'That's *strange*.'

If he'd been trying his hardest to make his guest feel uncomfortable, he couldn't have done a better job. 'We don't have anything like that where I come from,' he said. 'I get the impression from what the blind – what Cleander was saying that it's some kind of contest or trial, to see who's the best at running and fighting sort of things.'

Palamedes took a deep breath and let it go again. 'You could say that,' he said. 'But it's still misleading, the way you put it. The games – now then, let's see. Don't you even have chariot races where you live?'

'Chariot races?'

'Obviously not. This is going to be really hard to explain. All right. We have a tradition that when a great, important man dies, we honour his memory with competitions – games – of various kinds, all basically to do with strength or agility.'

'Ah,' said the Phoenician. 'Training for war. We do that.'

'Not exactly,' Palamedes replied. 'I mean, they aren't supposed to be *useful* or anything. But it's a way of finding out who's the better man without actually having to have a fight to the death. It's a competition – like war – but nobody gets killed. At least, only very occasionally.'

'I see,' the Phoenician said, clearly not telling the truth. 'These games, then, they're the same sort of skill you need to be good at fighting, but they're not actually fighting exercises.'

Palamedes nodded eagerly. 'That's it,' he said.

'Except for the running, of course.'

'What?'

'Running,' the Phoenician said. 'I think you mentioned something about running competitions. Well, surely that's not a martial art you'd want to *encourage*, is it?'

Palamedes frowned. 'Don't think of it as running as in running away,' he said. 'There's more than one kind of running, you know. For instance, there's running after. Chasing the fleeing enemy. That's a martial skill for you.'

The Phoenician thought about it for a moment. 'I don't know spit about wars and fighting,' he said. 'For which, let me add, I'm truly thankful. But I remember being told a few years back that when the enemy are running away and you're chasing after them, it's a bad idea to have your best runners at the front of your formation; anybody who runs faster than the man next to him is a traitor, as well as an idiot. Go figure. He opens up a gap in the line, which puts everyone else in danger; then he gets killed himself. Anything apart from a short, orderly pursuit is just giving the enemy a chance to turn a defeat into a victory.' He paused. 'Why are you all looking at me like that?'

It was Cleander who broke the silence. 'We don't do things the same way you people do. Obviously.'

The Phoenician shrugged. 'All right,' he said. 'But these games of yours, I'm still not clear about what they're *for*. I mean, these running competitions. What happens?'

Palamedes frowned. 'You scratch a line in the dirt,' he said, 'and then you pace out a certain distance, and you scratch another line.

Or you can pile up stones, that's just as effective. The first man to get from one line or one pile to the other wins. Simple.'

'I suppose,' the Phoenician replied. 'But what do they get out of it? Apart from travelling a short way in an uncomfortable fashion?'

'Prizes,' someone said. 'There's always prizes for the winners of the games.'

The Phoenician nodded. 'That makes sense. Only didn't Cleander say just now that the prizes are nearly always junk? Things people are only too glad to get rid of?'

'That's not the point,' said somebody else at the other end of the table. 'It's not the prize that matters, it's the fact that you've won it. Shows that you won, therefore you beat a lot of other people, therefore you're better than they are.'

'At running,' the Phoenician interrupted.

'Sorry?'

'You're better than they are at running,' the Phoenician said. 'Not necessarily at anything else.'

The man who'd been trying to explain frowned. 'Well, all right. I suppose that's true, up to a point.'

'Where I come from,' said the Phoenician, 'we tend to pride ourselves on *not* running, if you see what I mean. We don't run away in battle, we don't run after the enemy when we've won. And offhand, I can't think of any other times when running is useful; so, if it's not useful, why is it a good thing to be better at it than anybody else?'

There was a moment of troubled silence. 'It's not just running,' someone said. 'There's jumping. Jumping's good if you need to cross a river, say.'

The Phoenician smiled. 'Where I come from,' he said, 'we build bridges.'

'Chariot races,' said someone else.

'Same goes for chariots as men on foot: you don't want them charging ahead, or it's asking for trouble. That battle Cratus told us about proves that, surely.'

Palamedes was scowling. 'All right,' he said, 'wrestling. And boxing. They're both useful skills. They teach you how to fight.'

The Phoenician sucked his teeth thoughtfully. 'I suppose so,' he said. 'But there's fighting and fighting. Fighting for your country in a battle, with weapons – yes, I can see why you'd want to practise that, because it's useful. But fighting *not* in a battle, without weapons? Seems to me the only time you'd do that is if you picked a fight with someone, a neighbour, say, or a stranger in the market you decided you didn't like. Fighting like that isn't useful to a city. Quite the reverse, really. I'd say it wasn't something you'd really want to encourage.'

Palamedes sighed. 'You're missing the point,' he said. 'We never said games were practice for useful skills. In fact, we agreed that a while back.'

'Yes,' replied the Phoenician smugly, 'but you did say that games were to find out who was the better man. And I said, better at what? Being better at something that's no use for anything – antisocial, even – doesn't really count for much. It's like me putting on airs because I'm so much better at picking my nose than you are.'

'I can see we haven't been explaining this right,' Palamedes said. 'In fact, my heart's telling me that maybe this is one of those things you can't really explain to foreigners.'

'What he means is,' Cratus interrupted, 'games, or winning at games, is a reason for remembering someone after he's dead and gone. At least, that's why people take part in them. They hope that by winning, they'll make themselves famous and glorious enough that people will remember their names.'

'I see,' the Phoenician said. 'So it's all about –' Here he said a word in his own language that nobody recognised. 'It means remembering the past,' he explained. 'Making a record of the past, in fact, so that the deeds of great and glorious men may never be forgotten, and so that people can learn from the mistakes made by their forefathers and not repeat them.'

'Exactly,' said Palamedes, relieved. 'That's exactly what the games are for. So that great runners and jumpers and wrestlers will be remembered.'

'And great nose-pickers too?'

'If you live in a place where nose-picking is considered a great skill, yes. Why not?'

The Phoenician nodded. 'Fair enough,' he said. 'I was just asking. Only, I don't think it's ever going to catch on where I live. Whereas our way of going about this same thing, I think that's going to spread, and one day everybody'll be doing it.'

'You mean writing,' Cleander broke in, 'what we were talking about earlier. The little marks and squiggles.'

'That's it.'

'Well,' Palamedes said, 'each to his own. You look for immortality by making little marks on waxed boards.'

'And you do it by running between piles of stones.' The Phoenician shrugged again. 'Like you said, each to his own. But one other thing. These games of yours – why do you only have them when somebody dies?'

The next moment, the Phoenician was wondering what it was he'd said that everybody found so funny. 'Please excuse us,' Palamedes said. 'Private joke. But that's a very good question you just asked. Why indeed?'

'Which is where I'd just got to,' Cleander added plaintively, 'before I was interrupted.'

'What a bloody stupid idea,' King Leon said (the blind man went on). 'Holding games when nobody's died.'

'I don't think so,' I replied.

'I do,' Leon said. 'Think about it, will you? You're out in the fields ploughing or running your sheep through the raddle, and a herald comes up to you and says, Drop everything, we're holding games. And you ask why, and the herald says, Because everybody's still alive. I know what I'd tell him to do, in those circumstances.'

I sat down next to him. 'Leon,' I said, 'you're looking at this the wrong way. Games are for celebrating, right?'

Leon nodded. 'To celebrate the glory of the dead man, and make glory for the living.'

'All right,' I said. 'And people like games, yes?'

'Of course,' he replied. 'Both watching and taking part.'

I smiled. 'Now we're getting somewhere,' I said. 'Of course, the trouble with most games is, only the people within a day's journey get to take part.'

'Well, of course. You can't leave dead bodies hanging about while you wait for people to arrive from all over.'

'Absolutely,' I said. 'But if you had games when nobody's died, you could send out heralds beforehand, well in advance; make sure that all the best games-players got to hear about it. If they knew all the other first-rank runners and jumpers and charioteers were going to be there, they'd want to be there too.'

Leon scratched his ear. 'I suppose they would,' he said. 'But you still haven't told me what the games would be *for*. I know, they're to celebrate. Celebrate *what*?'

I shrugged. 'Whatever you like,' I said. 'Elis. Prosperity.'

'What prosperity? It's been a bloody awful year for onions.'

'Tell people they're celebrating prosperity,' I suggested, 'and they'll assume they're prosperous. Or, if they aren't, everybody else is. It'll make people feel good about themselves, and in turn they'll feel good about you. And the kid.'

'All right,' said Leon slowly. 'But my heart can see what they'll be thinking: this is Leon, they'll think, trying to make us all feel good so he can palm his useless son off on us. And they'll be right, too.'

'Fair enough,' I replied. 'All right, let's have games to celebrate the gods. Or just one god. Make it a festival.'

Leon sighed. 'Not another damned festival,' he said. 'There's too many as it is, if you ask me.'

'But none of them have games,' I replied artfully.

'That's a whatsitsname. Circular argument.'

'All right. But how about it?' I said. 'You send out heralds saying, Zeus has spoken to King Leon of Elis, promising prosperity and glory to him and his noble son. To celebrate, King Leon's marking the occasion with special games. Everybody's going to be there. If you heard that, what'd you do? Would you go?'

Leon nodded. 'Oh, of course I'd go. If only out of curiosity.'

'Well then.' I clapped my hands together triumphantly. 'There you are. I'll bet you, people will talk about nothing else for months beforehand, and years afterwards. And that's glory.'

Leon frowned. 'I suppose it is,' he replied. 'All right, I'll think about it in my heart. Though really, some god must have taken away my wits to let you talk me into anything after this damned war.'

'You think about it,' I said, standing up. 'That's all I ask.'

Well, he thought about it (Cleander continued), and I suppose some god must have put it in his heart to approve of the idea. Whether it was a good god or a mischievous one – well, you'll be able to judge for yourselves when I've done with this story.

First I heard of his decision was when the heralds came round the town-side fields calling everybody to Meeting. That was enough to cause a stir on its own; Meeting wasn't exactly a thing of the past back then, but there hadn't been one for years. Really, it's a throwback to the old Sons-of-the-Achaeans days, back when our grandfathers' grandfathers came down out of the north and pushed the Ionians out; in those days, so they say, they didn't have kings in the same way as we do now; the king was just one of the better sort chosen by the rest to be the leader in war and stuff, and if he wanted to do anything he had to call his peers together and ask them first. Doesn't sound a very efficient way of doing things, I know; but that's how we won the Peloponnese, apparently, so it must have worked for them.

Anyway. We all shuffled off to Meeting – years ago there was a special place set aside; by that time we remembered where it used to be, but a man called Coccys had built a house on it – and why not? Criminal to waste good land just for old times' sake. So we all hung around outside Coccys' house, wondering what to do next, until he came out and said why didn't we go through into his back orchard, it was big enough and we could sit under the trees in the shade. That sounded plenty good, so that's what we did.

Along came King Leon – it was a while before he showed up. Apparently he'd gone to the palace yard, expecting people to show up there, and stood around on his own for a while wondering why nobody else was there, till someone came and found him and told him what was going on. He had a short cloak on, and a spear and two dogs, like he was out for a day in the fields. Someone had told him that was the right way to show up for Meeting, but whether it's true that's how they used to do it, or whether someone was pulling Leon's leg, I don't know.

As soon as everybody had settled down – didn't take long, it was pleasantly warm and most people were feeling drowsy and content – he stood up on the back of Coccys' old apple-cart and started to talk.

'Friends,' he said (it should have been *Sons of the Achaeans*, but who cares?). 'I have something I want to share with you. Last night, some god came to me in a dream and told me that he was angry with us here in Elis.' That didn't go down well; people sat up and started to mutter, and Leon had to bang on the cart-bed with his spear to get their attention. 'This god told me, "You Eleans don't seem to care much about us gods, which is why we punished you in the battle, giving victory to lesser men. We punished you, but you're slow, you haven't understood. So they sent me to tell you what you ought to be doing; and if you do as you're told, we'll be pleased and things will go well for you. If you don't – well, your hearts will tell you about it soon enough, believe me."'

Well, he'd certainly got their attention. I wouldn't have gone about it quite like that, of course, but Leon wasn't stupid, he knew about people.

'"What you've got to do," the god told me,' said Leon, '"is hold a festival." "Excuse me," I said, "but we hold plenty of festivals already; aren't they good enough?" "No," said the god. "Think about it for a moment. You think gods are so different from mortals that what bores you doesn't bore us? What makes you think we take pleasure from listening to a bunch of wool-stuffed old priests mumbling old poems? You've heard them all before a couple of dozen times; well, what about us? We've heard them *thousands* of times, and they weren't anything special to begin with. You wouldn't burn down a temple, would you? Of course not. But you want to talk about impiety; which is worse? Burning down a temple – well, you burn it down, you build it again, no skin off our noses, really. But wasting the time and patience of the gods – there's times we're tempted to smash the lot of you with thunderbolts, just to make you shut up. That's the trouble with you mortals: you don't think."'

I was holding my breath here. Either people were going to think Leon had gone off his head and needed to be put out of his misery, or else some god had given him wisdom from heaven, and they'd believe him and do just what he said. One or the other; no half measures. Still, that was Leon.

'So I asked this god,' Leon went on, '"What would you like us to do? Just say it, it's good as done." The god smiled and said, "Not so hasty, Leon. What we want from you isn't going to be so easy. First you're going to have to persuade the Sons of the Achaeans, and you know yourself how awkward and difficult they can be, especially if you're asking them to do something new and different." "That's all right," I told him, "you'll give me divine eloquence to convince them with." And the god grinned at me and said, "We'll see."'

Leon was smiling too, and soon every damned idiot in that orchard had a big soppy grin on his face, though whether or not they believed him I couldn't say. That's where Leon was clever, see. It didn't matter whether what he was saying was *truly* true, it was true *enough*. The god may have been a real dream, or it may have been the god telling Leon's heart what to say. All as broad as it's long, really.

'So, anyway,' Leon went on, 'what the god told me to do was this: we're going to hold a festival, but it's not going to be a boring one. There won't be any standing around listening to some old fart reciting hymns; the gods want something to entertain them, so we'll give them something. We're going to have games.'

Dead silence. Even the sheep.

'Well, I was as surprised as you are,' Leon went on. '"Excuse me," I asked the god, "how can we have games? Nobody's died." And the god looked at me, sort of meaningfully, and said, "Well, if that's the only problem, I'm sure we can arrange something." I didn't like the sound of that, so I said, "It's all right, I'm just getting used to the idea; games with nobody dead. And you know what? The more I think about it, the more I like the idea." And the god nodded and said, "That's all right, then."'

I still wasn't sure about how he was going about it, but as far as my heart could judge, it was going down well. Mostly, I reckon, people were thinking, It doesn't matter whether the idea really came from the gods or not; if King Leon said it did, that's good enough for us. They were covered, you see, because a good man always trusts the word of his king, which is why bad kings can still have good subjects. If you didn't have a system like that, I think cities just wouldn't be possible.

'So,' Leon went on, 'that's how it's going to be. We're going to hold games, and we're going to send out heralds to all the greatest games-players in the world, telling them to come to Elis and put on a show for the gods. There will, of course, be prizes – proper prizes, not junk; we're going to show people that we're not paupers in Elis – but I reckon that winning at the Elean games is going to be the biggest, best prize of all on its own; better than bronze or silver, better than gold itself. Because people are going to remember these games, the games in Elis when nobody died. To start with, they'll remember them just because nobody'd died; then they'll remember them because all the greatest heroes in the world were there, like it was the old days of Thebes or Troy, or the Golden Fleece; and then they'll remember them for the wonderful things that were done there – because when great heroes compete with each other, they put themselves out more than when they're matched against the likes of you and me – and that's the memory that won't ever die. Those men will be as near as you can get to being gods themselves. And if that isn't a prize, somebody tell me what is.'

They were cheering him now, bless them; and even I was beginning to wonder if a god really had given him divine eloquence and he hadn't thought to mention it to me. And – well, if I was starting to believe him, when it was my idea to begin with, you can imagine how the rest of them were taking it. He was a clever man, King Leon, in his way; trouble was, either he didn't get the chance to be clever that way often enough, or he didn't realise what direction his talents lay in. It's often that way with clever people, like a man who's a natural shot with the bow but of course he wants to fight in the front rank, in armour, because even the world's best archer is of no account compared to a brave man with a spear.

But there was one man who wasn't smiling or cheering. I could see him from where I was sitting – put myself there on purpose so I could see him – and his heart wasn't happy at all. You've guessed it; Prince Oeleus, who reckoned on being king after Leon, because the boy wasn't up to it. Last thing Oeleus wanted was for Leon to do something that'd make him and Elis famous across the world. He wanted Leon to fail and get old and useless and die before his time, and Elis to be wretched and miserable and crying out for a good king who'd put things straight. Now that's what I mean, by the way, about good and bad kings and good and bad men. I have no doubts at all that Oeleus wanted to be king because he thought – well, he knew – that he'd be good at it, and good for Elis (because he was a good man, and he knew that too). But in order for him to get to be a good king, he was being a bad man and a bad prince, wishing misery and bad luck on Leon and Elis – so even before he was king he was a bad king, and how can good come out of a start like that? In fact, I'd say that anybody who wants to be king is likely to turn into a bad man, however good he may be; the things you have to do to get power make you unfit to have it, and there's no way round that that I can see. But of course, that hasn't got to do with anything, so forget I said it.

The point is, if we could rely on anything, we could rely on Oeleus making trouble, one way or another. I said as much to Leon that evening, after the dishes had been taken away and the girl was going round with the wine.

'Well, of course,' Leon answered me. 'You think I'm an idiot? Don't get me wrong, Oeleus is my own flesh and blood, and if the boy doesn't shape up then I need him to be the next king, otherwise he wouldn't still be here. You don't keep a wolf in your yard unless you figure one day you'll have a use for it.' But he looked depressed all the same, and maybe his heart was worrying about what he'd started. 'My guess is,' he went on, 'he'll try to make the games fail; but he can't do it openly – on his face he's got to be smiling all the time or else it'll turn people against him faster than you can throw a stone. People are like that, I've found. They don't like people who turn against something they want to see happen; but they get almost as much pleasure from seeing something fail as they do from watching it succeed. You think of how people talk about great men, heroes. While a hero's good, they're all for him; but still they're watching, like the wolf at the piggery door. As soon as he starts to show signs of failing, they're on to him like a hawk, pushing him down – not the man he used to be, they say, not half the man he was ten years ago, and once they're started on that game, there's nothing a man can do, however well he performs. They want him to fail. It'll be the same with our games, believe me. If things start to go wrong, there'll be more wanting them to fall flat than get back upright. And that's where Oeleus will take advantage.'

My heart knew he was right, but I didn't know what to suggest, so I kept my face shut.

'Which means,' Leon went on, 'we'll have to be very careful about how we handle this. It's like getting a city ready for war. You fortify all the weak points – because an enemy will smell them before he's even in sight of the walls. But you fortify the strong points as well, because if you concentrate all your strength at the weak places, you leave the strong points open to attack. We've got to figure out what the weak points and the strong points are, and guard all of them. Not just against Oeleus, either. You know that the gods will make a thing go wrong if there's any way it can go wrong.'

'That's true,' I said. 'And you're right, there's no point protecting your knees in a battle if you leave your head exposed, even if you're wearing a good helmet. On the other hand, you don't want to bash in a man's head if it means you leave your guard open.'

'Meaning?'

'Meaning,' I said, 'Oeleus won't want to attack our strong points if doing so leaves him vulnerable. It's what you were saying, about not wanting to make trouble openly. I think he'll try to make difficulties for the heralds, the ones who go around inviting people to the games. It's what I'd be doing, if I sat by his fire instead of yours.'

Leon grinned at me, a green-fig, young-wine sort of grin. 'Just as well you don't, then,' he said. 'But there's plenty who do whose hearts'll be telling them the same thing. And what can I do about what happens far away, in other cities? Nothing.'

'True,' I said. 'And who's to know in Elis what happens abroad? He can do what he likes there, and nobody here will think the worse of him.'

'Exactly,' Leon said. 'And that's why the most important thing will be choosing the heralds. They've got to be the bravest, wisest, cleverest men we can think of; and they can't be Oeleus' friends, either, or anybody who might be inclined to listen to him.'

I thought about that while the girl filled my cup. 'That cuts down the number we can choose from,' I said. 'Oeleus is more popular than you are among the better sort, and that's the sharp truth.'

Leon pulled a face. 'I know,' he said. 'Which is why I thank the gods I've got you.'

Honest truth: I hadn't seen it coming. I walked into it, like a bear-hunter into somebody else's trap. Some god took away my wits, I guess, because I should have seen it. But I didn't.

'Me?' I said, though I knew it was too late to get out of it now. 'What have I got to do with anything?'

A grin settled on Leon's face, like rooks on newly sown barley. 'Everything,' he said. 'You thought of the idea. You've just shown me you've got an excellent grasp of the situation and understand the difficulties. And, Zeus knows, you're a persuasive devil, because you persuaded me. I can't think of anybody better to take charge of this operation; including sending out the heralds, of course.'

'Of course,' I repeated; and inside me my heart was screaming, *Idiot! Idiot!* Which is all very well, but it should've warned me.

After that we talked about who we were going to have as our heralds. Leon didn't like some of the choices I made, but I insisted; if this was going to be my responsibility (or my fault), I had to have some say in the important decisions. Well, that's fair, isn't it?

Secrets are like those big round cheeses we get from Sicily (Cleander went on) – you know, the big island in the middle of the sea where the Cyclops lives – in that they're usually hard to swallow and extremely difficult to keep.

Pretty soon, everybody in Elis knew why I was going round the houses with a big smile on my face; and I've seen lepers and men with the plague more popular than I was. The reason wasn't hard to find: Eleans aren't stupid, they'd guessed about the same time as Leon and I did that Oeleus was going to make life very hard indeed for the king's heralds, as soon as we were safely over the border and out of Leon's jurisdiction. Accordingly, the houses I called on were generally empty when I got there. In a couple of cases, the doors were boarded up and the smoke-hole blocked with turf, just to make sure my heart got the message.

This threw out the plans I'd so laboriously agreed with the king. The men we'd decided on, the cream of the better sort in Elis, were all suddenly abroad, or sick, or dead (in some cases all three at the same time) and therefore not available to go heralding with me. I reported back to Leon, who wasn't the slightest bit happy about it, and together we worked out a new set of criteria for selecting heralds; basically, anybody who didn't get out of my way fast enough.

Actually, my first choice for a companion on this trip was the only man on my original list who agreed to go – my brother and best friend in all the world, Cratus. Well, he was then. These days, he's still my brother.

The two of us went to call on someone we both agreed might well be useful. Just as a precaution, we called at his house a couple of hours before dawn, creeping up by way of the river-bed just in case he'd set watchmen. As luck would have it, the watchdog sniffed us when we were fifty yards from the house and started barking like mad, but we were quick and managed to get our shoulders to the door before the gatekeeper had a chance to shoot the bolts.

'Good morning, Tachys,' I said.

Tachys, who'd obviously just woken up – he was standing in the hall with a wolfskin blanket wrapped round him, looking as if he'd just nibbled his way out of an egg – scowled at me and said, 'Go away, Cleander. I'm not going with you and that's final.'

'Tachys, Tachys,' I said, 'that's no way to greet an old friend. Besides, you don't even know why I'm here.'

Tachys shook his head. 'Don't need to know,' he replied, 'I can guess. And I swear to you, Cleander, whatever you ask of me the answer's going to be "No".'

'Really?'

'Absolutely.'

'That's your final answer, is it?'

'Yes.'

I nodded. 'All right,' I said. 'I ask you not to take part in the expedition I'm planning.'

I wouldn't have trapped him so easily if he'd been properly awake. But that was one of the reasons I tackled him when I did. Not a morning person, Tachys.

But we had to have him, no doubt about it. Tall, handsome, eloquent, resourceful, honourable to a fault, a fearless warrior, slow to anger but once angry, unstoppable; also well connected abroad, widely travelled, known to be first rate at handling people. The only reason I hadn't included him in my original selection was that a more miserable, depressing man never complained about a harvest. The thought of keeping him company from one end of the world to the other didn't appeal to me one bit.

He whined and moaned for a bit, but when I reminded him that he'd given his word, as good as sworn an oath, he realised he couldn't back out, even if he had been tricked into making the promise. That was Tachys all over; if you tricked him into swearing to kill his own son, he'd do it rather than break an oath. People like that worry me, no two ways about it; but on an expedition like the one we were embarking on, you need someone big and miserable you don't mind imposing on.

So; there were three of us later that morning when we headed out into the hills, looking for the next candidate. We found him easily enough; all we had to do was listen to our hearts warning us about extreme danger, and head for where we weren't supposed to go.

My uncle Sarpedon should have died when he was seventeen; there was this pirate, an Ionian, who'd built up quite an army out of runaways, criminals, bad people of every kind, and spent his time cruising up and down the coast of the Peloponnese picking off outlying farms and small villages. He was a spiteful man, this pirate – you can learn most of what you need to know about him from the fact that he wore a big necklace round his neck made up of the forefinger-knuckles of people he'd personally killed – and probably not right in the head, because he made a point of taking extreme and pointless risks, like in his heart he wanted to die. There are always people like that in the world. I've heard them called two-legged wolves, things like that, but they're not like any animal I've ever come across, far from it. They're all human, unfortunately.

Well, this pirate – I think he was called Dolon or Dolops or Doleus, something like that – fetched up on the north-west coast and managed to make a spectacular mess of a local army who'd set out to stop him; a proper army, not just a few farmers and their men, but chariots and fighters of the better sort. That was bad; it gave this Dolon ideas about making a name for himself, maybe even taking control of a small city (like Elis) and becoming a genuine king instead of a captain of pirates.

Now, there's my uncle Sarpedon: seventeen years old, tall, skinny, been the sort of kid who's always picking fights with boys older and stronger than he is and getting horribly smacked around for his trouble; Uncle takes it into his head to find this Dolon and kill him, by way of making a name for himself. Marvellous way to avoid reaching the age of eighteen, if you think about it calmly, but Sarpedon managed it. Say what you like about him, Fear's never managed to prise open the door of his heart. He found the pirate camp, waited till dark and sneaked past the sentries, ran off the horses to make a diversion, then waited outside Dolon's tent. When Dolon came bustling out, fumbling with his helmet straps and shouting blue murder at his captains, Sarpedon jumped on his back and cut his throat, quick and sure as an old priest killing a goat. Dolon falls down dead; of course, Sarpedon didn't really expect to get that far, so he hadn't given any thought as to how he was going to get out again. All he could do was run – he's fast, mind, and agile, he can change direction in a flash, dodge and duck and scramble under and over things. It must have been a sight to see, Sarpedon scampering about that camp like an escaped duck in a farmyard (you know how tricky they can be when you're rounding them up and there's just one left loose; there's ten or so of you after this one wretched duck, and you're tripping over things, running into each other, losing your tempers), and they nearly got him; they had him surrounded and were gradually closing in, when somehow or other he managed to slip right under the legs of one of those pirates and scuttle away. Nearly clear, he was, but an archer got off a lucky shot which nicked a vein in his leg. Only his heart knows how he kept going; by the time some of our people found him there can't have been enough blood left in his body to fill an eggshell. But he just lay there for days, not quite dying, until suddenly he sat up and announced that he was better now and wanted to go home. Amazing.

Well, you can figure it out for yourselves. In one scale, here's a man with no fear and an unhealthy abundance of good luck; in the other scale, he does crazy things just for glory or fun, which makes him extremely wearing to be with. Not my first choice, by a long way, but it didn't take much imagination to see where he might come in handy.

When we caught up with him, he was up a tree. At the bottom of this tree he'd tethered an old, sick ewe, and he was sitting on a low branch with a sword in one hand and an old, tattered cloak in the other, waiting for a big, ugly old bear that had taken to breaking into houses down in the valley.

'Go away,' he hissed, when we showed up. 'You'll frighten the bear.'

'The crows with the bear, Uncle,' I called back. 'It's me, Cleander. I need to talk to you.'

(Did I mention that during the battle, the one where Deistratus got killed, it was Sarpedon who waded through four – it was either four or five – at least four of the enemy when they were driving us back, and kept them busy with one hand while he dragged Deistratus' body out of the fighting with the other? Crazy thing to do, and he'd always loathed Deistratus while he was alive.)

'Go away,' he repeated. 'After I've got the bear, I'll come and find you.'

'It won't wait,' I replied. 'Official business. A mission on behalf of King Leon.'

He scowled horribly at me from between the branches. 'So help me, Cleander, if I don't get this bear because of you, I'll break both your arms. Now get out of here.'

My heart told me what to say. 'We'll go,' I said, 'if you'll promise to come with us on this mission. Otherwise we'll stay here under this tree shouting and banging sticks together so loud every bear from here to Corinth'll hear us. What do you say?'

I won't tell you what he said; the long and the short of it is he got his bear the next night, and showed us its skin when he caught up with us, back at Leon's house. He had terrible deep claw-marks across one shoulder and an ugly scar across his left cheek – ploughed through his beard like someone cutting the first rap in a field of beans. He was fifty-two years old then. Tachys was really,

really unhappy when he realised I was taking Sarpedon with us. I could see his point, at that.

Now, if it had been up to me, that would have been the party – me, Cratus, Tachys and Sarpedon. Tachys and me to do the talking, Cratus to watch out for Tachys and me – I'm cleverer than Cratus, but Cratus is wiser; anybody who knows us will tell you that – and Sarpedon just in case we ran into any mad dogs or large enemy armies. A small, well-balanced, carefully chosen party. I was quite proud of myself, given that I'd had so few people to choose from. In fact, I was congratulating myself and thanking my heart for the inspiration when we arrived back at the palace. There was someone sitting on the step, much to the annoyance and embarrassment of the two guards, who were trying their best to pretend she wasn't there.

But my sister Dusa was hard to ignore at that age; even if a man was able to keep his eyes off her, she'd probably kick his shins or bite him, just for wickedness. Her given name was Eurymedusa, but life's too short to spend the time it takes to say a name that long when you're talking about a girl who only comes up to your shoulder; so she was Dusa to family and close friends, Cimon's daughter to the world at large, and You-stay-away-from-my-sister to single men living in the city of Elis, if Cratus and I had anything to do with it.

'What the hell are you doing here?' I asked.

'Heard what you two are up to,' she replied. 'Hello, Uncle Sarpedon,' she added, grinning up at him. Needless to say, Uncle Sarpedon and Dusa got on famously. I suppose we should be grateful that the bad blood in our family seems to have been mostly concentrated in them, leaving the rest of us relatively normal.

'Hello yourself,' Sarpedon replied. 'Answer the question.'

'What question?'

'What he said.'

Dusa yawned. 'I hear you're all going on a jolly,' she said. 'Well, I'm coming too.'

Cratus and I looked at each other. Cratus was the first one to say it.

'No you're not,' he said.

'That's what you think,' Dusa replied. 'But you're wrong. I mean, if King Leon says I'm coming with you, I'm coming with you.'

I frowned. 'Not necessarily,' I told her. 'But what god would make the king say such a damned stupid thing?'

She stood up, nudging one of the guards out of the way. 'No god,' she said. 'Me. In fact, it was his suggestion. I just agreed, like a loyal subject should.'

I closed my eyes. The truth is, when she wasn't bored Dusa was a good kid. She was brave, straightforward, sharp as a new razor. But when she was bored, which was most of the time, she did things, just for fun. One of the things she'd been doing lately was making doe's eyes at the prince, the idiot boy we were going to all this trouble for. She was only doing it to annoy Cratus and me, and King Leon, and a dozen or so young men who tended not to think with their hearts or their brains, if you follow me. But another thing about Dusa: anything she did, she tended to do well. I could see how Leon might be extremely relieved to see her leave the country for a while.

'All right,' I said. Cratus looked as if I'd just jabbed him in the leg with an arrow. But I knew Dusa: dealing with her was like trying to get a hook out of a fish's lip – the more you pull, the deeper it goes in. My best chance was to make her welcome on the trip; then she might decide she didn't want to go, just to be awkward. But she knew my heart as well as I knew hers, so I wasn't holding my breath.

Uncle Sarpedon just went on grinning.

The one who took it worst of all, needless to say, was Tachys. Never knew a man relish misfortune quite so much as he did.

'It's insane,' he said, when we were hanging around the hall waiting for Leon to show up. 'As if we didn't have enough to contend with, you're seriously suggesting we take with us a sixteen-year-old girl with a warped sense of humour and the morals of a—'

Cratus gave him a look, and he subsided a bit. After all, she was our sister. If anybody was going to tell the truth about her, it'd be us.

'Anyway,' he went on, 'you can't allow it. It's too dangerous.

Quite apart from all the usual dangers of travelling – and they're bad enough to turn your hair grey, Zeus knows – we're quite likely to have to face attacks from Oeleus and his people. Taking a girl into a situation like that . . .'

I was beginning to wonder if I could face listening to Tachys all the way to the Outer Sea and back. I never knew anybody with such a burning compulsion to state the painfully obvious.

'If we take her with us,' I told him quietly, 'it'll be over my hamstrung corpse. But you just leave this to me, I'll handle it. All right?'

'It's between you and your heart, I suppose,' he grumbled. 'But you just remember—'

I trod on his toe to shut him up; Dusa had just strolled in, looking as if she had every right to be there. I never knew a little detail like two guards in armour to keep Dusa out of anywhere.

'In case you're wondering,' Dusa said, sitting on the edge of a table and swinging her feet, 'I'm not just coming along for the ride. In fact, if this crazy plan of yours works out in the end, it'll be all because of me. You should be grateful I decided to help out.'

Cratus shut his eyes. I nearly said something that would have made things a whole lot worse. Tachys, all due credit, just stood there like he was holding the roof up with his head.

'You've got an idea,' said Uncle Sarpedon, typically.

'Not just an idea,' Dusa replied, looking up at the sky through the smoke-hole. 'Some god must've put it in my heart, it's so clever. I'm going to be your Victory.'

For a moment, I didn't understand what she was getting at. Then Sarpedon burst out laughing and said, 'Like Dolonassa,' and I understood. I felt like I'd just put my foot in a wolf-trap.

Dolonassa was – what, my great-great-great-great-grandmother. By all accounts she was a raving beauty; she was also as tall as a man, taller than most, and when whoever it was who was king of Elis in her day – can't remember the name, sorry – managed to get himself thrown out by the Sons of the Achaeans for being vicious and useless, he used Dolonassa to help him get back in again. Apparently he had her painted head to foot in white glaze, the stuff potters use, handed her a spear all covered in gold leaf and sprinkled a whole palm-sized bag of gold dust in her hair. Then he stood her beside him in his chariot and set off for Elis, having first sent ahead a couple of his men to spread the word that the goddess Athena herself was bringing the king home, and anybody who didn't like the idea was at perfect liberty to raise the subject with her. That was the end of that particular mutiny; and I believe the king married Dolonassa to keep her mouth shut thereafter, though it didn't do him much good in the end, when his sons by his first marriage stabbed him to death in his bath. After that, so they say, she married our ancestor and made his life hell by beating him up whenever he tried to tell her off about anything.

Anyway, that's enough about her. What Sarpedon meant, and indeed what Dusa had got planned, was that Dusa would somehow dress up like Victory herself and go around with us on our journey. Every famous games player we visited, she would take him on one side and promise him Victory in the games, and that'd mean they'd be certain sure to turn up.

Oddly enough, the more I thought about this ludicrous scheme of hers, the more it appealed to me – mostly, I guess, because of the precedent; grandmother Dolonassa and the king, I mean. It was just the kind of idiotic stunt that will work, provided it's carried off right. After all, everybody believes that there are gods walking about among us all the time, disguised as farmers and merchants and blacksmiths' apprentices and ugly old women and anything else you care to mention. I believe it myself, because it's obviously true. Now, the idea of painting Dusa with white runny clay and lugging her around in a chariot didn't appeal to me at all; it might have worked once, long ago in Elis, but quite apart from anything else the Dolonassa story was widely enough known that sooner or later somebody would tumble to it, and then we'd be a complete laughing-stock. No; what I was thinking was, take Dusa with us and make out, by hints and suggestions, that she was the goddess Victory *in disguise*.

That night, when we were on our way back home from Leon's house and I put this idea to her, she pretended that that's what she'd had in mind all along. That was good; it meant she liked the plan and was happy to play along with it. Sarpedon, of course, was all for doing it the other way (or that's what he said; I guess he was just being annoying). Tachys was horrified by the very idea, goes without saying. And Cratus—

'Cratus,' Cratus said, 'would've tied all three of you up and dumped you in a barn till the god gave you your wits back; but there was only one of Cratus, and three of you, so I decided to keep my face shut. One of the worst decisions I ever made, that was.'

His tone of voice made the company round the table feel uncomfortable, like a cold breeze coming in under the door. Everyone sat still and quiet, waiting for something to happen.

CHAPTER FOUR

'If it's all the same to you,' said the Phoenician, anxious to seize his chance, 'I think I'll just wander off down the other end of the hall and get some sleep. Thanks for the story.'

He started to get up, got in the way of a stare from his host and another one from Cratus and sat down again with a faint sigh.

'You don't want to go to sleep quite yet,' Cratus said. 'The story's just starting to get interesting.'

'It's very interesting indeed,' the Phoenician mumbled. 'But I think I'm a bit too tired to appreciate it properly. Perhaps tomorrow. Or the next time I'm in the area, even—'

'Sit still and listen,' Cratus said. So the Phoenician sat still, and listened.

My brother said an interesting thing just now (Cratus continued), about how he's cleverer than me, but I'm wiser than him. I can't say I'd ever thought of it in those terms before, but yes, basically he's right.

That is, he's always been the one who comes up with schemes and plans and good ideas; they seem to sprout in his heart like seedcorn stored in a damp jar, and as soon as a new one pops its shell, off he goes telling everybody, badgering them into going along with it. Oh, he's an extraordinarily persuasive man, my brother; he could talk a hill-farmer into swapping his grain for a wagon-load of stones. Maybe he should have taken up your line of work, going from place to place giving and getting given presents. Once one of his ideas starts to roll, it's like a cart running away down a hill when you've forgotten to put the brake on. Unless you're quick enough to jump aboard and stop it before it's really begun to move, all you can do is run alongside it, watching it getting faster and faster as it races towards the pile of rocks at the bottom of the slope.

Not only is my brother clever in the way he comes up with ideas, he's shrewd too, or should that be cunning? Anyway, he knows just when to turn the idea over to somebody else to look after, round about the point where everybody's praised him to the skies for being so smart and come to the conclusion that a scheme that clever is bound to succeed unless somebody actively sabotages it. That's when he shoves the reins at somebody else and hops off the cart; so, when it crashes, it's the driver's fault and not his.

He doesn't mind me saying all this, you know. Deep down, somewhere in the hayloft of his heart, he knows it's true. Otherwise, do you think he'd be sitting there now, quiet as a cat, while I'm saying all these rude things about him?

Well, this particular cart was nicely under way before Dusa decided to jump on board, so she wasn't really his fault, strictly speaking. Still, that won't ever stop me from blaming him for everything. After all, he's my brother.

I remember going home that evening, dumping my shoes and hat on the floor and stomping into the inner room like I was trying to squash ants.

'What's up with you?' my wife asked. 'You look like you've had a bad day.'

'Don't ask,' I replied, pulling my tunic off over my head and managing to tear the seam.

'All right,' she said, and went back to the mending she was doing.

I sat there for a while, scowling at the wall. 'Well?' I said. 'Aren't you going to ask me what the matter is?'

'You said not to,' she replied, not looking up.

I sighed. 'Yes, but I didn't mean it,' I said. She nodded.

'One of those days,' she said. 'I have them all the time, but of course you never take any notice.'

I grunted and climbed into bed. 'Don't start,' I said.

She put down the cloak she was darning and looked at me. 'This isn't any good,' she said. 'Now you're going to lie there all night grunting and muttering, keeping me awake, and finally you'll get to sleep just before dawn, when it's time for me to get up. Tell me what's upset you, and then maybe we can both get a good night's rest.'

I closed my eyes. 'It's that brother of mine,' I said.

'Ah,' she said.

'If I had the sense of a small rock, I'd clear out of here,' I said, 'get on a ship and go found a colony or something. Sometimes I'll swear he does it on purpose, just to aggravate me; but that'd be like saying he's got the wit to see the consequences of something, and I'm here to tell you, he hasn't.'

'This is about these games-with-nobody-dead, isn't it?' she said calmly. 'Personally, I think it's a brilliant idea.'

'Figures,' I grumbled.

'And you've taken against it just because it was Cleander who thought of it, not you –'

I made a rude noise. 'If I started thinking up ideas like that, I wouldn't be here; I'd be over at the shrine, offering prayers for a speedy recovery.'

'– And so you're probably going to make trouble for him over it, which'll only end up falling back on you, like it always does. And then I'll have you sulking round the house for months, until it's all blown over or Cleander does something else you don't approve of . . .'

'Wrong,' I interrupted. 'I'm not going to be round this house for a very long time, sulking or otherwise. My dear brother, who you seem determined to defend at all costs, is making me go with him on this wretched jaunt of his. Gods alone know how long we'll be away for.'

'Oh.' She looked at me. 'That's a nuisance,' she said. 'Have you really got to go?'

I lifted my head. 'I'm afraid so,' I replied. 'You see, it's not just Cleander and me. For reasons known only to his heart, he's taking Uncle Sarpedon along as well.'

'Oh.'

'Quite. And that's not the really inspiring bit. Guess who else is coming along?'

She frowned. 'Your cousin Theagenes?'

I shook my head. 'If only. I wouldn't mind being bored to death; they tell me it's gradual and really rather soothing, in the final stages.'

'Worse than Theagenes? This sounds serious.'

'You bet. The silly fool's only agreed to take Dusa along.'

She bit her lip. 'Oh,' she said.

'You could say that. She didn't give him much choice about it, mind. But the idiot's got this idea about pulling a sort of Dolonassa stunt—'

'Surely not?'

'Would I make something like that up?' I replied. 'I'm not that imaginative.'

She sat down on the bed beside me, and started pulling a comb through her hair. 'Do you know where you're going yet?' she asked.

'No idea. Don't suppose Cleander has, either. I overheard him gabbing away to King Leon about all the great heroes he plans on visiting; I'm not even sure that some of the places he was talking about really exist.' I shook my head. 'Have you ever heard of Sardinia?' I asked.

'No.'

'Nor me. But Cleander's planning on going there.'

'Do you think he knows where it is?'

'You know Cleander.'

She sighed. 'Well, if you're not back in two years' time, I suppose I can always marry Stasilaus.'

I smiled. 'If he'll still have you,' I said. 'You've put on weight since then.'

'Look who's talking.'

Well, the rest of our conversation that night was purely domestic in nature, and of no interest to anybody. Perversely, though, the more she sympathised and agreed that yes, Cleander had got me into a really ugly mess this time, the better I felt about it all. It can't be that bad, I said to my heart; and all the time I was exaggerating, making it sound even worse than it actually was, just to get more sympathy. That in turn set me thinking about how much worse it could have been, which is next door to stepping back and saying, Well, it isn't as bad as it sounded at first. Come the next morning, I was almost cheerful about it all, until I left the house to walk into the city.

Unfortunately, the first person I happened to meet was Alastor, Oeleus' kid brother.

He had every right to be there, more than I did. I was taking a short-cut across an orchard that lay on the boundary between my neighbour Calliphon's place and a small farm that belonged to an old boy (his name escapes me) who was one of Oeleus' debtors. I don't know if you have anything like it where you come from; round here, when the small farmers run into difficulties – bad harvest, illness, disasters of that sort – and their neighbours can't or won't help them out, they have the option of going to the king or one of the princes, or any of the better sort, and getting what they need on a sort of permanent-loan basis. The way it works is that the king or prince never expects to see his capital again (if a man's reduced to asking for help in this way, you can bet he'll never be in a position to pay back anyway). Instead, the lender settles for a regular share in the debtor's surplus produce each year; a sixth, usually, though it can be more or less, depending on circumstances. But that's really just a pretence too, for the same reason. Anybody whose farm produces more than he needs is going to have put aside a bit of fat, so to speak, in case of hard times; it's the ones who live right on the edge who end up knocking on other men's doors. Besides, if you're in a position to lend to others, it's a certainty that you've got more than you need; you can't eat it all yourself, you'd swell up like a drowned man and die. No, what the lender gets out of it is rather more valuable to him than jars of flour or olive oil. He gets the loyalty and support of a free man, not to mention respect, gratitude, prestige – all those things we of the better sort tend to value most, gods bless our vainglorious little hearts. I'm in two minds about the system myself. On the one hand, it's a way for the powerful man to help his weaker neighbour without actively making things worse for him on a day-to-day basis, and I'm all in favour of that. Can't help thinking, though, that it's not good for us to get into the habit of dealing in people, the same way we reckon up our worth by how many head of cattle we own, how many jars of wine we stored last year, how many pairs of sandals we've got in the chest beside the bed. Put that sort of obligation on a man and he's not much better than a slave, or a hired worker. Still, that's easy for me to say. I've faced my share of dangers and hardships in my time, but starving to death for want of a bag of seedcorn hasn't been one of them, so what would I know about it, anyway?

That's beside the point. This orchard I was walking through belonged to this old man who was Oeleus' debtor, so in a sense Oeleus' brother was entitled to be there and I wasn't. Never a problem before, of course. Oeleus and I had always been on fairly civil terms, no earthly reason why we shouldn't be. But as soon as I saw Alastor and he saw me, I knew all that had changed.

He didn't snarl, or set his dogs on me (he had two rather fine boarhounds with him, as it happens; I don't know why I remember them so well, but I do). He smiled, said hello in a perfectly polite manner, and asked if he could help me at all.

'No, not really,' I said. 'I'm just cutting through on my way to the city.'

'Oh.' He looked at me as if the idea of a short-cut was some new kind of blasphemy imported from the nefarious East. 'Please, be my guest. You're welcome to come this way any time you like.'

'Thank you,' I said. By then, of course, it was too late to retrieve the situation. I had become the forgiven trespasser, enjoying the benefit of a licence that had been granted and could be withdrawn at any time. Just to hammer the point home as firm as a gatepost, he turned round and walked with me all the way to the boundary. He didn't make me turn out my satchel to see if I'd stolen any apples, but probably only because there weren't any apples on the trees yet.

I was walking up the road to the city, muttering to my heart under my breath, when I heard a familiar rumbling noise behind me; I jumped sideways without looking and just managed to avoid a four-horse chariot. I recognised the back of Alastor's head, though I couldn't make out the driver.

All in all, I wasn't in the happiest of moods when I reached the palace; and the sight of Dusa sitting under the old fig tree by the door didn't improve my temper.

'Must you do that?' I asked her.

'Do what?' she replied.

'Sit out in public like that,' I replied.

'Like what?'

I don't know what the convention is in your country; here, the rule is that men spend all their time outdoors and have dark, bronzed skins, while women never leave the house and are milk-white, like a dead body fished out of the sea. If you see a woman with a suntan, you assume she can't possibly be one of the better sort, she's got to be a peasant's wife who works in the fields alongside her husband. Inevitably, girls like my sister Dusa take a perverse pride in sitting outside in the sun, often without even a hat. Doesn't bother me, but some people get really upset about it.

'Please yourself,' I said. 'At least you've got the sense to sit in the shade this time of day. Your wits are feeble enough as it is without being fried.'

'Thank you so much,' she replied, getting up and brushing dust off her skirt. 'What took you so long, anyway? I've been here since just after sunrise. Really, I'd have thought you'd have shown a bit more enthusiasm than that.'

I didn't even bother to answer. 'Are you proposing to come inside with me?' I asked.

'Yes.'

'You do know women aren't allowed inside the palace? Apart from members of the household, of course, but you aren't.'

Dusa smiled at me. 'What a strange man you are,' she said. 'First you tell me off for being outside, then you tell me I'm not allowed to come in. I wish you'd make up your mind.'

The thought of a series of discussions of this kind, all the way round the cities and back again, made me cringe. Still, I hadn't entirely given up hope of leaving her behind. That's me, an optimist to the last twitch.

'If you want to try getting inside the palace,' I said, 'you go ahead. Just don't involve me, that's all.'

She laughed. 'The day I need your help for anything,' she said, 'you've got my permission to bury my ashes in an ants' nest. You, on the other hand, need my help rather a lot, so if I were you I'd mind my manners.'

Cleander and Tachys were already there; Sarpedon wasn't, but if he had been I'd have been worried, because he was always late for everything (except battles). King Leon was sitting on his bed – he'd pulled the curtain back – looking miserable.

'I was just telling your brother,' he said to me as I went up the hall, 'I didn't sleep at all last night, worrying about this scheme of his. Of course, it's too late to back out now, after I've announced it and everything. But what if it's a disaster? There's so many things that could go wrong, it's enough to poison a man's heart.'

Really, that wasn't the sort of thing I wanted to hear. It's one thing to be downbeat and gloomy about something yourself; when other people start acting worried and depressed, though, that's something else entirely.

'Like you said,' Cleander replied, 'it's done now, you've promised everybody the treat of a lifetime. If you cancel the games now, you'd better start packing up your stuff on a wagon and looking for somewhere else to live.'

Leon looked like a dog that's got a partridge between its teeth and really doesn't want you to have it. 'I'm not sure you're cut out to be a diplomat,' he said. 'And you're the bright one.'

'Well, if any of you had listened to me—' Tachys started; then he ran into the expression on Leon's face and quickly looked the other way. If Leon had been able to turn people to stone just by glowering at them, like the witch in the old story, we could have turned Tachys on his side, split him down the middle lengthways with wedges and used him for a lintel.

It was then that my heart told me what I had to do. It was against my better judgement; but just because a thing's ill-founded, that's no reason why a man should stand by and watch it get worse.

'Don't worry about Cleander,' I said, 'or Tachys, either. We've started this thing now, so we'd better make it work. And,' I added, 'it will.'

'Really?' Leon turned that into-stone glare on me. 'What makes you so sure, all of a sudden?'

'Because I'm going to make sure it does,' I said; and for some reason I said it so calmly, with such authority and unruffled determination, that for a moment, everybody believed me.

Including me.

Well, maybe a god took over my body and spoke through me. 'All right,' Leon said. 'When can you start?'

'Tomorrow,' I said. 'First light, to get a jump on Oeleus and his people. We'll go home now and get our things together – not that we'll need much. The less we take with us, the less there'll be to lose when we cross a river or get laid up in the mountains.'

And that, apparently, was that. We were going, after all. I was as surprised as anybody there. But these things happen, and it's not often that something unfolds the same way you folded it up.

Sarpedon arrived just as we were leaving. 'Tomorrow morning,' I told him, 'first red light of the dawn. We'll meet up at Caryllus' southern boundary-stone. Bring as little as you think you can get away with.'

Uncle grinned. 'Oh good,' he said, 'you're in charge now. I feel better already.'

Leon and Cleander both looked at me at the same time, like archers estimating range. 'That's right,' I said. 'It's my party now. Anybody got any problems with that?'

'No,' said Leon, before anybody else could speak; and after he'd spoken, there wasn't much point anybody else saying anything. I noticed that Dusa was grinning too, but nothing I was minded to say at that moment would have improved the situation, so I kept my face shut.

I went home, and got ready.

When our father died, rest his soul on the far bank of the River, and Cleander and I set about dividing up his property between us – some years after all this, by the way; let's not get confused about the order of events – I made a point of choosing the southern house (which was where I was living when all this happened) even though it's smaller, darker and more inconvenient. I just happen to like it, that's all.

Not that it's anything special, mind you; well, it's pretty much like this one, only smaller, of course, and shorter, but the same basic pattern, rounded at the back end, square at the front (why do we build them that way, does anybody know?) with an open porch in front of the double doors, overhung by the loft balcony. Downstairs is just the main hall, no inner room like you've got here; upstairs is the upper room, where my wife and I slept. I didn't keep a large household, no more than a dozen of us at any one time.

It didn't take me long to get my stuff together; my spare tunic and sandals (I wore my boots), the better of my two hats, my sword and two spears – couldn't be bothered to take a shield; in any kind of fight I was likely to survive a cloak wrapped round my left arm would do just as well; wine, flour and figs for three days, a wooden cup and bowl and a small skin of water. For presents, I took a silver belt-buckle I'd been given by someone I never liked much (it was a high-class buckle, but I never liked it for that reason), a short sword with enamel and silver filigree decoration, a couple of old-fashioned brooches that I knew my wife hadn't worn for years, a couple of slightly faded purple tunics and a big square-handled silver cup of the unlovely or prize-in-the-games pattern. I reckoned that would do to get me started; obviously I'd get presents in exchange as I went along. It's odd, isn't it, that no matter how far you go or how often you give and receive presents along the way, you generally find you come home with a collection of old junk that bears a striking resemblance to what you left home with—

'That's true,' Palamedes interrupted. 'I remember one time when I went south – Messene, Sparta, out that way; I'd had this quite hideous cauldron and stand given me, one of those copies of the genuine Assyrian article, and the best part of the whole trip was going to be losing this thing and maybe getting something better in exchange (well, that was a foregone conclusion, even if all I got was a year's accumulated toenail clippings). Turned out I was in luck. I palmed the cauldron off on the first people we stayed with, in

Bassae, and I got a rather nice silver-washed spearhead for it. We carried on, down the coast to Pylos, up to Limnae, then Sparta, Prasiae, Tegea and finally Mantinea, by which time I'd converted that cauldron, so to speak, into a quite superb old-style helmet, the conical pattern with the big cheek-pieces, that had apparently once belonged to Achilles himself. Anyway, I duly presented this to my host at Mantinea, and you know what I got in return? That rotten fake Assyrian tripod, the very same one I thought I'd got rid of when we set out. Turned out our host from Bassae had been to visit his married sister at Mila, and her husband had taken a trip to somewhere else, and it had ended up in Mantinea a couple of days before we did, where our host clearly reckoned it was the neatest thing he'd ever seen in his life. It was plain to see he was heart-broken to part with it, but since I'd given him such a classy present and he didn't have much nice stuff, he really didn't have an option. There was what you might call an awkward moment there—'

'Quite,' said Cratus. 'Well, these things happen, don't they? I'm sure you got rid of it eventually.'

Palamedes grinned. 'Oh yes, quite well, as it happens. Got a cartload of iron ingots for it from this extremely gullible Phoen—'

He stopped abruptly. The Phoenician smiled. 'It's all right,' he said, 'it wasn't me.'

'That's all right, then,' Palamedes said.

The Phoenician nodded his head. 'Actually,' he said, 'it was my father. Tell me, did it have three gryphons' heads with sort of stuffed expressions on their faces, and a big dent in the stand rim? That's the one. Still got it at home somewhere; my wife likes it.'

'Ah,' Palamedes said. 'That's all right, then. Sorry, Cratus, you were saying—'

Yes, I was, wasn't I? But that's all right (Cratus went on), it's your house, you just feel free to butt in whenever it takes your fancy.

Where was I? Oh yes, getting ready for the journey. I was damned if I was going to walk if I could help it, so I found the groom and had him bring out the chariot; might as well get some use out of the wretched thing, rather than leave it mouldering in the top barn. It was nothing to get excited about; big and lumbering, only a two-horse four-wheeler, in fact rather better suited to plain old getting-from-here-to-there than warfare, which is probably why it had come my way, while Cleander got the prestige four-horse with the big handles.

There was plenty of room in that old trundler for my stuff and the presents, and still space for one, maybe even two passengers. We got it rigged up, checked the boom and the pins, slapped a bit of goose-grease on the axles and inspanned the horses. I had six horses at that time; five mares and a stallion. I chose a couple of grey mares that weren't much use on the farm (part of my wife's dowry, so they were getting on a bit, but they were steady enough, which is what you want if all you're doing is bouncing along the roads) with my favourite black mare on the leading rein as a change. Finally, on impulse, I dashed back into the house and dug out my bow and a sheaf of arrows. I know it's not something to be proud of, but I was a good archer; I figured we might get a shot or two at some deer along the way – a bit of fresh meat makes a change when you're on the road, and makes a good present when you're calling on strangers.

I stood there in the chariot, asking my heart if I'd forgotten anything. Stood to reason there was *something* I'd forgotten, because there always is, isn't there? But I was reasonably sure that whatever it was, it couldn't be anything important. Last of all I waved to my wife, who was round the side of the house picking figs. She waved back, but didn't seem inclined to stop what she was doing, so I picked up the reins and moved off. Not what you'd call a heroic sort of leavetaking, but I was in a hurry and besides, I've never been a great one for fuss.

I should've known I'd be the first one at the meet-up point. I stood about for a bit until my legs started to ache, then I tied up the horses to a spindly old olive tree, made myself as comfortable as I could under it and lay down. I must have closed my eyes and gone to sleep, because the next thing I knew about was somebody's foot prodding me in the ribs.

Cleander, I thought as I came to, and I'd already opened the gate of my mouth to tell him what I thought of him, punctuality and manners, when I opened my eyes and realised it wasn't him at all.

Fool's luck only takes you so far, my father used to say; after that you have to get out and walk. Actually, that's one of his more intelligible utterances. There's some of them I've been trying to figure out these last forty years, and I still can't make any sense of them.

'Hello,' I said, for want of anything more sensible coming immediately to mind.

The man standing over me grinned unpleasantly. 'Hello yourself,' he said. 'Get up.'

I could have pointed out quite truthfully that the point of the spear he was resting on the hollow of my throat made getting up uncomfortable, even potentially dangerous. But I guessed he wasn't in the mood; instead I sort of rolled sideways and pulled myself up against the tree. His friends were methodically unloading the chariot and outspanning the horses, while a bored-looking man was driving out the axle pins with a drift and a small hammer.

'The wheels are the only bits worth having,' the man explained, following my line of sight. 'Nice bit of copper on those wheels. The rest's just fit for firewood.'

He sounded so disappointed in me, my heart wanted to apologise. But I didn't feel much like talking.

'Nice sword,' he went on. 'I'll have that. Those boots new?'

I shook my head. 'My feet sweat, too,' I pointed out.

'Never mind,' he replied, 'they'll do for my oldest boy; bit big, but he'll grow into them. He's at that age where you turn your back on them and they're a span taller.'

I took that to mean that I was supposed to take my boots off. Since the man's spear-point was once again sticking in a relevant area, I thought it'd be sensible to do as he said. While I was at it, he went on, I might as well take off my cloak and tunic; not for him, he was at pains to point out (and I could see his point; he was rather magnificent in a bright purple tunic and a blue wool cloak with a gold and amber brooch), but his father could use a second tunic with the cold weather coming on. I got the impression that his father either wasn't fussy or was grateful for anything he got.

Well, it was a warm day, I didn't really need clothes any more than I needed an extra hole in my body, so I followed his suggestion. That just left the gold ring on my right hand, which he pulled off himself to save me the trouble.

'That'll have to do, then,' the man said with a sigh, as if reproaching me for wasting his time. 'There's nails in the chariot that would probably straighten and do a turn, but I expect we'd have to burn them out, and we haven't got time. Mind how you go on the road; there's loose flints, and you haven't got anything on your feet.'

Then he bashed me over the head with the butt of the spear – to keep me from following and strangling them all with my bare hands, I suppose – and I was out of it for a while. Next time I came round, Cleander was standing over me.

'What the hell do you think you're playing at?' he asked me.

My head hurt, and I felt a bit of a fool lying there with no clothes on. 'Go to the crows,' I replied.

Cleander frowned; then he grinned. 'You got robbed,' he said.

'Wisdom's your friend today, I can tell,' I replied. 'Here, give me your cloak before I frighten the horses.'

He scowled and popped the brooch. 'What horses?' he replied. 'They seem to have taken them.'

'I didn't mean my horses, rest their souls,' I said.

'We've come on foot,' Cleander said. 'We assumed you'd bring the old chariot or a cart.'

I closed my eyes. 'Wonderful,' I said. 'So either we go back for a cart or we walk all the way to the end of the world. What an auspicious start this is turning out to be.'

'We'll walk,' said Uncle Sarpedon, leaning over Cleander's shoulder and prodding at the cut on my head. 'That's not serious,' he said. 'Can't have put up much of a fight if that's all they did to you.'

'I didn't put up any sort of a fight,' I told him. 'There were six of them. Got more sense.'

Uncle Sarpedon looked at me as if I was something he'd trodden in.

We trudged back to Uncle Sarpedon's house – it was the nearest – in gloomy silence. Even Dusa was relatively quiet (Dusa, neglecting an opportunity to be unbearably amusing at her brother's expense: that ought to tell you just how depressed we all were).

I hadn't been inside Uncle Sarpedon's place for the best part of ten years, back before his wife died and both his sons left to join a colony in Ionia. Of course, I hadn't realised it had been so long. I certainly wasn't prepared for what I saw.

Uncle's house was full – jam-packed, crammed, piled up to the rafters – with junk. Everywhere you looked, there were *things*, so many of them that in places you just had to step over them, like a man crossing a river on stepping-stones. Now, if that makes it sound like Uncle Sarpedon was rich, forget it, please; when his father's land was divided up between him and his brothers, he got the rocky, sour-soiled end the rest of them didn't want, and (since there were four sons in the family) not very much even of that. He hadn't married well – typically, the dowry was mostly armour and weapons and a chariot – and the seven acres he'd inherited from his mother's side was the only good land on the whole patch, and that was on the other side of the valley from the rest of his holding. Also, Uncle had never taken much interest in what little he had got. Given the choice between getting his own hands dirty and hiring a couple of no-goods off the road come pruning or ditching time, he could be relied on to make the wrong decision. He could never be bothered, too busy practising sword-drill and spear-casts and shield exercises, bashing dust out of the ratty old quintain he'd set up in the courtyard or hauling his shepherd down from the sheiling during lambing and making the poor bugger throw spears at him (sharps, mind, not blunts) so he could practise his dodges and parries.

So, if Uncle wasn't rich, how had he come by all the countless things that were packed into his house? Well; first, he'd always been a great traveller, a compulsive goer-on-visits, and over the years he'd called on a lot of rich and generous friends who took a pride in giving genuinely valuable presents. Without meaning to, he'd always had the knack of doing well out of giving and receiving, in terms of both quantity and value; accordingly, a lot of the stuff in his house was the proceeds of his various quests and expeditions.

Even more of it was loot; his share of the plunder of several cities and the gods only know how many small towns and villages. He'd done well there, too; where most men of his rank would have wanted to take their share in women, Uncle had always gone for the more 'honourable' kind of plunder, stuff that'll still look good, and therefore preserve the memory of his glorious deeds, twenty years later. So he had any amount of tripods, cauldrons, bits of imported furniture, big cedarwood chests full of clothes that he'd never thought to open since the day he got them; and don't forget all the armour and weapons he'd stripped from the bodies of the men he'd killed. Put together, his collection of metalwork was worth a fortune just on metal value alone, but I'm not counting any of it as wealth, because nothing on earth would have induced him to part with any of it, and if that's your attitude, you might as well not have the stuff for all the practical good it'll do you.

So; he'd acquired it, one way or another, and then, apparently, just stacked it against the wall or dumped it on the floor. You think I'm exaggerating; you tell them, Cleander. I'll swear, there was stuff there that looked as if it had been lying in the same place on the deck for ten years. I guess he only thought of it, when he considered it at all, as evidence, some kind of tangible proof of what he'd done over the years; it might just as well have been notches cut in a tally for all he cared about the things themselves. Bizarre, I call it—

'Excuse me butting in,' the Phoenician interrupted, 'but there's a case in point for you, Palamedes. About what we were discussing earlier. This man had to keep a house full of useless objects to remind him of his deeds – and all that wealth in metal and fabric and so forth, completely wasted – when if he'd known about writing, he could have written it all down, still had a record of the score, so to speak, and been able to walk across his floor in a straight line into the bargain.'

Palamedes grinned. 'It's a fair point,' he said. 'But suppose he'd done what you seem to be suggesting – given away all his trophies and plunder and got things he wanted in return; and say he'd scratched down all about his deeds on a wax tablet instead. Where would the proof be?'

The Phoenician frowned. 'Sorry, I don't follow,' he said.

'How could he prove he'd done all the things he said he'd done, if he had nothing to show for it except a bit of wood with some scratches on? I mean, he could have made the scratches and never left his house or gone to the wars. A stranger from another city, or his own descendants after his death, they wouldn't know whether he was a truthful man or not. If they couldn't be shown actual things he'd brought away from a war, they'd have to take what he said on trust.'

'True,' the Phoenician said. 'But I could go around collecting bits of old armour with holes punched in them, and I could hang them up on my wall and pretend I'd stripped them off the bodies of great heroes I'd killed in battle, and you wouldn't be any the wiser.'

Palamedes frowned. 'I suppose you could, at that,' he said. 'But who'd do such a thing?'

'The same sort of man who'd write out a false tablet, I guess,' the Phoenician replied.

'All right,' someone else said. 'But your scratched bit of wood wouldn't mean a thing to me. I mean, if you'd died and I was going through your stuff and I found a bundle of bits of wood with wax on them, I'd assume they were firelighters. But if I went into your house and saw helmets and shields and spears all over the place—'

'You'd assume I'd made a living repairing damaged armour,' the Phoenician said with a smile. 'The truth is, things on their own can't tell you very much, not unless there's words to go with them. The point about writing is, it preserves words, like flies caught in those amber beads you get from way up in the north-east. If you preserve a man's words, it's – well, it's as if he's still alive and talking to you, maybe a hundred years after his death. But stuff's just stuff.'

There was a moment's awkward silence; then someone else down at the far end of the table spoke up. 'There's another alternative you haven't considered,' he said. 'And as far as I'm concerned it's the most important one of all. Glory isn't things you leave behind, or some sort of tally or message you scratch on bits of tree-bark. It's how other people remember you. It's having people telling stories about you – and repeating the words you said – when you've long since flaked away to ashes and the sheep have scattered the stones of your cairn. And that only comes if you've really done something worth remembering, so all this talk about proof isn't really relevant.'

The Phoenician nodded. 'If they remember you right,' he said. 'But what if they don't? Suppose there was a great battle, everybody fighting bravely, great deeds of valour done on both sides; but one side's completely wiped out. Now, the survivors on the other side go away and tell their tale, and they're remembered all right, but what about the equally brave men on the losing side? They're forgotten; or maybe even worse, lies are told about them and repeated over and over again for generations. But if you write stuff down, you're talking directly to a man long after you're dead, without having to rely on other people to be truthful and have good memories.'

There was a murmur around the table after that. 'I'll admit,' Palamedes said, 'the more I hear about this writing business, the more interesting it sounds. But it's no good me being interested; if nobody else can understand my scratches, it'd be like having a lock without a key to fit it.'

A longer silence; which Cratus eventually broke.

'If it's all the same to the rest of you,' he said, 'can I carry on with the story now, please?'

Thank you (Cratus said). Now, where'd I got up to? That's right, Uncle Sarpedon and his junk.

I don't think Uncle was in the habit of entertaining guests. We had to find our own places to sit down, wash our own hands and feet – had to fetch our own water, come to that, while the half-dozen or so oafish-looking men he had hanging around the place just stood there with their mouths open – and generally make shift for ourselves while Uncle hopped about like a bird on a thin branch, looking out suitable bits of kit to make good my losses.

Well, I had my choice of armour – only I wasn't reckoning on taking any armour, so he had to put it all back again. He more or less forced me to accept a helmet and a huge old-fashioned sword with a pommel that dug into my wrist. They were both as green as moss, and I think something small and furry had been living in the helmet. To wear I got a very old purple cloak, with gold thread fraying wildly round the neck, and a couple of homespun tunics out of a box whose lid was white with mildew. As for the one pair of boots I managed to prise out of him, you didn't have to be particularly observant to realise that the previous owner had died in them; there's nothing quite like caked-on blood for cracking leather.

By then, of course, it was too late to set off, though we made several half-hearted attempts at suggesting it, on the basis that a night under the nice clean stars was greatly to be preferred to trying to sleep wedged in the cracks between Uncle's metalwork collection.

Maybe it was the excitement of the day's adventures, or the weird surroundings, or the foul, stale bread we had for dinner; but I had a rather peculiar dream that night, as I lay on my side under my new-to-me cloak between a large, ugly tripod and a stack of spears.

I was lying there (in my dream, I mean) when this dark figure appeared at the back of the hall. Now, in my dream there was an inner room in Uncle's house, and this figure walked through the door from the inner room into the main hall; it was dark in the hall, but there must have been a whole bunch of lamps burning in the inner room, because as the door opened a beam of light shot out, and because the figure was standing in front of the light, I couldn't see who or even what it was.

'Hello?' I said. 'Who's there?'

No reply from the figure, who just stood there; but I saw myself, and Cleander, and the rest of our party (including some other people I didn't know – oh yes, and the prince, Leon's boy) stand up and walk towards the light, past this figure and into the back.

'Hello,' I repeated; I was wondering, if I'd just seen me going through the door, then who was dreaming this dream anyway? 'What's going on?'

Well, the figure in the doorway didn't look like it was going to be any help, so I (whoever I was at this stage) got up and went to see for myself. I put my head round the door; but now the light was behind me, in the hall, and the inner room was as dark as a bag.

I turned round and made a grab for the figure; I caught hold of a handful of long hair and realised it was a woman. Then I caught sight of her face, and I knew, the way you do in dreams, who she was; it was Athena, and I was pulling her hair like a naughty boy tormenting his sister.

I tried to let go, but the stuff was sticking to my hands like cobweb. 'I'm really sorry about this,' I said, or words to that effect.

'Don't worry about it,' the goddess replied. 'After all, who would you rather be, the man who wins the prize or the man who calls out the names of the winners?'

Didn't make a whole lot of sense to me, either. While I was trying to figure it out, Athena grabbed me by the hair (I'd apparently managed to come unstuck from her by this point) and dragged me back into the hall; only it wasn't the hall, it was this big, enormous building, like a temple, only bigger; and I was looking at an absolutely huge statue of a man sitting in a chair. When I say huge, I had to crane my neck till the back of my head was squashed against my shoulders just to see its head; and it was made of ivory, gilded to show up the hair and the clothes. Strangest thing you ever saw. But that wasn't the really crazy part. It was who the statue was of—

Yes, quite. Modesty forbids.

'See?' said Athena. 'Cleander was right after all.'

I hadn't got a clue what she meant by that, but I let it pass; after all, she was a goddess, and she still had me by the short hairs, literally. 'That's nice,' I mumbled.

I could feel her smile at me; and then the statue started falling to bits, right in front of my eyes. The head went first. Great big chunks of gilt ivory as big as chickens came tumbling and bouncing down, like a rockslide on a cliff face. After that the shoulders split and fell apart, followed by the rest of the body, till there was nothing left but two big heaps of white rubble. Again, I didn't need to be told; my funeral cairn, and Cleander's.

Well, that really put the wind up me, seeing my own grave like that. By now, the temple had fallen down as well, and we were in the open air; just me, Athena and those two piles of stones about a couple of hundred paces apart. There was a big crowd of people hanging about watching, and I figured out what it was – funeral games for Cleander and me. Anyway, there were runners getting set beside my cairn, and on the mark they started to run.

Let me put it this way. I was there all right, but I also knew in my heart that it was just a dream, the way you do; and that part of me was just thinking really hostile thoughts about Uncle Sarpedon's ewe's-milk cheese when the goddess grabbed my shoulder and hauled me round so I was staring her right in the face. And it wasn't her any more, it was Dusa.

At that point, I'm delighted to say, I woke up.

I knew it would be pointless trying to go back to sleep after that. I just lay there, waiting for the dawn and trying to figure out in my heart what the dream could possibly have meant. I was still figuring when someone shook me hard by the shoulder, and I realised I'd fallen asleep after all, though not for long.

'On your feet,' Uncle said. 'We've got a whole day to make up somewhere, thanks to you.'

I had plenty of time to mull the dream over in my heart that day as we tramped along the road to Mantinea – Uncle insisted we should walk, probably because none of his horses were fit to draw a chariot – but the more I thought about it, the more confused I got. All I can say is, if the dream was a god telling me something, the god was mumbling.

Someone else who wasn't too thrilled about walking was Tachys, our hardened traveller. About midday he mentioned his feet. A little later, he mentioned them again, along with a passing reference to his ankles and the dryness of his mouth. It was, he observed, a hot day. Inexperienced travellers, he pointed out, had been known to overdo it in heat like this, leading to exhaustions, strange visions and death. Experienced travellers like himself, he mentioned in passing, preferred to sit out the midday heat under a shady tree.

Uncle Sarpedon decided to reason with him. 'Shut your face,' he said. Uncle Sarpedon could be very persuasive when he wanted to be. We didn't hear any more out of Tachys for the rest of the day.

We slept very well indeed that night, slumped on the ground like a drunk's clothes (we were supposed to have set a watch, in case of thieves, but somehow we didn't get round to it; and all our things were still there when we woke up), and, come dawn, we felt reasonably refreshed, if a trifle stiff around the calves and knees. We set off at a smart pace and covered a respectable amount of ground before it was time to stop for breakfast.

'We aren't stopping for breakfast,' Uncle Sarpedon announced. 'No time for that, sorry. Thanks to Cratus we're a day and a half behind.'

I wasn't the only one who didn't like the sound of that. 'Be reasonable,' Dusa said. 'If we don't eat we'll get worn out, and then we'll be even slower. And besides,' she added, 'who appointed you captain of the march?'

Uncle looked offended. 'I'm only trying to help,' he said.

'Please don't. You're being extremely annoying.'

That was the first cross word between those two; up till then they'd been thick as curdled milk, hanging back a few yards behind the rest of us and nattering away, just softly enough that the rest of us couldn't hear what they were saying. Uncle Sarpedon was certainly taken by surprise.

'But you're all so *slow*,' he said unhappily. 'You dawdle. Gods, we'll be old men by the time we reach Athens, at this rate.'

Cleander looked up. 'Athens?' he said. 'Who mentioned anything about going to Athens?'

'Well, aren't we?'

'Why would we want to go there?' Cleander said. 'I thought we might just hang about for a boat at Rhion to carry us over the Gulf, and then head straight for Thessaly. At this rate, we could be there within ten days.'

The rest of us exchanged looks. 'Cleander,' I said, jumping in because I was the most tactful, 'the Gulf and the ferry are due north of Elis.'

'I know that. So?'

'Well,' I pointed out, 'we're going south.'

Cleander scowled at me. 'Nonsense,' he said. 'We're going north. You can tell by the position of the sun.'

Uncle made a growling noise. 'It's true,' he said, 'you can. And if you try the experiment, you'll find we're heading due south. Why, where did you think we were headed?'

Well, Cleander tried to make us go back. Luckily for him we were all too tired and hot to argue the point as forcefully as we'd have liked, and besides, there wasn't a well handy to put him down. So we had to make do with yelling at him till he gave way.

'After all,' I pointed out, 'there are plenty of good games-players in the southern Peloponnese. We were going that way anyway; we'll just have to do them first, that's all.'

Then followed a brisk, occasionally heated discussion, the outcome of which was that if we were going south (Cleander refused to admit this as a proven fact) we were much closer to our first stop than we would have been if we were going north, and were therefore making better progress than we thought we were, so that was all right. We'd know soon enough which direction we were travelling in, Tachys pointed out, because if we were going south, before the day was out we'd be paddling in the Alpheus river, not to mention being able to see the sea. Cleander replied that there was a perfectly good river, and a perfectly good sea, two days' march north of Elis as well, so that wouldn't prove a thing. At this point, Uncle Sarpedon offered to break Cleander's nose, but the consensus was that that'd only slow us up even more.

We still weren't unanimous about it when we resumed our march – 'Knowing where you are isn't like a Council meeting,' Cleander said, 'you can't be in a certain place just because a majority of those present vote that you are' – but I was sick of arguing, Dusa was bored, Tachys was depressed and Sarpedon would probably have shed blood if the argument had gone on any longer, so moving on was the only sensible thing to do.

It was just starting to think about getting dark when we reached the river. No sea, not in any direction, but an undeniable river, which Tachys solemnly assured us was the Alpheus (we didn't ask how he knew). We'd come down from the hills into a flat, grassy plain, with olive trees and white poplars scattered about, and on our right was a steep hill covered with pine trees. There was a small, old-looking thatched hut beside the river, but no signs of anybody living there, so we guessed it was a shrine or temple of some sort. Nice enough spot, if you like rustic.

I was wondering if Tachys' obsessive piety would be outraged if we dossed down for the night inside the temple, when I noticed that Dusa had stopped still and was standing with a dead-sheep expression on her face, staring at the landscape.

'Dusa?' I said.

'Sorry,' she replied, without looking away. 'Do you know, I've got the strangest feeling about this place. My heart tells me I've been here before.'

'Have you been here before?'

She lifted her head. 'No,' she said.

'Well, there you are, then.'

'But my heart's really, really sure it's seen this place,' Dusa said. 'Like in a dream or something.'

Oh, for crying out loud, said my heart. 'Come on, Dusa,' I said. 'We're going to have to get you a thicker hat.'

'Shut up, Cratus,' she replied, a preoccupied frown on her face. 'Yes, this is definitely it. I'm sure of it.'

'Sure of what?' Cleander asked.

'This place.' Without taking her eyes off the view (which was all right, but nothing all that special, I promise you) she sat down and rested her chin on her hands. 'This is where we've got to hold the games.'

'No it's not,' Cleander said. 'We're going to hold them in Elis, just outside the city, where we do the funerals. It's all settled.'

'Then you'll just have to unsettle it,' Dusa said. 'I've remembered now. Hercules showed this place to me once.'

Tachys frowned. 'Impossible,' he said. 'He's dead. Isn't he?'

'In a dream,' Dusa said. 'He brought me here in a dream. Right here, where we're standing now—'

I'd had enough. 'Dusa,' I said, 'this is all very good and I'm glad you're practising for when we meet the games-players and you pretend to be a goddess or whatever. But there's a time and a place. Doctors and executioners don't practise on their close relatives, and neither should you.'

'I said shut up,' Dusa said. 'Right here, just behind where you're standing, Uncle, there should be a stone.'

There was. 'Proving nothing,' I pointed out. 'This is the northern Peloponnese; it'd be more like a miracle if there *wasn't* a stone . . .'

'Look at it closely,' Dusa went on – she was looking the other way – 'and you'll see a mark on it, like it was a wet clay tile and someone had trodden on it. It ought to be the size and shape of a man's foot.'

'She's right, you know,' Sarpedon said. 'Damn big foot, mind,' he went on, putting his own not inconsiderable foot inside the mark.

'That sounds right,' Dusa said. 'It's Hercules' footprint. He made it while I was watching, in my dream. He said we should mark out a race-track six hundred times the length of the footprint.'

'Hercules told you that?' I asked.

'In my dream.'

'Then he must be as batty as you are,' I said. 'Stop mucking about, Dusa. This is all a wind-up, isn't it?'

She stared at me for a moment with completely hollow eyes; then grinned at me. 'Had you going there, though, didn't I?' she said. 'Gods, you should see the look on your face.'

Well, we forgave her for her excruciating wit, eventually; and although Tachys was extremely upset and shook his head till I was afraid it would come off, we spent the night in the little shrine (it was empty apart from a small rock) and left there just before dawn the next day. It was while I was waking up, still sweeping out the sleep from my mind, that my heart asked me how come, if Dusa was playing tricks on us, she'd known about the stone with the footprint on it, which she couldn't possibly have seen.

CHAPTER FIVE

'Excuse me,' said the Phoenician, 'but I've got to go and take a leak.'

There was a nice convenient channel running under the wall of the house. When the Phoenician got back, there was an argument going on.

'I'm sorry,' Cleander was saying, 'but he's doing it on purpose, to annoy me. And he's succeeding, too. He knows I can't see to bash him any more, so he carries on and says what he likes, and it's not fair.'

'Not fair,' Cratus repeated in a sing-song voice. 'Not fair, not fair, not fair. I've had to listen to that all my life, since we were snot-nosed kids. Listen, I tell it how I remember it, that's all.'

Cleander was clearly upset. 'It's not all, not by a jarful,' he said. 'This Phoenician's listening to you, and he's going to go away thinking that it all happened like you said. And it didn't, and I don't want people thinking it did when I'm dead and gone and not there to straighten them out.'

'Tough,' Cratus said. 'But since we're the only two people left to tell the story and our hearts don't agree about what happened – which is putting it mildly – I'd say it'd be just as unfair if you told the story – your version of the story – and left our guest with a false impression of me.'

Not for the first time, the Phoenician wished he knew exactly who these two men, Cratus and Cleander, were. At first he'd assumed that they were members of the household, poor relations or retired hangers-on. Somewhere along the line he'd revised that impression and concluded that they must be ancient retainers, probably inherited by Palamedes along with the fixtures, fittings and live and dead stock. At this point he was tending towards the view that they were simply old friends of Palamedes or his father, who hung around the big hall because they liked it better there than at home.

Trying to achieve such precision among Greeks was, of course, a very efficient way of boiling one's brains; in Greece, he'd learned over the years, you were a fusion of who you thought you were and who everybody else thought you were, qualified to a certain extent by such factors as wealth, military prowess and whether people liked you. Come to think of it, he'd never actually seen or heard any proof that Palamedes was the King of Elis – he didn't wear a tiara, like proper kings back home, but people generally did what he said; and when his father had referred to 'trading with Elis', he'd meant going to visit Palamedes, or at least whoever was living in this house at the time. Since it didn't actually matter very much, he decided to compromise; Palamedes was a king, if not necessarily *the* king, which meant that Cratus and Cleander could have the word 'courtier' scratched on their lids (there was, to the best of his knowledge, no Greek word for 'courtier') and he wouldn't have to think about it any more.

'I know,' the Phoenician piped up. 'How about if we forget all about the rest of the story and I keep an open mind about the both of you?'

Cleander lifted his head. 'Too late for that,' he replied. 'It's started now, you'll have to listen to the whole thing and then make up your own mind.'

'Oh,' said the Phoenician. 'Only, I really don't want to cause any more trouble between you two; and besides, it's late, and I'd love just to go to bed—'

'And,' Cleander went on, 'I insist on being allowed to tell the next bit, because it's too important to let *him* twist it round and make it all sound bad.'

Cratus yawned ostentatiously. 'You go ahead,' he said. 'The next bit isn't really all that important anyhow.'

Our first visit (said Cleander) was to the King of the Triphylians—

'Hold on,' the Phoenician interrupted. 'I thought you were at war with the Triphylians.'

Palamedes held up his hand to indicate that he was going to answer. 'We were,' he said. 'But the war finished.'

'Just like that?' The Phoenician looked confused. 'But it was a terrible defeat,' he said. 'Cratus said so himself; his uncle Deilaus –'

'Deistratus.'

'– Deistratus was killed, along with that other man, the charioteer's father. And Cratus killed the crown prince. Don't tell me that after all that you just walked into the palace yard and said "Hello".'

Palamedes frowned. 'Why not?' he said.

'Because . . .' The Phoenician shook his head. 'Oh well,' he said. 'I suppose it's all to the good, really, if you don't hold grudges.'

Someone at the opposite end of the table laughed. 'Put it another way,' he said. 'If we *did* hold grudges, it'd be impossible to live. Dammit, when we aren't at war with the Triphylians, it's the Achaeans or the Mantineans—'

'Or with the Triphylians against the Mantineans and Bassae—'

'Or with the Achaeans against the Triphylians and the Mantineans—'

The man grinned. 'Anyway, it's complicated,' he said. 'If we worried about that sort of thing, like remembering and laying down in our hearts what happened in the war before the war before last, we'd all be wiped out in a year or so.'

'But surely,' the Phoenician replied, 'as far as I can make out, one of the main reasons you have wars is so you can do great deeds that will cause you to be remembered. And I assume that means remembering the names of the great warriors you kill.'

'Sure,' said Palamedes. 'But not the wars themselves.'

'I understand,' the Phoenician lied. 'Sorry, I interrupted you.'

That's all right (said Cleander). Anyway, we reached the palace just in time for dinner – fortuitous, really, because we'd eaten all our food, and since Cratus contrived to get his bow and arrows stolen, we couldn't hunt; and you *can* live on nuts and berries, but it's unbelievably boring.

So there we were, making our first call on a great games-player. Not the king, of course; he was well into his seventies, past all that. His son had been a fine discus-thrower, but he was dead, so that ruled him out. That left the king's younger brother Ischomachus, who was reckoned to be one of the finest boxers since Castor and Polydeuces.

(Castor and Polydeuces? Long before our time. They were twin sons of Zeus by some mortal woman. Depending on who you believe, either they're immortal or they died in my great-great-great-grandfather's time. Anyway, Castor was the greatest boxer ever. Sorry, Polydeuces. Well, one of them, anyway.)

Ischomachus wasn't there that evening; he'd gone up into the mountains to take a look at his pigs. They say that every man's heart has a special joy, something that speaks directly to it in a way that nothing else can. For some men it's love or wealth or power, glory in battle, the beauty of the sun on the sea or the dew on a rose. With Ischomachus, it was pigs. He doted on them. Now, a good man ought to take an interest in his pigs. They're a very efficient way of providing meat all year round, they'll eat any damn thing and live anywhere, and the bits you can't eat you can make things out of. They make a big song and dance about how Prometheus was the great friend and benefactor of mankind because he stole fire from heaven in a fennel-stalk and brought it down to us here, but for some reason whoever it was that smuggled the first pig off Olympus never achieved the same level of recognition, and I call that a shame and a miscarriage of justice. With the possible exception of these new-fangled chickens you're starting to see everywhere you go, the pig's quite possibly the most useful animal going.

Well, I happen to like pigs. Nothing wrong with that.

Next day we set off up the mountain. The king sent a boy with us to show us the way; he was thrilled to be out in the fresh air in the company of so many terrible and ferocious Elean warriors. ('Do you really eat the kidneys of the men you kill in battle?' he asked. 'Yes,' we replied. 'Doesn't everybody?' He couldn't do enough for us after that.) He took us what he called the 'short way', which was pretty well straight up the side of this sheer cliff into which some crazy optimist had cut terraces for olives – bizarre, since they're quite well off for good land in those parts, unlike so many places.

I tell you, it was an absolutely magnificent piggery. You've never seen the like. It was way up on a spur, looking out over the valley – you could see for miles. As we approached the top, we passed the quarry where the stones had been cut; someone had been to a lot of trouble. The outer stockade was all whitethorn, and inside that there were a dozen sties, each with fifty-odd brood pigs; naturally he kept the boars in a separate pen round the back. All the buildings and fixtures were new and well maintained, all the gates sat sweetly on their hinges; I've seen scruffier temples.

It was just on feeding time when we got there, and the noise of six-hundred-odd pigs all filling their faces was one of the most raucous, deafening sounds I've ever heard outside a general assembly of the Sons of the Achaeans. In the corner of one of the pens there was a big bald-headed man covered in mud and pigshit; he was raking muck with a long wooden rake.

'You there,' Tachys called out – we'd agreed that he should be the chief herald for the day. 'Where's your master?'

'What?' the man grunted, sounding just like a pig himself.

'Your master. Prince Ischomachus.'

The man leaned his rake against the sidewall. 'Who wants to know?' he replied.

Tachys frowned. 'That's for us to tell Ischomachus,' he said. 'And unless you want a kick up the backside for keeping his guests waiting, I suggest you go and fetch him.'

The man smiled. 'Expecting you, is he?'

'What's it to you if he is or if he isn't?' Tachys was well annoyed by this stage. 'What's your name, anyhow?'

'Ischomachus.'

'Oh.'

Maybe I should explain, for the benefit of our Phoenician friend; maybe they do things differently where he comes from. In these parts, one of the rudest, most offensive things you can do to a man – well, a man of the better sort, anyway – is ask his name, straight out and to his face. It's just not done. Well, maybe that's a little too sweeping; if someone turns up on your doorstep and you invite him in and feed him and pour wine down his neck for three days and he still hasn't volunteered the information, I reckon you'd be within your rights to make a polite enquiry; that's if you're the host, of course. For a guest to go asking names is really bad form, believe me.

(Why? Don't ask me. If you want my opinion, it's another of those Sons-of-the-Achaeans things – the idea is, any Achaean is as good as any other, so what does it matter who he is? When someone comes to your home, first thing you do is give him food and drink and something to wash his hands and feet with, that's a basic duty we owe to Zeus. Who the stranger is really doesn't matter all that much.)

Of course, theoretically Ischomachus had made the first breach of protocol with that who-wants-to-know crack. But there was no getting round it, we'd made an awful start; why the boy who'd showed us the way didn't warn us, I don't know. I was all for apologising and getting out of there before we started another war; Sarpedon looked like he wanted to cover up our gaffe by killing Ischomachus and burning the steading to the ground. Cratus was looking the other way, a talent he's been developing all his life. As for Tachys – well, for two pins I reckon he'd have jumped in one of the sties and let the pigs eat him alive, out of pure shame.

'Excuse me,' Dusa said, 'but are those Argive saddlebacks?'

I nearly fell over; but Ischomachus scowled, then grinned all over his face. 'That's right,' he said. 'Fancy a girl knowing that.'

'Less of the fancy-that, if you don't mind,' Dusa replied. 'What are you feeding them on?'

If someone had tapped me on the shoulder right then and I'd woken up, I'd still have been asking my heart what the hell was going on; because even in a singularly odd dream I'd never have thought of Dusa as an expert on pigs. In real life, it was enough to make your eyes hurt.

But Ischomachus answered her – acorns, he said, and beanhelm, and there was a whole lot more of it but when it got technical I lost track – and she stood there nodding, as if he was her apprentice and she was testing him. Then she was asking about yields and litter sizes and the gods only know what, and he was chattering away; and the next thing we knew, we were inside the house (which made my place look like a toolshed) being fed on roast pork and barley meal, washed down with some of the nastiest neat wine I've ever had to swallow in my life. All good friends, in other words; although it was pretty clear that we were only there because we were with Dusa, and it'd have been rude to make us stand outside while they went indoors and talked pig.

While we were still eating, Ischomachus jumped up mumbling something about afternoon feed. When he'd gone, I grabbed Dusa by the wrist.

'How the hell do you know so much about pigs?' I asked her.

She grinned at me. 'I don't,' she said.

'Don't be funny with me,' I said. 'You knew they were Argive saddlebacks, whatever that means.'

She lifted her head. 'Actually,' she said, 'that was pure luck. But my heart reminded me of a really boring old man Father had to stay once – you two sloped off out of it, but I had to stay and pass the wine round – and he talked about pigs all night. I remembered Argive saddlebacks, and took the chance. After all, there was nothing to lose.'

I furrowed my brows at her. 'What about all the rest, then?' I said. 'All that other stuff, those questions you asked him.'

She grinned. 'Just what I've overheard people saying,' she said. 'Some of us do have ears, you know. I always listen to people, you can learn so much that way.'

'Oh,' I said. 'Well, it seems to have done the trick.'

'Maybe.' She yawned. 'It was a gamble. I reckoned that since he was the sort of man to build a piggery like the King of Assyria's palace, he'd probably be prepared to talk to anybody so long as it was about pigs. And with me being a girl, it'd be a great novelty.

Now, though, it's up to you. I'm all talked out, anyhow. And I never want to see another pig as long as I live, understood?'

'They're quite nice animals, actually,' I said, 'once you get to know them.'

Anyway; when Ischomachus came back in, I launched an offensive at once. It was an honour, I said, to meet the greatest living boxer, the undisputed master of the art, and so on. Since he couldn't possibly know what I was flattering him for, he didn't suspect it was all hot air and garlic, and immediately he started preening himself like a fighting-cock.

'I'm out of practice, though,' he said. 'Haven't had a bout – a proper one, that is – for years. Thought there'd be some fun at the prince's games, but there was nobody else there who could box worth spit; it was hardly worth my while wrapping my hands. And apart from the prince, nobody's died around here lately.'

'Ah,' I said. 'It's odd you should mention that.'

And then I gave him the whole speech, the one I'd been rehearsing with my heart as audience over the last few days of footslogging. I did it well, though I say so myself. I talked about glory, and how good opinion won in the games is like the ambrosia, the food of the gods; if men eat it, they become immortal and death can't get a grip on them, like a wrestler who's oiled his skin. I put it to him that it was a waste of the gifts of the gods that a great games-player like himself should be denied opportunities to use his wonderful skill just because Triphylians of note were so slow to die; also, if the games are for honour, who better to honour than the immortal gods themselves, rather than some mortal man? I said that by the time we'd finished our journey – the journey alone, I told him, would be enough to win us our place in the minds of men for ever – every games-player in the world would be heart-full of longing for the contest we were arranging, it would be the most extraordinary assembly of great and glorious men since the Trojan war. Poets, I told him, would be singing about the games at Elis a thousand years hence, and wouldn't it be a shame and a travesty if all they could say about the boxing was 'Ischomachus, however, was not present'?

And so on. I had to keep going because our gentle pig-fancier was lapping all this up like a dog who's knocked over the milk-jar. His eyes were shining like the harvest moon, and he was twitching slightly, like a cat that's just about to jump on a mouse.

'I'll be there,' he said eventually. 'Count on it. What an absolutely wonderful idea. Some god must've put it into your heart, I'm telling you.'

'Absolutely,' I replied; and then I told him about King Leon's dream – not the one he told the Sons of the Achaeans about, mind you; a different one that I'd made up specially for the purpose. Or at least, a god probably put it into my heart, and if he could put it into my heart, no reason to believe he didn't put it in Leon's, too. So for all I know, what I told him may have been perfectly true.

Ischomachus was so thrilled, in fact, that the only way he could properly express his excitement was in pork; he dashed out and dashed back in with a couple of fat young suckling-pigs, squirming and squealing in his arms, and we had another enormous meal of roast pork, followed by more of that unspeakable wine. Then Ischomachus and Sarpedon suddenly discovered they'd both been in a battle once, on the same side (fortunately); we had the whole battle, blow by blow, glorious feat of arms by glorious feat of arms, until it was too late to go back down the mountain that night, and Ischomachus went back out to find a pig to kill for dinner.

What with pigs and the immortal deeds of heroes, I'd had enough by that stage; I ate as much as I could, just enough to be polite, propped myself against the edge of the table and went to sleep. When I woke up, everybody else had gone to sleep too, on the benches or on the floor under blankets; I crawled on to a bench and closed my eyes, with the feeling that at last we'd made a start, that the adventure was under way, everything was going to work out. My heart could see the successful outcome, the way a man in a forest can see the edge if he climbs a tall enough tree, and although I recognised that we still had a hell of a long way to go, somehow it all seemed so much more possible now that we'd actually netted a games-player. If we could convince Ischomachus, especially after the catastrophic start we'd made, winning over the rest of them was at least possible. Bear in mind, nobody had ever done this before, so when we started there was no reason to believe it could be done, we'd been marching on hope all the way. I tell you, once you know that a thing can be done, has been done before, it's much easier to do it. I suppose that's why we take the trouble to remember the achievements of our forefathers, so we'll know that all the things they did are possible – what someone's done before, someone else can do again. Think what it'd be like if each generation had to find that sort of thing out for itself. Wouldn't that be unbearably lonely, without the past to keep us company?

For some reason (Cleander went on), we all had headaches the next morning.

We said our rather muted goodbyes to Ischomachus, reminded him yet again of the time and place of the games, and said we'd see him there. Then we set off down the mountain.

Fresh mountain air on the morning after has different effects on different people. Sarpedon and I soon felt much better. Dusa was in turns quiet, querulous and noisily sick. I don't know how Cratus and Tachys were feeling, since they were lagging behind. Anyway, going down the mountain was rather less of a chore than going up it.

At the foot of the path we met someone we knew.

'Hello, Alastor,' I called out, before he had a chance to dodge off the road and out of line of sight. 'Fancy meeting you here.'

'Cleander.' He smiled at me. Now, we'd always got on pretty well, Alastor and me; my wife's best friend when she was a girl was Alastor's sister-in-law's cousin, while he and I were both nominal members of some college of priests – another of those Sons-of-the-Achaeans things, doesn't mean we ever had to dress up in white sheets and murder goats, it was all to do with family grazing rights and access to shared water supplies. Anyway, whenever we'd had occasion to spend time with each other, we'd found we had a lot in common, in terms of interests, experiences and ways of looking at the world. Two more such meetings and we'd have been friends, rather than just cordial acquaintances. But you didn't have to be the Oracle to know why he was here, or why he was planning on going up the mountain.

'This is jolly,' I said, giving him a friendly hug that left me standing directly in his way. 'I wish I'd known you were coming out this way. We could have travelled together.'

He looked at me for a couple of heartbeats. 'Actually, I'm not travelling alone,' he said.

'Really? Where's the rest of your party, then?'

'Oh, they went on ahead. I'll catch up with them later.' He made a small sideways movement, which I matched exactly. 'So you've been to see Ischomachus, have you?'

'That's right.'

'Interested in boxing, are you?'

I grinned. 'You bet,' I said. 'I love a good fight.'

'Really.' He tried moving the other way, and I matched him again. 'This is something to do with these games-with-nobody-dead, presumably.'

'In a way,' I replied. Not a very strong answer, but it was the best the god was prepared to give me at the time. 'How about you?' I asked.

'Duty call,' he replied cheerfully. 'Since I was in the neighbourhood. Oh, didn't you know? He's my – now then, let's get this right – third cousin twice removed. On my mother's side.'

I hadn't known that. 'Oh,' I said, brilliantly.

At the time, it felt like being kicked in the nuts by a mule; all that time, effort and patience, most probably gone to waste. Later, as we discussed it among ourselves on the road, it was possible to take a less dismal view; like, if forced to choose between a man who promises you immortal glory and your third cousin twice removed, who would you choose?

'Anyway,' Alastor said, 'mustn't keep you. Take care.'

'And you. Oh, by the way.'

'Hm?'

'Your cousin,' I said. 'Have you met him before?'

Alastor shook his head. 'It's a big family,' he said.

'Right. Well, a word of warning. He's a scruffy-looking man, it's fatally easy to mistake him for the hired help. So if you see a big, bald man all covered in pigshit—'

Alastor laughed. 'Nice try,' he said.

'Honest.'

He shook his head. 'Be seeing you,' he said, and went on his way chuckling.

We were in two minds what to do next. Tachys was all for traipsing back up the hill again and confronting the two of them, arguing it out like a debate, fair and square. Inevitably, Sarpedon's suggestion included murder by the wayside and bodies buried under loose piles of shale. Cratus shrugged, and said, 'What's the point?'

'Dusa?' I asked.

'Let's move on,' she replied. 'We'd better make tracks if we want to keep ahead of him.'

I agreed with Dusa and, by default, Cratus. Sarpedon tried to insist that at the very least we should break Alastor's arms and legs and cut out his tongue, but the consensus was against him.

Nevertheless, we had a fair bit to talk about as we walked toward Bassae. The optimistic faction held that Alastor couldn't possibly be related to every single games-player of note among the Achaeans and Danaans, and since what we had to offer was so desirable that once we'd spread the word it'd take a miracle of eloquence to talk anybody out of it, we should just take him in our stride. The bleaker outlook reckoned that the least we could do was try to figure out the sort of arguments he'd be likely to use against us and see if we could pre-empt them with arguments of our own (though that probably wouldn't help much, since the last word is always twice as loud). A minority view pointed out that the mountains around Ira were known to be infested with thieves and outlaws, on whom the violent death of a stranger could easily be blamed. We were still considering the various issues when, a couple of days later, we walked into Bassae.

Nice place, Bassae. We stopped at the well and asked directions to Prince Onesimus' house, and an old man went with us to show us the way. It was impressive enough: two thick stone pillars framed the porch, and the doors had genuine-looking Assyrian bronze hinges.

'That's a man who believes in appearances,' Dusa said. 'Also first impressions. We'd better tidy ourselves up and think what we're going to say.'

In the end, we decided that when you're anxious to make a good impression, a present is worth a thousand words; so we unslung the packs with the presents in and tried to decide what would be most suitable.

'Assyrian door furniture,' Tachys said, 'suggests a taste for imported goods and show. I vote we give him the Tyrian silver bowl with the ships embossed on the side.'

'Too small,' Cratus replied. 'A man who builds a house like this likes *big* things. Also, if we give him the Thracian cauldron, it means I won't have to carry the damn thing any further. It's rubbed all the skin off my shoulder.'

'That piece of junk?' Dusa said scornfully. 'Oh, come on. It's going to be hard enough as it is without deliberately insulting the man.'

I frowned. 'I happen to like that cauldron,' I said.

'Do you?' Dusa gave me her get-well-soon look. 'Never mind,' she said. 'We won't let on if you don't.'

'If you ask me,' Sarpedon interrupted, 'you can't beat a good sword when it comes to presents. Valuable and desirable, doesn't take up much space when you're not using it, and in a tight spot . . .'

'Be quiet, Uncle. All right, we'll give him the cauldron, agreed? That's settled, then,' I said, as the rest of them all started to talk at once. 'Now then, strategy. If we blunder in saying the first thing our hearts tell us to, we're going to get off to a lousy start, just like we did with the pig man. Dusa,' I went on, turning to her, 'what do you reckon?'

I knew I was bound to offend the rest of my companions by asking her opinion first; but so what? Her observation about the door-hinges had impressed me no end; also, she'd been the one who got us out of trouble with Ischomachus, thanks to the insight some god put into her heart.

'Me?' she said (making trouble, as usual). 'Well, if you really want my opinion, I'd stress the point that these are going to be the *biggest* games ever. That's all, really.'

'All right,' I said, 'that's what we'll do. Tachys, I'll need you to join in after I've made the initial attack and he's come back at me with the "Yes, but . . ." Cratus, you stand by in case Tachys and I get ourselves in trouble. Sarpedon, keep your face shut. Dusa—'

'Yes?'

'Just don't *start*, that's all. Agreed?'

I didn't wait for an answer. Didn't take me long to work that one out: leadership is the art of asking everybody for their opinions and then doing exactly what you intended doing in the first place.

The doors were opened for us by Prince Onesimus' porter, one of the grandest mortals I've ever had the privilege of encountering. I think he was squinting when he looked at us, the way you have to if you want to focus on something extremely small. According to this remarkable object, the prince wasn't in; he was outside in the *palaestra*, exercising.

I hadn't heard that word before, and asked what it meant; but I must have mumbled or something, because the porter didn't seem to hear me. Fortunately, the god put it into my heart to keep myself between the porter and Sarpedon; my uncle fancied himself as something of an ear-doctor and generally prescribed a short, swift flight through the air as a sure-fire cure for deafness in porters, stewards and the like.

The *palaestra* turned out to be a threshing-floor, just like the ones back home; except that instead of a bunch of men bashing ears of barley with jointed wooden sticks, we found one enormous individual trying to jump from one pile of stones to another.

('Wouldn't it be easier just to walk?' Dusa asked.

'Quiet,' I replied.)

In each hand he gripped a heavy lump of iron; as he crouched and bent his knees before each jump, he'd swing these objects out in front of him, presumably to add to his momentum. All he was wearing was a thin coat of olive oil and a narrow band of sheepskin around his forehead.

'Hello,' I said.

He looked round, saw us and immediately, too fast for deliberate thought, adopted a rather more heroic posture. 'Hello yourself,' he replied, looking first, briefly, at me and then at Dusa. 'Travellers?'

I opened my mouth to speak, but Tachys (of all people) beat me to it. 'That's right,' he said. 'We were just saying what a wonderful place you have here.'

'Yes,' Onesimus replied.

'And this –' Tachys waved his hand vaguely. 'This is where you train? For the games?'

'Yes.'

'What a good idea. I expect one day all games-players will have something like this.'

'Only the rich ones,' Onesimus replied.

It was one of those moments when you look to your heart to suggest something, only to find the door wide open and nobody home. I couldn't think of anything to say. Tachys was standing quite still, with his mouth tight shut. There was a fair chance Dusa might say something quite soon, but I doubted very much whether it would help. Sarpedon was growling softly like a dog that can smell a fox, something he did a lot. And that only left—

'You know,' said Cratus, not even looking at Onesimus, 'we could have something like this at home. All we'd have to do is pull down the old house – you know, the one out on the thirty-acre; level it off, root up those vines out the back, it'd be ideal.'

I hadn't the faintest idea what he was talking about. True, we had a thirty-acre plot; or at least we had a mountain whose base covered well over thirty acres, but the only possible use we'd ever been able to think of for it was asking a god to uproot it and use it to imprison uppity frost-giants under. Also, I doubted very much whether Cratus really wanted the old house pulled down, since he lived in it.

On the other hand, it looked like the god had put an idea in his heart. Who was I to argue with the gods?

'It's a thought,' I replied cautiously.

'And when we've done that,' he went on, starting to sound disturbingly excited, 'we could chop down those useless old olive trees, terrace up the ends and build a chariot circuit. It'd be nicely handy for the stables.'

Just as I was reminding myself that the ideas the god puts into our hearts aren't always necessarily any good, Prince Onesimus turned his head sharply and looked at us. 'You're thinking of having your own chariot circuit?' he asked.

'Why not?' Cratus shrugged. 'After all, how can you get better if you don't practise? And it's not as if we haven't got the space.'

A little fold of skin twitched between Onesimus' eyebrows. He was worried.

'Actually,' he said, 'I've been thinking about doing something like that here.'

'Really?' Cratus asked politely.

Onesimus nodded. 'I was thinking about pulling down those barns there –' He gestured in the direction of four large, newly built barns, each one the size of my house, each with an untarnished gold thatch. 'Then I could have a bank dug for spectators, over where the sheep-pens are now.'

I'll say this for Cratus, he can convince you he's what he isn't better than any man I've met, when he's in the mood. He pulled this face; it made him look like a god who's been asked for advice about when to plant leeks. 'Could do, I suppose,' he said. 'Though it'd be a pity to lose a nice run of barns. Still, if you're cramped for space here—'

'Oh no,' said Onesimus quickly. 'Not in the least. You see that hill over there, the round one with the three tall pines on the top? That's all mine, from here up to just beyond the hill. And if you look over there' – he turned a right angle and pointed – 'that wood there, on the horizon, that's my western boundary. And I've got three more patches on the other side of the city, too.'

Cratus did a marvellous study in bored deity. 'A bit awkward to get to, nevertheless,' he said. 'Pity you don't have a couple of long meadows or orchards beside the house, really.'

Onesimus' face lit up. 'Actually,' he said, 'that big meadow down there to the right is mine, and so's that elbow-shaped piece there, and the hog-back ridge that comes round the back—'

Cratus gave him an indulgent smile. 'It's wonderful what you can fit in with a bit of ingenuity,' he said. 'Of course, it'll be easy for us, since our place is so flat; just grazing land and black-earth, you see, so we don't have to worry about hills and dips getting in the way.'

At the back of my mind, a little god was asking me to consider what was going to happen when this clown did come to Elis, and decided to stay with us while he was there. Even if I turned out of my house completely and gave him the run of it he'd still be mortally offended, imagining we'd put him in one of the shepherds' huts. But we'd deal with that as and when it happened, I told him; we could always pretend we'd been caught conspiring against the king and had all our land taken away from us. Something along those lines, anyway.

'Come into the house,' said Onesimus. 'Maybe you'd like something to eat.'

We followed him. Just as I was about to duck in through the door, Dusa pulled me back by the elbow.

'I know about how important the mission is,' she whispered, 'not to mention the sacred laws of hospitality. But if that fool doesn't stop staring at me, I shall say something I won't regret but you might.'

'Don't you dare,' I replied.

'But he's such a—'

'I know. But think, if there were only decent, sensible, intelligent people in the world, how lonely it would be. Keep it to yourself, Dusa. That's an order.'

She looked at me and made a suggestion about where my orders could be stored when not in use, but I didn't feel inclined to follow it; it'd have been undignified and very bad for my health.

The house of Onesimus, Prince of Bassae, was somewhat magnificent; the sort of place you'd imagine a god building for himself if he suddenly came into a substantial inheritance. Let's start with the hall itself. Needless to say it was enormous; places for fifty at the tables, and each seat had its own individual purple coverlet and matching purple-upholstered footstool – you'd never believe there were enough oysters in the sea to produce enough shells to make that much purple. The staircase to the upper room rose out of the hall like the mast of a ship. At the back of the hall, as far as I could see – I've never been much good at seeing things over extremely long distances – was an enormous door, leading to the inner room; it had two massive locks on it, which explained the two winnowing-fan-sized bronze keys (with ivory handles) that hung from the belt Onesimus was carrying in his hand. The thresholds and doorposts were polished oak, like the hall-pillars (each one made out of a single giant growing tree that hadn't been an acorn since Zeus was weaned). There were no fewer than five braziers, all solid bronze, not to mention the bronze wall-sconces; my guess is that they needed all that light just so Onesimus could revel in the purpleness of his soft furnishings even in the middle of the night.

And oh, the *things* – tripods and cauldrons standing in a row like sentries all down one wall; tapestries and hangings above them, enough to make sails for the thousand ships that went to Troy; naturally, when we presented him with his gift, Onesimus had to make that an excuse to show us round his treasury out the back, under guise of putting it away safely and choosing us something fitting in return. Armour – if he'd lived to be eighty he'd have been able to wear a different suit every week. Swords – well, Sarpedon was either in hell or heaven, I can't say which. Tableware – stacked in mountains, it was; easily a hundred and fifty plates, as many cups, sixty-odd jugs (he told us the exact figure, but I wasn't listening), yet more tripods and cauldrons and mixing-bowls, iron spits and fire-dogs; also big jars full of bronze nails; two dozen ploughshares (unused, still in their grease); saws, hammers, axes, shovels (wooden and bronze), scythes, hooks, pruning-knives, wheel-rims, two dismantled chariots, half a dozen enormous great blooms of pig-iron; twenty tunics, as many cloaks, twenty or more belt buckles, half a wall of boots and sandals, a whole jar of spare hobnails; three ship's masts, an anchor, a hundredweight of blankets, enough rope to tie Elis to Corinth, jars – you just couldn't imagine that many jars, and the gods only knew what was in them, could've been flour or wine or oil or gold dust for all I know. The thought that one man could own so many *things* was enough to make your head spin. I tell you, it was enough to put you off the whole idea of wealth. Yes, I know: wealth is the gods' way of showing your worth, of marking out the better sort from the rest. But I ask you, in all conscience, what in the world could one man want with *six* small circular tables?

'Remind me to call here again,' Sarpedon muttered, 'some time when I have a spare army.' I could tell he was a bit upset; Onesimus' treasury made his own collection of useless junk look positively meagre.

'Now then,' Onesimus was saying (he'd become a lot more talkative once he was surrounded by his things). 'What can we find that'd make worthy presents for such distinguished guests?' Blather,

I don't need to tell you. He hadn't a clue how distinguished we were, apart from Cratus' parcel of lies. He just wanted an excuse to make us feel small by giving us excessively generous presents.

It was almost comical to watch him, wading about knee-deep in his jam-packed store of objects, picking something up off one pile or heap, shaking his head and putting it back. It was all done on purpose, just in case we'd missed this or that exquisite artefact. Eventually, after he'd fingered pretty well every single thing in the storeroom (this took a very long time, as you can imagine), he handed us our allotted pieces of clutter: for me, a bronze and amber brooch, with one of the three amber studs missing; for Sarpedon, a slightly bent silver cup, easily big enough to contain one small mouthful; for Tachys, an ancient and slightly bald ferretskin arming-cap, with distinct traces of the original owner's sweat inside the brim; for Dusa a rather fine ivory-handled mirror, lacking the mirror; and for Cratus, a solid gold bracelet as big as your closed fist. Somehow, I got the feeling that it was my brother who'd made the best impression.

Well, after we'd all looked thrilled and made the required just-what-I-always-wanted noises, we were herded back into the hall, where the men were lugging about enough meat to last the whole of Elis through a hard winter.

'Got to keep our strength up, after all,' our host said to Cratus.

'Oh, quite,' my brother replied, as three men set about the carcass of a huge ox with big curved blades.

'That's what people don't realise,' Onesimus went on, flopping down into a robust-looking ivory and sandalwood chair. 'If you want to do well in the games, you've got to plan your whole life round it. Eat the right food, sleep the right amount every night, do the right exercises. There really isn't time for anything else.'

I must have started grinning, because Dusa kicked me on the ankle and gave me a poisonous look. But what did she expect, when this character was so obviously already knee-deep in the lime before we'd even said a word?

'You're right,' Cratus replied smoothly. 'And when you think how rarely an opportunity comes along to make use of the talents the gods have given us—'

'And which we've worked so hard at cultivating—'

'Of course, that as well. Anyway, it's enough to make you weep. After all, you could spend years getting into peak condition, be at the very pinnacle of your readiness and abilities, and then find yourself waiting for years before you get a chance to compete in an actual event. What a waste, that's how I see it.'

Onesimus sighed so deeply I was afraid the doors were going to blow open. 'That's so true,' he said. 'Take my own father, for example. Wonderful boxer. Wasn't anybody to touch him in the whole Peloponnese – well, nobody to touch him twice, if you get my meaning. But who's going to remember him? Nobody. And why? Because he never got the chance to fight in a proper games, that's why.'

'Nobody died,' Cratus murmured.

'That's right. That's it, exactly, nobody died. No uncles, see – any gods' amount of aunts, but no uncles. And his father; well, we make old bones in our family, the old boy was nearly eighty when he finally went on, and by then my father was in his sixties, well past his prime.'

Dusa clicked her tongue. 'Some people can be so thoughtless,' she muttered under her breath. Fortunately Onesimus didn't hear, though I think he may have noticed the little squeak of pain she made after I stamped on her toe.

'Oh, of course they said to him, Don't worry, there's plenty of wars, you can show off your prowess in battle. Well, they always say that. But it's not the same; you don't necessarily use the same muscles, the same routines, the same footwork in fighting that you do in boxing, let alone other games. Like, take jumping, my speciality – when the hell do you ever need to jump your own length in a battle? You could spend your whole life in the field, fighting every day of the year, and never have to jump over anything wider than an irrigation ditch.'

Cratus was beginning to worry me; any moment, I thought, and the strain of keeping a straight face is going to make him crack his jawbones. 'They just don't think, do they?' he said. 'But then, how can you expect them to understand? They aren't games-players.'

'True.' Onesimus craned his neck slightly so as to be able to see over the enormous boulder-sized cut of prime steak that had landed in front of him on the table. 'But so what? The vast majority of people don't fight in battles, either; I'm talking about your small-time peasants, your seven-acre men who spend their lives dragging a bit of stick through a thin layer of dirt. They don't fight and they don't play games. But you ask them about Hercules or Achilles or Diomedes, they'll tell you all about them; and Castor and Polydeuces and Hippolyta, too. What I'm saying is, you and I understand, yes, because we're games-players ourselves; but there's only so many of us, a small handful compared to all the hundreds – thousands, even – living in the Peloponnese. And the fact is, my friend – sorry, I didn't quite catch . . .'

Cratus frowned a little but replied, 'Cratus. I'm from Elis.'

'Cratus, right. I'm sure I've heard of you. The fact is, it's not a few games-players who're going to keep your memory alive when you're dead and ashes. It's not even the better sort, sat round the fire in a hall somewhere. Oh, we've got our house poets and our genealogies, we know more or less who our great-great-great-great-grandfathers were; but what's the good of that if the family dies out, they all get killed in a war or die of the plague or the line simply dwindles away? They go, and all the memories go with them; and suddenly your ghost is shivering on the wrong bank of the River, completely forgotten and alone. You know what they told me when I went to the Oracle once? They said that so long as enough people remember your name, you'll live in the Elysian Fields, never know want or pain or fear, never grow old or waste away. But when they forget you, then Hades' guards come and take you away and throw you out of the gates back into the darkness, out there with all the hundreds of thousands of dead men who nobody remembers, in the dark and the cold; and once you've been there a while, it gets so that nobody can even see you any more, you can't hear, you can't even talk. You're awake, but you're nothing, for ever. I tell you, Cratus, I don't think I'm that much of a coward – I'm not brave, but I'm not feeble either – but that thought really frightens me.'

We were all quiet for a bit after that; and in my heart I felt sorry for this Onesimus, as I pictured him pounding away day after day in his *palaestra*, endlessly jumping and running round and throwing the discus, as if every scrap of effort he put into it was somehow a blow struck in the battle against that darkness and that cold. It wasn't, of course, and he knew it; but the fear would take him every time he stopped, and he'd drive himself on to more jumps and more sit-ups and knee-bends, like a field-hand whipped on by the overseer.

'I know,' Onesimus continued, 'what do you expect if you choose to be a games-player and not a fighter? You ask me that, and I can't really give you a good answer. But I'll tell you this, friend, and you'll have to make your mind up as your heart sees fit. I never could see the point in starting a war and killing other people and seeing your people die and maybe even getting killed yourself, just so you'll get to have peace and light after you're dead. I don't follow the argument. I don't see how the one follows on from the other. Now, you'll say I'm contradicting myself, saying one thing and something completely different the next moment. But here's the truth: I'm not a good fighter, I haven't got the reflexes or the upper-body strength. More than that, I haven't got the heart. But I'm a *good* games-player; not because I was born the son of a king, or even because I've spent my life training and eating red meat and drinking milk. It's because the gods gave me the skill as well as the strength and the endurance. I think I ought to be allowed to earn my memories doing what I'm good at. Otherwise, what's the point of them giving me all this to begin with?'

He was making me feel uncomfortable, at that. I could see now the reasons for all his wealth and show, his mountains of food and his purple cushion-covers. If he couldn't be remembered for his jumping and his prowess at throwing a flat bit of polished wood across a disused threshing-floor, then he'd try his best to be remembered for his wealth, his tasteless and vulgar display of appearances, his things. He was like a squirrel, burying nuts for the winter; every item of superfluous, unused junk was a stone in the cairn he was trying to raise for himself, to cover his still-unburned body. My heart was confused, then and there; was this man so afraid of the dark that every damned thing he did was just an attempt to wriggle his way into the light, to stay there an extra month or so?

Eventually, Cratus found some words. 'Well now,' he said, 'I think I might be able to suggest a better way. Would you like me to tell you about it?'

Onesimus blinked. 'By all means,' he said.

'All right. Better still, why don't you listen to my brother Cleander here? He's the one who's organising it all. What do you reckon, Cleander?'

So I said my piece; and honestly, it was like when a man's about to be hanged or beheaded, and at the last moment one of the king's squires comes down from the palace into the yard and tells him it's all right, the king has decided that he doesn't have to die that day.

'Think of it,' Cratus picked up, when I'd ground to a halt. 'There'll come a time when Elis and Bassae and Corone and Lampsacus and all the places we know are deserted and fallen down, just like the places that are ruined and forgotten in our time – we see the stones, sure, we can just about trace where their great houses and storerooms and treasuries were by the patterns in the grass, but we haven't the faintest idea who they were beyond the names of a few kings; all we know is, they lived here long ago and they don't live here any more. This very hall, now – oh, I know, I don't suppose you'll find its like anywhere this side of Athens or Eretria – but I'll wager you there'll come a time when people will walk over a grassy meadow and wonder whether it was here or in the next valley that the mighty Onesimus lived, the one who could jump and throw the discus further than any man before or since. The palace won't be there any more, not even the city; there'll be nothing left except a name, an idea, the flavour of great things done by great men, standing up through time like those patterns we see in the grass. That's what you and I are after, aren't we, that shape in memory, the pattern that'll put them in mind of what they could do themselves, if they had the strength and the determination, and the gods putting the will in their hearts.'

I was embarrassed half to death, I'm telling you, sitting there with my mouth open, like a gate left unlatched by a careless goatherd. Bless my heart, I was thinking, since when was my miserable brother so eloquent about something he'd have had me believe was nothing but foolishness? He knew and I knew why we were there: because the King of Elis had a dead fish for a son, and something had to be done about it before it was too late. And yet here he was – there you were, Cratus, damn you – reaching out and pushing back the darkness, like the light from these very braziers. Quite the poet, my brother, don't you think? I hated you right then, I'll tell you straight, because you could lie so easily about something that mattered so much, to that poor fool Onesimus and every living man.

Cratus smiled (but of course his brother couldn't see it). 'You reckon I was lying?' he said.

'Of course,' Cleander said impatiently. 'Of course you were. You never believed in the mission, even for the purpose we were doing it for. Of course you didn't believe a word you were saying, about memory and living for ever in the Elysian Fields. How could you? Everything you were saying was a lie, you were pretending you were a mighty games-player too. We games-players, you were saying to him, but you were manipulating an idiot, like a child with a puppet made out of pomegranate-rind.'

'Is that so?' Cratus said. 'Well, then.' He shrugged his shoulders. 'Let's ask the Phoenician. After all, he's a stranger here, he doesn't know us from a piece of old cheese and probably doesn't care one way or the—'

Someone sniggered. The Phoenician was fast asleep.

CHAPTER SIX

'It only goes to show,' said Cratus sadly, as the baskets of bread were handed round next morning, 'how pointless the whole thing is, when you get right down to it. No offence, my friend, but when you dozed off last night, you proved my point. Thank you for that, anyway.'

'Mmm?' The Phoenician's head felt rather fuzzy, and both light and sound bothered him. 'Sorry, did I miss something important?'

Cratus laughed, while Cleander scowled horribly. 'Not in the least,' Cratus said. 'And like I just told you, you gave us all a splendid demonstration of what I'm trying to persuade you all of. I mean to say, there we all were, trying our hardest to preserve the memory of Prince Onesimus, so the poor beggar won't have to spend all eternity in the freezing darkness, and you defeat all our best efforts by closing your eyes and taking a nap. So much for immortality.'

'I'm sorry,' the Phoenician said. 'And besides, I do remember what you were telling me about Onesicles—'

'Onesimus.'

'That's right, him. He was the rich show-off who gave you all such rotten presents.'

Cratus nodded gravely. 'That's right,' he said. 'You remember that about him, and I guess you won't be far wrong. Or at least,' he went on with a slight grimace, 'that's how tales get about, as my old grandmother used to say.'

Cleander grunted. 'No she didn't,' he interrupted. 'It was the old peasant woman. Our grandmother was just quoting her.'

'So? When she said what the old woman said, she said it. Don't be so damned picky. Doesn't matter anyhow, it's just a saying. Probably doesn't mean a thing to anybody outside our family.' He turned sharply towards the Phoenician. 'Does it?' he demanded.

'Sorry,' the Phoenician replied, 'I didn't quite catch all of that.'

At that point, Palamedes joined in. 'Cratus is right,' he said. 'Things have different meanings depending on what's gone before. Like the rat pies.'

Everybody looked at him.

'Rat pies,' Palamedes repeated. 'My great-grandmother used to make a special sort of cake for Spring Festival, and she called them calm-cakes. When my grandmother was a little girl, she could never bring herself to eat them, because she thought they were ferret-cakes – you know, made out of ferret-meat; that's why festival cakes are called rat pies in our family.'

(The Phoenician looked blank for a moment; then he realised it was a sort of unintentional pun – *galen*, meaning calm, and *galena*, meaning polecat. He felt quite proud of himself for having spotted it, in a foreign language, when his head hurt.)

'What I'm trying to say is,' Palamedes went on, ignoring the stares, 'someone in our family knows what I mean by rat pies, while the rest of you are looking at me like I've gone daft in the head. Because of memory, you see; knowing the background, what's gone before. If I hadn't explained, our friend here might well have gone back to his own country and told everybody there that in Elis they eat rat pie. And of course we don't.'

'Well,' someone put in, 'not often, anyway.'

'Ignore him,' said Palamedes. 'And have some breakfast, it'll buck you up no end. Here, try some of this.'

The Phoenician noticed a dish of some kind of pastry, hovering to his left on a level with the bridge of his nose. 'Thanks,' he said, 'but I'm not hungry. Maybe just some plain wheat bread, and a cup of water . . .'

Well (Cratus said), we were tempted to hang on there for a day or so, enjoy our welcome, wait for Alastor to show up . . . It'd have been entertaining to hear what our new friend Onesimus had to say to him when he tried to snatch the promise of immortality away from him, no doubt about that. But we were behind our schedule, and the distance we had to cover wasn't getting any less. So we said, Goodbye, see you in Elis; and that clown Onesimus was genuinely sorry to see us go, I'll swear to it. I suppose he wanted us to hang around for a month or two watching him prance about his *palaestra* all covered in olive oil and sand.

Before he let us go, he insisted on giving us four – I'll repeat that, four – mules and a spare pair of boots each, not to mention about a year's supply of fine-grade wheat flour, dried figs, olives, a cheese the size of a cartwheel with the plaster around it still damp, a whacking great big basket of apples and two big jars of wine. For two pins and an olive-pit, he'd probably have come with us himself; but we managed to dissuade him from that. It'd have been like going out hunting with a big, young, friendly dog that races off barking at the first sniff of a hare three hundred paces away.

The next leg of the journey was short enough, Bassae to Mila, one brisk day or two leisurely ones. Mila was very much an afterthought; we didn't even know for sure that there was a games-player there, though it seemed like a reasonable bet. And as luck would have it, there was: Prince Stenyclarus, shepherd of his people, a wolf with the discus and the javelin, so everybody we met assured us, and the only possible explanation for why we'd never heard of him was that all of us had spent our lives huddled in a small cave at the top of some remote and inaccessible mountain.

That sounded promising, so we got a move on and limped off a very stony, rutted road into Mila just as it was getting dark. We asked a woman filling her jars at the well, and she pointed out Stenyclarus' house – one of two large, rather slab-sided buildings that stood side by side in the square.

That told us all we needed to know about politics in Mila: two palaces meant two princes, sharing the rule of the city between them. Now, I don't know about you, or what it's like where you come from when a king dies and two sons inherit jointly, but in these parts it's either a total success or a desperate failure. The good thing is, you can usually tell which as soon as you pass under the gatehouse.

In Mila, though, there didn't seem to be any indications either way. The gate was still open even though it was dark, with a bored-looking man-at-arms leaning on his shield who didn't bother looking up as we walked by; good sign. But the street was almost empty and most of the houses had closed doors, nobody hanging about outside in the porch; bad sign, possibly. In truth, no way of knowing.

'Still,' Dusa said, 'we can start from the assumption that there's going to be rivalry between Stenyclarus and his brother, friendly or otherwise. That ought to mean he'll be interested in a way of boosting his own prestige, especially if he can do it without overtly treading on Brother's toes. He ought to be interested.'

Well, we banged on the gate, first with our fists, then with our spear-butts. It was a long time before anybody came.

'More guests,' the doorkeeper snarled at us. 'You'd better come in.'

Alastor and his people? Possible. But one of my reasons for stopping in Mila was because I was sure Alastor wouldn't; he'd assume we were heading straight for Pylos, and so get there before we did. I wanted to be one step behind Alastor for a while, so that we'd be getting the last word. Probably not Alastor, then. Could be anybody.

Wasn't.

It shows how my mind was elsewhere – I didn't recognise them at first. Oh, I knew that I knew them from somewhere, but not straight away. In other words, they recognised me as the man they'd robbed in Elis before I realised that they were the men who'd robbed me.

Given that the god gave them this advantage, they should have made better use of it. If I'd been them, I'd have tried something a bit more subtle than they did – I might have jumped up and pointed me out as a bandit who'd waylaid them, or a sworn enemy in a blood-feud, anything to discredit me. I suppose they weren't subtle people; not much call for guile and subterfuge when you make your living behind a spear.

By the time my memory had caught up with me, the leader (or at least the man I'd spoken to) was on his feet, waving his knife at me. On balance, he'd have done better to have removed the large chunk of roast pork from it first. A moment later the rest of his party were on their feet too, while the host was sitting up with a bemused look on his face and asking what was going on. The bandit leader, however, wasn't in a chatty mood. His heart was telling him to get out of the hall, which would mean going through or over us.

That was the point where I got shoved out of the way and fell sideways over a bench, bumping my head quite hard. I don't know how long I was out of it, but what brought me to was a big man with a sword in his hand standing over me looking ferocious. Fortuitously, I had the angle and the presence of mind to boot him sharply in the nuts before he could get beyond the staring-and-growling stage that he clearly regarded as an indispensable prologue to a respectable fight.

With him out of the way, at least I had a clearer view of what was happening, not that that was something I'd necessarily have wanted. The centre of attention was my uncle Sarpedon, who seemed to be enjoying himself no end. Where the sword came from I don't know; we'd all left our weapons with the doorkeeper, so either Sarpedon had bashed one of our host's men-at-arms to get it, or it was a spare he'd got hidden away down the side of his tunic. Whichever; the first I saw was his hand going up over his head, the sword gripped firmly just behind the hilt. Then someone got in the way, but the sound was quite enough for me to know what Sarpedon was up to. There's no other noise like it, not even the crunch of a pig's carcass being jointed.

I couldn't see Tachys. Dusa was sprawled over a bench, presumably where someone had shoved her. I saw her grab a big silver jug for the purpose of bashing heads, but she hesitated and stayed where she was. Cleander was in some sort of trouble with a short, stringy man who had his back to me. Worst of all, there were men-at-arms squeezing their shields through the door and heading straight for us.

I could only think of one thing to do; so I did it.

'Stop it!' I yelled, at the top of my voice.

And stop it they did; though that may have had more to do with the half-circle of spear-points bearing down on them than my magnificent tone of voice. Hard to say, looking at it objectively. Of course, I'm a biased witness, so you mustn't count on getting the plain truth out of me.

Talk about a mess. I've thought about that scene a few times over the years, mostly from our host's point of view. What he saw, when the blurred movement stopped and he had a clear view, was one dead man lying face down on the floor of his hall, another man curled up in a ball in the corner by the doorway, covered in blood; he saw an arm – well, a hand and a wrist – lying almost at his feet, like the bones you don't fancy yourself so you sling them to the dog. He saw them, and he saw us, two parties of strangers who'd come into his home and started a fight for no reason he knew.

He looked round, with an expression of distaste on his face the like of which I've never seen, then pointed to the dead man, and the arm.

'Who did that?' he asked.

One of his men-at-arms took a step forward. He was wiping blood off his face from a very nasty cut that ran from his cheekbone to the corner of his mouth; he'd have a real horror of a scar there for the rest of his life. 'He did,' the man said, pointing at Sarpedon with his spear. 'That old bugger there.'

Our host looked at Sarpedon. 'Well?' he said.

'Sure,' Sarpedon replied. He was breathing a little heavily, but grinning. Not a mark on him, of course, unless you count someone else's blood. 'That was me.'

I could feel the situation going bad on us. 'I can explain,' I said, but someone prodded me hard in the ribs and told me to shut my face.

'All right,' our host said. 'And who the hell are you?'

'Sarpedon of Elis. You've probably heard of me.'

'No.'

'Oh.' Sarpedon looked hurt. 'You do surprise me.'

'Please,' I said, managing to anticipate the spear-butt this time, 'let me explain. These men attacked me—'

'No they didn't. You attacked them.'

He had a point. I could have put it better, I suppose. 'Not here,' I said. 'These men robbed me on the road just outside Elis.'

He frowned. 'And you are?'

'My name's Cratus. This is my brother Cleander and my sister Eurymedusa. Oh, and our travelling companion, Tachys.'

Stenyclarus nodded. 'What about him?' he said.

'He's my uncle.'

'Excuse me.' It was the leader of the bandits. 'Excuse me, but that's not true, what he's saying about being robbed by us. I've never seen any of them before and I've never been to Elis. Come on, do we look like robbers?'

That was a fair point, too; but then again, they hadn't looked like robbers when they robbed me. Come to that, I'm not sure what robbers do look like.

'All right,' Stenyclarus said, rubbing the bridge of his nose with the flat of his hand, like a man who knows he's getting a headache. 'So why did they attack you? Unprovoked, soon as look at you.'

The robber shrugged. 'I have no idea,' he said. 'Perhaps Madness lodged in their hearts, these things happen. Or—' He snapped his fingers, as if inspired by a sudden insight. 'If they're from Elis, maybe they attacked us because we're Triphylians. There was a war recently, you know.'

'Was there?' Stenyclarus raised an eyebrow. 'First I've heard of it.'

'Actually,' Cleander interrupted, 'that's perfectly true, there was a war. But we've just been with the Triphylian king, he gave us presents and sent us on our way.'

'Really. Oh well, maybe you're right.' Stenyclarus took a deep breath and let it out through his nose. 'But I think that's beside the point. What I see as the point is, you people come bursting in here, you attack guests of mine with swords, kill one and maim another, beat up my retainers, allegedly because these men are supposed to have robbed you in Elis.' He scowled like thunder. 'Is that about it?'

I nodded. 'Let me try to prove it to you,' I said. 'I can describe the things they stole from me. Maybe they've still got some of them with them.'

Stenyclarus shook his head. 'I don't think so,' he said. 'You could have been snooping round my stables before you came in here, going through their panniers; or maybe you met up with someone they'd been with, who described what they were carrying. And anyway,' he went on, 'that's not the issue here. It's none of my business what any of you got up to in Elis. But it's my business when blood gets shed on my floor.'

'Just a moment,' someone interrupted; I looked round and saw it was Tachys. 'Sorry to butt in, but that's *not* what happened. As soon as we walked in, that man there jumped up and came at Cratus here with a knife. Then Cratus got knocked over, and the rest of them came at us; that's when Sarpedon pulled out that sword and started hitting people.'

'That's true,' Stenyclarus admitted. 'Yes, that's a valid point, I suppose. You, what do you say to that?'

The bandit looked a bit worried, but he recovered well. 'I beg your pardon,' he said, 'but that's not how it happened at all. Some strangers came in, I stood up to welcome them, same as anybody'd do—'

'Really? I didn't, and it's my house.'

'It's what we do where I come from,' the bandit replied.

Stenyclarus shrugged. 'Carry on,' he said.

'That's about it. This one barged at me, I grabbed at him to keep my balance, he fell over. Then the madman started slashing at us with his sword. Ask him, by the way, exactly why he had a sword hidden under his cloak, if he meant no harm.'

'What about you?' Sarpedon snapped at him. 'You were waving a knife.'

'I didn't wave anything. I was still holding my knife, I was eating my food with it. That's not the same as waving, and you know it.'

Stenyclarus closed his eyes, as if he was hoping that when he opened them again, it'd all have gone away. 'All right,' he said to the bandit, 'suppose I believe you. What do you want me to do about it?'

The bandit looked shocked. 'Hang them, of course,' he said. 'He murdered my nephew, he cut off Theoclymenes' arm. In your house,' he added, 'under your roof.'

'Oh, sure.' Stenyclarus looked very weary. 'So I string up five perfect strangers, and next thing I know I'm locked into some ghastly blood-feud with half the families in the Peloponnese. I don't think so.' He turned round. 'And what if I believe you?' he said, looking at me. 'What's your suggestion?'

I thought quickly. 'I don't think it's up to you to do anything,' I replied. 'I'd say this dead man and the other man's arm cancels out the robbery. Just send us on our way, and them too. If anything still needs to be sorted out, we'll do it somewhere else, where it won't concern you.'

The bandit looked appalled. 'Now just a moment—' he started to say, but Stenyclarus shut him up with a gesture.

'That sounds more like it,' he said. 'At least, you're on the right lines. Here's what you're all going to do. You're all going to get out of my house and off Milaean land by sunrise. And if I ever lay eyes on any of you again, I'll kill you on the spot. Fair enough?'

'No,' the bandit shouted.

'Absolutely,' I said.

'Then it's a deal,' Stenyclarus said. 'You, take this lot and walk them to the southern boundary.' (This lot was us.) 'And you, take these men to the northern boundary. If you see any of them again, kill 'em on sight.'

'What about Theoclymenes?' the bandit protested. 'He's just had his arm cut off, he's in no fit state to move.'

Stenyclarus shrugged. 'Carry him,' he replied. 'Do whatever you like, just so long as you go away and don't come back. But hear this, all of you. I won't have fighting in my house, and I won't have my people beaten up or put at risk. That's all there is to it.'

'What a dreadful thing,' the Phoenician said. 'First these people robbed you, then they set on you again, then they nearly got you hanged. That's awful.'

Cratus smiled. 'You think so?' he said. 'Well, all due respect, but that's because you've only heard me tell the story. Think about it. In my opinion, we were very lucky indeed.'

'Lucky!'

Cratus nodded. 'It was clear enough to me that he hadn't believed a word I'd said. He didn't believe a lot of what the bandit said, either – my guess is, he thought we were the two sides in some feud or other, and neither of us were ready to tell him what was really going on. He got rid of us simply because he didn't want to get mixed up in whatever we were involved in. Wise choice, if you ask me; he only had a limited number of men, and remember, it was a split city. Last thing he wanted was to get sucked into some faction war where his brother might have gone in on the other side as a pretext for getting shot of him. If the same thing had happened in a strong city – Bassae, say, or here – chances are we'd all have been lynched, or locked up till he found out if anybody was ready to pay a ransom for us.'

The Phoenician looked disturbed by that. 'It can't be right,' he said. 'After all, you were all respectable people – well, possibly not Sarpedon, but the rest of you. And they were bandits. Surely that'd have come out sooner or later.'

Palamedes shook his head. 'Why so?' he said, leaning across the table. 'I expect the bandits told him they were respectable people when they first called in; or more likely, Stenyclarus assumed that, because that's what you automatically assume. In fact, the world wouldn't work if you didn't.' He smiled. 'You make it sound as if it's always possible to scrape right down to the truth, whereas in reality it's only very rarely you come across something your heart can really be sure is true. And that's just life, the way the gods have ordained things should be.'

The Phoenician shook his head. 'Then it makes everything we've been talking about seem a bit meaningless,' he said, 'don't you think? I mean, if you can't tell truth from lies or good from bad when events are happening right in front of your eyes, how the hell can you be sure that anything handed down in memory's going to have even a tiny speck of truth in it?'

There was a moment's bemused silence. Then Cratus said, 'Are they all as naïve as you in Phoenicia?'

'We have writing,' said the Phoenician stiffly. 'And laws, and judges. If this terrible thing you've just told me about had happened in my country, the prince would have arrested everybody and held them for trial; then he'd have sent out his men to find out what really happened, if there'd been a robbery or not, if the bandits had committed any other crimes in other parts of the country; the district magistrate for your city would have sent a written –' (here the Phoenician used a word the Greeks didn't understand) '– to confirm that you were who you said you were, with all the relevant information about you. The truth would have come out, quickly and efficiently, and the matter would have been dealt with in accordance with law and justice.'

There was a long silence; after which Cratus said, 'Apparently, the answer to my question is "yes". No offence,' he added quickly, 'but anybody with half a brain can see the flaws in that system. Each to his own, I suppose, but I'm glad I don't live in your country. And to be fair,' he added with a grin, 'I'm sure your people are glad that people like me don't live in your country. Anyway, it's just as well we're not all alike, or it'd be a very boring world.'

The Phoenician looked like he wanted to say something else, but he didn't. Cratus poured himself a drink, and went on with his story.

From Mila (Cratus continued), we went to Pylos.

Everybody, me included, was thrilled to bits at the thought of going to Pylos. Sarpedon pretended he'd been there once, when he was very young, but we didn't believe him; he seemed just as excited as the rest of us, which suggested he hadn't been there either. Didn't matter; we knew all about Pylos, because we'd all been brought up on stories about the glorious sons of Nestor, the great palaces, the lofty granaries and water-towers, the streets so wide that two chariots could pass each other without slowing down. As for our mission, we knew we were on to a good thing, because there was no more famous chariot-racer in the whole of the Peloponnese, or among all the Sons of the Achaeans, than Demophoon of Pylos.

The only thing that could possibly go wrong, that we could think of in our hearts, was Alastor getting there first and having time to do a really thorough job of turning the king against us; but that was a risk we were prepared to take, since we'd have the tactical advantage of the last word, and anyway, it was such a remote possibility that we couldn't force ourselves to worry about it. Demophoon wasn't just famous for racing chariots; mostly he was known for his wisdom, a trait that ran in the family, since his great-great-however-many-times-grandfather Nestor had been the wisest man in the world at the time of the Trojan war, and people said that Demophoon was just like him in that respect, once you'd allowed for the fact that the men of today are necessarily inferior to the men of the past.

So we didn't dawdle, but we didn't rush either. We followed the coast most of the way, keeping ourselves to ourselves since we still had all that food that Onesimus had given us, and stopping anywhere would only have meant delay. All of us wanted to get to Pylos, as if some wonderful thing was waiting for us there; a hot bath, a warm bed covered in sleek fox-furs, a hearty meal that *wasn't* just enormous chunks of spit-roast pork, a true oracle from the gods, the divine ambrosia. At Pylos, all our troubles would be over.

And yet – at nightfall on the last leg of the journey, we were only a couple of thousand paces from the city (according to Tachys, who'd never been there but had been told the way in detail by his grandfather); we could have pressed on, but we didn't. Our hearts told us to put off the fulfilment of our desires just a little longer, so that we could savour them when we were fresh and easy. There was a wonderful feeling of contentment around our fire that night; we lay on our backs gazing at the stars, like herd-boys up in the mountains in summer, relishing the freedom and the space. I remember listening to Sarpedon telling Dusa how to make a shield – I can't imagine she wanted to know, but she made plenty of interested noises, as Uncle described in loving detail how you steam the willow laths to curve the frame, then boil the seven oxhides to make them malleable before tacking them in place; then finally the sheet bronze, slapped on before the boiled leather's had a chance to harden, so that all eight layers will fuse into one. There was something spellbinding about the sound of his voice, the assured way in which he described the process, even I couldn't help taking an interest. Tachys was fast asleep all this while; I expect that if he'd been awake he'd have been fretting over some anticipated problem, which would've spoilt the mood. As it was, his soft snoring was a soothing background, like crickets or the distant drone of a shepherd's pipes.

Cleander, who was lying on his stomach beside me, rolled over and grinned; I could see his face, red with the firelight.

'Pylos tomorrow,' he said.

'Yes,' I replied – didn't seem much else I could say.

'Pylos to Corone,' he went on, 'then a bit of a hike to Sparta, across the Eurotas to Amyclae and Therapne, round the foot of the mountains to Prasiae, then up the coast to Tegea; Argos, detour to Troezen before heading up to Corinth, then Megara and Athens. We're getting there, you know.'

I nodded. 'Slowly but surely,' I replied drowsily. 'Barring accidents.'

'Yes, well. Let's not go asking the gods for attention. You know, if we handle it right, we might be able to get Demophoon to come with us.'

'You reckon?'

Cleander nodded. 'It's worth a try,' he said. 'And – well, the King of Pylos, you don't say no to him in a hurry.'

'True,' I said. 'What's he like, do you know?'

'A good man, by all accounts. Very wise.'

'Ah.'

Of course, he knew precisely as much about King Demophoon as I did, namely spit; but it did us both good, I think, to talk about him as if we'd known him since we were kids scrumping apples together. By the time we both dropped off to sleep, we'd talked him into coming with us and providing an armed escort of a hundred men-at-arms, plus fifty mules laden with food and presents and a couple of large portable pavilions. He was a pushover. It was all very encouraging.

That night, for some reason, I dreamed about making love to a drunk woman, who giggled a lot and fell asleep at exactly the wrong moment. With hindsight, I don't think the dream signified anything at all.

We were all awake before dawn the next day (Cratus went on), excited as children whose fathers have promised to take them to the city. We combed our hair and beards, brushed the dust off our knees and set off for Pylos.

We went slowly, strolling rather than marching – we didn't really want to arrive too early, when the king's house would still be waking up and the hall would be full of servants rolling up the bedding and pulling out the benches, and Demophoon would be briefing his stewards with the day's work. On the other hand, if we were too late, there was always the chance of missing him; if, say, he wanted to walk up to the top steadings to look over the pigs or the goat-pens, or see how the olives were coming along. If we missed him at the start of the morning, we might have to wait until he'd got home and heard the day's petitions and lawsuits; by which time he might be in a foul mood and not receptive to what we had to say.

But we reckoned we'd pitched it about right when we climbed over the little scatter of rocks that Pylos had been hiding behind all morning, and started to walk down through the home fields. I shall always remember that first glimpse of the place, as the land rolled back and the site rose up towards us.

Pylos had been burned to the ground; it wasn't there any more. Oh, it was plain enough where it had been; there were dark shapes and lines in the lie of the coarse grass, here and there the occasional spike of stone or timber poking up, like an arrowhead that's gone right through and out the other side. The plain was empty; not so much as a wild goat or a hare flolloping around among the bumps and tussocks – apart, that is, from a mob of crows, pitched in the middle of a square outline, picking out grass-seeds.

None of us said anything. There wasn't any point in talking.

We walked down through the skeleton of the home fields, boundary-stones half sunk in grass, olive and fig trees with this year's burgeoning crop sharing the branches with the pecked and shrivelled husks of the previous crop gone over. Through some instinctive sense of what was right and proper, we entered the dead city through the main gate – you know that Pylos means gate, don't you? – and followed the memory of the main street up to the grassy rectangle where the palace had been. That was when we saw the signs of burning: blackened log-ends poking out from under wreaths of firewort and creeper, here and there a green and sparkling door-hinge or nail-head poking up through the grass, as if a new city was coming into bud. We found bones too, men and horses and pigs and goats – wasn't there a story about something like that? That's it – when Jason went to Colchis to get the Golden Fleece, the bad king burned the dragon Jason had killed, picked out the monster's teeth and sowed them, and men sprang up out of the earth like barley-shoots. Well, the crop had failed at Pylos; like the field out back of our place which my father said would only grow stones, only dead men seemed to grow in the ashes of Pylos.

'Bugger,' Sarpedon said. It was the first word anybody had spoken since we came over the crest.

Dusa sat down on the ruins of the central pillar of the hall – it had crumbled down to just the right height for her to perch on – and cupped her chin in her hands. 'Pity about that,' she said. 'I wonder what happened.'

'Anybody's guess,' Sarpedon replied. 'Could have been war, or pirates, or just a stray spark from the fire catching in the bedding and taking in the thatch before anybody woke up. Given a stiff breeze, it could spread across the roofs as quick as bad news. No way of telling, really.'

'Somebody's bound to know,' Cleander said. 'I mean, a city like Pylos doesn't just vanish without somebody knowing what became of it.'

I shrugged. 'Does it matter?' I said. 'One thing's clear enough, we aren't going to find any games-players here. Or, come to that, any food to see us through to Corone.'

'That's a very good point,' muttered Tachys. 'Food, and a change of boots. The sole of my left boot's almost completely worn through.'

I sighed. 'Some people have no consideration,' I said.

'Well, it's important,' Tachys said irritably. 'All right, maybe it's not as important in the eyes of the gods as the fall of Pylos, but it's a damn sight more important to me than a load of burned-out houses. And what if I go lame and slow us down and we never get to Athens? The whole mission could turn on something like that.'

'Oh, shut up, Tachys,' Dusa said. 'You're not helping.'

'All right,' Tachys replied, 'I'm just saying, that's all. I'd hate for generations yet unborn to remember that the great adventure of the games all failed just for want of a pair of boots.'

Sarpedon stood up. 'I'll patch your boot with your tongue in a moment,' he said. 'Come on, let's get out of here. This place is starting to get on my nerves.'

Mine too. I was trying to picture the city as it was, trying to get an image in my mind based on these flat marks in the grass, but I couldn't. I'll tell you something, my friend; that's the image that came into my mind when you were talking yesterday about this scratching-marks business of yours, where you scribe the little signs in wax? That's what I reckon that must be like, the overgrown ruins of walls and streets laid out in the flat; tells you there was once a city there, but you'd never be able to picture it – the colours, the smells, the sound of the people's voices. There was nothing left of Pylos except a fact; and that'd only be there until the wind and frost broke up what the locals didn't filch to build barns with.

Well, anyway.

We held a brief assembly (Cratus continued), like a very small convocation of the Sons of the Achaeans, and decided to miss out Corone altogether. Instead, we'd head straight for Sparta, trying to keep up a good pace and hoping we could make the food we'd had from Onesimus last out. There was no reason to suppose it wouldn't, if we went easy on the rations; and once we reached Sparta, of course, that particular problem would be solved.

'Assuming Sparta's still there,' Dusa grumbled.

Why we decided to miss out Corone, I have no idea. I guess it seemed like a good idea at the time, though I can't remember why. It'd only have been a short hike out of our way; there was a games-player there (Eurycleides, a reasonable discus-thrower and long-jumper), not to mention food and, of course, boots. I guess we felt we'd come into a desperate situation and needed to take desperate action, even if it wasn't particularly appropriate.

Anyone here been to Sparta? Not by road, I'll bet. What we should have done, of course, was pottered across to Corone and begged passage on a ship going east; hopped off again when we reached the other side of the gulf, spared ourselves that gruelling tramp across the head of the bay. We'd still have had the long trudge round the Taygetus mountains, of course, but we'd have been that much fresher when we started. All in all, we got that part of the journey badly wrong; no excuses, some god took away our wits and that's all there is to it.

Nevertheless . . . I often wonder what becomes of the people who make up proverbs; everybody knows the words themselves, but who the hell remembers the man who first thought of them? Well, if ever you hear the proverb 'You have to climb a lot of hills if you want to get to Sparta', please bear in mind that I made that one up, and give credit where it's due.

(The point being, yes, we had a very rough journey, thank you very much, but whichever direction you come from and whichever route you take, you're going to eat a lot of dust and wear out a good pair of boots getting there, simply because of where it is. We didn't make the best possible fist of getting there, but we could have done worse.)

And you know what? It was worth it. There's no place like Sparta in the whole world for gracious living (or you could call it nauseating decadence, but only if you're dead miserable, like our colleague Tachys. Tachys didn't like Sparta one bit). The city lies in a flat, pleasant plain under the shelter of the Taygetus mountains, with the Eurotas river running in smooth, elegant curves on the other side. The best place to take in the beauty of the city is the hill on the other side of the river, near the village of Amyclae; it's where the great hero Menelaus and his wife, Helen of Troy, are reckoned to be buried, and if you've got to be buried somewhere, I guess there are worse places. From there, you look down over a steepish slope covered with yellow flowers, across the plain with its olive-groves and patchwork of fields, past the silvery silt of the river-bed to the town and the grandeur of the mountains beyond. Just gazing at that view gives you a feeling of well-being, of peace, plenty and easy living – which, of course, is what Sparta is all about.

It's not just the landscape, or the buildings, for that matter; it's the people. Now, I don't know why it is, though I can hazard a guess or two, but some places are inhabited by mostly ugly people, while in other places they're all tall and rounded and good-looking. Sparta's one of the good-looking places. You don't see many sun-burned women in Sparta, or cripples, or men with only one remaining tooth; no twisted backs or bandy legs or goitres or unsightly birthmarks. You don't see children with sticks for arms, or little old women permanently bent in two at the waist. There are a lot of people living on that plain; from the vantage-point I've described to you, it's hard to pick out a patch of workable land that hasn't been neatly trimmed and hemmed and put to use, and all the Spartans we came across were pretty much the same. They moved slowly, talked slowly, took their time, like men savouring a good meal – here in Elis we scurry about like ants a lot of the time, as if the hopeless odds against a man being able to make a living oppress our hearts and make us frantic. Not in Sparta. It's the same difference you find between a mountain stream tumbling down over rocks, and a broad, lazy river winding through a level plain. The Spartans know where they're going and know they've got plenty of time to get there. It's a nice attitude; it's a nice city. I liked it a lot.

So picture us, if you will, trudging wearily across this pretty wonderful plain, and suddenly catching sight of a sparkle in the sky. None of us could think what the hell it might be, but a few hundred paces further on we ran into a woman filling a pitcher at a well, and we asked her.

She grinned. 'You're not from around here,' she said.

'No, we're not.'

'Ah.' She thought about that for a moment. 'Chances are,' she said, 'what you saw was the sun catching the gilded pillars of the Great House. On a clear day you can see it from miles away. Proper beautiful it is, close to.'

Well, we were too polite to call her a liar to her face, so we changed the subject. 'As it happens,' said Cleander, 'we're on our way to see the prince. Prince Theopompus. Where might we find him?'

She grinned again. 'At the Great House, most like,' she said. 'That'll be easy enough to find, I reckon. Just go through the gates and follow your nose.'

She was right about that. There was no danger at all of mistaking the palace for anything else; and that's not to say the other buildings there were plain or drab, not at all. But the palace – well.

The exterior was enough to make you think you'd died and ended up in the Happy Islands. Surrounding the courtyard, where we tied up the mules, there's this wonderful orchard, marked off with crisply trimmed hedges, and it's full of precisely ordered trees lined up like members of the household at a ceremony; pears and apples and figs and pomegranates, with rows of vines interplanted between the files of trees; and another vineyard on the other side of the courtyard, with a fountain in the middle, feeding a stream that runs out across the courtyard and under the threshold of the house, and comes up again out in the street, so that people can fill their pitchers from it.

I kid you not; the palace doors were solid bronze, burnished to perfection, and sure enough, the pillars on either side were covered in thick gold leaf. Once you stepped inside, the first thing you noticed was the colour of the walls – they were a sort of dreamy sky blue, painted plaster, with a narrow gilded frieze right at the top. On either side of the door were these incredible life-size statues of torch-bearers, marble painted in brilliant colours. The seats run all the way up along the walls – it's a *big* hall – each one with its own tapestry coverlet and footstool, as far as the doors that separate the hall from the inner room and stairs.

'This is incredible,' Dusa said, in an unusually subdued voice.

'Yes,' I said.

At this point, someone noticed we were there and pointed to us. At once a big, rather stout young man with thinning blond hair jumped up out of his seat at the far end and came towards us, making welcoming noises.

'You look like you've come a long way,' he said. 'Sit down, have something to eat and drink, take the weight off your feet. Or would you rather have a bath first, and then have something to eat?'

We opted for the bath first. Now, in other places when we'd had the chance of a bath, some female or other swooped down and hauled Dusa off into the inner room, where as often as not she had to make do with standing in a cauldron and having luke-warm water poured over her head. No such fussiness in Sparta; no, she got a proper bath of her own, with a gaggle of maids to shroud her in towels when she got in and out. You never saw such baths, by the way, and the olive oil for sloshing on afterwards was that lovely smooth green stuff you get from the first press of the nearly ripe olives, not the kitchen surplus we're used to. When we looked round for our dusty old clothes there was no sign of them. In their place were soft woollen tunics and cloaks, still smelling of cypress from the press.

After all that our heads were spinning a bit, but nobody seemed to notice, and we found ourselves sitting on chairs up at the top of the hall with the quality, not parked down at the draughty end. A girl came round with a silver jug and basin to wash our hands in; some of the young men brought up a table, the housekeeper brought out a great big basket of perfectly fresh wheat bread, while someone else carved long, thin slices off a smoked ham.

We were hungry, no doubt about that; and the food was first rate, and so was the wine that came after it. While we were filling our faces, the prince (we assumed it was him) sat watching us with a satisfied little smirk on his round face – you could see he enjoyed watching hungry people eat as much or more than eating himself. When we'd demolished everything they put in front of us and done severe damage to another basket of bread and plate of sliced ham, he asked us if there was anything else he could get for us; some apples, say, or a plate of honey-cakes.

We were tempted; but there would be time for that sort of thing later. As far as I could tell, the polite thing to do at this point would be to introduce ourselves, state our business and hopefully find out who we were talking to.

After I'd said my piece, the stout young man nodded a few times and thought for a moment. 'Games-players,' he said. 'Right. I reckon you'd better talk to my brother about that, he's the games-player in our family.'

'Prince Theopompus,' I said.

The stout man nodded. 'But you're out of luck, I'm afraid,' he said. 'See, he's away right now.'

'Oh.'

''Course,' he went on, 'you're more than welcome to wait here till he gets back.'

'When are you expecting him?'

He thought about that, too. 'Definitely he'll be back in time for the vintage,' he said. 'Possibly before that, even. All depends; winds are a bit changeable this time of year.'

'Oh,' I repeated. 'That's a pity. We've got a long way to go yet, you see, and time's getting on.'

He frowned. 'Surely you can hang on till vintage,' he said. 'It's what, no more than a couple of months. You're more than welcome.'

Prince Theopompus, we found out eventually, was in Crete. Why he was there, I have no idea to this day; maybe he just felt like going there, for a change. His elder brother King Bias, the man we were talking to, wasn't a games-player, and he didn't know of any other games-players in the neighbourhood – he looked genuinely unhappy when he told us that, as if he'd have liked nothing better than to have had twenty chariot-racers brought to us on a chafing-dish, with a mint and watercress garnish. The best he could do, he said, was pass on our message to Theopompus as soon as he got back – he made me go through all the arguments in favour about four times, to make sure he'd got all the details straight, hadn't missed any of the nuances or anything. He was positive his brother would be thrilled beyond measure to take part; in fact it was a sure thing, a guaranteed certainty. We didn't believe a word of that, naturally; he was just trying to be nice, and the lengths he went to in stressing the point suggested that Theopompus had far better things to do with his time, not least of which was cleaning the wax out of his ears with his little finger.

In fact, the longer we stayed in the house of King Bias, the more obvious it became that we were wasting our time. It stood to reason – why should a Spartan be interested in anything anyone else had to offer, when everything at home was the best of its kind? That didn't explain why Theopompus had gone to Crete; but the implication was that his motive was to confirm his instinctive belief that the rest of the world wasn't worth spit. As for the idea that someone from a place like this would ever drag himself all the way up to Elis in the hope of winning fame and glory – forget it. You might just as well expect Apollo to leave the golden houses of the immortal gods and try to get a job as a minstrel in a village manor-house somewhere up our way. Put in cold, crude terms: there was nothing in Elis, tangible or otherwise, that a Spartan could conceivably want.

Not that King Bias would have dreamed of saying that; it was one of those things that doesn't have to be said and probably can't be put into words anyway. The more he spoke, the more painfully obvious became the vast, unbridgeable gap between ourselves and this kind, patient, soft-spoken young man. It was a division on the same scale as the one that separates me from my shepherd. I happen to like my shepherd; he's very good at his job and we get along perfectly well. But we both know that when the sun sets, I go home to the Great House, while he curls up in a corner of the steading on a pile of reject fleeces; and if I dragged him into my hall and sat him down and poured wine into him, he'd think I'd gone mad, with good reason. What made it all the worse in this case was that King Bias was treating us not just as equals but as honoured guests, which made us feel all the more uncomfortable; hence the fact that we got out of Sparta the next day, and were extremely glad to be on our way.

CHAPTER SEVEN

There was a games-player in Amyclae (Cratus continued); Thootes, a high-jumper and discus-thrower – extremely good at both events, by all accounts, but only a very minor princeling, and therefore fated never to win anything. He was thrilled to bits to be asked and promised faithfully to be there; then, as we were leaving, he fell off the pen-rail he was sitting on and broke his leg.

A pattern, I felt, was beginning to emerge.

Anyway, from Amyclae we went to Therapne, only to find that Alastor had got there ahead of us and had persuaded the prince (Hippolochus; two-horse chariot) that we were lunatics turned out of Elis for bringing disgrace on a noble house. Hippolochus was very kind and polite, and told us to go to the crows in the nicest way possible. We thanked him, said that if he should happen to change his mind he'd be more than welcome, and went on our way with what little dignity we had left.

We struck out half a day on the Argos road until we came to a suitable spot – one of those weird old chambers, dome-shaped like a beehive or a dovecote, where the Giants used to bury their dead. I don't know about you, but they give me the creeps. Your voice echoes inside them, for one thing, as if the damned building was agreeing with everything you say and repeating it after you, like those dull old men you try to avoid talking to in the square. They're also invariably as dark as a bag inside – reasonable enough for a tomb, I suppose – and I don't like the fact that you have to go down on your hands and knees to crawl through the entrance tunnel.

We were stuck in that horrible old tomb for the rest of the day – I can smell it still, if I close my eyes – until eventually we saw Alastor and his men strolling along the road. We'd poked a hole in the side wall of the chamber, like burglars breaking into a house.

The mules nearly gave us away at the last moment; after standing still, good as gold, all afternoon they suddenly got restive and started pawing the dirt – one good bray and we'd have been wasting our time. Fortunately, the god had put it into Cleander's heart to grab some apples out of the jar when we were leaving Hippolochus' palace, and he shovelled them into the mules' faces and shut them up.

Even then; well, if ever you need to ambush anybody, don't hide in a beehive tomb, because crawling out inconspicuously is exceptionally difficult and you get your clothes absolutely filthy. Actually, Tachys and I got stuck and had to be pulled out by Dusa, who wasn't impressed; but we were 'not needed on the expedition', as they say, since Sarpedon and Cleander between them were so utterly terrifying, with their sudden whoops and flashing blades, that we'd only have got in the way.

To do them credit, Alastor's men showed more common sense than most people would have done in their position: they dumped the stuff they were carrying without a word and ran like hares, leaving Himself standing there like a boundary-marker looking mustard at us.

'What the hell do you think you're playing at?' he asked.

Uncle Sarpedon made a wonderful growling noise, like a stray dog; fortunately, Cleander got in front of him so Alastor couldn't see the blood-curdling faces he was pulling, else Alastor would probably have burst out in giggles and then there really would have been blood in the dust.

'Friendly warning,' Cleander replied. 'Go home. Stop buggering us about. It's hard enough as it is without you interfering.'

Alastor grinned. 'You aren't going to kill me,' he said. 'You've got more sense.'

It was Cleander's turn to pull a ghastly face. 'We wouldn't, no,' he said. 'But the ruthless band of thieves and cut-throats reported in this area . . .'

'Oh, sure.' Alastor lifted his head. 'You mean the ones you attacked without provocation back in Mila?'

We weren't making much of a job of it, I could tell. Cleander was taken off guard by that, and like a fool allowed Alastor to see it. 'You hear a lot, don't you?' he said.

'I've got donkey's ears, like King Midas,' he replied smugly. 'Really, you're making too much of my part in your failure. So far I've hardly had to lift a finger, you've done it all by yourselves. Amazing, really,' he went on. 'If anybody had told me that anyone, even a bunch of deadheads like yourselves, could make a mess of inviting fanatical games-players to a chance-of-a-lifetime event, I'd have hurt myself laughing. But by the gods, you've managed it. I'm impressed.'

I couldn't let that pass. 'Hang on,' I interrupted. 'Forgive me, Alastor, but you make it sound like you think this games thing is a good idea.'

He nodded. 'It is,' he replied, 'no doubt about it. Brilliant idea. Amazes me nobody's thought of it before. Really and truly, I hope that you don't make such an utter balls-up of it, or I don't do such a wonderfully thorough job of spoiling it, that the whole thing dies a death and can't be resurrected later. It'd be a dreadful waste.'

Cleander nearly fell over. 'You *like* the idea?' was all he could manage to say.

'What's not to like?'

We let him go after that, before he could hurt us any more.

We went to Prasiae, following the nice, well-marked road. The road isn't the quickest way from Therapne to Prasiae. Guess who was waiting for us when we got there?

The Prince of Prasiae was no great loss; a marginal boxer and wrestler, I can't even remember his name now. What did get on our nerves was being arrested and shut up in a cowshed while whatever-his-name-was's men went through our luggage in search of the various items Alastor claimed we'd stolen from him. Since Alastor had a fairly shrewd idea of what was in the presents stash – as you'd expect; he'd owned half of them himself at one time or another, we all had – it was hardly surprising when his description of his lost property fitted (item) one small bronze cup embossed with a ploughing scene, handle slightly bent, (item) one silver-gilt dagger with old-style gate-shaped hilt, enamelled, some enamel missing, (item) one gold grasshopper brooch, end of pin snapped off. The rest of his stuff, he explained, we must've disposed of along the way or buried somewhere under a tree-stump. It wasn't the things themselves, of course, it was the sentimental value – some of them had been given to him by dear friends (which was true, in a sense, of the brooch; he'd had it from my father, who got it back many years later, minus the pin-end).

Unfortunately, the Prince of Prasiae was one of those interfering, can't-leave-well-alone types who takes an interest in justice, even when it's nothing to do with him. We were hauled out of our cowshed, lined up in the city square with a couple of dozen day-labourers and jobbing tradesmen gawking at us, and told how utterly wicked and contemptible we were. If it wasn't for the generosity and nobility of spirit of our victim, who'd made a point of stressing that we were of the better sort (or what passed for it in Elis), he'd have had us strung up from the rafters as an awful warning. Instead, this fatuous idiot said, he'd let us off lightly by confiscating the stolen goods (to be returned to their rightful owner) and the rest of our surplus property, doubtless the loot from other malfeasances, which were forfeit to the majesty of the Zeus-descended lords of Prasiae.

Well, we were dragging our feet out of town, with our one remaining mule, when Alastor came scurrying up behind us with a complicated look on his face. And you know what? He apologised. Although (he said) what he'd done was entirely fair in the context of the game, and in any case we'd started it by jumping out on him and scaring off his no-good companions, nevertheless he felt that the prince had been unduly harsh, not to mention greedy and rapacious, in leaving us with so little; without at least a few presents to give, he went on, we wouldn't be able to claim hospitality on our journey home, and he didn't want our deaths or destitution on his head. As a token of goodwill, therefore, would we please accept (item) this charming bronze cup, (item) this attractive dagger, and (item) this exquisite gold brooch?

And you know what? We took them, and were grateful. We didn't say so, of course, we weren't that demoralised; but by that point our hearts were so empty that this simple act of kindness cut us to the quick. When I say 'we' and 'us', of course, I'm not counting Uncle Sarpedon, who expressed a strong wish to see Alastor eat all three items, even though he'd just had dinner. But Cleander and Dusa didn't say anything, just mumbled and looked away. I think I rustled up a very small smile from somewhere, like a hill-farmer giving alms at the Lady's festival. And Tachys—

Tachys asked Alastor if he could go along with him. Now, under normal circumstances, those would have been the last words ever to pass through the gate of his teeth. But remember, we'd just spent a very long time shut up in a cowshed with Tachys, and he'd helped pass the time by explaining to us exactly what we'd done wrong from the moment each of us was born. The thought that, if the food ran out or his boots fell to bits, Tachys might favour Alastor with a similar explanation was almost enough to cheer us up as we parted company.

'To the crows with both of them,' Uncle sighed, as we flopped under a lonely fig-tree a thousand paces or so outside the town. 'Doesn't matter any more, in any event. One less straggler, one less whining voice on the way home—'

'Who said anything about going home?'

It was Cleander, of course, who came out with this wonderful remark. Who else?

I lifted my head. 'Of course we're not going home,' I said. 'Perish the thought. May the gods scrub the stains of it off the floor of my mind. Of course, we've got nothing to eat, almost nothing to give as presents, that bastard – beg pardon, those two bastards – following us round like a sausage-maker's dog. Apart from that, everything's just fine. Onwards to glory, say I.'

Cleander gave me that look of his, the one I've somehow managed not to strangle him for since we were both kids. 'Fine,' he said. 'So you'd rather go crawling back to King Leon while there's still good leather left on your soles, and tell him we gave up because of one miserable setback? I can picture him now. What was it, Cratus? he'll say. Attacked by pirates, all your gear washed away by a river in spate, got the fever and had to be carried home on a shield? No? What was it, then? Must've been something really serious—'

For once the gods put exactly the right words into my mouth. 'Shut up, Cleander,' I said.

'He's right, you know,' Dusa chimed in.

'Of course I'm right,' I said, 'only this clown here—'

'Not you,' said Dusa. 'Him.'

We all looked at her, as if the god had suddenly turned her into a rosebush.

'Don't all look at me like that,' she said. 'Oh, come on, Cratus, why do you think I insisted on coming on this jaunt in the first place?'

'To annoy me,' I said.

'Mostly, yes. But why else?'

I shrugged. 'Curiosity? To see the cities of the Sons of the Achaeans and understand their minds?'

She smiled. 'Don't be ridiculous,' she said. 'No, I came on this trip to look after you two, make sure you didn't come to harm or pack the whole thing in the first time you stubbed your toe or missed breakfast. And that's what I intend to do.'

I'd have laughed out loud if she hadn't been glaring at me. But it was like the story of the other Medusa, the one who could turn people to stone with a single glance.

That's the odd thing about my sister. Ninety-nine days out of a hundred, she was nothing but a pest, a tomboy, an unmarried sister with nothing much to do except annoy anybody ill-advised enough to get within range. The one remaining day, she'd suddenly get serious about something – no way of knowing what it was likely to be, it could be anything from whether we ought to go to war with the Triphylians, the fact that we were wasting the last few apples of last season's crop because we weren't laying them up right in the store, the fate of a three-legged dog or a poor man being bullied off his land by a rich and powerful neighbour. Whatever it might be, once Dusa got serious about something, the best thing to do was either agree with her or catch a ship to Egypt. She wouldn't give up; she was like a young dog with a rat. Persuasive? Why the god should choose to put such good words in her mouth, I don't know – if he wanted the point made, why not put them in the mouth of someone people would listen to, rather than some girl? But maybe that's something gods do to show off, or to make things challengingly difficult for themselves (or think of how Apollo put the truth in the heart of Cassandra, and then made it so nobody would ever believe her; a way of giving fair warning to people he wanted to destroy. Strange people, gods; I'm glad that generally speaking we don't have much to do with them).

Anyway; I'd known Dusa long enough to understand that once she got that look in her eye, there wasn't much point arguing. She'd win the argument, no question about that, and it's embarrassing for a man to be worsted in argument by a woman in front of his kin. It's like seeing a great prince shot by some peasant with a bow – you know that he was the better man, and if they'd have come to blows he'd have won; but somehow the lesser has overcome the greater, and although his death can have no meaning he's still dead.

And besides, it wasn't just a matter of persistence, or even just a knack of being able to win arguments. There were times when Dusa was genuinely right.

And you can all take that look off your faces, thank you. Let me try to explain it to you, before you put me down as a lunatic. Now, as is tolerably well known, the god made women's minds separately from those of men, and different in many ways. Men's minds are like the river or the deep water; the current runs slow and steady under the surface, guiding him firmly and straight along the right course. Women's minds are like the wind, swift but blowing from many directions, as likely to send them off course as to take them where they're meant to go; they puff out the sails of the ship until you'd think they were full to bursting, but if you look there's nothing in them except air. There are times when the god puts a quick, sharp, clever thought into a woman's mind – they call it intuition – and as many times when he fills her mind with mist and salt spray, whereas the thoughts he puts in a man's mind are long and deep, and perhaps it may take him many years and a lot of bad experiences to understand what they really mean.

But just occasionally, the god seems to make a mistake, like a drunken herald; and he puts a woman's thought into a man's mind or the other way round; which is why some men sometimes do stupid, ill-considered things, and some women occasionally come out with wise, sensible advice. I don't know why, but Dusa seemed to get more than her fair share of these misdirected thoughts – possibly the top of her head looked like a man's when seen from directly above, it's as good an explanation as any – and always when she was in that serious mood of hers. Our father had an uneasy feeling that at times the god chose to speak through her, or maybe whisked her off asleep into the clouds and took her shape, as the gods are known to do (which explains why people sometimes appear to do things that are entirely out of character; but of course, it's not them but the god. A man's character is one of the few fixed and unchangeable things in the world). Anyway, he was the sort of man who doesn't take chances, so whenever Dusa gave him that grim look and told him to do something, he invariably did it, on the offchance that it was a god talking, not his little girl.

Anyway; if there's a point to this digression, it's that you should always try to listen to what's said to you, no matter who says it. Listen to the actual words themselves. Women, day labourers, foreigners, children, it doesn't matter, you've got to pay attention, just in case.

'All right,' I said, leaning back against the tree and closing my eyes. 'Uncle, what do you reckon?'

Sarpedon clicked his tongue. 'I think we ought to go home now,' he said, 'before we come to harm and make fools of ourselves. On the other hand, I've always wanted to go to Argos.'

(And that's a case in point, because if ever there was a woman's thought in a man's mind – but nobody else noticed. Dusa just nodded, and Cleander said, 'Well, there you are, then.' They weren't listening, you see.)

'All right,' I said, 'we'll go to Argos, try our luck there. If it's no better, we'll call it a day and go home. Agreed?'

'Interesting place, Argos,' said Sarpedon, 'so I've heard.'

'Really?' I sat up a little. 'What's so interesting about Argos?'

'I don't know,' Sarpedon replied, 'I haven't been there yet.'

So off we went. Since Tegea was directly on our way to Argos, we decided we had nothing to lose by going there first; Tegea had not one but three games-players, brothers, all chariot-racers (they have plenty of space for horses and chariot-races in the flat plains of Arcadia). There was a chance that we might be able to persuade one of them to listen to us, even if the other two were dead set against.

When we got there, we were amazed. In fact, we wondered if we were in the wrong place.

'This can't be right,' Sarpedon muttered as we walked under a splendid high-arched gateway and up a wide street towards what was obviously a rather fine palace. 'I know about these people, I've fought wars against them. They're nobody. Are you sure this isn't Argos?'

At some stage, apparently without mentioning it to anybody, the Tegeans had found prosperity. Not to mention extreme wealth. The street was paved with lots of identical flat stone slabs, with a gutter running down each side. Many of the houses couldn't have been more than ten years old; on some of them the whole of the thatch was still golden yellow. As for people, the place was full of them.

'Where did they all come from?' Sarpedon demanded, of nobody in particular.

Now, although we knew there were three chariot-racing brothers, we only knew the name of one of them: Thoas, which coincidentally was also the name of the previous king, against whom Sarpedon had fought his war. It took us some time and no little embarrassment before we finally figured out that all three princes were called Thoas, just as every male child in the royal family had been for the last nine generations (named, someone later explained, in honour of their ancestor, the celebrated hero Thoas. Before you ask, I haven't got a clue who the celebrated hero Thoas was, either). Anyway,

Cleander and I exchanged quick don't-ask glances and tried to act as if this was all perfectly normal; I guess the Thoases were used to it, in any event, because they didn't seem to take offence.

To the point; yes, they'd be delighted to come and race chariots, under any pretext whatsoever. It so happened, they told us while shovelling fine white bread and roast mutton into our faces, that a couple of very strange men from up our way had passed through Tegea only a day or so before, strongly urging them not to go chariot-racing in Elis. They'd been so very passionate and persuasive about it, they said, that all three brothers had at once made up their minds to find out if there were going to be any chariot-races at Elis in the near future, and go to them; wasn't it lucky, they went on, that we should drop in and give them the information they needed?

As gifts, we gave the Thoas brothers one embossed bronze cup, one silver-hilted dagger and one magnificent but slightly damaged grasshopper brooch. They were very pleased with the presents – 'You just don't see *old* things like this any more,' Thoas assured us, beaming – and in return gave us a whole bunch of stuff, a lot of it so good that I'd have kept some of it if only that had been possible – genuine imported Assyrian and Egyptian metalwork, a harp, a couple of gold collars, and other things just as good. Perhaps we were too enthusiastic to be tactful, and they guessed from our reaction that we'd been expecting junk; anyhow, Thoas nudged Thoas in the ribs and said, 'Why don't we tell them the story,' and Thoas nodded and said, 'Yes, why not.' Thoas didn't seem to object, so they told us.

All this stuff, they said, and a whole lot more, including some they'd used to finance the improvements to the palace and the city, was part of a ransom they'd been paid by some mad foreigners. The weird thing about it was, they said, that the ransom wasn't for a living man, or even for the body of someone killed in a recent war; it was for a jarful of old bones that someone had dug up under his floor. They were not, Thoas put in, ordinary bones; they were enormous, and at first the man hadn't thought they were real bones at all. He'd thought they were a carving of some sort, because they were set in stone, like the comb in set honey. Maybe they were a carving, Thoas went on, for all he cared they could be a carving, or just some old, very long bones. Didn't matter a damn. Anyway, the man who found them slung them out behind the house along with the rest of the spoil, where they were noticed by this madman. He almost foamed at the mouth, he was so excited; he scurried away and came back a few days later with some other madmen, and nothing would do but they had to have these bones. The man who found them was all set to let them take the nasty, heavy things away and save him a job; but Thoas here got to hear of it and had the foreigners brought in, just to see if they were as crazy as everybody made out. Well, no sooner had the foreigners realised who we were than they started talking about gold and ransoms. We thought they thought we were going to hold them to ransom, but luckily, before we could say, No, we don't do things like that in Tegea, Thoas realised that they were actually talking about ransoming the bones.

Well, we all stuck wise-owl expressions on our faces and said that it wasn't really on; these were, after all, extremely long bones, and a good long bone is hard to find in this degenerate age. The foreigners went berserk; they all started yammering at once and offering us gold and nice things by the cartload. Thoas and I were all set to have them gently slung out – after all, fun is fun, but not when it gets out of hand – when one of the maniacs mentioned something about having brought the first instalment with them, just in case; so we humoured him and let him go to fetch it, and back he came with – sure enough – an ox-cart stuffed tailgate to box with the most wonderful stuff you ever saw. Thoas nearly burst into tears, but we managed to keep our faces straight and said, All right, three more like that and you can have the bones; at which the loons grinned at each other as if they'd just tricked us rotten, and we parted the best of friends. Sure enough, the ox-carts came rolling up full of goodies, and left full of bones. And that's the end of the story—

'What are you grinning at?' Cratus said. 'It's not that funny.'

The Phoenician tidied his expression up a little. 'Sorry,' he said. 'But you don't know, do you?'

'Don't know what?'

'About Tegea.' The Phoenician sat up straight. 'Which, incidentally, isn't there any more. Well, it is, but you wouldn't recognise it now. It's just a village; no walls or palaces, certainly no princes called Thoas. The Spartans captured it, you see; they wanted some of the Tegeans' land. But every time they tried to take it by force, the Tegeans gave them a damn good hiding and sent them home again.'

'I'm not surprised,' Cleander put in. 'Like my brother says, it's a big city.'

'Was a big city,' the Phoenician replied. 'Anyway, the Spartans sent a message to the Oracle, asking why it was that they always lost against the Tegeans; and the Oracle said that so long as the Tegeans kept hold of the bones of – well, some hero or other, I can't recall the name offhand – so long as they had these bones, the hero himself would defend them and nobody would ever defeat them. Then, about twenty-odd years later – and this is what I was told – a Spartan prince sneaked into Tegea, stole the bones (which were of monstrous size) and took them home with him to Sparta; whereupon the Spartans knew they were going to win and led out their entire army for a full-scale assault on Tegea. They won, hands down, and that was the end of that. Now the Spartans have become terribly brave, without the Tegeans to beat them up at regular intervals, and have started conquering cities all over the place.'

There was a brief silence.

'Oh,' said Cleander.

'That's a pity,' Cratus said. 'It was a fine city, and they were very kind to us when we needed it most.'

The Phoenician, who'd been grinning like a dog, bit his lip and mumbled something. After a while, Cratus carried on with his story.

We left Tegea (Cratus said) feeling thoroughly pleased with ourselves – I wish you hadn't told me that, about the Spartans; I liked them too, you know – and headed north, towards Argos. We hadn't gone more than a day's march when we came across a most distressing sight: a man lying in the road, covered with blood, apparently dead.

'He's still alive,' Dusa said, after taking a closer look.

'Oh,' I said. 'Well, that's all right, then.'

Dusa gave me yet another of those looks. I pretended I hadn't seen it.

'Cratus,' she said. 'We've got to do something.'

At this point Uncle Sarpedon bent down and looked too. 'We could take his boots,' he said. 'There's plenty of wear left in them.'

'Uncle!'

Well, there wasn't any point in arguing. I could have told her, no good ever comes of picking up strays on the road, making yourself responsible for someone who could turn out to be nothing but trouble, somebody's enemy, that's how innocent men get caught up in blood-feuds; but that would only have wasted still more time. At least the bastard wasn't wearing only one sandal—

'Huh?' said the Phoenician.

'Oh good, you *are* paying attention.' Cratus smiled indulgently. 'Sorry, Sons-of-the-Achaeans joke. In our rich and colourful heritage of myth and story, a stranger encountered on the road who's only wearing one sandal is going to turn out to be the exiled prince out to avenge his dead father, sure as flies in summer. And what does the usurper who killed said father do, on encountering a one-sandalled man on the road? Have him killed on the spot? No fear. No, he invites him home, plies him with food and drink, tells him all about the one weak spot in the magic spell that makes him otherwise completely invulnerable, gives him detailed instructions for finding the magic sword that's the only weapon capable of killing the hundred-headed dragon who guards the royal treasury, practically orders him to seduce his beautiful daughter – well, anyway, you can bet next year's vintage that by the time the story grinds to a halt, the evil but naïvely warm-hearted usurper's head will be hanging from a hook in the city square, and the one-sandalled man will be in the palace, commissioning new tapestries for the upstairs room. I guess that the germ of truth these stories are intended to pass down from one generation to another is, if you find a one-sandalled man lying in the road, jump on his head with heavy boots on.'

'Ah,' the Phoenician said. 'Actually, we have remarkably similar stories where I come from, except that with us, it's babies found floating down rivers in wicker baskets.'

'We have some of them, too,' Palamedes interrupted. 'Though generally speaking, babies found abandoned on hillsides are more usual.'

'Indeed,' Cratus said gravely. 'And that, my friend, raises a rather interesting point. We've all agreed, I think, that the only way a mortal man can hope to cheat death is by being remembered for his great deeds and wonderful adventures; and we remember Perseus and Bellerophon and Theseus and Jason and a score of other one-sandalled foundlings, so that they may never wholly die, but will live for all time in the Happy Islands. But if you stop for a moment and think just how remarkably similar all these stories are, how many common ingredients they share, doesn't it raise just the tiniest blemish of doubt in your mind that maybe the stories aren't true? That maybe there never was such a person as Perseus or Bellerophon or Jason? That somebody *made them up*, just for the sake of the story? And if that's possible, if you can't believe in the truth of tales of ancient valour – well, the whole principle comes crashing to the ground like a tower built on a sand-pit.'

'But who would do such a thing?' Palamedes asked. 'Who'd deliberately make up a story he knew wasn't true? And more to the point, who'd want to listen to a story they knew wasn't true? It'd be a waste of time, surely. Not to mention dangerous for the man who made it up; if people realised what he was doing, they'd be bound to get very angry.'

Cratus shrugged. 'Very true,' he said. 'But people do the strangest things.'

The Phoenician noticed that the blind man, Cleander, was getting up. 'It's all right,' he announced, 'my dear brother hasn't mortally offended me. But I've got cramp in both legs, and unless I walk it off I'll be in agony. You carry on the story without me. I know it all already; I was there, after all.'

'Take care,' Palamedes said. 'You there, move the trestles so he can get through. Do you want me to send anybody with you?'

Cleander laughed. 'Palamedes, I've been blind longer than most of the people here have been alive; and I've known this house longer than you have. I can find my way twice round the orchard and back without breaking my neck, I promise.'

Anyway (Cratus went on), there we were looking at this mess we'd found lying in the road. And if you've all done with interrupting me for a while, perhaps I can get on and tell you what happened next.

We were standing there, like I said; and suddenly we heard thudding hooves and jingling harness, and there was a chariot coming up behind us, alarmingly fast. Of course, I jumped clear, since I've never had all that much confidence in other people's ability to control horses; Cleander did the same, displaying an unusual level of common sense. Dusa, though, took one horrified look at the chariot and started dragging at this stranger's arm, trying to pull him off the road before the chariot ran him over.

It was one of those moments when the god empties your mind of calm, rational thoughts and fills it with a buzzing swarm of panic and instincts. Instinct told me to grab hold of Dusa and get her out of the way, but Panic had pegged my feet to the ground, making any impulsive notions I may have been harbouring somewhat irrelevant; in other words, I stood as still as a tree with my mouth wide open, watching to see what would happen.

Dusa wasn't making much headway with shifting the stranger. That just left Uncle Sarpedon. Now maybe, after a lifetime of experience, he'd found a way of keeping the god out of his mind at awkward moments like that; in any event, he seemed quite calm, though paying strict attention. When it was pretty clear that the chariot wasn't slowing down so as you'd notice, he stepped over the stranger's body and stood quite still, arms folded, right in the middle of the road.

I'll swear by the River that by the time the chariot stopped he must have been feeling the horses' breath on his face, but he didn't budge so much as a finger's width. Quite remarkable; not to mention completely idiotic. But that was Uncle for you. Now that I'm his age, it makes me shudder to think of doing any of the stuff he did. I suppose being as mad as a pedlar's dog must have helped.

The man driving the chariot didn't seem happy. 'You,' he shouted, 'get out of the road.'

Sarpedon looked up at him. 'No,' he said.

Now, up to this point, the men in the chariot (there were three of them) had acted reasonably sensibly. It was plain enough that they were set on killing the stranger, whose rather dilapidated condition they were presumably responsible for. Well, given such intention, running him over with a chariot was as good a way of going about it as any, better than most, and nobody in his normal mind would've anticipated some lunatic deliberately getting in the way. Having had the bad luck to encounter such a lunatic, they did the right thing in slowing down and not flattening him too – if they had, we'd have had no option but to kill them, though as you can imagine, getting involved in a blood-feud in the middle of a foreign country while surrounded by enemies wasn't something we'd have enjoyed particularly much. So; right up to that point, they'd come across as sensible, rational men. A pity, then, that they had to go and spoil it.

The mistake the driver made was leaning forward over the rail and smacking Uncle Sarpedon across the face with the goad. Now, I wouldn't do a thing like that under any circumstances, unless I was deliberately setting out to start a war or a ten-generations feud. You probably don't get the full significance. Well, to hit a man with a goad or a cattle-prod is really rather serious; far more than if you smacked him with a stick or a regular weapon. By using an instrument you'd normally only use on slaves or cattle, you're actually taking away his status as a free man, let alone a man of the better sort. Not clever. In fact, downright rude.

Which is why what Sarpedon did next was entirely justifiable; even I can't really argue with it, though I maintain that he started the whole thing by standing in the road like he did.

Before the driver had the chance to lift the goad clear, Sarpedon grabbed it left-handed, yanked it out of the man's hand and turned it round. Then, blithe as a three-year-old, he vaulted up on to the chariot-boom, boosting himself up there with his right hand (I couldn't have done it even then; shows how fit he was), danced right down the boom, leaned forward over the driver's head and whacked him just over the right eyebrow, very hard indeed. The man on the driver's left tried to prod at him with a spear; that was a mistake, because Sarpedon took the spear away from him with his right hand and stuck him through the junction of neck and collar-bones with the butt-spike, then spun the spear across the back of his hand so as to be in position to skewer the third man, who died before he'd even had a chance to get his sword out.

'Uncle,' I wailed. 'What the bloody hell do you think you're playing at?'

Sarpedon twisted round – the way he was able to keep his balance standing on the boom was really very impressive – and gave me a look of pure, refined mustard. Then he pulled a little apologetic face. 'He hit me,' he said.

'Yes, but—' I gave up. Wasn't much point agonising about it all now. No point crying over spilt blood, as the saying goes. 'So now what do we do?'

Rather more carefully and awkwardly than he'd got up there, Sarpedon got down again. 'Well,' he said, 'it's rather a delicate point of protocol. Since it was a fair fight and they started it *and* it was a blood insult, we're definitely within our rights taking the weapons. The chariot's pushing it, I'll grant you, but the way I see it, since they were actually using the chariot *as* a weapon—'

'Uncle!' I yelled at him. 'That's not what I meant.' I could see it was useless shouting at him, so I shouted at Dusa instead. 'This is all your fault,' I told her. 'If you hadn't insisted—'

She wasn't listening. 'Uncle,' she said quietly, cutting me off short like she was pruning a vine, 'do you think he's well enough to be lifted up into the chariot? Only the bleeding looks like it's stopped – the last thing I want to do is start it off again.'

I made one last effort. 'Dusa!' I shouted. Not a blind bit of notice.

Sarpedon gave the stranger a quick examination and said that, in his opinion, while putting the man in the chariot might lead to further bleeding and subsequent death, not putting him in the chariot would most definitely cause his immediate demise, and the likeliest cause of death would be bronze poisoning.

'What?' Dusa said.

'Over there.' Sarpedon pointed back down the road. You didn't have to be far-seeing Polydeuces (or Castor; I can never remember which of those two is which) to see the sunlight glinting amber on sword-blades and spearheads. 'I suggest we go away before they get here.'

The god put it into my mind that on this one occasion, Uncle was probably right.

And that's how we got involved. So easily done. I don't suppose you could have brought a quart pot to the boil in the time it took us to change our lives beyond all recognition. If you were quick, maybe you could have skinned and jointed a hare, or cut down a small olive tree. I have an idea that the gods punish us for wanting to be masters of our own destinies by ordaining that all the most irrevocable things men can do – ending lives, or creating them – can be done quickly, blindly, in a haze of passion, when the mind is empty and the heart is full. It takes a whole day to make a good pair of boots or a gate or a bronze cauldron or to plough the waste in a vineyard.

Five of us in one two-horse chariot; Cleander drove, Uncle Sarpedon and I held the stranger up, and Dusa clung on to the rail like a young kid on top of the hay wagon. If we'd turned over or lost a wheel, all five of us would've been killed – and Cleander was driving with the sheer blind recklessness of a very frightened man, so it's a wonder I'm here to tell the tale.

I don't know how long we kept the pace up for, but it seemed to last all of this life and a hefty mortgage on the next. When finally we persuaded Cleander to slow up, I was shivering like a man with a bad fever, and my clothes were wringing wet with, among other things, sweat. But slow down we eventually did, at a place where the road passed through a little wood. We all got out – that was a wonderful feeling, getting out of that chariot – and while Cleander and Sarpedon cut the horses loose and dragged the chariot off into the scrub where it'd be hard to find, Dusa and I got the stranger out of sight. We found a nice sheltered dip, laid him on his back and had a look to see if he was still breathing.

To our great surprise, and the disappointment of one of us, he opened his eyes after a while and muttered something about being thirsty. As if we hadn't done enough for him already. If he'd had a scrap of decency in him, he'd have offered to fetch water for us.

'It's all right,' Dusa said, exaggerating shamelessly. 'You're safe now.'

'No we aren't,' I pointed out. 'We're hiding in a wood, with a bunch of armed men no more than an hour behind us. If that's your idea of safe—'

'Be *quiet*!' Dusa snapped at me, so ferociously that I took a step backwards. 'Ignore him, he's my brother,' she added, as if that explained everything.

I didn't even try to reason with her, because my heart told me I'd be wasting my breath. You see, she had that look in her eyes – not the serious one, a different one, but if anything rather more ominous.

Now, there are some young women who must have an invisible stuffed bird hanging round their necks – you know, the sort they put up for archery practice. Fortunately, Dusa wasn't like that. I say fortunately; mixed blessing, because she was quite the opposite. Where the dizzy sort of girl has the invisible stuffed bird, she had a warranted triple-proof solid bronze cuirass, the sort that comes with a little dent in it to show you that when it was made, they shot an arrow at it point-blank and failed to puncture it. That's how come we'd never managed to marry her off. Not for want of trying. Four times we actually got as far as setting a date and organising the torch-bearers and the musicians. Once, we were so close we'd actually spent a morning picking rose-petals for the bridal bed. Every time, though, there was that moment when she frowned, lifted her head and said, No, this is a very bad idea – and that was that. Finish.

Oh, she fooled around a bit with boys and girls her own age, but mostly just to annoy Father and Cleander and me; as for actually falling in love, she'd done that precisely once, which is how come I recognised the signs so clearly. That was a story, and no mistake; she fell for this man (he was nearly twice her age) who was staying with us; he was the third son of a family from the northern side of Elean territory, a bit of a waste of space by anybody's standards. He was bored with just farming and pottering about, he told us (what he really meant was, he wasn't any good at it), and he wanted to go abroad, maybe travel round a bit, take service as a soldier with the

Lydians or the Kings of Tyre, come home with wealth and glory – but of course he didn't have a ship of his own, so did we know anybody who was fitting out a ship and was looking for company on the voyage? For some unaccountable reason, my father took a shine to this buffoon; at least, until he found out that Dusa was absolutely besotted with him and not particularly bothered who knew it. That's the point at which versions of the story differ. Afterwards, Dusa told people they'd been secretly married, and a few months after he left she got word that he'd been killed fighting for the Tyrians against the Sicels (or the other way round; who cares?). Father's version was that he'd found the man a place on a ship and given him a very useful cargo of presents and the like, everything the young adventurer needs, on condition that he never came back to Elis. What I heard, a while later, was that he'd taken Father's stuff, swapped it with another man on the ship for his allotment at a colony, and was making a very pleasant life for himself in Ionia.

And now, here was that look again; and I thought, Oh, Dusa, not *now*, for the gods' sakes. But I didn't say anything to her, for fear of making things worse. Instead, I sat down and pretended to feel neighbourly concern for our injured guest.

He'd been in a fight, no doubt about that. He had a clip to the side of the head, just above and alongside the left eye; showy and gory, but nothing serious. What had put him down was the deep puncture, probably from one of those imported Assyrian-style thin-bladed swords, level with his navel on the right side. He'd bled like a pig from that – I expect you could have made a whole string of sausages out of what he must have dripped between getting that wound and when we found him. And yet it was only a little mark, compared with the showy slice off his head; which only goes to prove what they say about appearances.

He repeated his request for something to drink; and since I wasn't going to budge, Dusa went off to find some clean water. That gave me a chance to ask some straight questions.

'My name,' he started to say; then he thought about it for just a heartbeat, and went on, 'My name is Pentheus.' And I thought, Oh gods, melodrama; because obviously he wasn't called that – sorry, it's an Achaean thing; Pentheus means 'man of sorrow', and nobody's actually going to call a kid that, are they? It'd be like calling your best mule Steal-Me. 'Where are you from?' he added.

'Never you mind about us,' I replied. 'Where are you from and what've you done?'

'Done?' He looked at me. 'I was set upon by bandits—'

'No, you weren't.'

He frowned a little, then winced because frowning hurt. 'All right,' he said, 'it wasn't robbers.'

'Feud?' I asked, trying to make myself sound sympathetic.

'I suppose so,' he replied. 'At least, the beginnings of one. I killed someone in Tegea, and his brothers came after me.'

I sighed. 'Figures,' I said. 'What was it? His wife? Sister? Boyfriend?'

He looked shocked. It was as convincing as made-in-Elis Egyptian beadwork. 'Nothing like that,' he said. 'I was avenging an insult to my honour. It was a fair fight.'

He was about twenty-five; old enough to know better, anyhow. 'Try again,' I replied. 'Or if you're too tired and weak to talk, let me have a go, see what the god whispers in my ear. Well, for one thing, your boots tell me you don't live in Tegea; those soles have been even further than mine. Likewise, either those were originally someone else's boots, or your feet have shrunk.' He opened his mouth, then closed it again. 'Now then,' I went on, 'that smack on the head's not the first you've had to put up with, because there's a scar just like it on the other side; also this one, on the ball of your shoulder. Suggests to me that you've been in a fight or two, but not wearing armour, like you would if you'd been in the wars. Let's see your hands.'

He scowled at me, but didn't resist.

'Well now,' I said. 'Either you're very rich or very poor, with hands like these. No calluses, look; it's been a long time since you did any cutting or pruning, or took a mattock out on the fallow.' Then I saw something and grinned. 'Oh, now *that's* interesting,' I said. 'Hard skin in the top joints of the first three fingers of your left hand. I'll bet if I look at your right wrist, there'll be a few scars there.'

He looked mustard at me. 'So I'm an archer,' he said. 'So what?'

'So nothing,' I replied. 'It's not necessarily a bad thing to be. But put it all together: an archer who doesn't do any work, far from home and found lying all bloody in the road.' I smiled at him. 'If you ever were set on by bandits, it was because they caught you trying to sneak off with more than your share. Is that what happened?'

He gave me a cold, nasty stare. 'You couldn't be more wrong,' he said. 'But why should I bother telling you the truth? You wouldn't believe me.'

I shrugged. 'Suit yourself,' I replied. 'Doesn't matter a bit, anyhow. Thanks to my dear sister and my dear uncle, I find myself in the thoroughly rotten position of being on your side, or at least, on the opposite side from the people who were trying to kill you, and who'll now be trying to kill us. On balance, I'd far rather you turned out to be a dispossessed prince or a wandering hero, just so I don't feel such a complete and utter clown.'

He scowled some more; then his face sagged. 'So what're you going to do?' he asked.

'Do?' I smiled again. 'I'm going to believe you, of course, for the reason stated. After all, I could be jumping to quite the wrong conclusions about what I've seen. Two words of advice, though.'

'Yes?'

'First,' I said, 'I'm going to find it a whole lot easier to believe you if the story you tell me and the others takes account of the points I've mentioned. Clear?'

'Yes.'

'Second,' I said, 'I put it to you that you're married to a beautiful girl who lives somewhere a long way away, and very much in love. Is that right?'

He frowned, then nodded. 'Yes,' he said.

'Wonderful,' I said, 'how the god tells me these things. Maybe I ought to set up my own oracle.'

'Well, you certainly have the knack of telling people things they don't want to hear.'

The sound of snapping twigs and rustling leaves told me Dusa was coming back (did any of you ever meet a female who could walk quietly in a wood? Thought not. And the silly thing is, the patron deity of hunters is a woman).

Anyway—

Cratus suddenly lowered his voice. 'Talking of people coming back,' he whispered, 'here's my brother. Can I just mention, he's never heard about the talk I had with the stranger. Can we keep it that way, please?'

CHAPTER EIGHT

Now then (Cleander said), where had my brother got up to?

The stranger's name was Pentheus, and he had a remarkable story to tell, like something out of the fall of Troy or the wanderings of Ulysses. It affected me, I can tell you; but that was nothing compared with what it did to my sister. I'll try to tell it as near as I can to the man's own words – it's been a few years, of course, but I've got a reasonable memory – I can still recite you stories I heard just the once when I was a boy, except you really wouldn't want to hear them, because they were fairly dull.

Anyway; this is what Pentheus told us.

I was born (Pentheus said) on the island of Aegina, where my father was the king. He had five sons – three older than me – and two daughters. We were well off; I don't know if any of you have ever been to Aegina – No? Well, it's a flat, fertile island with good grazing and fine vineyards. To tell the truth, we were a lazy family, spent more time hunting than farming. My brothers and I used to go and shoot wild goats up in the hills, and that was about all the work we ever did.

I expect you're wondering why I'm here, all bloody and in need of the help of strangers, if I'm a king's son in my own country. Well, here's what happened.

When we weren't hunting, my brothers and I, we used to practise games-playing. I was a reasonable runner and long-jumper, my brothers Ialmenus and Ascaphalus were better runners and competent charioteers. Our eldest brother, Lycomedes, was actually a top-class boxer, and if you go to Aegina any time, you'll find plenty of people who lisp when they talk because they're missing a few teeth; ask any of them, if you can make out what they're saying, they'll tell you the same thing. Even our kid brother Hyrtacus knew how to pass for a competent wrestler. But the real games-player in our family, believe it or not, was my elder sister, Actis; she could run and, most of all, she could drive a two-horse chariot.

Actis was actually the eldest, a year older than Lycomedes. She didn't look much, being too fond of the open air; brown as a nut, she was, and all muscle and bone. But she could easily have got married if she'd wanted to – a king's daughter, it goes without saying; only she didn't want to. What she liked best, after games-playing, was camping out in the hills with a lot of other big, brown, bony girls her own age, in honour of some women-only goddess we weren't even supposed to ask her about. Likely story, we all thought; they used to go off with a big cart loaded down with jars of wine and nice things to eat, and come back five days later all dirty and ragged and foul-tempered – one time I'll swear I saw blood under her fingernails before she had a chance to go in and wash, so the gods alone know what they all got up to. Anyway, whatever it may have been, Actis reckoned it was much better fun than getting married and raising a family; so my father decided to make the best of it and endow a temple for this goddess of hers, with Actis as the priestess; which made it a bit more respectable, and gave us all an excuse for why our sister was twenty-two years old and still hadn't got a husband.

My other sister, Chariessa, was short and dumpy, married a nice young man from Troezen when she was fourteen, and was dead a year later. These things happen.

Well, like I just told you, we loved our games-playing and all dreamed like crazy of getting a chance to take part in some real games; but the only people on the island who were grand enough to merit games all steadfastly refused to die, and there we were, getting old and musclebound, with not much likelihood of getting a games. That was annoying, I guess, but we were realistic about it. And you can't expect people to drop dead for your own convenience, can you?

And then, quite unexpectedly, someone did. And it wasn't even an Aeginetan, though he was family of a sort; my brother Ascaphalus' father-in-law, who happened to be on the island visiting, and who was a great man in every way (not to mention a miserable old bugger, and no loss, so we didn't even have to feel guilty about feeling pleased, if you follow me).

It was an especially good time for me; my wife, Periboea, had just given birth to our second child – we called him Nicephorus, for luck—

('Excuse me?' the Phoenician asked.

'It means "Bringer of Victory",' Palamedes explained.

'Ah. Right. Sorry.')

Have you quite finished? (Cleander said). Thank you.

Anyway (said Pentheus), we decided to add the celebrations for Nicephorus' birth on to the funeral for Phorbus – Ascaphalus' father-in-law – and make a really big party out of it all. We invited everybody on the island, just about. We wanted to make it the most memorable bash in the history of Aegina. We succeeded, too.

Fortunately, Phorbus died in the early winter. Because Aegina's so close to Athens, there was time to issue invitations to some of the really top-flight games-players on the mainland as well as the local talent, before the body went off and had to be got rid of.

Now, it so happened that there was a Corinthian family visiting relatives in Attica at that very moment, and they were all red-hot games-players; four brothers, about the same ages as we were. Even on Aegina we'd heard of them, and so we were dead keen to get them to come too. They were the sons of Laops – Ctemon, Phorcys, Hephaestodorus and Axius. Our hearts told us that it couldn't have worked out better if we'd broken into the workshop of the Fates and fiddled about with the threads ourselves.

Well, the big day came round. No fewer than four ships from Athens came in early in the morning, all low in the water with celebrated games-players and their horses and chariots and lucky weights and big, fat stocks of presents; but no Laopides, which nearly spoilt the whole thing for us. Anyway, we'd more or less given up on them and were about to do the actual cremation when someone keeping lookout from the top of a store-tower yelled that a ship was coming in. We stopped the proceedings to give them time; and, sure enough, it was the Corinthian contingent, who were late (they said) because they'd had problems getting the loan of a ship at such short notice. Anyway, they were there, which was all that mattered.

First, of course, we torched the old man. He lit up just fine, bless his poisonous heart; then we did all the right things – quenched the ashes in good wine, scooped up the mud, covered it with best-quality beef fat, double-thick, in a gilt bronze bowl, heaped up the barrow round it and made good. We even managed to do all that stuff without grinning.

Then, on to the serious business of the day. The first event was boxing. Poor Lycomedes went out in the first stage – literally, on a door, having failed to get out of the way of a very hard, straight left hand belonging to an Athenian whose name escapes me. One of the Corinthians won the prize, after flattening his brother with a tap on the cheekbone that would probably have killed me; but the other Corinthian – can't remember which one – was back on his feet again a moment or so later, and whining because he hadn't been given another chance.

Wrestling next. The Corinthians didn't take part in that; but my brother Hyrtacus had a rough ride from an Athenian called Teleides, who nearly snapped the poor kid in half. Luckily, Hyrtacus kept his temper, and the god put it into his heart to let the Athenian try too hard; then, when this Teleides was about to break our brother off at the neck like a bunch of grapes, Hyrtacus put his weight on one foot and used the heel of the other to stamp down hard just inside the back of the Athenian's knee. Well, they both went down, but the difference was, Teleides hit the ground with his nose, and that was the last he knew about the funeral of Phorbus.

So that was all right. After that came throwing the weight, about which I remember nothing; and after that the foot-race, in which I came fifth out of a field of twelve. A friend of mine won it, with a Corinthian second and an Athenian third. I was all set to make fourth place right up to the point where we were running for home, lengthening the pace – at which point the god robbed me, putting a big, pointed stone right under the sole of my right foot at a very inconvenient moment. That allowed the youngest Corinthian, Axius, to nudge past me. Worse than that, I did my ankle no good at all and had to sit out the long-jump, which I'm sure I'd have been placed in – only my brother Ialmenus made a better distance than my normal practice-jump, so you can see it wasn't all that strong a field, in spite of the distinguished company.

But we were feeling quite happy, my brothers and I; we'd won one event, I'd been placed in another, and we had our secret weapon for the biggest event of all. Our sister Actis was going to run in the chariot-race.

Well, maybe it was asking for trouble; but even if we'd tried to stop her, we wouldn't have done any good. As it was, we managed to persuade her to dress up and hide her hair under a hat. In an old tunic and cloak of Lycomedes', she looked just like a man, thanks to her deep tan, bad girl's arms and excessive height. We announced her as Acteus, a cousin of ours from the hill country, and I don't think even Father guessed what was going on.

It was one hell of a field; there was an Athenian called Hippocleides who was the clear favourite, but if I hadn't known about our sister I'd have gone for either Phorcys or Hephaestodorus, the Corinthians, even though they were obviously having to run borrowed horses and chariots. I'd heard a few things about them from some of the Athenians I knew slightly. By all accounts, they relied more on technique and good position than the quality of their outfits, so the fact they weren't running their own teams wouldn't make any serious odds. Hippocleides, on the other hand, was held not to be anything special as a driver, he just had an exceptional pair of horses and a chariot that had been boned right down, until one man could lift it right off the ground.

The poor fools, I thought; because not only did Actis have the best pair of horses ever seen on Aegina – they looked like they were only fit for dog-food, but they drew together like they were two parts of the same animal – but she was also the canniest tactician who ever bored her brothers to sleep by chuntering on about inside lines, clipping curves and forcing the pace on the straight. No doubt about it: Actis could take both the Corinthians any day, blindfold and driving the miller's donkey. The only problem that we could see was how to lay heavy bets with the Athenians without making them suspicious.

All told there were five chariots in the race – the two Corinthians, the Athenian, a neighbour of ours called Haemon, and Actis. That's a lot of chariots in a small space; but Actis wasn't bothered at all. She let the Athenian and one of the Corinthians, Hephaestodorus, do all the early work while she held back in third place (old Haemon wasn't really bothering) and secured the inside track. The other Corinthian, Phorcys, was clearly thinking along the same lines; but for some reason he was perfectly happy to let Actis lead him, and seemed to be content just to follow up her line exactly.

As anticipated, Actis made her move at the turning-post—

'I'm terribly sorry,' said the Phoenician, 'but I'm not following any of this. What's a turning-post, and what's all this stuff about lines and tracks?'

Cleander closed his eyes and opened then again. 'You don't have chariot-races in Phoenicia,' he said.

'No.'

'Fine. All right, the basic thing to bear in mind is the shape of the track. At the far end there's a single marker, either a wooden post or a pile of stones. At the other end there's a line scratched in the dirt. First past the scratched line wins. But first they've got to go up one side of the track – imagine a skein of wool looped over a woman's hands, and her fingers are the two marks. You do have skeins of wool in Phoenicia, don't you?'

'Yes.'

'Splendid. So, they go up one side, round the turning-post, back down the other and across the line. Now, if you think about it, the chariot that goes on the far outside – furthest away from a line running up the dead centre of the track, if you like – has got further to go than the chariot running the innermost line; so the trick is to get on the inside, be the closest to the post at the halfway mark, and then hold the inside line all the way back to the finish. That way you've got less distance to cover, so you're more likely to win. Does that make any sense, or do you want me to explain it again?'

'No,' the Phoenician muttered, 'that's just fine. You carry on.'

Actis made her move at the turning-post (exactly as I told you just now), and put on speed to haul ahead of the Athenian and Hephaestodorus the Corinthian down the home straight, edging them off from the middle. She was doing just fine; the Athenian was outside the line anyway and had nothing much left in reserve, so it was just Hephaestodorus and her. But then the Corinthian, who'd let her push past him on the inside, tightened his line and jammed her right up against the middle while reining his horses back and slowing down. Actis had no choice but to slow down too; otherwise she'd have been pushed back off the track and into the stones and rubbish in the middle, which would've done her wheels and horses no good at all. While this was going on, of course, the other Corinthian, Phorcys, pulled out all the speed he'd been holding back, hauled round the both of them and went sailing ahead.

They'd planned it all before the race, you could see that; though how they knew Actis was the one they'd have to take down, rather than the Athenian or Haemon, I couldn't say. Anyway, we were angry about it but there it was. Nothing to be done except grin and bear it.

But our sister wasn't like that. She didn't cheat, and she didn't hold with other people cheating. So, instead of reining back like a good little girl, she sideswiped Hephaestodorus' chariot as it moved in on her, and gave the man himself a mouthful of goad to chew on.

'Oh gods, now what's she doing?' I heard Ialmenus moan beside me; at which point Hephaestodorus let go of his reins to grab his busted jaw, and everything went horribly wrong. Exactly how it happened, what hit what, I couldn't tell you. If you want me to guess, I'd say either his reins fell under the hooves of her horses, or her wheel got lodged in front of his; anyway, the result was that both chariots went over, locked together, rolled; his boom snapped, but it was too late by then, the damage was done; and, to make matters worse, her team dragged the tangled mess another thirty paces before they slowed down.

He was thrown out after his chariot turned over; he was dead when he hit the dirt, snapped neck. She wasn't so lucky. Because they were so close to the middle anyway, she got swiped against the sharp stones in the dead ground – like when a harness-maker shapes leather with a heavy-toothed rasp. I remember seeing her hair come out from under her hat, and one arm sticking out at the side, bent right back the wrong way.

Actis was still alive when we got there, but the mess was so badly tangled that we couldn't get her out. There was a big spar of splintered wood right through her stomach, poking out the other side, and half her face had been wiped off on the stones. She tried to say something, but her jaw was shattered. We didn't dare move anything, she was so hopelessly caught up and pinned down, so much a part of the chaos. So we just sat on our heels and waited until she died.

While we were waiting, we were sort of dimly aware of someone shouting and yelling in the background, but it wasn't until after she'd died and we were getting up, noticing the cramp in our knees, that we realised that the shouting was aimed at us, and it wasn't very friendly.

Turned out to be the Corinthian, Phorcys. His brothers were holding his arms; he was straining, like an excited dog on its leash, trying to pull away and get at us. To begin with we couldn't imagine what he was so upset about; then we remembered, his brother had been killed too. He was howling something about murder and revenge; I thought, that's a point, I suppose, properly speaking he's responsible for her death, maybe we ought to do something about it – but it was a vague idea, too big and difficult to deal with at that precise moment, when we had other things on our minds and in our hearts. Then I realised: he meant that our sister had murdered his brother. Which was absurd.

I wasn't in the right mood to argue the point; but my brother Lycomedes was. He jumped up and stalked over to face the Corinthian. What the hell was he talking about? If anybody was to blame it was Hephaestodorus, for cheating and recklessly dangerous driving. At that, this Phorcys struggled so hard he nearly got away from his brothers; that was an evil lie, he shouted, our sister had hit his brother with a goad; that was insult-with-injury-with-intent-to-degrade, reason enough for him to kill us all even if his brother wasn't lying all smashed up dead. Perhaps it was injudicious of my brother to pull a face and say, He was cheating, he had it coming; anyway, Phorcys got away from his brothers and made a grab for Lycomedes' throat. Another mistake; Lycomedes was the boxer, remember, and a moment later Phorcys was on his nose in the dust. Then things started to get out of hand.

This really isn't the time, I remember thinking; but then one of the Corinthians tried to hit me with his walking-stick, and to tell you the truth I was glad of it; I suddenly had an opportunity to turn all that anger and horror and shock into a definite act, aimed against one specific person instead of the whole world and the gods. I hit him good, and he went over.

Then some fool drew a sword. I'm not sure who, although I have a bad feeling it was me; but I can't remember for sure, because everything was confused and a mess, like a couple of chariots rolling together. Maybe that Corinthian got up and whacked me across the shoulders with his stick when I'd turned my back on him, and got me mad that way; if it was me, then some god clearly took away my wits and put madness in my heart. The next thing I remember for certain was the look on the Corinthian Axius' face; it shocked me so much I stopped what I was doing and took notice, and saw that we were all holding weapons, including me; and apparently I'd just cut Axius across the back of the left hand, because his fourth and fifth fingers were dangling by a strip of skin, and blood was draining out of him like water from a burst pipe.

That stopped the fight, anyway; we were all too dazed and dizzy to move. Some Athenians bustled the Corinthians away; presumably they bound up Axius' hand before he bled to death. I remember asking a perfect stranger, 'Did I hit him?', but I can't remember what he told me, or whether he answered me at all.

Anyway, that was the end of the games. The foreigners hung about for an hour or so, just standing in a group talking quietly. We got Actis' body and took it home, and didn't go out of doors again that day. Someone else must have cleaned up the mess, taken down the stand and the jumps and barriers and things, carted off the smashed chariots, seen to the horses. It's just as well that there are always people to take care of such things, or they'd never get done.

We hardly said a word to each other that night, or the next day; it was a long time before talking returned to our house, and even then the race, the deaths, our sister were never mentioned. I think two of the maids turned out Actis' things from the upstairs room. I gathered later that some fool proposed holding games for her funeral, but luckily none of us got to hear of it, or there'd have been more blood shed.

We burned her early one morning; just father, my brothers and me, not even our mother. It was something that had to be got out of the way, like a mistake covered up before the master gets home. I don't recall anybody saying out loud, From now on, she never existed; it somehow didn't need to be said. I tell you, it was the same sour mood that you get when a joke goes badly wrong, nobody laughs, someone gets angry or hurt. You just want to forget about it and hope the grass will grow over it, as you might say.

A couple of months later a herald arrived from Corinth. He looked absolutely terrified, as well he might; he was there, he said, to demand settlement for the life and honour of Hephaestodorus, who'd been shamed and murdered by our late sister.

Father heard him out in complete silence, without moving a muscle. Then, when the poor fellow had said what he'd come to say, father sighed.

'Get out,' he said.

The herald did just that, quickly and efficiently, and we shoved the matter out of our minds.

Well, a whole year went by. Most of the time we loafed about feeling bored, my brothers and I; somehow we didn't feel like games-playing any more, even hunting seemed like too much effort.

My kid brother Hyrtacus got married, but it was a quiet wedding. Just after harvest, my wife said she wanted to go to visit her father on the other side of the island. It would only be for a month, she said, and she took our children with her. Two months later she sent a messenger to say that she'd be staying there a bit longer. I sent back that that was fine.

One night we were sitting in the hall, my father and brothers and me, my sisters-in-law and the children and a few of the household – we'd taken against having a lot of people round us, so most of the men slept in the city. Anyway, we'd cleared away the tables and were sitting round waiting until it was time to go to bed – a musician may have been playing, I can't remember. Suddenly my brother Ialmenus looked up and asked if we could smell burning.

We said no, we didn't think so; but when he asked again a little later, we agreed that maybe we could. Father said did we think one of the houses in the city was on fire? None of us was particularly keen to get up, but eventually Ascaphalus sighed and said he'd better go and take a look. He shoved on his hat and boots and went to the doors; then he looked back at us and said they appeared to be stuck.

'What do you mean, stuck?' Father asked.

'I mean, I can't get them open,' Ascaphalus replied.

Father made an impatient noise. 'Here, let me see,' he said. A moment later, he was looking very thoughtful. None of us said anything; but the burning smell was quite strong.

'You two,' he said to Ascaphalus and me, 'get a bench, we'll try ramming it open.' We all got behind the bench and gave the doors a fearful thump; they shifted a little, but not much. That was the point at which I noticed a little blue feather of smoke seeping through the thatch.

'Who the hell do you think it is?' Lycomedes asked. The rest of us couldn't be bothered to answer. After all, it was obvious enough.

'They must have blocked the door with stones,' Father said, 'or billets of wood. Hyrtacus, go upstairs and look out of the gallery – careful, mind, they'll probably take a shot at you if you poke your head out.'

Hyrtacus turned white as linen, but nodded and scampered off.

Some of the women started asking questions – what was going on, who was it? Father told them to be quiet. My little nephew Gortys, Ialmenus' son, started to cry until his mother slapped his legs.

'It's them all right,' Hyrtacus reported back. 'They've got a mob of men with spears on the courtyard gate – they were holding torches, I could see them clearly enough. I think there's others posted round the house, but it was too dark to tell. I don't think anybody saw me.'

Father nodded. 'Can you tell where they've lit the fire?' he asked. 'And what they're blocking the gate with?'

'I couldn't see,' Hyrtacus replied. Father got angry and told him to go back and take a proper look. He went away; we waited a while, but he didn't appear again. Then his wife started to scream and sob, said why didn't we go and see what had happened to him? She wasn't helping.

'I think we can assume,' Father said, 'that they've got archers covering the gallery doors, so we can't get out that way. It's got to be either through the roof or under the walls. Any views on which?'

It was getting very smoky and hot in the hall, and we could hear the flames; by the sound of it they were spreading quite rapidly along the crest of the roof. Pretty soon we'd have falling timbers to contend with, as well as the smoke.

'Under the wall, then,' Father said. 'All right, let's get started.'

No need to tell us where; a few years before, some cheeky bastard had the nerve to break into the house and steal things – he didn't get through to the inner room, so all he ended up with was a lousy old bronze cauldron, which he was welcome to. What really vexed us at the time was the damage he did where he dug under the wall. Now it looked like he might have done us all a serious favour.

We'd blocked his hole with rubble and packed earth, but we'd made a pretty slack job of it. We all got swords and iron spits and set to prising up the waste. We were halfway down when a rafter fell slap in the middle of the hall; it killed my mother outright and pinned down Lycomedes' wife and daughter.

'Leave them,' Father shouted, 'there isn't time.'

Lycomedes hesitated for a moment, then went on digging, hard as he could. I've wondered about that, but I guess he did the right thing. After all, a man can always get another wife, more children; but his father and his brothers can't be replaced.

We knew we were losing the race quite some time before we actually gave up; right up to when the smoke was too thick even down at floor level, and with timbers and blazing thatch pitching all round us, we kept at it, though we couldn't see each other, or what we were doing, and the noise was so loud we couldn't hear anything else. Then the moment came when I realised I was the only one still digging; and a heartbeat or so after that, I was through.

Fresh air came up through the hole like blood from a cut vein, and I shoved my head into it and gulped it down like a thirsty mule at a river. The sheer joy of breathing painted out everything else from my mind, until a clump of burning straw landed square on my back and made me howl with pain and terror. That was enough for me; I shoved myself through that hole – it was just big enough, if it'd been any smaller I'd have kept pushing anyway, even if it meant ripping an arm off – and just when I thought I was stuck and was bound to die ridiculously, my bum burned away while my head was in the clear, out I came like the stopper from a jar.

The first thing I saw when I opened my eyes was a face staring at me. I didn't know who it could be. Then he started yelling, and at the same time he was trying to draw a bow, but in his excitement he'd let the nock of the arrow slip off the string, and he was fumbling to get it back again. I squirmed up out of the hole and tried to get past him, but I caught my foot on the edge of the hole and went down flat on my face. He dumped the bow and made a grab for me; I put up my hand to fend him off, saw I still had a sword in it and stabbed him in the groin. He left me alone after that.

I didn't have a clue where to go; just 'away', my heart was telling me, and that seemed about all I could cope with in the way of advice. I kept running until I saw the courtyard wall, hopped over that and found myself in the orchard (I'd lived in that house all my life, but until I nearly ran into an apple tree, I didn't even know where I was). That struck me as a good thing; the orchard backed on to the house of Cacodaemon – I'd known him since before I could walk, even. But when I crept round to the door and banged on it, nobody answered; and then there were people in the street, just standing and watching, holding torches and lamps, and I decided I didn't want to hang around. That proved to be a wise decision; someone threw a spear at me – missed plenty wide, but I remember squeaking in terror and bolting for the darkest patch of darkness I could see. After that I kept on running.

At some point, if I remember correctly, I tripped over a root or ran into a wall; anyway, I managed to knock myself out cold, and that's what saved my life. The Corinthians had brought three whole shiploads of men, and once they realised that one of us had got out they sent the lot of them to look for me. But they were looking for a running man, not an idiot lying stunned, so they went straight past me in the dark and never knew I was there.

I came round just before dawn, and lay for a while asking my heart what I should do next. At first my heart told me they'd probably all gone by now, I should get back and see if by any miracle any more of us were still alive. But then I found I was too scared for that; better to get up into the hills, where I'd be safe. I knew where the steadings and caves were, where I could find food and water, clothes and weapons from the stores we leave up there for our shepherds. If there was no sign of them after a day or so, I'd come down.

Just as well the god put that thought into my mind; I spent the next few days dodging Corinthians through the hills – and more depressing still, as often as not they had Aeginetans guiding them. After a really uncomfortable day wedged up a tree, during which I had a chance to eavesdrop on the conversation of one of the hunting parties (their guide was a man I used to go netting partridges with, may he burn in hell for ever), I realised what had happened. Not content with killing my family and burning our house, the Corinthians had decided to take over the island. And as if that wasn't bad enough, the Aeginetans, my father's loving people, the sheep of his fold, didn't seem to mind a bit

On top of everything else, that was so bad I almost wanted to laugh. All the years I'd been growing up, living among them, and I hadn't know it: they hated our family, were delighted to see the back of us. The raid itself had been organised by some of the better sort in the city; according to what I heard, they'd *invited* the Corinthians to come over, put the idea into their heads. But for giving them the satisfaction, I nearly got down out of the tree there and then and let them take me in. Really, I couldn't see the point in bothering any more.

But the god put better ideas in my head, which is why I'm here today, for what little I'm worth. I say that; I may not be much good to myself – or to you people – but the sons of Laops value me very highly. I think the only reason I carry on living is to spite them – if they were to stop chasing me and sending men to find me, I'd probably curl up in a ditch and cut my wrists.

Well (said Cleander), that was the story he told us.

I'd been too wrapped up in the story to notice what effect it was having on the rest of us. When he stopped talking, I looked round. Dusa was gazing at him with a sort of drowned-in-honey expression on her face. Sarpedon was frowning. Cratus – well, I don't know what he thought he looked like; he had a silly grin on his face, hidden under tight eyebrows.

'So you're a games-player, are you?' he said. 'There's a coincidence.'

For that, he got enough mustard from the rest of us to spoil a whole ox. Pentheus just smiled sadly. 'Not any more,' he said.

'But you know all about that sort of thing,' Cratus went on. 'That could be very helpful to us.'

'I don't mind helping in any way I can,' Pentheus replied humbly. 'After all, you saved my life.'

'Yes, didn't we.' Cratus stroked his beard. 'Just a couple of points, though. What about your wife, and – what was it, a son and a daughter?'

'Two sons, actually.'

'I stand corrected. What about them, though? Did you just up and leave them?'

Pentheus nodded. 'That's right,' he said. 'I wasn't in any position to help them; if I'd tried to cross the island to my father-in-law's house, I don't suppose I'd have got very far; and even if I had, all I'd have done was put them all in extreme danger.'

'Fair enough,' Cratus said. 'But your son – sorry, your two sons – don't you think that the Corinthians would be concerned about two potential heirs to the throne living right under their noses on Aegina? If I was them, I'd have thought getting rid of them would be a really high priority—'

'Cratus!' Dusa growled. 'For the gods' sakes!'

Pentheus lifted his head. 'It's all right,' he said. 'Look, to tell you the truth, I haven't got the remotest idea what's happened to any of them. I don't even know if they're still alive. All I do know is, if they're alive, they've got a far better chance of staying that way if I stay off Aegina and don't try getting in touch with them in any way. And since you seem so fascinated by that side of it, yes, it tears my heart to pieces thinking about them, not even knowing, but since there's spit I can do about it, I keep my face shut and my heart closed. All right?'

'That's reasonable, I guess,' Cratus said blandly. 'All right, next point—'

'Cratus!'

'With you in a moment, Dusa, just asking our guest some questions. Now then; you say your people had come to hate you—'

'*Cratus!*'

'Yes,' Pentheus said. 'At least, that's what I heard them saying. And the way they all helped look for me would tend to suggest there's a grain of truth in it.'

'Quite so. But do you know why they all took against you like that? What was it – high rents, foreclosing on mortgages, forcing them to join in pointless military adventures?'

'I don't know,' Pentheus replied, 'and that's the truth. All I did gather was that they resented the fact that my brothers and I spent so much time practising games, and they reckoned we never did any work – soft hands, they said we had, and we didn't know one end of a plough from the other.'

Cratus looked thoughtful. 'I can see that wouldn't make you popular,' he said. 'But actually helping your enemies—'

'My guess is,' Pentheus said with a sigh, 'that what really offended them was when we let Actis take part in the race. Thinking about it, I can remember hearing a fair bit of muttering over the years about how it was wrong, a girl games-player, and no good would come of it. I guess that when Actis got her just deserts, as they'd have seen it, they were afraid the bad luck would pass over from us to them; so they decided to get rid of us.'

At that point, I felt Cratus had done enough harm for one day. 'In any case,' I said, 'what's done is done. What we should be thinking about is, what are we going to do next?'

'Absolutely right,' Cratus said, grinning. He was being insufferable.

'You sound like you've got plenty of good, sensible suggestions to make,' I said. 'Go ahead. We're listening.'

Cratus lifted his head. 'I'm assuming,' he said, 'that we're proposing to take this lost sheep with us. Right? Thought so – and stop pulling faces, Dusa, or the Gorgon will come and you'll be stuck like that for ever. All right, let's think for a moment, see if we can figure out what difference it's going to make.'

'Go on,' I said.

Cratus nodded. 'First,' he said, 'there's presumably a risk of more run-ins with the man's enemies, particularly now that Uncle Sarpedon's been so free with the old pitiless bronze. For all we know, he may have started off a blood-feud that'll make our new friend's troubles look positively bland in comparison. But like you said, Cleander, that's done, nothing we can do about it now. So. All we can do is press on, take a few sensible precautions – setting a watch at night, for a start, and I volunteer our new friend Pentheus to take first watch, followed by Uncle Sarpedon, so they can both have a chance to reflect on the effects they have on other people.

'Apart from that – well, what about it? We've still got our job to do. We've still got Alastor and our good friend Tachys to make it just that bit harder for us. We've still got one hell of a way to go. And,' he added, with a meaningful glance at Pentheus (I say meaningful; damned if I knew what it meant), 'we've now got an expert former games-player to help us along with useful inside knowledge and technical advice. After all,' he added, 'a man who's been practising games all his life, he's bound to know a thing or two about the great games-players of his generation – just the sort of information that could make all the difference when we go cold-calling.'

Well, that actually did seem pretty sensible, and we all nodded (Pentheus included, though he looked thoughtful and didn't say anything).

'How are you feeling?' Dusa asked him.

Pentheus pulled a face. 'Could be worse,' he said. 'I'll be all right so long as—'

'You aren't going anywhere,' Dusa interrupted. 'We'll stay here, give you a chance to rest. When was the last time you had anything to eat?'

Cratus and I looked at each other. 'All right,' I said, 'we'll stay here till morning; and then we really do have to get on.'

Dusa scowled at me, as if everything was my fault, including Pandora's box and the war between the gods and the frost-giants. 'Why?' she said. 'A couple of days won't make any difference to anything. The only thing is, we ought to get him to some shelter. It can't be good for him, lying out in the open air.'

'What makes you an expert all of a sudden?' Cratus asked. Honestly, you'd think he was trying to provoke her. Fortunately, Sarpedon jumped in; and since he clearly knew a great deal about wounds (how to cause them, mostly, but he also knew a bit about patching them up), she shut her face and listened.

'Lugging him from door to door trying to find someone who'll take us in, with him in tow, is going to do more harm than a night under the stars,' he said. 'The bleeding's stopped, and the wound doesn't look like it nicked anything important. A day or so of rest and he'll be back on his feet again.'

'Uncle—' I said.

'But,' Sarpedon went on, 'if you drag him along before the wound's started to knot, you'll start the bleeding off again, cause all sorts of problems – and that really will slow us up. Now, get some cheese and bread from the panniers, and a finger's length of that blood sausage.'

At least he didn't specify which finger.

It was very boring being cooped up in a wood with a wounded man and a drooling girl. I stuck it out for the rest of that day and the following night; then I announced that I was going to walk down to the nearest village, see if I couldn't scrounge some milk, maybe some cold beef or some bacon. Cratus immediately volunteered to go with me, make sure I didn't come to harm if I ran into bandits or Corinthians. Truth of it was, he was even more bored than I was.

Well, the village was a morning's walk on down the road; miserable little place, with a stockade all round it, two dilapidated store-towers, a few houses, a well and a smithy. Naturally, we headed for the smithy, went in and sat against the wall.

'You're not from round here,' the smith told us, after we'd been there a while. He was putting rivets into the blade of a broken sickle. I could have done a better job myself.

'That's right,' I replied. 'We're on our way to Argos.'

'Ah,' the smith said. 'Well, you're on the right road.'

We knew that perfectly well; but it seems to be an integral part of being a smith, this business of telling people what clearly they already know. He went on with his work, keeping the sickle-blade clear of the sett so that all the force of the blow went through to the rivet-head. It's an art, peening rivets; most people try to hit them square on top, but really you nibble round the edges with a series of light, precise taps until you've turned over the head completely. This smith seemed to understand the principle of it, though he wasn't putting it into practice all that well.

'How far is it to Argos?' I asked, after another long silence.

'Don't know,' the smith replied without looking up. 'Never been. Never needed to go, neither.'

Cratus smiled at him. 'If you got the chance, would you go? Or are you just not particularly interested?'

'Can't be bothered,' the smith replied. 'And I got a whole heap of things to do. What the hell would I want to go to Argos for, anyway?'

'To see the games,' piped up a voice from the corner. I looked round and saw a tiny little old man huddling in the far corner like a spider in a web. He was wrapped up in a tatty old cloak that was more holes than cloth, and the tip of his nose poked out over the top.

'What games?' I asked.

The old man laughed. 'It's true,' he said, 'they ain't from round here. *The* games, boy; the Argive games, in honour of Hera.'

Cratus frowned. 'Who died?' he asked.

This time the smith laughed too. 'Ain't nobody died,' the old man said, 'least, nobody I heard of. We don't wait for people to die in these parts 'fore we have games.'

'Have 'em every year,' the smith said. 'Waste of time if you ask me, mind, all that effort and sweating and running about, and they don't actually *do* anything. So they can jump a finger higher than anybody else? So what?'

'Every year,' I repeated.

'That's right.'

'And how long's this been going on for?' Cratus asked.

The old man shrugged. 'Five years,' he said, 'maybe ten. Don't reckon as how they keep tallies.'

Cratus and I looked at each other. 'And when are these games?' I asked.

'Soon,' the smith replied. 'That's a job I got to do, make up a throwing-weight for some horse-taming git who's going to the games. Just a big lump of bronze, and a handle on it. Talk about a waste of good material.'

I took a deep breath; it helps me keep my temper. 'When you say soon—'

The old man scratched his nose. 'When the Pleiades set,' he said. 'Round the time honest folks are starting to plough. Damn foolish time to be away from home playing games, but that's Argos for you.'

'And do many people go to the games?' I asked. 'People from away, I mean? Or is it just for the Argives?'

The old man thought for a moment. 'Mostly just the Argos folks,' he said. 'Few from away – heard tell that one year they got folks from as far away as Asine and Troezen. But who'd go out of his way just to play games in a foreign city, right at the start of ploughing?'

'Right,' Cratus said. 'It'd have to be someone with nothing to do and no brains to do it with.'

The smith turned over the sickle and studied the rivets for a while. 'Where did you boys say you were from?' he asked.

Well, we got out of there as soon as it was polite to leave, and headed back the way we'd come.

'To the crows with it,' I snarled, as soon as we were away from the village. 'That just about ruins everything.'

Cratus looked at me. 'You reckon?' he said.

'Well, of course. This big idea of mine, it isn't new at all.

According to that old fool in there, they've been having games-with-nobody-dead in Argos for ten years.'

'True,' Cratus replied. 'But we didn't know that.'

'Well, of course we didn't. If we did we wouldn't be here, wasting our time.'

Cratus frowned. 'You're missing the point,' he said. 'We didn't know. Nobody else we've met so far has known. As the man said, it's only a few Argives and the occasional offcomer – guest-friends of the Argive princes, probably.'

'So?'

'So,' Cratus said patiently, 'if nobody knows about it, it doesn't matter.'

'What?'

'Oh, for crying out loud.' Cratus sat down and pulled me down with him. 'Think about it,' he said. 'What's the difference between something happening that nobody knows about, and the same thing not happening at all?'

'What?'

'All right, I'll use shorter words. Suppose we'd never come here, right? And suppose for some reason we missed out Argos and went straight on to Corinth. We'd never have heard of these Argive games. Neither would anybody else. As far as all of us are concerned, they might just as well not exist.'

'But we know they exist,' I pointed out.

'Really? What if the old bugger was lying? Making it up?'

'Why should he want to do a thing like that?'

'That's not the *point*,' Cratus said angrily. 'The point is, we've only got his word for it. Nobody else knows – nobody who matters. And if nobody knows, then it's all right. Something nobody knows about might as well not exist. It's really very simple when you think about it.'

I thought about that for a moment. 'You mean,' I said, 'we shouldn't tell anybody, even though we do know? We should pretend—'

'Yes.'

'Oh.' I shrugged. 'All right, then,' I said. 'We'll do that.'

Cratus grinned at me. 'Well done,' he said. 'Now, look on the bright side, will you? It proves it can be done. It proves that people will go to games where nobody's died.'

I lifted my head. 'That doesn't help us,' I said. 'We aren't telling anybody, remember?'

'That's not the *point*—'

'Yes it is,' I insisted. 'We can't go around saying, Come to the games in Elis where nobody's died, they're just like the ones in Argos. And they say, Oh, do they have games in Argos where nobody's died? And we say, no, of course not. No help at all.'

Cratus looked at me. 'You know,' he said, 'the fact that you and I are brothers never ceases to amaze me. Your very existence accuses our mother of adultery. Nevertheless, I will try to explain. The fact that these games have succeeded, that they've managed to keep them going for ten years, suggests to me that the very idea of games where nobody's died isn't quite as bone-headed stupid as I thought it was when you first suggested it. I find that a great comfort.'

'Do you,' I said.

'Yes.'

'I see. You won't believe me, but you'll believe a bunch of Argives you've never met, and an old fart you got talking to in a smithy.'

He smiled. 'Of course,' he said. 'I'm your brother.'

I was about to say something about that when I noticed the expression on Cratus' face. Anybody could tell that the god had just put something into his mind. Now, I wasn't in the mood to listen to Cratus trying to be funny, but you'd be a fool not to listen to a god. 'What?' I asked.

'I've just had an idea,' Cratus replied. 'These games.'

'Yes?'

'Well, if they're when the Pleiades set, that's no more than a week or so away. We could go.'

I didn't follow. 'Go where?'

'To the games, of course. Oh, come on, brother, even you aren't that slow. Where better to find games-players who'll be prepared to go to games where nobody's died, than games where nobody's died?'

'But I thought you just said—'

'Right,' said Cratus, standing up. 'That's settled, then.'

CHAPTER NINE

'Just a moment,' said the Phoenician. 'I've been to Argos, several times. I never heard of anything like that.'

Cleander looked surprised. 'Really?' he said. 'That's odd. I suppose they must have stopped holding them there at some stage over the last fifteen years. After all, just because they did something once doesn't mean they'll carry on doing it for ever.'

'Even so,' the Phoenician said, 'I'd have thought someone would have mentioned it.'

'Why?' Cratus asked. 'I mean, I don't suppose you ever asked.'

The Phoenician nodded. 'That's right, I didn't. But didn't we agree a while back, the whole point of games is so that people who are good at them get remembered? That's not likely to happen if nobody talks about them.'

'Maybe they only talk about them if you ask,' someone suggested.

'All right; but first you've got to know to ask; and if you know already, why bother to ask?'

Nobody appeared to have an answer to that. Finally Palamedes said, 'So, what exactly are you saying?'

The Phoenician looked uncertain. 'I'm not sure,' he said. 'I was just pointing out that if the reason for having games is to be remembered and so cheat death, the Argives were wasting their time.'

'Maybe they were,' Palamedes agreed. 'Of course, the same thing goes for anything a man does to try to get himself remembered. Take war, for example; you could have a wonderfully brave and strong man who fights to the death surrounded by hundreds of the enemy, kills half of them before he dies himself, makes it possible for his king to escape or his people to close the city gates in time. But nobody on his side was watching, and the enemy aren't likely to tell stories about a man who made them look like a bunch of idiots. All that effort and heroism, for nothing. Maybe it was the same with the games at Argos – they did their best, but nobody was interested. Or,' he went on, 'take you and your patterns-scratched-on-waxed-boards. You could scratch down records of all sorts of wonderful things, but how are you going to make sure people ever look at them? You can't.' He shook his head. 'And you know, when I think about that it makes me wonder. You'd think someone – the gods, I suppose, there's nobody else could do it – you'd think the gods would see to it that the more splendid a man's deeds are, the more people will hear about him and remember him. But it doesn't seem to work that way. I remember a man when I was a kid, he could lift this enormous great big stone that the smith used as an anvil. Lift it clean off the ground, he could; but I can't remember his name or anything else about him, while I know all about Theseus of Athens, who first got famous for lifting a big stone. What if my man's stone was bigger and heavier? There's no justice in that.'

The company around the table looked at him, as if wondering where all this was leading. Nowhere, apparently, because Palamedes tilted his cup, found it empty, and shouted for the jug.

Well (said Cratus, after Palamedes' cup had been filled), you just heard my brother, who seemed to reckon I was suggesting something odd, possibly bad. That's the difference between him and me. I thought it was just common sense.

After all, as I said to the others when we got back to the camp in the woods, if you're looking for a ploughshare, you go to a smith; you don't wander through the villages on the offchance that someone might have a spare they don't want tucked up in the rafters. If you want games-players, go to the games.

'Seems reasonable to me,' Sarpedon said. 'Only thing is, what's to stop them telling everybody about the games in Argos? If they do that, everybody'll be in on the secret, and we'll all look like fools.'

'Not necessarily,' I replied. 'Besides, does it really matter that we didn't have the idea first? As I see it, our job is to make sure that we get as many games-players to go to our games as possible. Once we've done that, anything that goes wrong is someone else's fault.'

'Dusa?' Cleander asked. 'What do you think?'

Dusa looked round. 'Sorry,' she said. 'What were we talking about?'

Cleander and I looked at each other; *got it worse than we thought*, our hearts said to each other. 'These games in Argos,' Cleander said. 'Did you get that bit?'

'Yes,' Dusa said. 'Cratus thinks we should go. I agree with him. Stands to reason.'

'Oh.' Cleander sighed. 'All right then, we'll go. If we make a diversion and go to Asine first, then head back to Argos from there, we should arrive just in time.'

'Excuse me,' said Pentheus.

We'd forgotten – Cleander and Sarpedon and I had forgotten – all about him. 'What?' I asked.

'Sorry to be a nuisance,' he said, 'but I'd really rather not go to Argos while these games are on. You never know, the Corinthians might be there, if they have foreign games-players. I don't want to run into them. And if not them, maybe there'll be people who know them, or know me.'

Cleander looked angry. 'That's not on at all,' he said. 'We're here to find games-players, remember. We aren't going to manage that by skulking around in the dark with our cloaks over our faces.'

'Pentheus is right,' said Dusa firmly. 'It's too dangerous. We can't go.'

Cleander made a rude noise. 'Then we might as well go home,' he said. 'Look, if we go about calling on kings and princes, and this man's the surviving Prince of Aegina, then yes, there's a risk someone's going to recognise him.'

'You're all missing the point,' Sarpedon said. 'It's not as if we can just dump Pentheus and be rid of all our problems. Oh, we can dump him all right – might be a good idea, at that – but it won't change the fact that we fought and killed his enemies, which means that his enemies are now our enemies. Now he's not the only one who's got to be careful where he goes and what he does.'

That really depressed us all. I mean, the god had put the same thought in all our minds, but we'd ignored it because it didn't taste nice. Now we had to deal with it.

'End of discussion, then,' Dusa said. 'We go home.'

A part of me – the sensible part, I suppose – was very much inclined to agree with this suggestion. Unfortunately, it was outnumbered and shouted down. Why? Well, the first thought that occurred to me was that if Dusa was allowed to take her new pet home, like a kid who finds a bird with a damaged wing out on the hill, next thing we knew she'd be married to him, and we'd have to support the rogue for the rest of his life. I didn't want that.

'No, we don't,' I therefore said. 'Don't even think about it. We've come this far, we're going on. For gods' sakes,' I continued, as my brother and uncle stared at me as if I was out of my head, 'are you suggesting we ought to scurry home and hide under the bed the rest of our lives, just in case some nasty men come looking for us? I don't think so. More to the point,' I added, 'how is anybody supposed to know that it was us who killed those people? We got them all, didn't we? If anybody comes up and accuses us of killing them, we just look blank and deny everything. But I can't see that happening unless they plan to waylay every party of travellers in the Peloponnese.'

Cleander rubbed his eyes; he looked tired. 'But what if they catch us with *him*?' he said, pointing at Pentheus – very bad manners, don't you think? 'They may not know us, but—'

'Who's to say we didn't meet him later, after somebody else killed those people? All right, they may not believe us; but anybody who's rational enough to stop and ask questions is also going to be rational enough not to risk getting involved in an unnecessary feud by harming strangers when they can't be sure they're picking on the right men. Besides, it's him they want. And if the situation arises, we hand him over and go on our way.'

Of course, Dusa made a hell of a fuss about that; but for once we didn't allow her to bully us. After all, there were three of us, grown men, against one girl – close odds, but still in our favour.

'Look,' I said to her, 'this is the deal. Either we dump him now, or we take him with us, reserving the right to dump him later. Which would you rather?'

She scowled like the Gorgon and didn't say anything, which experience has taught me means, Oh, all right then, in female. So that was settled.

We went to Asine.

We'd now reached the stage familiar to all you seasoned travellers where one city starts looking pretty much like another. You know how it is; first time away from home, you start off thinking how wonderfully different everything is – gods, you say to yourself, in these parts they roof their cattle-stalls with osiers and have an entirely different way of lacing their boots, isn't this incredible? And after a while, once you've trudged far enough and seen enough of the cities of mortal men, you tend only to notice the similarities, the basic shapes that are common to all human settlements – here's the city gate, here's the square, here's the well, here's the palace wall, big deal. I don't know if either way of seeing things is right, or better than the other, although you could say that since the latter view comes with age and experience, it ought to be wiser and therefore more valid. But I don't know. Don't care much, either.

We might have been more aware of our surroundings if Asine hadn't been such a dump. It was a small, fairly new city. The wall was low and rather shoddily built, a bit bowed and out of true in places. The houses were small, too. The people we saw in the streets wore plain, old clothes. The palace would have been a medium-sized barn in Sparta. The two princes seemed pleased to have company; our presents actually impressed them, but what we got in return was low-grade locally made rubbish. There was something about the place that was extremely and depressingly familiar, but I couldn't put my finger on it at first.

Then I realised what it was. Asine was just like Elis.

I suppose it's only to be expected when you've been away for any length of time. The further from home you get, the harder it becomes to remember who you are.

Prince Demodocus, the younger and chattier of the two princes, thought the idea of a huge and magnificent games-with-nobody-dead was quite wonderful; like the Argive games, he said, only bigger and better. We nodded and looked grave, like a nestful of owls. Prince Demodocus explained that although he was a moderately good archer and boxer, the best games-player in Asine wasn't a prince, or even a son of one of the Better Houses; his name was Sclerus, and he'd just shown up at the door one day looking sad. Eventually he'd come out with a tragic story about being a nobleman's son in Crete who'd been abducted by Tyrian pirates – no offence, friend, I'm just telling you what he told us – and sold as a slave in Corinth; after a few years, he'd run away and come south, making his living as a day-labourer, which is probably a worse hardship than slavery – you serve many masters, not just one, and you don't have the slave's security of knowing you'll be fed come nightfall. The princes weren't too sure about harbouring a runaway; but then they reflected that it was all right because, after all, the man was a prince in his own country. So they asked him if he felt like staying with them for a month or so, to get a good rest and eat a few solid meals. That had been five years ago.

But it didn't matter (said the princes) because, for one, he *was* a prince in his own country, and also he was an absolute prodigy when it came to running, jumping, throwing weights and wrestling – which of course proved that his story about his royal origins was true, because nobody who's not of the better sort can be good at games; known fact.

Far from being a pest (they said), this Sclerus had become one of the most admired and popular men in Asine, all because of his wonderful ability to run, jump, throw things and damage people in the name of healthy fun. Crowds gathered to watch him practise. Girls wanted to marry him. Young men invited him on boar-hunts. Needless to say (the princes added), he was still very sad, what with being a stranger in a foreign land, deprived of his rightful inheritance; but it was a real credit to him that he managed to stay so cheerful all the time, especially when he was invited to someone's house for dinner. The ability to smile in the midst of misfortune, the princes said, is the unmistakable mark of the true man of quality.

When we asked if we could meet this Sclerus (who was out when we called, visiting a family of admirers in the city), the princes smiled and said, Of course; but if we were thinking of trying to lure him out to our games, we'd be disappointed. For all his wonderful prowess, they explained, Sclerus hadn't even been to the Argive games. He'd told them the reason why – he didn't want to run into any acquaintances from his younger days, he said, who might recognise him and mock him for his afflictions or (even worse) pity him. After all, he who had once been a prince was now nothing but a wandering hireling, and it would shame him almost to death to be seen in such a state by someone he'd once presumed to call his equal.

While we were listening to this load of old rubbish, trying to keep our faces straight, I kept glancing sideways at our new friend Pentheus; but he sat there perfectly still, with an expression on his face like it'd been flayed off the bone, stuffed with basil and juniper berries and put up in the rafters to mature.

Well, we still had a few days to go before it was time to leave for Argos; and the Princes of Asine apparently weren't sick to death of the sight of us yet; so we decided to accept their invitation to hang around and go with them to Argos. That suited me; we were reasonably safe from Pentheus' enemies while we were in the palace, we were on hand in case Alastor and Tachys showed up, and (best of all, as far as I was concerned) there was a chance that this obvious rogue Sclerus might serve, as it were, as a mirror in which my dear sister might see a true image of young Pentheus. Also, the food, though plain, was reasonable and I'd had enough of walking to last me. Just sitting down was nice.

I can only assume that Sclerus found out that there were strangers staying at the palace, because he sent word that he'd been invited to stay a day or so with his friends in the city. I may have smirked to myself when I heard that, but of course I kept my face properly shut. Not for me to go making trouble for someone who'd never done me any harm. But Pentheus, of all people, seemed to have contracted a burning desire to meet this Sclerus, and nothing would do except that Demodocus, one of our hosts, should take him to the house where Sclerus was staying, so he could see him.

I frowned when I heard that; but again, none of my business. Where Pentheus went, of course, Dusa had to go too, as nurse and guardian; and where my sister went in her unstable state of mind and heart, I was going. Cleander didn't want to be left in the house with nobody but the older prince, Aristippus, to talk to (Aristippus was large and solid and knew at least two words, 'yes' and 'no'), and Sarpedon came along – well, I don't know, maybe he thought there was a better chance of getting into a fight in the city than in the palace. Anyway, he joined us, and off we went.

We found this Sclerus holding court – no other word for it – on the threshing-floor of a large farm just outside the walls. There was a crowd there all right; the family, the farmhands, a mob of kids of various sizes, and a quite disproportionate number of young women. They were watching Sclerus practising the long jump, and quite a performance he was making of it, too. He had a pair of stone jumping-weights – the kind you hold in your hands and swing in front of you to add momentum to your jump – and for a few minutes all he did was wave these solemnly backwards and forwards through the air, a manoeuvre that seemed to me to have little therapeutic effect, but which did show off the muscles of his chest and shoulders to great advantage. He had a piper playing to help him with his rhythm, a young lad with rather more enthusiasm than skill.

When he'd finally done flexing, he actually condescended to make a jump.

You know how it's done; you start off by squatting down, as if sitting on a chair that isn't really there; then you swing the weights back as you topple forwards; then, just as you're about to lose your balance and go down smack on your nose, you swish the weights forward and up, kick with your legs like a frog to boost yourself up in the air, push your feet out in front, let go of the weights and land on your toes. If you've got it all right, you make a nice clean mark in the dirt with your heels. If you've got it wrong, you either flump down on your bum hard enough to jar your spine out of your ear, or you topple forwards and smash your chin.

Sclerus was – well, competent. He didn't fall over or damage himself, and he cleared seven paces, which isn't bad. But neither is it astoundingly brilliant, especially if you're using the big weights. Certainly it wasn't good enough to warrant the rapturous applause of his audience. Anyway; I was bored, and I'd seen enough. I looked round for Demodocus, to suggest we go back to the palace.

But while I was looking the other way (don't you hate it when that happens?) Pentheus must've slipped past me, through the crowd and on to the floor. First I knew of it was when this sort of buzz went round the crowd; I looked, and saw Pentheus blithely picking up the discarded weights. He'd pulled off his tunic and sandals and was heading for the mark.

Then Dusa was tugging at my arm. 'You can't let him,' she said loudly, 'he's not well enough, he'll hurt himself.' Well, I don't think any other argument could have persuaded me, but she'd hit the spot, like a first-class archer.

'Nonsense,' I said. 'If he wants to try his luck, let him.'

Don't suppose I could have stopped him anyway; the crowd wouldn't have stood for it. They were gawping with happy, happy faces, which was more than could be said for Sclerus (he was shooting mustard at Pentheus as if he could burn him to death by sheer malevolent glaring). Anyway, after a couple of desultory wafts of the weights, Pentheus jumped.

It was very quiet after he'd landed. Even I was impressed; the jump was a shade under nine full paces, which is longer than I've ever seen, that's for sure. A moment or so later, the silence turned into frantic cheering and yelling, and Pentheus had to scramble up a ladder into the hayloft to keep from being pulled to bits by all those ecstatic girls. The poor thing.

'So?' I muttered, to myself more than anybody else. 'The boy can jump. So can a frog.' But it wasn't over, not by the length of a good furrow.

Once Sclerus had quit breathing fire, he stomped over to the ladder, climbed up a couple of rungs and challenged Pentheus to a wrestling match. Pentheus poked his head down out of the loft, agreed and came down the ladder. The crowd pulled back. Someone darted forward with a rake to level out the dirt. Dusa was babbling away about opening up half-healed wounds and how *could* I just stand there when a man's life was in danger? Fortunately, the noise from the crowd was so loud I could legitimately pretend I couldn't hear her.

It's a cold fact that most really high-class wrestling matches are extremely boring to watch, since for most of the time the two opponents dance round each other in circles looking for an opening, and even when they stop prancing about, nobody gets snapped in half or thrown through the air – if they're good wrestlers, they're too good to lay themselves open to anything like that. No, they just grab each other round the waist and heave until one of them gives in or falls over. That's upright wrestling, of course. Ground wrestling is for kids and dogs.

I have a confession to make at this point. It's not something I'm proud of. But they say that shame is like a dead rat under the floorboards; you keep it stashed away in your heart for long enough, it'll smell the place out. So please, don't make matters worse by laughing or jeering, because I think I've punished myself enough for this already.

Very well, then, when I was young – too young to know any better – I was a bit of a games-player myself. To be precise, I dabbled in wrestling and heavy wrestling for a year or so. In fact, to be cruelly accurate, it's all Cleander's fault. You see, when we were kids, he was much bigger and stronger than me, and naturally enough tended to use me the way a dedicated swordsman uses his stout oak post bound with straw; he used to bash the shit out of me as a way of honing his martial skills. This is, of course, the way of things, as ordained by our ancestors and by Nature herself, so I had no right to complain; nevertheless, there were times when, as I picked myself up out of the dust only to be kicked back down again, I wondered if there might not be another way.

I found it in the teachings of an old man who came to visit us once. He was a prince and a famous warrior, so what he was doing wasting his time on a snot-nosed kid I don't know. But he sat watching one day as Cleander worked me over – he just sat there, on the tailgate of a cart, as if we were putting on a show for his benefit – and as I limped away, all dusty and snivelly, he beckoned me over and asked if I fancied learning how to wrestle. Now, at that age – I was, what, eleven? – the word 'learn' had unfortunate connotations of boredom and irrelevance; but then this old man, whose name's leaked out of my mind many years since, explained that not all learning is a waste of time, some of it can be used to inflict salutory pain on elder brothers. That got me interested; and for the next few days I suffered at the old man's hands instead of Cleander's.

At the end of it, though, I discovered that for some perverse reason the god had hidden away in the dark rafters of my heart a knack for wrestling; and once I'd paid back Cleander, capital and the debtor's sixth (for which I got into deep and painful trouble, thereby learning a lesson about justice as well as wrestling), I decided to carry on and practice a little more, since at last I'd found something I was actually good at. In the end I grew out of it, along with a number of other nasty adolescent habits; but (and here's the point of the story) even now I can remember enough to know a good wrestler from a lucky one, and to spot who the winner of a fight will be before the first grip's taken or the first tooth loosened.

There's two kinds of wrestler – strong and skilful. Sclerus was strong, no doubt about that. Whether there'd be enough of Pentheus left to fill a small jar depended entirely on his level of skill. I couldn't wait to see the outcome.

First came the oil-bath; then, when both men were properly shiny and sticky, they solemnly rolled over three times in the dust, to give each other something to grip on (one of my strongest memories of wrestling matches was the awful embarrassment of having to roll over in the dirt in front of a crowd of people I'd have to talk to afterwards). As they got up, I noticed Sclerus surreptitiously wiping his oily hands down his waist and thigh – this is, of course, cheating, since it makes it harder for the other man to get a grip; but of course I didn't say anything, and I don't suppose anybody else there knew enough about the game to understand what he was up to.

Sclerus, being bigger and stronger, immediately went for the heave. He ducked his head down low, butted Pentheus in the stomach and tried to grab him round the thighs to lift him off the ground. To his credit, though, Pentheus was ready for that; he brought his knee up under Sclerus' chin before he had a chance to get a grip, there was an aesthetically satisfying crunch, and Sclerus wriggled out of the heave in a hurry. There was blood at the corner of his mouth, which suggested that he'd bitten his own tongue.

To my surprise, Pentheus immediately tried the same manoeuvre on Sclerus – a shrewd move, since it was the last thing Sclerus was expecting. It was all very good in theory – Pentheus got a good grip, his head nuzzled well into Sclerus' groin to stop him using the same tactic he'd just used on Sclerus, but he just didn't have the strength for the lift itself (not that all that illegal oil made it any easier). Sclerus, meanwhile, had got his arms round Pentheus' neck – you lay yourself open to that, no matter how good you are – and was proceeding to pull his head off at his leisure.

That wasn't doing Pentheus any good; so he let go and grabbed for Sclerus' right leg, taking hold around the inside of the knee. That made it easy enough for him to lift Sclerus' right leg off the ground, at which point he rolled sideways, putting them both down. It was an elegant way out of an awkward situation, but it hadn't got him anywhere, and it was plain enough for anybody to see that Sclerus had given him a hard time with the neck grip.

I was just starting to feel quietly confident when Pentheus pulled off a manoeuvre I'd only ever heard about, and never expected to see in real life. It took me entirely by surprise, so you can imagine the effect it had on the crowd, not to mention Sclerus.

In theory, it goes like this. You face off against the other man, then crouch down, actually turning your back on him. The tricky part is grabbing hold of his wrist with both your hands as you make the turn – get that wrong and the next thing you'll see is the Ferryman's boat nudging towards you through the reeds. But if you manage to catch hold and hang on, you then use your own crouching-and-turning movement to pull the other man over your shoulder and through the air, slinging him off you like a big, heavy sack. It's called the Flying Mare, and I never dared try it myself, so I'm going purely on what other people have told me.

I guess that's what Pentheus did to Sclerus; I'm guessing, because they were turned sideways on and away from me, and it was all too quick anyway. All I saw was Pentheus apparently cringing away, followed by Sclerus sailing gracefully through the air, crashing head-first into a fence-rail and flopping like a dropped cloak.

Damn, I thought. That certainly seemed to be that; Sclerus wasn't moving, and Pentheus was slowly getting to his feet with a big, happy smile on his face. My fond dream of taking Pentheus' shattered and mangled corpse somewhere quiet and dumping it in a ditch thinned and faded like the smoke from a fire. Even so; it was the first Flying Mare I'd ever seen, and even if I wasn't impressed, my heart was. I suppose it's part of being human, you can't help feeling good when you see the little man make a fool out of the big man, even if you happen to be the big man's mother.

But if I thought Sclerus was through, I misjudged him; credit where it's due, either stamina or cold, blind fury got him back on his feet again, and after a stagger or two he managed to stay there.

'All right,' he said, mumbling past a thick lip. 'Heavy wrestling. What do you say?'

Pentheus shrugged. 'All right,' he said.

Dusa, who'd been hopping up and down with bloodthirsty joy, froze open-mouthed, then shrieked 'No!' at the top of her voice. The reaction of the rest of the crowd, however, showed that she was in a minority of one.

Do you know what heavy wrestling is, as opposed to upright wrestling? No? Well, that's fair enough. After all, you're from a much more refined and advanced nation, as you've been at pains to point out. It figures you don't go in for heavy wrestling; and all credit to you, it's a decidedly uncouth practice, not to mention crude and dangerous. I guess that's why we Sons of the Achaeans like it so much.

Heavy wrestling isn't really wrestling at all; well, you can wrestle if you like, but you can also punch, kick, bite (in theory you're not meant to, but I've never seen a games-player penalised for it) – pretty well anything that can cause pain or injury without the use of tools. Skill helps, to a certain extent; but heavy wrestling is mostly for very big, strong, nasty men who like to break bones.

It didn't take an expert to predict how Sclerus planned to fight. He had longer arms and longer legs; he'd rely on kicks and punches. Pentheus, on the other hand, would want to get in close and grapple.

Now usually, a contrast of styles like that makes for a long, boring match – the big man launches his blows, the little man stays out of his way, and nothing happens until someone makes a mistake or trips over, after which the contest is short and very one-sided.

Sclerus did just as I'd expected. He came out 'jabbing and grabbing' as the saying goes, trying to land a punch or get a grip on wrist or forearm, so he could pull Pentheus in close for a knee to the groin. Pentheus danced out of the way all right, but he danced round, not away; instead of trying to keep his distance, he was constantly trying to get in closer. It was a good tactic and he carried it out well, but Sclerus had the wit to see what he was doing and after a few passes managed to anticipate; he feinted with his fist and lashed out with his knee at where he reckoned Pentheus was going. He wasn't far out, either. Needless to say, Pentheus doubled up – but the god put it into his mind to take advantage of his misfortune by grabbing Sclerus' ankle before he could get his foot back on the ground. Sclerus wobbled as Pentheus shifted his grip to the foot itself, got both hands to it and twisted it sideways, like a man killing a chicken.

That's a truly horrible noise, a joint grinding and tearing. Sclerus looked more astonished than agonised; he was still upright, pivoting on his one good foot, and he clubbed his two fists down hard on the back of Pentheus' neck. Pentheus felt that all right; he straightened up, trying to push Sclerus over as he went; failed, and made a quick grab for Sclerus' left hand. He only got hold of one finger, but that was all he needed. The sound the bone made as it broke was a sharp click, like a well-made lock turning.

This time Sclerus screamed; but instead of falling over, he grabbed Pentheus round the shoulder with his right arm, for support as much as any hope of damaging him. It was almost as if that was what Pentheus had been playing for all along; he let his feet go, taking Sclerus down with him, then rolled on to his back, got his foot right into the pit of Sclerus' stomach and kicked for all he was worth. Sclerus shot through the air, landed on his belly, skimmed a yard or so through the dust like a flat stone on water and then lay completely, definitively still. Not hard to see why, once you'd noticed the angle of his head on his shoulders.

It was so quiet, you could have heard a rat scratching itself. I don't think Pentheus realised he'd killed Sclerus until he'd slowly and awkwardly hauled himself back up on his feet. I imagine he was wondering why everybody was so quiet after he'd just pulled off a flawless Eagle-and-Fox throw (starting, I may add, from a very difficult and unorthodox position). Must've thought we were a miserable lot, or we'd all wandered off somewhere during the fight.

Then he saw the body. He looked at it curiously, as if he'd seen something similar once upon a time, but couldn't quite place what it was. Then, in what I can only describe as a thoroughgoing breach of good taste, he walked slowly over and prodded it with his toe. Finally, he smiled – though it wasn't one of your regular smiles, having little to do with happiness.

'Well,' he said, 'that's the way it goes with me and games-playing.'

Then, I suppose, he noticed for the first time that he was bleeding. Odd that he hadn't noticed it before; maybe he'd seen it but assumed it wasn't his blood. It was the stab-wound that he'd had when we first picked him up off the road, opened up again.

All this time I hadn't stopped to think what effect all this was having on Dusa.

When I thought of it and turned round to see how she was getting on, I expected to find her shoving her way through the crowd with a strip torn off the end of somebody's cloak for a bandage. Wrong. She was standing quite still, pale as milk, with a look of horror on her face and tears running down her cheeks like a leak in a rainwater tank. Ah well; they look a bit like us, sound like we do when we're young, eat the same food and smell roughly the same in hot weather, but women are no more like us than the gods are.

It was at this point that Pentheus fell over; and, since he was nominally ours, Cleander and I nudged through the crowd and picked him up. It was rather spooky, pushing past all those still, silent people. Maybe they'd never seen anybody get killed before, or they were still debating with their hearts whether to cheer or send out for a rope. In any case, it seemed wise to us to get our wretched encumbrance out of their way before they reached a decision on the matter.

'Put him in the cart,' someone said; it was Prince Demodocus, who was looking shocked and washed out, as if he'd just lost family. Maybe he had, in a way; this Sclerus had been living in his house for five years, and there was a case for making out that he and his brother were thereby bound to take revenge for the death, even though it was accidental and in the course of a game. It looked to me as if Demodocus was trying very hard not to let that thought occur to him, since we were also his guests, and there comes a point when the rules get so hopelessly complicated that you'd have to be Nestor or Tiresias or someone like that to make head or tail of them (although this doesn't stop the Furies from haunting your dreams if you fail in your duty, something I regard as bitterly unfair).

The cart, which belonged to the farmer, though I don't suppose anybody asked him if we could borrow it, was duly wheeled out of the barn and a couple of sleepy-looking mules were backed into the collars – still nobody was moving in the crowd, though they were watching us like crows in a tall tree watching a slowly dying goat. Cleander jumped up on the box with Demodocus beside him. Sarpedon and I lugged Pentheus up over the tailgate, and we hopped on the back, at which point I noticed that Dusa wasn't with us. Fortunately, Sarpedon had noticed that too. There are times when a recklessly brave uncle has his uses, because I don't suppose I'd have been too happy to go back into that crowd for anything.

Anyway, Sarpedon strode off and reappeared a moment later towing Dusa along behind him like a tuna-net; he bundled her up on to the cart and stayed down himself, to provide a rearguard. Thus arrayed, we rattled out of the yard and through the town. Nobody followed us, thank the gods.

'Now what?' Cleander asked. Demodocus shrugged.

'I'll send some men down for the body later,' he replied. 'It's up to us to burn him, I suppose, since he didn't have anyone else in these parts. Properly speaking, we ought to send someone to Crete, let his family know.'

It was in my heart to ask him why, if he was so concerned about the man's family, he hadn't sent a message home during the five years Sclerus had been living with him; or, come to that, why he hadn't sent Sclerus himself to reclaim his birthright. But even I'm not stupid enough to ask questions like that out loud.

'Your friend,' Demodocus went on, 'how badly is he hurt? That looks like a stab-wound to me, not something you'd get in a wrestling match. Did he fall against something in the yard there?'

Of course, none of us had mentioned the circumstances of our meeting with Pentheus, or explained his state of health – well, it's not the sort of topic of conversation that arises spontaneously, and wise guests don't volunteer information, just as good hosts don't demand it. Cleander and I looked at each other.

'Difficult to say,' Cleander replied. 'I didn't see anything sharp or pointed lying about, but everything happened so fast back there—'

'Quite,' Demodocus said; and you could almost hear him debating with his heart as he drove the mules – if there was a material possibility that Sclerus had somehow palmed a knife, or hidden one somewhere in the yard, and stabbed Pentheus with it while nobody was looking, then Sclerus would be the author of his own misfortunes and Demodocus wouldn't be obliged to do anything. Obliquely raising the point and having heard nothing to contradict it, he could tell himself he'd made appropriate enquiries, and found the matter to be beyond proof. Well, it's exactly how I'd have argued it, if I'd woken up in the middle of the night and found the Sisters standing over me waving burning torches.

The prince unloaded us at the palace, gave his brother an admirably brief account of what had happened, which didn't seem to bother him in the least, and went out again to collect the body. For some reason, presumably to do with honour, both Cleander and Sarpedon offered to go with him, and he accepted. As soon as they'd gone, Dusa scuttled off into the inner room, leaving me alone with Pentheus.

'Well now,' I said. 'If I'd known bad luck followed you around like a blind puppy, I'd have made sure we left you where we found you.'

'Thank you so much,' Pentheus replied. 'If you're not going to help me, would you at least get me some water and something to bind this up with?'

'Of course,' I said. 'In fact, I know the very thing.'

Happily, nobody ever bothered to sweep or dust up among the rafters, and there were some quite magnificent spiders' webs up there if you cared to look. Pentheus took some convincing, which only went to show his ignorance; there's nothing like cobweb for stopping the flow of blood. I sacrificed the hem of an old cloak I found in a trunk in a corner, and ripped it up for a bandage. You see, I can be as nice as anything if I try.

'You don't like me,' Pentheus said, as I tied off the bandage.

'I can see how much it distresses you,' I replied. 'But I see it as a way of maintaining balance, which is the principle on which the cosmos operates, according to some. You see, my sister likes you far more than you deserve, so I dislike you rather more than your dealings with us merit.'

He scowled at me. 'That's not fair,' he said. 'I haven't done anything to encourage her. Short of spitting in her face, what else could I have done?'

'The spitting idea is good,' I answered, 'and we'll keep it in reserve in case we need it later. Right now, though, I think you may have solved the problem already, which is why I've put nice healthy cobwebs in your wound instead of wolfsbane.' I smiled pleasantly. 'I think she may have gone off you a bit, after seeing you kill that man. What on earth possessed you, anyway?'

He frowned. 'It was an accident,' he replied, 'in a fair fight.'

'Sure,' I said. 'Only you're talking to a wrestler here, not that I ever went in for the heavy stuff. You'd made two winning plays – the twisted ankle and the finger-break. You could have left it at that, but you didn't; you made the Eagle-and-Fox, and you killed him. Why?'

Pentheus was quiet for a moment. 'He didn't seem to want to give up,' he replied. 'You know as well as I do, it's a fight to a submission, not any specific injury.'

I lifted my head. 'Like hell,' I said. 'You could've given a little twist to either of those holds and had him weeping with pain, and you knew it at the time, too. Dusa knows it, what's more; she's seen me wrestle often enough. More to the point, she's seen me do things like you did, though I never went so far as to kill anybody, or even leave them permanently damaged. Oh yes, I know what it feels like, that urge to add a little more pain. You know you've done enough, but you've got the man helpless under your hand, and Anger snuggles into your heart and says, Go on, hurt him a little more, you're allowed to. Maybe it's because he's thrown you well and made you look a fool, or he hurt you with one of his plays, or maybe you just don't like him very much, the way he walks or wears his tunic. Dusa's seen me give that extra little tweak or twist, in the tiny moment after the man's opened his mouth to say he's through, but I'd turn the words into a scream, just because I could.' I sat back and rested my head against the wall. 'Maybe that's why I quit wrestling – because I didn't like what I was doing to people, or I didn't like the way my sister looked at me once or twice. Anyway, the point is, you can't fool her or me.'

He looked away. 'I can see that,' he said.

'Good. So what was it? You don't have to answer, but I'm curious. Do you get pleasure out of hurting people? You wouldn't be the only one.'

He looked mustard at me. 'Gods, no,' he said. 'I've had enough people try to hurt me in my life, of course I don't enjoy it.' He leaned forward to put his head in his hands, but the movement hurt him and he leaned slowly back. 'The truth is,' he said, 'I was showing off. I wanted to make the Eagle-and-Fox play – I was looking for it all through the bout, but he didn't give me an opening. So I created one.'

I nodded. 'It wasn't the obvious play from where you'd got to,' I said. 'So I believe you. But why was it so important? You wanted to humiliate him? To look good in front of the crowd?'

He lifted his head again. 'No,' he said. 'I just wanted to be the best, that's all.'

'To be the best,' I repeated.

'That's right.' He smiled wanly. 'You know that bit in the Trojan story, where the King of Lycia tells his cousin about what it means to be a prince; where he says that in return for all the privileges, the palace and the gardens and orchards and land, and the respect of the people – do you know the bit I'm talking about?'

I nodded. 'And the prince explains that in return for all that, the prince is obliged to fight always in the front rank, always to be the best. Is that what you really believe?'

'Yes.'

I frowned. 'But you're not a prince,' I said. 'You're a stray, a landless man, an outsider. You don't have that obligation.'

He looked at me. 'But I should have,' he said. 'I should be a prince, a man of the better sort. Dammit, I can do what a prince does; I can fight and play games, I lower my head to no one. If I wasn't meant to be a prince or a king, how come the god gave me a better man's skills? How come I'm minded like a prince, if I'm meant to be a beggar?'

I sighed. 'And that's why you insisted on making the grand play,' I said. 'Because you wanted to be the best. And now you've killed someone, and we're on a razor's edge in this city – we never asked to get involved with you, so why should we have to put up with the consequences of your actions?' He tried to speak, but I overrode him. 'I'll tell you one thing,' I said, raising my voice a little, 'whether or not you were meant to be a nobleman when the Fates twisted your thread, you've got the heart and mind of a games-player. And that, coming from me, isn't a compliment.'

He started to get angry; but Anger couldn't seem to get a foothold in his heart. 'I think you're right,' he said. 'I measure everything against myself; is it too high for me to jump or too far for me to run, can I take that man in a heavy bout or would he take me? That's a games-player's heart for you, I guess, always competing.' He grinned. 'Always striving to be the best, no matter what. It's probably just as well there's so few of us, and we get so few chances to be what we are.'

'When somebody dies,' I said. 'But of course my brother and I are going to change all that.'

He closed his eyes and stretched his legs out. 'I'll miss the Argive games now,' he said. 'I'm sorry, that probably makes me sound like what you think I am. But I didn't mean to kill anybody, and I'd have liked to play in the games.'

I stood up; I was starting to get cramp in my knees. 'Games are ambivalent,' I said, 'like all things are. It's like the Good Strife and the Bad Strife, in the poem; Bad Strife makes you greedy and jealous, Good Strife makes you strive to better yourself. But they're both the same thing, it's just a matter of whether you come at it from the light or the shadows. Listen to me,' I added, 'a moment ago I was telling you to stay clear of my sister, now I'm spouting poetry at you. I'm beginning to wonder which one of us got banged on the head today.'

He laughed. 'You're a games-player too,' he said. 'You understand.'

'Good Strife and Bad Strife,' I answered.

'Fair enough,' he said. 'But which of us is which?'

CHAPTER TEN

'I'm not doubting your word or anything like that,' the Phoenician said carefully, 'but are you sure you're telling us exactly what you and he said to each other all those years ago? Or are you making it up – the actual words, I mean, not the gist of it all.'

Cratus frowned. 'You mean, am I lying?'

The Phoenician wished he'd never started this. 'I wouldn't say lying—'

'That's just as well.'

'It's just—' the Phoenician blundered on, feeling like a man walking further and further into a quicksand. 'Well, if it was me, I'm sure I couldn't tell you the exact words I used talking to someone thirty years ago, or precisely what someone else said to me. So if I was telling a story like you're doing, I'd use the sort of words he and I would've been likely to use, and I'd do my best to get across the meaning of what we were saying, the best I could remember it.'

Cratus' frown grew slightly deeper. 'In other words,' he said, 'you'd lie.'

'I beg your pardon?'

'You'd make up stuff and pretend it was what was actually said. Yes?'

'That's one way of putting it, I suppose.'

'Yes or no?'

'All right, then,' the Phoenician admitted. 'Yes.'

Cratus' frown dissipated a little, like a swarm of wasps scattered by a slight breeze on a still day. 'Thank you,' he said. 'I'll try to bear that in mind if ever I have dealings with you or your countrymen. Are you trying to tell me that you *can't* remember conversations?'

'Yes.'

'Oh.' Cratus looked surprised, but shrugged it off. 'In which case I'm sorry for you. It must make life difficult, having a bad memory.'

The Phoenician told himself not to let any of this irritate him – it's a primitive culture, they're like children compared to us. 'I think my memory is perfectly normal,' he replied. 'Obviously you've got an exceptionally good memory. And you, Cleander, as well. Maybe it's something you Sons of the Achaeans all share.'

'My heart tells me,' Palamedes interrupted, 'that it might be something to do with your scratches-on-wax you keep going on about.'

The Phoenician stifled a sigh. That was another topic he really wished he hadn't raised. 'How so?' he asked, as politely as he could.

'Stands to reason,' someone else put in. 'It's like muscles. If you do a lot of arm work, like a smith or a shipwright, you build up strong arms. If you have an accident and you're laid up six months and can't work at all, your arms wither and get puny. Same with the memory. If you don't use it, because you store all kinds of stuff that needs to be remembered actually outside your head – like on bits of wood, or whatever it is you do – then maybe your memory withers, because you aren't using it.'

'Possibly,' the Phoenician replied. 'Though I'd turn your analogy round: you people live in cities, you have to remember a lot of things, far more than you would if you were just wanderers or nomads. But where we developed the scratches on wood to help us remember things, you have to store it all in your heads; so your memories have grown stronger, like the shipwright's arms.'

Palamedes laughed. 'I'll say one thing for you people,' he said, 'you're rather more tactful than we are, as a rule. You phrased that so you could uphold the honour of your people without actually insulting us. Very good. Does that mean you're going to take Cratus' word for it that he can remember those conversations, from all those years ago?'

'Yes,' the Phoenician replied. 'I am.'

Palamedes shook his head. 'Rather you than me,' he replied. 'These days I'm hard put to it to remember what month we're in. Still, it's all right, because it doesn't really matter. What difference does it make whether they're exactly the right words or just something similar? It's whether it's a good story that counts in the end. If it's a boring story nobody'll remember it, no matter how accurately it's told.'

If Cratus is going to sulk (Cleander said, after a while), I suppose I'd better carry on with the story. While we're on the subject, I can remember nearly every word of conversations I had – what, fifty years ago. Nearly remember, mind; only problem is, I can't always be sure which are the bits I'm remembering and which are the bits I've forgotten and mended, so to speak, with words of my own. Am I repeating what I heard fifty years ago or what I put in to patch up the bit I found I'd forgotten forty years ago? Search me.

Anyway, there we were. The business with Pentheus and that rogue – Sclerus, yes, I'd forgotten that was his name till Cratus reminded me just now – that business had more or less sorted itself out, more by luck and forbearance than judgement on our part. We got away with it, is about all you could say about that.

Cratus wasn't the only one who was worried about Dusa getting infatuated with Pentheus; but that looked like it had sorted itself out too. When she finally came out from the inner room, she didn't say a word to him or even look at him, just grabbed a basket from one of the men and started handing bread round – looked away when it was his turn. We didn't say anything, of course. Best left alone, the whole thing.

To my heart's astonishment and great joy, the atmosphere in Demodocus' house was actually improved as far as we were concerned by a visit from Alastor and Tachys. They'd lost our scent around the time we ran into Pentheus; they'd been chasing round trying to find us, and turned up looking tired, ragged and disreputable in the middle of the night. We were all still up – one of Demodocus' people was telling a good story, and we'd lost track of the time – when we heard what sounded like a frenzied banging on the doors, as if a crowd of people were trying to break them down. Demodocus jumped up and sent a boy for his sword and shield; we all grabbed weapons or things we could hit with before the doors were opened. Of course, we knew who it was, but we kept our faces shut. Turned out that Tachys – of course, Tachys – had fallen over a stone in the road and damaged his ankle; he'd hobbled a day and a half, and then Alastor and one of the men had had to carry him. As a result, Alastor was in a bad mood and forgetful of his manners; he pushed in, rather than waiting to be asked, and started ordering Demodocus' people about, sending them for wine and a bowl of water and chairs and what-have-you, as if he was in his own house. The fool. To begin with he didn't notice we were there until Dusa, showing the first signs of life we'd had out of her since the wrestling-match, jumped up with the wine-jug and greeted them both as old, dear friends. These men, she explained sweetly, were our fellow-countrymen from Elis, friends of ours from way back. Rather self-consciously, Demodocus warmed up his welcome a little, giving the distinct impression that if we hadn't vouched for them, he'd have had them put in the barn for the night. I think Tachys was wise to what she was up to, but he was too far gone in self-pity to care; Alastor, on the other hand, missed the point completely (spending any length of time with Tachys in a complaining mood can do that to a man, we knew that from experience); he scarcely waited until he'd stopped eating and drinking before he launched into his Terrible Warning to our host, about how we were trying to snare respectable people into joining this idiotic scheme of ours.

Clearly they hadn't heard of the Argive games.

Anyway, by any standards Alastor overstated his case. My guess is, he let his heart run away with him, working out his store of irritation and bad temper in his attack on us. If he'd been himself, I'm sure he'd have noticed that he'd lost the sympathy of his audience at a very early stage, but fortunately for us the god blinded him to

Demodocus' mustard frowns – embarrassment first, followed in short order by downright anger – until he'd baled all the malice out of his heart and was waiting for a response.

Demodocus started by saying that it was a pity Alastor lacked the manners to refrain from insulting his guests and friends to their faces under his roof; having a rather more traditional view of hospitality, he went on, he was prepared to put it out of his mind if we were (of course, we said; we were gloriously magnanimous about it) and offer Alastor and his friend the welcome of the house for the next day or so, until we all set off for the annual games at Argos . . .

I remember one time when Cratus and I were young men, watching Cratus getting his face slapped by a girl. He really wasn't expecting it – he thought the treaty was as good as made, all over bar the libations, and then whack, right across the cheek; she was wearing one of those old-style heavy coiled-wire gold rings, as I recall, which must have stung like anything. Anyway, the exhibition of stunned dismay on his face was the closest thing I've ever seen to the look on Alastor's face when Demodocus mentioned the Argive games. Demodocus decided to interpret it as a request for further details, and started telling him all about the games, with particular reference to what a good idea it was, games with nobody dead. He concluded by saying that he was extremely pleased to have been invited to the games at Elis, which sounded just like the Argive games, except that they promised to be bigger and better; doubtless, he said, we'd all of us meet up again then, at which time he'd be pleased to accept Alastor's hospitality in return for his own.

The kindest thing you could have done for Alastor at that moment was take him out the back of the house and bury him in the dung-heap, like you do with a dead dog. I almost felt sorry for him – except that it'd have been wrong in the sight of the gods, who ordained that we should love our friends and hate our enemies.

They were both fairly quiet after that, apart from the occasional groan of misery from Tachys and a few sneezes from Alastor after he ate too much garlic. For our part, we were feeling quite pleased with ourselves – I for one was glad to see Dusa looking a bit more like her old, troublemaking self – which may explain why, although I noticed Alastor staring at Pentheus when he thought nobody was looking, I didn't think anything of it. I suppose the gods were trying to be fair. I hate it when they do that.

If you'd told me when I was a kid that one day I'd visit Argos . . . Just goes to show how much we lose when we grow up. It's an interesting balance, that; the gains and the losses. Try to work it out from a practical point of view, as if you were looking at a patch of waste land on your boundary, trying to decide whether to take it in hand, build terraces – you'd figure out likely yields and returns, ask yourself if it's worth the effort and the seedcorn. Well; we gain so much as we take our lives in hand, but the expenditure – and the losses . . . If you could make a decision, standing on the boundary of childhood, looking at the future, which way would you go? Would you risk the losses to make the gains, or would your heart ask you if there was anything you stood to gain that'd make up for what you stood to lose?

Well, fortunately the question doesn't arise, or else the chances are you'd have to walk halfway to Tegea to find a grown-up. The point being, it was only after we'd set out, and we were bumping along the Argos road in one of Demodocus' chariots, that my heart suddenly pointed out to me where we were going – Argos, for the gods' sakes; the oldest city in the world. The nurse of heroes. The second cradle of the Sons of the Achaeans. And all I could think about was games-players. If the little boy I once was had seen me then and known what was in my heart, he'd have knocked my eye out with a stone.

On the way from Asine to Argos, we stopped in a small village under a hill. Demodocus jumped down and waved to us to follow him, and we trudged up the hill till we came to the top. There were a few blocks of stone there, poking up out of the dirt.

'See that?' Demodocus asked.

'Sure,' Cratus replied. 'What is it?'

Demodocus smiled. 'Tiryns,' he said.

Tiryns . . . You could have knocked me over by blowing in my ear. Of course, I knew that Tiryns was somewhere near Argos – the three great strongholds of the Sons of the Achaeans: Mycenae, Tiryns, Argos. But it didn't make sense.

'Where's the rest of it?' I asked.

Demodocus pointed down at the dirt. 'There,' he said. 'Buried. Or scattered about there.' He waved his arms towards the village below, with its clutter of houses, barns, storage towers and low stone walls parcelling out the home fields. 'Look at any of the houses around here, you'll find bits of the stones the Giants used when they built Tiryns – far bigger than any stones we use nowadays, and they cut them as straight as a plumb-line and fitted them together without mortar. When I was a boy, a few of us came up here with an old man, and he showed us where to dig; we dug right down into this hill, and just when we were about to give up and go home, we broke through into the ceiling of a house – deep in the hill, I promise you, you've never seen the like. Well, we lit some torches and dropped down through; the old man said that when he was our age, he'd come here with his father and they'd found gold and bronze and all sorts of treasure, stuff the Giants had made, just lying about on the floor. That got us interested all right, but there was nothing like that; instead there was this enormous room, one room that was bigger than the entire palace at Asine. It had the most incredible painted pictures on the walls – painted on plaster, and if you touched them, they just turned into dust and fell on the floor like spilt flour – men and women and chariots and horses, men jumping over the backs of bulls, flowers and processions and I don't know what else; all things the Giants made, before the Sons of the Achaeans ever came here. I tell you, we're children compared with what they must have been.'

'Evidently,' Cratus said. 'Which begs the question: if they were so strong and clever, and their city was so beautiful, why the hell did they bury it under the ground and go away?'

Demodocus smiled. 'I haven't the faintest idea,' he said. 'It's not like at Mycenae; friends of mine have been there, poking about like we were doing, and they told me that all they found was old ash and cinders and blackened stones, as if the whole city had been burned to the ground.'

I scratched my head. 'None of this makes sense,' I said. 'I can see where even a great and splendid city might burn down; well, we went to Pylos—'

'Pylos?' Demodocus raised an eyebrow. 'What about it?'

'Have you been there?' I asked.

'No,' Demodocus replied. 'Always wanted to, never got round to it. Why?'

'Don't bother,' I told him. 'It's gone. Burned down. Nothing but ruins.'

'You don't say.' Demodocus looked astonished. 'What happened?'

I shrugged. 'No idea. Can't even tell you when it happened.'

'My grandfather went there,' Demodocus replied, 'so it can't have been that long ago. Oh well, that's one ambition I'll never realise. You've told me something I didn't know, anyway.'

'There you are,' I said. 'And I can see how a city might burn down and be destroyed, like I was saying; but who in their right minds would go to all the trouble of burying the ruins under all this dirt? It'd take years and years and thousands of people.'

'The Giants weren't like us,' Demodocus said. 'And since we don't know anything about them, it's pointless speculating, because we'll never understand them. When I first came here, I guessed that the Giants had decided to go away but planned on coming back some day; so they buried their beautiful city to keep it safe, the way you might bury your family treasure during a war, or if you were likely to be away for several years. That bothered me, actually; what if the Giants came home, and found out that we'd been digging holes in their roof? Anybody as big and strong as they obviously were, you wouldn't want to make them angry.'

Dusa yawned and stretched, a sure sign she was getting bored. 'Well,' she said, 'if there's no gold and treasure left, we might as well be getting on.'

I smiled. 'You aren't curious, then?' I asked her.

'It's a few bits of stone,' she said, 'and a pile of dirt covering some fallen-down old buildings. So what?'

I shrugged. 'It's very old,' I said.

'So will I be, if I stay here much longer. Come on, let's go to Argos.' She stopped, and looked back. 'Argos is still there, isn't it?' she asked. 'We're not going to get there and find that someone's taken it away and put it somewhere safe, in case it gets stolen or dropped or anything?'

Demodocus nodded gravely. 'Argos is still there,' he said. 'At least, it was last time I looked.'

Dusa frowned. 'I bet someone said that about Pylos,' she said.

Argos is big (Cleander continued). It lies on the south-western slopes of one of two mountains that flank the road to Sparta, looking out over a plain that's so fat and rich you wouldn't want to stand on it for too long, for fear your sandals might take root and start growing up your legs.

Big, but not pretty. Excuse me if I sound like I've been out without a hat; some cities smile at you when you walk up to them. Argos frowns. It's not sure it wants your sort in it. I'm talking about the city now, not the people; by and large, the people are all right. But Argos the city's been there so long that it doesn't necessarily think the same way its people do. My heart tells me it looks down its nose at you as you walk under the gate; it's seen the likes of Atreus and Agamemnon and Orestes in its time, and it's not sure you measure up to its high standards.

You can ignore it; you can stick your tongue out at the walls, say, 'I'm coming in, and there's nothing you can do about it.' But that stare of disapproval, it'd get to you after a while, if you were planning to stay there more than a day or so. My guess is that when a city gets too big and too old, it gets ideas above its station, starts imagining that the people are there to look after it, not the other way round. When it gets to that point, maybe a good fire, or burying the bugger, would be the right way to go.

About the Argives, though. Living in a city that's so old and so grand and so very big – someone told me there's the best part of five thousand people living in Argos; can you imagine that, five thousand people all living together in one place? Crazy – you'd think they'd be grand and standoffish and distant. Not a bit of it. I was feeling a little apprehensive about having anything to do with them, but the fact is, they're just straight, simple folks – it's as if they're grimly determined to be ordinary, living in the shadow of all that grandeur. It makes you feel like you're in some great man's house and you're talking to his household and his servants, the lower orders, while you wait for the great man himself and his sons and retainers to come back from the hunt.

You're here for the games, then; that's what everybody said to us, as soon as they saw we weren't locals. And when we said, Yes, thank you, that's right, they all beamed at us with big smiles you could have stored a winter's supply of grain in; they were delighted that we'd come to their games, even more so when we told them where we were from, how far we'd come – we didn't get around to pointing out that we hadn't come all that way just for the Argive games, but that was what they all assumed. The more I heard and saw, the happier I felt; it was as plain as anything, the games meant so much to these people, made them feel quite ridiculously proud and good about themselves. If we could get anything like this sort of feeling going in Elis, the whole scheme might actually work.

The drill was, Demodocus said, that we should go to the palace, pay our respects to the king, give him his present, in the usual way; he'd then invite us to stay with him while the games were on; we'd thank him kindly for the offer, but say, No, if it's all the same to you we're planning to stay with some friends of ours down in the city. That way, he'd be free of his obligations of hospitality without having his house turned into a cattle-stall.

We'd actually be sleeping in a tent. This wouldn't be a hardship; Demodocus had brought along the tent his grandfather had built for taking to the wars – it was a great big thing made of proofed hides neatly sewn together, with plenty of space for all of us, our gear, the chariots and horses, the lot. Everybody pitched their tents in a ring around the plain where the games were to be held; it's a lovely place and exactly right for the purpose, just outside the town looking up the hill, where there's a flat spot under the lee of the rise. That means the spectators can sit on the slope and get a good view of what's going on in the middle, rather than the neck of the man in front.

I remember next to nothing about the King of Argos, I'm afraid, and not much more about his palace. I'm sure they were both impressive enough if only you could get to see them, but there were so many people milling about the place that all I could see of the palace were the beams of the roof, while we were whisked in front of and past His Majesty as if we were jars of olives on our way to the press. I think he was called Tisamenus; the kings of Argos usually are. I suppose it's got the benefit of continuity, having all your kings with the same name, and the convenience outweighs the confusion.

We all lent a hand getting the tent up – Demodocus thanked us for our help, because of which (he said) the job had taken twice as long as usual. The king had given us a sheep, a couple of goats and two big jars of wine and flour (everybody got the same; shows what a rich man he was), so we killed the sheep and dressed it out, made the bread and sat down to dinner. We'd had a long day and we were all happily tired, if you know what I mean.

After dinner we went and called on the tent next door, which belonged to a man called Gorgias, who told us he came from Lerna, a small place to the south-west we'd passed through on our way. He was happy enough to meet us and we got on well; but I couldn't help noticing the interest he was taking in Pentheus, as if he'd come across him before but wasn't sure if he remembered him. That made me feel a little apprehensive, but I told my heart that Pentheus, like the rest of us, was here as the guest of the Prince of Asine, who seemed to be both known and respected in Argos, so it was unlikely that anything bad was going to happen; besides, one of the rules of the games was that nobody was allowed to carry on feuds or grudges or wars while the games were on, or while travelling through Argive territory to or from the games, and I got the impression that everybody took this rule very seriously. Even if we did bump into some of Pentheus' enemies, it was highly unlikely there'd be any trouble; and it ought to be within our capabilities to give them the slip before the truce ended. I told my heart not to worry about it.

This Gorgias, by all accounts, was a mighty boxer. He certainly had a boxer's face, but that's no guarantee of ability, just of participation at some time or other. I could get a boxer's face any time I like, just by picking a fight with twelve strong men or walking into a water-pump. Rather more convincing proof was his habit of stopping in the middle of whatever he was saying, blinking a couple of times and then starting again, saying the same thing but in a different way. They say that when a man's been bashed on the chin many, many times over the course of many years, his mind gets dizzy and loses its way along a path of thought. My brother Cratus dabbled in boxing when he was a young man. I thought I'd just mention that, in passing.

We asked Gorgias if he was taking part; he said he wasn't quite sure yet, it depended on whether someone else whose name escapes me turned up in time. If he didn't get to play, he added, he wouldn't be absolutely heartbroken, since he'd heard that the Corinthian champion was going to be there, and this character had an unfortunate habit of killing his opponents, or at the very least knocking out all their teeth and at least one eye. There was no malice in it, Gorgias went on; it was just that the Corinthian's fist was harder than anybody else's skull. The lad had taken to boxing, so the story went, after his father had come upon him at ploughing, hammering a loose nail back into the plough handle with the heel of his hand.

Were any of us taking part, Gorgias asked; I was about to say no when Pentheus spoke up, taking care to avoid looking where he might see Demodocus' face or cut himself on Dusa's eyes. He quite fancied having a go at the long-jump, Pentheus said, and maybe, possibly one of the wrestling events, if there were still places.

Gorgias replied that he was sure there were, and told Pentheus what to do in order to enter; Demodocus stood up in the middle of the explanation and made let's-go-home-now noises, but it was already too late; and when the rest of us trooped back to the tent, Pentheus nipped smartly off under the pretext of being sick; he was heading for the tent of the games-marshal, as described to him by the annoying, helpful Gorgias.

'It's all right,' Dusa said icily, and in a loud, clear voice, 'perhaps this time he'll be the one who gets his silly head knocked off, and that'll be a stroke of luck for the Peloponnese.'

I should have been pleased to hear a remark like that coming from her, but I wasn't; it was said with that chilly, razor-sharp distaste that tells you plain as a bell that here's a woman in the third or fourth stage of the usual cycle of infatuation, the part where passionate attraction turns to utter distaste; it can last anything from a few days to half a year, but it always turns back again. In fact, I hadn't realised until she said it exactly how deep the little flying hooligan had stuck his arrow in my sister.

(Have you ever noticed, by the way, that the nastiest and most offensive of the pests sent by the gods to afflict us always seem to have wings? The Furies, the Harpies, the Diseases, Rumour and Love, all winged like eagles and able to swoop down on us out of a limpid blue sky, so fast there's nothing we can hope to do about it?)

I didn't sleep all that well, and when I did finally slip away, a dream came and stood over me all the time.

Annoyingly, the dream took the shape of King Leon; and he was crying his eyes out, so that the tears ran down his cheeks and were caught up in his beard like sheep in a thorn fence. He was crying, he told me, because of the death of his son, a homeless and landless exile cast out of his kingdom and inheritance by greedy noblemen and the hostility of the people. After drifting aimlessly through the Peloponnese, the dream said, the poor boy finally met his end lying beside the road, gut-stabbed and broken-headed, while strangers stepped over him on their way to the famous games at Argos.

I woke up with a crick in my neck and a slight headache to find that it was almost dawn and my companions were already up, washed, oiled and breakfasted, and that Pentheus wasn't there; he'd left a short while before I opened my eyes, and gone down to loosen up with the weights in good time for the long-jump.

I told my heart not to worry about that for now, and went out with the rest of them to watch the opening ceremony. For one thing, I was curious to see what they did; how do you start off games without a funeral? I'd already given the matter some thought, but the best I could come up with was a sacrifice and a hymn or two; you can't go wrong with a sacrifice, because it lets people know that sooner or later there'll be roast meat going the rounds, which encourages them to stick around and get their share.

The Argives, it turned out, had solved the problem rather elegantly, and I resolved to steal the idea and use it myself.

I was standing outside the tent, taking a breath or two of fresh air and gazing sleepily at the field, when someone blew a trumpet, terribly loudly, not far away from me. While I was still wincing as if I'd been hit with a wet fish, a rather splendid procession set off from the marshal's tent; first, some very grave-looking old men with long white beards, then a couple of priests prodding three white oxen, followed by a gaggle of healthy-looking young men, clearly the games-players themselves. While they were marching slowly and gracefully across the field, some other men were quickly putting together an altar – basically a big, jagged rock (someone told me later that it was one of those rocks that fall out of the sky from time to time; they're either the blades of Zeus' thunderbolts or, as some people would have you believe, the gallstones of the gods) with a little wooden ladder and a low platform of planks for the priests to stand on. When the procession reached the altar, the priests stepped up and made the sacrifices; then the grave old men lined up in front of them and repeated a ferocious-sounding oath, all about how they swore to judge the contests fairly and without favour, on pain of terrifying-sounding punishments on the other side of the River. After they'd done that, the games-players took their place and swore an even longer and grander oath, saying that they were the flower of the Sons of the Achaeans, come together to honour Hera of the Argives with offerings of their skill, strength and goodwill, and they swore to do their very best, without cheating or losing their temper; if they kept their oath, they said, may Hera grant them to live for ever in the minds of men; but if they broke it, may She wipe out their names from mortal memory as the sea wipes away footprints in the sand. Then the trumpeter made another loud and raucous noise, and the spectators – there were ever so many of them, several thousand at least – all started cheering at once. It was really rather moving, the whole thing.

'Come on,' Demodocus said, 'let's cross over to the hill and find somewhere to sit. If we're not quick, we'll end up at the back and won't be able to hear the boxers.'

Well, that would never do – where's the fun in a boxing match if you can't hear the bones break? – so we scuttled along behind him like baby ducks, and he found us a place to sit where we could see everything.

'Just a moment,' I said, once we'd sat down and arranged our things where we could get at them. 'It's just occurred to me. Aren't you taking part? I'd assumed—'

'Me?' Demodocus smiled. 'I don't think so. I took part last year and got comprehensively beaten. The standard here's very high, you know.'

That didn't please me, since he'd readily agreed to take part in *our* games; that implied that our games weren't going to be anything like as good as these. If that attitude was shared by the rest of the Argives, chances were these fine games-players weren't going to bother tramping all the way to Elis, and we'd have wasted our time coming.

I put those thoughts out of my mind, however, because the first event was about to begin.

A herald stepped up and called out a list of names for the foot-race, while two of the judges solemnly paced out the distance and marked the limits of the course with little piles of stones. Then they beckoned to a group of porters, who carried out the prizes for the race on a big figure-of-eight shield. Some prizes: there was a beautiful helmet, gilded, made in the Argive fashion with a tall one-piece crown, broad earflaps and a high crest; a magnificent silver belt with a purple sash; and an enormous four-handled gold cup for the winner. I looked at the stuff and nearly burst into tears, thinking of the sort of junk that we'd be able to offer.

What can you say about a foot-race? The fastest man won, closely followed by the next fastest, with the third fastest not so far behind. After it was over and the winners had caught their breath, they were ushered over to the big gilt and ivory chair where the king was sitting, and he handed them their prizes, while the herald called out their names and where they were from. I made sure I'd committed the names to memory – I can't have done all that wonderful a job, because I can't recall any of them now – and poured a drop of wine into a little horn cup that Demodocus had put there for me.

Next up was the boxing; and there among the competitors, looking as scared as a polecat in a deep ditch, was our friend of the previous evening, Gorgias. They decided who was going to fight who by drawing tallies; each man made a distinctive mark on a bit of sheep's horn, and all these tallies were put in a helmet. The judges pulled out two at a time, and that's how they decided the pairings. I kept my eye on Gorgias; when he heard the name of his opponent, he closed his eyes and let his head drop forward a little, like a man who hears he's about to be put to death.

The Argives don't box quite like we do; they allow stabbing with the fingertips and blows beneath the neck, which are reserved up here for the heavy wrestling matches. Now, unlike most people, I don't find boxing particularly interesting to watch; strikes me that in the average boxing match, all you get to see is two men walking in circles round each other for the time it takes for an experienced man to yoke up a pair of oxen, followed by a very quick flurry of movement, followed by one of the two men falling over. Blink and you'll miss the good bit; and even then, you really do have to know what to look for. That's why it's important to be near the front, so you can hear the crunching noises. It's the only reliable way of keeping track of what's happening.

The first round of fights were all pretty typical of this pattern, and were soon over. The second round lasted a little longer, but not much; in fact, it was only the last fight of all that made any kind of spectacle. To my surprise, and moderate joy, one of the two finalists was none other than our neighbour Gorgias. The other man was some huge giant by the name of Dercyon. I can't remember where he was from, but it wasn't Corinth.

Even from where we were sitting, I could tell that Gorgias was petrified, if only because of the trouble the heralds had in getting him to keep his hands still while they bound them up with the rawhide bandages. There is, of course, quite an art to wrapping a boxer's fists; ideally, you want the turns to overlap, leaving one edge of each turn exposed, thereby producing a surface like the edge of a rasp. This makes it much easier to inflict those helpful cuts around the eyebrows that drip blood in the other man's eyes and blind him at crucial moments. If ever you're watching a boxing match, spare a glance for the man who's waiting to fight the winner. Chances are he'll be fiddling with his bandages, the knot gripped in his teeth, as he struggles to get the lie of the turns just right.

When Gorgias walked out into the middle, he had an expression on his face like a servant on his way to confess that, yes, he was the one who left the pen-gate open and let the goats get into the vineyard. The other man, this Dercyon, looked very calm indeed; so calm as to be just this side of dead. I couldn't see the match lasting very long, so, although I was dying for a leak, I resolved to sit tight and watch, so I wouldn't miss the action.

Bad mistake on my part. Gorgias sensibly resolved to take the initiative while he was still reasonably fresh, get his punches in while he still had them, and try to put Dercyon down with a lucky shot before he had a chance to get going. Predictably, Dercyon decided to sit out the storm and let Gorgias wear himself out; some of the punches he managed to take on his hands and arms, but the ones that got through and landed on his face didn't seem to trouble him unduly. Even a smart, loud smack on the chin had no more effect than a thumb's length of head movement. In a way it was quite awe-inspiring, watching a human being soak up all that force without even blinking.

Gorgias wasn't a fool; he knew that as soon as he slowed down, he was going to get hit very hard. So he didn't slow down. If anything, he got faster and more furious. That was pretty inspiring too, after it reached the point where his muscles must have been completely exhausted and it could only have been fear and the god breathing strength into his heart that kept him moving. It was as if some god had scooped the moment up in his hand and was holding it clear of the flow of time. There seemed to be no reason why either of them should ever stop doing what they were doing, and even the gnawing pain in my bladder didn't seem to matter terribly much.

How long this strange state of events went on for, I really couldn't say – it was like those bits of your childhood that, in recollection, seemed to have lasted for ever, but when you think about it you realise it was only one or two years at most; when the end came, I'd virtually lulled myself to sleep. With hindsight, I guess that Gorgias must somehow have managed to land a considerable number of blows on exactly the same spot, and it was the cumulative effect rather than one mighty freak punch that made Dercyon suddenly stagger. Anyway, stagger he did; and just before he went down, he let fly with an enormous swishing slash, which quite by chance connected with Gorgias' chin. If his fist had made contact, I reckon Gorgias' head would've been snapped off his shoulders like an apple off the tree. Instead it was Dercyon's forearm that did the damage, and the thick pad of muscle cushioned the blow enough to save our new friend's life.

However it happened, the outcome was that both men were asleep before they touched the ground, and both of them landed nose-down in the dust at precisely the same moment. Oddest thing you ever saw; and I don't think you'd ever see the like if you lived to be a hundred and watched boxing every day of your life.

There was complete silence from the crowd for a heartbeat or so; then everybody started muttering at once. From the spectators' point of view it was a terrible outcome; the amount of wealth in the form of wagers riding on the event was probably enough to ransom the King of Egypt, and nobody had the faintest idea who'd won. It would be up to the judges to decide, and I for one didn't envy them the job. Actually, they were very sensible about it; they sent out a herald to announce that since both men had hit the ground simultaneously, by the ancient rules of boxing neither of them could have won, and the contest was therefore void. This meant that all bets were off, and although nobody won, nobody lost either, and everybody kept their tempers. My guess is that the judges saved a fair few lives that day.

It's a curious thing, though; we watched a lot of games, played by a lot of very fine games-players, but the only event I remember at all clearly was that boxing match; and it's stayed in my mind not because the fighters displayed any unusual degree of skill or did any great deeds, but simply because of a bizarre turn of luck. I can't help thinking, where's the point in being the best, when a moment of pure farce drives out all your glorious achievements and leaves you in the dark, on the wrong side of the River?

After the boxing came the wrestling.

'It's a curious thing,' Sarpedon whispered to me as the herald called out the names. 'If I was on the run from a serious blood-feud, only a step or two ahead of the enemy's hired killers, I'm not sure I'd care to be standing in the middle of a public place with a man shouting out my name so everybody could hear it.'

I couldn't help but agree; all the more so because it was common knowledge that there were men from Corinth present, and weren't Pentheus' enemies supposed to be Corinthians? On the other hand, there was the truce; so long as the games were on, he was as safe as it's possible for a mortal to be, if you discounted the threat of death or mutilation at the hands of his fellow wrestlers.

As it turned out, Pentheus' time in the middle was very short indeed. He'd been drawn against the Argive champion, one of the king's younger brothers, and all we saw of him was a vague blur as he was bounced round the middle like one of those sewn-up bladders kids use for playing catch. After the prince had finished with him, we collected what was left and lugged it back to the tent to make up its mind whether it was going to live or die, while we went back and watched the rest of the match.

Actually, he wasn't badly hurt at all; no broken bones, just a few bruises and a fairly serious case of squashed pride. I was afraid that the public defeat and humiliation might have a bad effect on Dusa – why it is, I don't know, but eight times out of ten a spectacular hiding makes the heart grow fonder – but I kept a close eye on her and there didn't seem to be any danger signs. She didn't go back to the tent; instead she stayed put and watched the wrestlers smash and crush each other into bloody messes with obvious signs of enjoyment. That's a woman for you, I suppose.

As I think I mentioned just now, I've forgotten most of what happened in the games. I was preoccupied, I guess; what with Pentheus, and Dusa, and trying to commit all the names and cities of the players to memory, and wondering how we were going to set about recruiting them once the games were over. Potentially, we had a chance there to conclude our mission in one dramatic splurge of recruiting. If we could secure enough of the players who were taking part at these games, it was as good as grain in the jar that they'd go home and spread the word for us, in effect do our job without any help from us, and probably better than we could do it. We were as close as a man tickling trout – we could see the quarry, we could reach out and touch it, if only we could be sure of keeping hold of what we grabbed. Or we could get it wrong and throw away all the work we'd done since we left Elis, if we somehow managed to give offence. Then the word would spread through the whole Peloponnese like rot through a jar of figs, and wherever we went after that, we'd be given our dinner in the barn and immediately sent on our way.

Small wonder, then, that I didn't have much mind left to pay to what was going on in the middle. My dear uncle, on the other hand, was completely engrossed in it all; Dusa was thoroughly relishing anything with blood in it; even Cratus looked as if he was enjoying himself. At first I felt a bit annoyed, as if they'd all bunked off during the middle of haymaking and left me to pick up and load the wagon. That passed, though. It stood to reason that if we were going to charm and seduce all these games-players into joining us, at least one of us would have to know such details as who won what and who beat the stuffing out of who. Otherwise we'd be bound to say the wrong thing sooner or later and find ourselves in deep trouble. Looked at that way, it was a fair division of labour. They watched the games, I did the thinking; each doing what the god made him good at.

I was running through a standard form of words in my mind when I heard shouting and various other noises coming from the direction of our tent. For some reason I assumed that the tents were on fire and jumped up to investigate. I was therefore in position to see Pentheus running like a hare, with three or four men chasing after him. One of them was holding a sword, and another had a hunting-spear with half the shaft broken off.

A heartbeat or so later everybody on the field was watching too, which must have been mortifying for the games-players in the middle – don't ask me which event was going on, all I can remember was that it was some sort of race; ironic, really. To begin with, I don't suppose any of them could believe what they were seeing; nearly everybody we'd talked to had made a point of mentioning the truce, how sacred it was, how nobody would ever possibly dream of breaking it. Even thieves and cutpurses, they'd told us, didn't bother to run if they were caught stealing during the games, because nobody would dare chase them. Then, when it became painfully obvious that the impossible was indeed happening, everybody jumped up at once and surged forward, I assume with the intention of grabbing the truce-breakers and tearing them limb from limb.

CHAPTER ELEVEN

Credit where it's due (Cleander said), it was an extremely fine piece of tactical thinking on Alastor's part. He'd figured out that the only offence that would justify breaking the truce was breaking the truce . . .

So what he'd done was send the wretched Tachys over to our tent, while everybody was busy watching the games, equipped with a small, sharp knife. Tachys cut himself just above the hairline (where even a small nick will bleed like a fountain and make you look as if you've just been set upon by a dozen drunken centaurs), then ran from tent to tent yelling that Pentheus had drawn a sword on him and attacked him. Because everybody was watching what was going on in the middle, he had to run quite some way before he found anybody to pay him any attention; but as luck would have it, the first man to hear him was an Argive priest, very serious about the truce and the reputation of the games. This priest came bursting out of his tent with a sword in his fist, and by the time he reached the door of our tent, he'd accumulated a number of like-minded people intent on avenging the sacrilege in blood before the Lady Hera noticed and got upset.

At some stage in his career, Pentheus must have acquired a sense the rest of us don't have that warned him about the approach of armed, angry men; that or the god told him, or he heard the yelling. In any case, he escaped from the tent by slitting open the back wall (with my razor), and headed for the middle in the hope of being rescued. This was a miscalculation on his part; as soon as it became known that the pursuers were chasing a truce-breaker – fairly quickly, because someone recognised the priest, which meant that whoever he was after had to be the bad guy – everybody present apart from us wanted to get a piece of him (a finger, maybe, or a bit of skin).

If I'd been Pentheus, I'd have gone in for the foot-race rather than the wrestling. He was *fast*. Not only that; he made a fine show of jumping over obstacles (folding chairs, jars, rocks, slow-moving people who were still sitting on the ground) without slowing down or breaking his stride. It was without doubt the most spectacular display of skill and fitness of the whole event.

Demodocus – I felt sorry for him. He stood like one of those statues they put in front of temples; he was so absolutely still you could have used him for a column and rested a roof on his head. I think he was too shocked even to be angry.

Cratus nudged me in the ribs. 'I think it's time we were leaving,' he said.

Brother or not, I was inclined to agree with him. I don't think I'm a particularly callous or unfeeling person, but it seemed fairly certain that there was nothing we could do to help Pentheus even if we felt inclined to do so (remember: at that point we didn't know that Alastor had set him up), and if we stayed put there was a better than even chance that anybody associated with Pentheus was going to come in for some of the leftover outrage and fury once Pentheus himself had been reduced to his component parts.

'Good idea,' I said. 'Dusa—'

She wasn't there.

You know the story about Pandora and the jar; how she was given it by the gods, and when she broke the seal, all the evils and troubles that beset mortal men flew out to plague us for ever? Well, I'm prepared to bet that right up in the neck of that jar, along with Plague, War, Hunger and Death, was Sisters. Now, obviously I can't see any of you, but I'll wager that you're all sitting there nodding gravely, because you know I'm right. Personally, I shall never forgive the gods for that. I don't care what mankind had done to offend them; there was no call for them to go doing something like that to us. Just not fair.

'It's all right,' Sarpedon said quickly, before I had a chance to speak. 'Cratus and I'll go look for her. You head back to the tent, pick up as much of our stuff as you can; we'll meet up by that well on the Corinth road.'

I really didn't want us to get split up at that moment; but neither did I want to plunge about in the middle of a lynch-mob searching for a madwoman. To be honest with you, Cowardice found the gates of my heart open and slipped in without any serious opposition from the long-term residents.

'All right,' I said. 'See you there.'

The hunt – quarry and hounds – was out of sight by now, and the field was deserted. As I made my nervous way across the square, I couldn't help thinking how desperately sad it all looked; the middle, the marker-stones, all the bits and pieces that people had left behind as they raced off. It was as if it was all trying to explain to me how pointless, how idiotic the whole idea of games-with-nobody-dead, games-playing, what I'd been trying to do, doing anything was. In that deserted space I felt as if I was the last man alive, and that everything had gone wrong all across the world.

As I walked, a dream seemed to walk beside me; he was asking me to consider what it would be like going home, trying to explain. King Leon would be asking, Where's all the games-players you promised me? My father and sister-in-law would be asking, Where's Cratus and Dusa? What did you *do* out there, to lose all of them . . .?

He wasn't a very nice dream, and I wished he'd go away; on the other hand, at least he was prepared to speak to me, and by implication he was suggesting that I might possibly make it home somehow. That was some comfort, being the only evidence I had that such a thing might be possible.

There wasn't a lot left of our tent when I got there. Most of it had been trampled flat. I picked up everything I thought I'd be able to carry – a jar of flour, a goatskin bag with some cheese and olives, a sword, a cloak and a spare pair of boots, a few other odds and ends – looked around just in case I'd missed anything important, and crept slowly away.

I reached the well and sat down on the parapet. There didn't seem much point in waiting there very long; my brother, sister and uncle were undoubtedly either dead or awaiting execution, my host was probably leading a search-party to find me to add me to the carrion collection. I resolved to count up to a thousand then set off for Corinth, which was in the opposite direction to home and therefore the line they'd be least likely to take when they came after me.

I'd got as far as seven hundred and forty something when I realised there was somebody staring at me; an old woman, with a jar tucked under her arm.

'You using that well?' she said.

I stood upright. 'No,' I said, 'sorry. Here, let me turn the handle for you.'

She glowered at me. 'I'm perfectly capable,' she said.

Gods, I thought, now I'm offending perfect strangers. 'I'm sure you are,' I said. 'Just offering to help, that's all.'

She scowled a bit more. 'I may be old,' she said, 'but I can still wind a well, thank you very much. If you get out of the way, that is.'

I got out of the way. She gave me a further and fouler look, and tried to turn the handle.

'It's stuck,' she said accusingly. 'What you been doing to it?'

'Nothing,' I replied. 'I never touched it.'

'It wasn't stuck before *you* came along,' she said. 'And now the to-the-crows thing won't turn at all.'

'Would you like me to try?' I said. She clicked her tongue at me.

'Try all you like,' she said, 'you won't shift it. It's stuck.'

And it was, too. When I thought I felt the rope beginning to strain, I let go, not wanting to add damaging a well to my already impressive list of crimes and malfeasances. 'You're right,' I said, 'it's stuck.'

'I know it's stuck. Now I'll have to go home and get our Euthydromus to climb down it and sort it out. And he's not as young as he was, neither.'

Apparently old age and the passing of time were my fault now. It's amazing the number of bad things you can do and not even know you've done them. She sluiced me down with a little more eye-venom and hobbled away; I picked up my burdens and got ready to leave.

'Cleander,' said a voice. 'Is that you?'

Weirdest voice you ever heard. Sort of ringing and reverberating, not in the least bit human. A god, therefore, calling me by name; and the disturbing part was, it seemed to be coming up from the bowels of the earth, where generally speaking nice gods don't go.

'Cleander,' the voice repeated. 'Is that you up there? Can you hear me?'

I felt uneasy, not having anything to give the ferryman for rowing me across the River; then I thought about the stuck winch-handle, and the god opened my eyes. I looked round to make sure nobody was watching, then stuck my head down the well.

'Pentheus?' I said.

'Thank the gods,' the voice replied. 'I was beginning to think I was in trouble down here. I can't get back up.'

I took a deep breath. It smelt rather strongly of well, but that was the least of my problems. 'You are,' I replied. 'Goodbye.'

His yelp of dismay echoed up the wellshaft and came at me like a clap of thunder. 'You can't just leave me here,' he said. 'I can't climb up the rope, it's all slippery. You've got to pull me up.'

'No,' I said.

'But if you don't, how am I going to get out? I could die down here.'

I smiled. 'Even you ought to be able to manage that without screwing it up,' I agreed. 'Best of luck, anyway.'

'Cleander!'

Really, I was minded to walk away and leave him there. If it hadn't been for him – so all right, he wasn't responsible for all our troubles, just the overwhelming majority of them, including the loss of my family, the fact that I was alone and destitute in a strange and hostile city; things like that. On the other hand; on the other hand, he was the only man I knew in Argos who'd be pleased to see me. And I could always kill him later. Besides, if leaving Pentheus there didn't count as poisoning a well, I couldn't say what would, and poisoning wells is a great sin against heaven.

'How did you get down there, anyway?' I asked.

'They were chasing me,' he replied. 'I had a bit of a lead, but they were gaining. So I saw this well, grabbed hold of the bucket and jumped.'

'I see,' I replied.

'Right now,' he went on, 'I'm hanging from this rope with my feet braced against the sides. Are you going to help me or not?'

'Only because drowning's too good for you,' I replied. 'Hold tight, and I'll see what I can do.'

So I pulled, as hard as I could; and just as I was starting to hope that there was really nothing I could do for him (in which case I could go on my way with a clear conscience) I heard a joyful shout from down below. 'It's all right,' he said, 'I've got my footing now. There's stepping stones let into the sides. Keep pulling.'

(A smart idea, that; so that when someone's got to go down the well to free a stuck bucket or mend a broken rope, they can be sure of getting out again. They're clever people, the Argives.)

As I pulled I started thinking, if Pentheus has somehow managed to survive, maybe – just possibly – Cratus and Dusa and Sarpedon might make it too; after all, why would the god save a born pest like Pentheus, and destroy my family? Didn't make sense. Then again, very little of what the gods do makes sense, so it wasn't the most convincing of arguments. That said, I was feeling a bit more cheerful by the time Pentheus' head appeared over the lip of the well.

The first thing he said was, 'Where are the others?'

'I don't know,' I replied. 'I'm supposed to meet them here.'

He crawled out snake-fashion and flopped on to the ground. I helped him up.

'We can't stay here,' he said.

'You can't,' I agreed.

'You aren't going to abandon me,' he said – it wasn't a plea or a question, it was a statement of fact. 'I know, I'll hide somewhere nearby while you wait here for the others.'

I grinned. 'You could hide down the well,' I said.

'Not likely. What about one of the houses? I expect all the people are away at the games.'

I shook my head. 'I've got a better idea,' I said.

'Really?' His tone of voice was hardly flattering. 'What?'

'My heart tells me,' I replied, 'that if the lynch-mob comes back this way, they'll be looking for a long, skinny games-player, as opposed to a couple of clod-busters on their way out to the fields. So long as we act normal—'

He frowned. 'How do you do that?'

'What do you mean? Just – well, you know. Normal.'

'Sorry,' he said, grinning sheepishly, 'but I don't. I haven't exactly led what you'd call a normal life, so I don't know the rules.'

'Oh for— Look, just try to do what I do, but don't draw attention to yourself. You think you can manage that?'

'Remains to be seen.'

'Put this on.' I shoved the spare cloak at him. By chance or divine intervention, when I'd gone back to the tent I'd grabbed the first cloak I could see; it turned out to be Sarpedon's travelling cloak – old, threadbare, carefully and repeatedly darned, just the sort of thing a poor, hard-working smallholder would wear. I looked rather more prosperous and well-bred in my own cloak and tunic; I, however, had the advantage of an honest face, not to mention a clean conscience. As a finishing touch, I shoved my beat-up old leather hat down on to his ears as far as I could make it go, and covered my own head with a bit of knotted rag.

It's wonderful how our hearts can run in two opposite directions at once. There was one faction inside me that knew for a fact that Cratus and Dusa and Sarpedon had come to a bad end, and waiting for them here was a pointless risk. The other faction was convinced it was just a matter of holding still and biding time, and everything would be all right. In the middle was a third faction, stronger than both the other two put together, that refused to believe in or acknowledge what was going on, and seemed to regard the situation as some kind of dream or far-fetched joke. My mind was inclined to favour a compromise view, whereby our situation was grave but not nearly as bad as it could be, provided we acted sensibly, kept our cool and refused to listen to the siren voice of

Panic – but the fact is, the truth isn't a resolution passed by a council of the Sons of the Achaeans; just because such-and-such is the way we think things should have turned out, we can't alter the way things have actually happened by taking a vote.

'Now what?' said Pentheus, under the shade of my hat.

'We hang around here,' I replied. 'We're two old friends who haven't seen each other in a while. Quite by chance we've met beside this well, and now we're catching up with each other's news.'

'Right,' Pentheus said. 'That's what normal people do, is it?'

'All the time.'

We stood there for I don't know how long; long enough to prune a row of vines, long enough to heat a thick bar of bronze to forging red – I haven't the faintest idea. It just seemed a very long time, that's all. And all the while my heart was telling me, This is taking too long, if they were coming they'd be here by now, something really has happened to them and maybe you're never going to see them again. Now that really did frighten me, as I stood there pretending to be someone I wasn't. My brother and sister; I could no more imagine what it'd be like without them than I could imagine a day without sunlight. Every day of my life, near enough, I'd seen them, talked to them, argued and lost my temper with one or both of them. I don't suppose the thought had ever occurred to me that a day might come when they wouldn't be there. Well, how could I imagine such a thing? It'd be like a world where all the colours are different. Oh, people die, we all know that, just as we know that in Ethiopia the sun burns men's skins black, and we know that there are people who have just the one enormous foot, bigger than an old-fashioned figure-of-eight shield, which they shelter under from the fury of the noon sun. These are things we know to be true, on the assumption that this certainty will never intrude into our lives, and so it is with the death of those close to us. At the same time we know it's true and we believe it won't happen, in the same way that we believe we'll live for ever. We believe in the past and the future as we believe in the gods – there but not there, real but real in a different way. Not the sort of real that has any business with us.

Now the thought was so close that I could almost feel it brushing my ear, and it made me fidgety and nervous. I was hopping from one foot to the other, glancing round all the time without even knowing I was doing it, until Pentheus remarked that I was the one who was supposed to know how to be normal. That didn't help; all it did was make me try *really hard* to behave normally. I guess that if there'd been anybody there to watch, they'd have grabbed stones and started chucking them at me, assuming I was a crazy man.

Just when I thought I was going to burst with worry, like a badly patched wineskin, someone tapped me on the shoulder. I swear to the gods, I hadn't heard a footstep or anything like that.

'Cleander?' It was Dusa's voice. 'Oh, it is you. Why are you wearing that silly bit of cloth on your head? And who's—?'

Pentheus took off his hat – my hat, but I never did get the confounded thing back. Pity; it was a good hat. Anyway, the next thing I knew about was a sharp pain in my toe as Dusa trod on it while leaping into Pentheus' arms. I stood there, registering the pain in my foot and another pain directly related to the spectacle of my sister embracing the man who'd ruined all our work and nearly got us killed. 'What's *he* doing here?' someone asked in a horrified voice; I assume it was Cratus, but I didn't bother checking at the time.

'Can we go now, please?' Pentheus mumbled.

'Yes,' I replied. 'And for gods' sakes,' I added ferociously, 'try to act natural.'

My brother, sister and uncle all stared at me as if I was demented.

'There is absolutely no point,' I insisted later, as we huddled round the largest fire we dared light, 'in going on any further. It's completely out of the question. The only subject worth discussing is, how do we get home?'

They all looked at me and said nothing. None of us had been particularly talkative the rest of that day, once we'd given brief accounts of our various adventures directly after the games broke up. Pentheus' story was brief and unconvincing (though of course it later turned out to be true) – he'd been in the tent, having oiled and scraped, and was just pulling on a clean tunic when he heard yelling and trampling, which set off a basic survival instinct. He had no idea why they'd come for him, he hadn't done anything wrong.

Rather better received was Cratus' version of how he'd shoved his way in and out of the crowd until he quite literally walked into Dusa; if the crowd hadn't been so thick, he'd have knocked her over. She'd set off with some idiotic notion of trying to rescue Pentheus, which had lasted just long enough to propel her into the thick of the crowd. At that point she'd realised that she didn't really want to be there, but by then her chances of getting out again without serious help were next to nothing. Eventually, by standing still and letting everybody else shove past them, they'd managed to get out of the crowd and head for the well. That, in essence, was that. I asked Sarpedon what he'd been up to all this time, but he just scowled and changed the subject, and none of us were in the mood for an argument, so I let it go.

'The way I see it,' I said after a while, 'we've got two choices: north or south. Whichever way we go, we'll have to stay well away from Argos and all the places we went through on our way to Argos from Asine. That would make me tend to favour going north, more or less the direction we're headed in at the moment, until we reach Mycenae. After that, home'll be due west; Orchomenus, straight across the mountains . . . It'll be a hell of a journey, but at least we'll stay clear of big cities where they may have heard of us. Don't ask me what we're going to live on, by the way, because I don't know. But people do live in the mountains; we can beg, or steal, maybe even work, there'll be olives and figs to pick before we get home. It sounds pretty grim, sure enough, but there's no point lying to our hearts about it, we're in a pretty grim situation.'

I looked round. Cratus didn't seem to be listening. Sarpedon was nodding, with a face as long as a ship's mast. Pentheus was fiddling with the strap of his left sandal, which was frayed almost through.

'There's another way,' Dusa said.

I was about to tell her to shut up when my heart said to me, Go on, you might as well hear her out. After all, things are so bad, what have you got to lose? 'Go on,' I said.

'All right. We go north, just as you said; but instead of heading west, we carry on until we reach Corinth. There we talk our way aboard a ship and get a lift all the way home. Beats walking.'

You can tell how far down my heart was; I hadn't even considered a ship. 'You said "talk our way aboard",' I said. 'How are we supposed to do that?'

Dusa shrugged. 'Haven't a clue,' she replied. 'But it's got to be easier than walking right across the middle of the Peloponnese on an empty stomach.'

Sarpedon lifted his head at that point. 'I know someone in Corinth,' he said.

We all looked at him.

'Really,' he went on. 'Man called Oxyxiphus; I saved his life in a battle once. He'll help us out, if we can get that far. He'll give us stuff for presents – jars of wine and rolls of cloth, that sort of thing. We can give-and-receive our way round the coast. There's people do that sort of thing for a living, so they tell me.'

I frowned. 'Really?' I said.

'I believe so. The drill is, you find a man with a ship and give him a present; he lets you sleep on his ship and store your stuff under the bench. You've got to row, of course.'

I couldn't see it myself. 'Just you and the man who owns the boat?' I asked.

'No, of course not. There'll be thirty or forty others, all doing the same thing. Straight up, it's a way of life for some people during the off season. Quite fancied it myself when I was a good deal younger. Well, I'd have had my own ship, of course. But the idea's the same.'

'Are you sure?' Cratus asked. 'I mean, if this is just some story you've heard somewhere—'

'No,' I interrupted, 'come to think of it, he's right. You remember those foreigners who stayed with us when we were kids? The short, dark men with the smelly hair?'

'"Short, dark men with smelly hair",' the Phoenician repeated. 'Thank you very much.'

Cleander grinned feebly. 'We were younger then, remember. And not many of them – sorry, not many of you people came as far as Elis in those days. Thinking about it, I guess they used to get as far as Pylos and the Messenian coast and do their giving-and-receiving there, and any stuff that got as far as Elis came to us from

Pylos by way of the Triphylians. We got it when everybody else had finished with it, so to speak.'

The Phoenician nodded. 'I can believe that,' he said. 'But surely you had—' He said a word the rest of them couldn't understand. He tried again. 'I'm sure you must have had people who gave-and-received for a living who weren't Phoenicians; Sons of the Achaeans, I mean.'

'We did,' Cleander replied. 'But it didn't occur to us that they were – well, quite so cynical about it. We thought they were wandering sons of noblemen out for adventure. That's what they told us they were.'

'Really,' the Phoenician said.

Anyway (Cleander went on), that's what we decided to do. Everything depended, of course, on Sarpedon's friend still being alive, and willing to put himself out on our account; also on news of our dreadful activities not having reached Corinth by the time we got there. That was a bigger gamble than Sarpedon's friend; Corinthians go everywhere, everybody goes to Corinth, so sooner or later all the news in the world ends up there. Still, thinking about it calmly, there was no way anybody could prove we were who we were unless they were actual eye-witnesses. Would the Corinthians want to get involved with somebody else's feuds? Unlikely, we assured ourselves, until our hearts got sick of hearing us and told us they were convinced. It's remarkable how you can fool yourself into ignoring risks when you have to. Nobody else could have talked us into doing what we proposed to do, but we managed it.

We suffered a lot, getting from Argos to Corinth. An old man once told me that you had to be wilful or stupid to starve in open country, provided you knew which berries are safe to eat and how to kill small, stupid animals. I disagree. Between Argos and Corinth, you'll find a great deal of bare rock, plenty of sheep and goats (and mean-looking shepherds with big, ugly dogs), a few fig and olive trees and about a million small boys who pass the time by scaring away birds and reporting the advent of strangers to their betters. Hunting, gathering and theft won't feed you; so, if you're obviously poor and no good and so not fit to claim the hospitality of the better sort, that leaves work or begging.

We tried work, but nobody wanted us. It has to be admitted, we looked like trouble. Itinerants don't go around in packs of five; thieves and bandits do. Accordingly, even begging wasn't easy. Thinking about it, I can see why not. If I'd answered the door to find four villainous-looking men in my porch, I'd have shut and barred it quick as you like – nobody with any sense wants to be outnumbered by unvouched-for strangers in his own house, thank you very much. A lot of the people we called on – middling smallholders for the most part, living out in the open in a fortified house with gates and a tower – acted very hostile indeed, and we were glad to get away in one piece, hungry or not.

It was after we'd been thrown out of one such place that Cratus made the suggestion.

'Come on,' he said, after we'd all looked at him as if he was mad. 'If everybody's going to assume we're thieves and robbers anyway, what've we got to lose? And we won't actually hurt anybody.'

'No,' I said. 'Absolutely not.'

Cratus sighed. 'It's that or starve,' he said. 'And I don't want to starve, thank you very much. What've we got to lose?'

Sarpedon, who was sitting under a rock trying to stay cool in the midday heat, made a snarling noise. 'Our pride,' he said. 'And our honour.'

Cratus was starting to lose his temper. 'Fine,' he said. 'Well, we'll have your pride roasted on a spit and basted in honey for our dinner tonight, and your honour lightly fried with onions for breakfast tomorrow. Then we'll rob somebody.'

To my surprise, it was Pentheus who seemed most upset by the suggestion. 'I'd rather die,' he said. 'For the gods' sakes, I haven't come this far to end up becoming what I look like. If I'd thought it'd come to that, I'd never have bothered in the first place.'

So we put the idea out of our minds, and as soon as it was cool enough to continue we carried on trudging. But the mountains didn't get any lower or softer, and by the time we reached the hill where they reckoned Mycenae used to be, we weren't feeling quite so high and mighty.

I say used to be – we'd assumed there'd be something there, even if it wasn't a great and powerful city like it's described as in the songs. But there was nothing to see; a shepherd we asked the way from pointed to a hill with a few stones sticking out of it, like our ribs.

'Lot of pride and honour under that hill,' Cratus muttered as we started walking again. 'Pity we can't dig it up and eat it.'

I think it was Cratus' incessant whining more than the hunger itself – oh yes, and Dusa had started too – that finally got to me. Anyway, I called a halt and made them all sit down.

'Well?' Sarpedon said. 'You aren't actually considering it, are you?'

I sighed. 'I don't think we've got all that much choice in the matter,' I replied. 'It's that or split up and go our separate ways – we might stand a chance begging if we're on our own, but nobody's going to open the door to us as a group. We can't go on like this, that's for sure.'

'Thank you,' Cratus said.

'About time,' Dusa added. 'There was that fat old man with a donkey loaded down with cheeses we passed a way back. If you'd decided earlier, we'd all be stuffed with cheese by now.'

Sarpedon looked at us, then grunted. 'I suppose that if you're going to do this incredibly stupid thing, you'll need someone to make sure you don't do it completely wrong.'

'So you agree?' I asked.

'I suppose so,' Sarpedon replied wretchedly.

'I don't,' Pentheus said.

Cratus scowled. 'Nobody asked you,' he growled. 'Which reminds me: what the hell are you doing still following us about? We've saved your life – again; now why don't you go to the crows and stop bothering us?'

'Leave him alone,' I said. 'I haven't got the patience or the energy to deal with either of you, so just keep your faces shut and let me think.'

'Why you?' Cratus objected. 'Since when have you been giving orders to free men?'

'Since when were you capable of thinking?' Sarpedon snapped. 'I know I'm not,' he added with a wry grin. 'Not until I've had something to eat and washed some of this dust off my face, anyway. If Cleander wants to play at being Agamemnon, I say we let him.'

And that, my friends, is how we took the last step down the ladder. We'd gone from being the emissaries of the King of Elis, better than most and equals of any, all the way down to fugitives and vagrants; but at least, up till then, we hadn't done anything wrong, we'd been the victims of bad luck, other people's malice and the rather distasteful humour of the gods. Now, to complete the process, we were going to do something to deserve our wretchedness – become what we looked like, as Pentheus had said. Oddly enough, as soon as we took the decision, we all started to feel a whole lot better – even Pentheus, who didn't take long to join in the ensuing staff meeting, in the course of which he displayed a remarkable degree of insight into and understanding of the craft of highway robbery.

'What we really want to do,' I said, after we'd discussed various alternatives, 'is find a narrow place between two rocks. I know, it's just the sort of place where people expect an ambush. But that's only because it's the sort of place where ambushes happen. For a reason.'

Sarpedon shook his head. 'For one thing,' he said, 'look around. See any suitable places? Thought not. For another, that's the sort of place you'd choose if you were planning on what you might call the traditional approach – jump on the buggers, cut their throats and be on your way. Great location for that sort of thing, no good for what we're planning. If you aren't figuring on killing anybody, there's no advantage in it. Quite the reverse: you'll panic them into fighting, because they'll be expecting to be murdered if they don't.'

Then Pentheus joined in. 'I know what I'd do,' he said quietly.

We stopped talking and looked at him. 'All right,' I said, 'don't keep it to yourself. What would you do?'

He smiled. 'It's a matter of making the best use of our resources,' he replied. 'Now, what we need is an open stretch of road with a little light cover—'

And that's how come Cratus, Sarpedon, Pentheus and I found

ourselves crouching in a mulching-trench on the edge of someone's vineyard, right on the outskirts of a tiny village half a day's walk from Mycenae, staring at the road and trying not to think about the cramp in our knees. We were there a very long time, and for a bronze brooch-pin we'd have given up and carried on walking, except that it'd taken so much strength of will to get us in that ditch in the first place, somehow we'd have felt small if we'd simply got up and walked away.

Then, finally, we saw what we'd been hoping for: an old man and a young lad (grandfather and grandson, by the looks of them) leading a pair of heavily laden donkeys along the road. There were jars on the donkeys' backs, and both men had satchels over their shoulders, the sort you carry your food in. There had to be something to eat.

They were chatting quietly as they walked, and so didn't hear the soft groaning right away; in fact, the old man nearly trod on the beautiful young girl lying in a crumpled heap beside the road before he noticed her.

'Help, help,' she repeated, in between groans. Honestly, she wouldn't have fooled me for a heartbeat. Fortunately, the gods put simpler thoughts into those fools' hearts. They stopped and rushed over to see what the matter was. Bad mistake.

Pentheus dropped a bit of cord round the young lad's throat, Sarpedon waggled our sword a couple of times under the old man's nose, while Dusa got up and dusted herself off, looking extremely embarrassed.

'You're thieves,' the old man said, as if thieves were some kind of fabulous monster found only in Lower Egypt.

'Yes,' Sarpedon replied, pulling the satchel off over the old man's head. 'And, like jewellers and sandal-makers, we prefer to work in silence. Indulge us.'

The old man looked so hurt and sad it was nearly enough to burst your heart. Cratus, meanwhile, was twisting the stoppers out of the jars.

'Wine,' he said. 'More wine. More wine. Gods, you people must drink a lot in these parts. Mind you, if I had to live here, so would I.'

'All wine?' I asked? The old man nodded. 'Except the big one. That's olive oil.'

'Marvellous,' Sarpedon grunted. 'We can drink ourselves to death rather than starve. Let's see what's in your satchel.'

'Nothing,' the old man replied, sounding a bit confused. 'Well, there wouldn't be,' he added. 'It's nearly evening.'

Logical, of course. If we'd robbed them in the morning, it'd have been different.

'You haven't done this before, have you?' the old man added.

'It's that obvious, is it?'

He nodded. 'Which is a good thing, surely,' he added. 'I mean, robbing people well isn't really something to be proud of.'

I sighed and flopped down on the ground. 'Let them go, for pity's sake,' I said in disgust. 'We're wasting our time, no point in making things worse than they already are.'

Sarpedon grunted and lowered the sword, while Pentheus removed the cord from round the boy's neck. 'Sorry,' he said.

The old man massaged his throat where Sarpedon had pricked it a little. 'That's all right,' he said, 'no harm done. You boys look like you're having a rough time.'

I laughed. 'That's no lie,' I told him.

'Mossus, put those lids back on the jars.' The boy nodded and got on with the job. 'Tell you what,' the old man went on, 'my place is just down the road from here. We haven't got much, but I expect there's enough to feed us all if you don't mind last year's barley.'

We looked at each other like idiots. Finally, Dusa had the sense to say, 'That's very kind of you,' or something like that. Then we followed the old man home.

On the way, of course, I did my best to make amends by explaining that really we weren't thieves and low-lifes; on the contrary, we were noblemen and respected citizens in our own country. The old man just smiled, as if he'd heard that one many times before.

'Noblemen,' he repeated. 'Not princes, then?' He grinned, and before I could answer he went on, 'Doesn't matter to me in any case. Far as I'm concerned, you're poor buggers like me and you could do with a feed and a sleep on some clean reed.'

'We're that all right,' I said.

'Of course. Words lie, eyes don't. Next time, though, make it princes. Sounds better.'

The old man's name was Glycus, and his grandson was Mossus. Both of Glycus' sons had died years ago (we didn't find out how) and Glycus' wife had died the previous spring.

It was a tidy little smallholding – well, not so little; Glycus had built it while both his sons were alive and at home, and they'd made a good, thorough job. There was a shoulder-high outer wall with a good, straight gate; inside that were the house, a couple of barns, a well and a tower. He'd built it with defence in mind more than convenience – it was quite some way to his fields and his steading, but he'd chosen a high place with a good view and its own water.

'These parts haven't always been quiet,' he explained. 'Used to be a good few wild men running about here; you wanted to be able to bar your gate and lock your door at night, and see who was coming before they saw you. Things are better now, though; they pushed the wild men out, sent them packing west. Haven't had any trouble since before Mossus here was born.'

I asked who these wild men were; Glycus was a bit vague on the subject – he wasn't all that interested in them – but I got the impression that they'd been the last surviving descendants of the people who once lived in the great city of Mycenae; the Giants, as we always called them, except they weren't big and strong. In fact, they were shorter and slighter than the Sons of the Achaeans, though that aside there wasn't much to tell between them and us. For some reason, I found it very hard to take; I believed him, I just thought it was sad and not at all like what I'd always believed. You always think that the people in the old stories were big and strong and clever, better than us; according to what the old man told us, not a bit of it. And yet they built huge cities and wonderful palaces, had gold and silver and bronze treasures the like of which we don't know how to make any more – and they did such things, like crossing the Sea and sacking Troy.

Sometimes, you just don't know what to think.

That night, after we'd eaten rather too much of Glycus' spare food and drunk a jar of his quite palatable wine, he told us a story.

I can't remember exactly how the subject came up. All I remember was, someone (may have been me) had said something about Mycenae, how we'd expected to see something there if it was such a famous city in the old days. Glycus grinned like a thirsty dog and passed the jug round.

'I can tell you a thing or two about the old city,' he said, 'if you're minded to listen. But I don't reckon you'll believe it.'

At that stage in the evening, we weren't all that fussed about truth. 'Try us,' said Cratus. 'You never know, we might surprise you yet. Some of us,' he added, 'will believe anything.'

Glycus laughed. 'All right,' he replied. 'But don't you go getting mad at me if you figure I'm trying to give you short measure.'

When I was nothing but a little kid (Glycus said), my grandfather, who was an old man then, asked me to give him a hand with shearing his six or eight raggety old sheep he used to keep up on the rough side there; ain't nothing but rocks, now as then, and it's a long walk there and back again. But I was young, didn't have nothing better to do; so I went with him, helped him pen up those old sheep and held 'em down while he did the shearing – he was the best shearer I ever did see, he could take off a fleece whole in the time you or I'd take to prune back a vine. Anyhow, he was mighty glad of the help, and when we got back home he said he'd give me something for my trouble. Now, it hadn't been no trouble; but nobody but a fool ever said no to a present, and I knew the old man still had a thing or two stashed away in a big old trunk in the upper room, that nobody but he was allowed to look in. Naturally, this made me and my brothers mighty curious to know what was in there, so you can guess how keen I was to have something out of that old box.

He went away and came back with a bit of old rag, all waxed up with wool-grease, wrapped round a short dagger. I tell you, my eyes nearly bust out of my head looking at it – I didn't have any kind of knife of my own, and this wasn't just a knife, it was one hell of a thing. There was gold, real gold, on the handle, and pictures made of gold and white and blue stone cut into the blade; there was two men fighting on one side, and a man in a chariot stabbing a lion on the other.

'Is that really for me?' I asked, and the old man said, Yes, it was. Reckoned he'd always meant for me to have it, soon as I was old enough to take care of it properly; he'd had it from his grandfather when he was a boy, and he'd had it from *his* grandfather, and the gods only knew how far back it had gone like that. 'Kind of like a tradition,' the old man said. 'And when you've got a grandson of your own, always supposing he's any good, mind you give it to him the same way.'

(And I did, too; gave it to Mossus here the year before last, and if he's lost it or given it away, he's got the wit not to have told me about it.)

'Another thing goes with it,' grandfather went on, 'is a story; and you can't have the one without the other. You still want the knife, son?'

I nodded like crazy, because of course I wanted that knife, and I liked grandfather's old stories too. 'Sure,' I said. 'I'd really like that.'

He gave me a big toothy smile. 'You're a good boy,' he said. 'Well, this is the story, and it goes back at least as far as the knife does, maybe even further. See, that knife came from Mycenae – that's what they used to call the old city that's gone now, buried under the hill. You heard any stories about the city, son?'

I shook my head. 'Not really,' I said. 'Dad told me once about King Agamemnon and going to Troy, but that's not really about the city, Agamemnon just lived there.'

He nodded. 'That's the truth,' he said. 'But this story's not about him or his time; it's a good few years after that, when the Sons of the Achaeans first came into these parts.'

'That's us,' I said.

'You bet. But the folks who lived in the old city, they weren't Sons of the Achaeans – least, they spoke the same tongue as we do, more or less, but they were different in a whole lot of ways. Cleverer, they reckon, and richer, and lived a whole lot longer than we do – because they were closer to the Golden Age, I guess, so they hadn't got so much bad in them.'

I reckon I must have looked like I didn't follow, because he stopped and said, 'You ain't heard about the Golden Age?' and I said no, I hadn't. So he told me; how when the gods first made men it was the age of gold, and folks lived hundreds of years and never got sick, and they didn't have to work hardly at all, just picked fruit from the trees, and all the rivers ran with honey. But they turned wicked in time, though not so wicked as we are, and the gods took away the age of gold and turned it into the age of silver, which wasn't so good as the last one but still pretty good, considering. Folks still lived a long time and didn't get sick often, and though they had to do a little bit of work, it wasn't much. And they were all wise and didn't fall out or fight or steal. Now, grandfather reckoned that age of silver was when they built the old city, and those silver men were the ones who lived there; and he reckoned that the age of bronze, which is where we're at now, was when the Sons of the Achaeans came into the Peloponnese from the north; which would be around the time this story comes from.

Anyway, the old man told me that his great-great-grandfather, or however many greats it was, he was a boy when they came this way, travelling in big old ox-carts as high as a house for years on end, never stopping in any one place above a year. Now, being curious, I asked the old man if they were the ones who buried the old city, which is what someone told me once – that the Sons of the Achaeans drove out the wild men from the city and buried it so they'd never come back. But grandfather lifted his head.

'That's what people say,' he told me, 'but it isn't so. Truth is, the only reason why those old Achaeans kept moving on is because the old-city folks kept throwing them off their land and pushing them away; they were strong and powerful, we weren't nothing but simple folk, didn't understand about war and fighting. It was the same here; the King of Mycenae told us we couldn't stay in these parts, we'd have to move on, but since it was late in the season already when we arrived here, he said we could spend the winter here and take off come the spring. Well, we didn't mind that, it was better than trying to cross the mountains in the cold weather, and it was more kindness than we'd come to expect. We halted the wagons and put out our stock where we were told we could graze them, and settled in for the winter.

'Before the winter came, though, word reached the king that there were wars going on all round – north, east and west, and nobody knew who in hell the enemy was. It wasn't our people, the Achaeans, nor theirs; it was people from across the Sea, who'd come over in ships from away somewhere, and all they cared about was gold and silver and metal, things they could steal and take home in their ships. Now, at first the king didn't pay no heed to these stories; but then he heard from a cousin of his that some of these people from the Sea had marched right up under the walls of Tiryns and burned it to the ground, just to get the gold and stuff and because they really didn't hold with cities much.

'That worried him, sure enough; so he called up all his men and set them to guarding the gates and the walls, and in due course the enemy came. Never did find out who they were or where they were from; never did find a way to beat them, either. Now, our people took to the hills as soon as they heard these folks were coming, and they had the wit not to come out again till after they'd gone. All they found was ashes and cinders and fallen stones; there were places, the old man told me, where the fire got so hot it melted the stone into glaze, and it was all clear and shiny like black water. They didn't find a single man alive; just a few old women and some dogs. That was where my great-however-many-times-grandfather picked up this pretty knife; it was lying under a dead man in a fallen-down building, where the roof-timbers had fallen on him and stopped him getting burned up.

'Anyhow; the enemy never came back this way, though folks from away told us they'd showed up in other parts of the Peloponnese, Pylos and Asine and Sparta; tried to burn Athens, but the Athenians managed to drive them away. By all accounts, they were the only ones that did. It wasn't all at once, mind – they'd come and burn one or two cities a year and then go home again, and some years they went to the islands, or across to Egypt or Syria or Phoenicia, burning cities there till folks reckoned that pretty soon there wouldn't be any more cities left for them to burn. And all this time, nobody ever said they'd met one of these people, or spoken to them, or even seen one up close; nobody ever found out what they called themselves, or what things were like at home that they felt the need to come out burning and killing. All anybody ever called them was the raiders, or the pirates, or the bastards from the Sea.

'Well, when it seemed like it was safe enough, our folks moved down into the valleys and started building houses and walls, clearing the fields and planting out vines and trees. That's how we got started in these parts, and we've been here ever since. I did hear tell once as it was the King of Egypt who finally put a stop to all the raiding and burning, when all of those raiders ganged up and attacked him; he fought a great battle against them in the middle of the sea, fighting on ships like they were dry land, and all of them as wasn't killed were drowned. Maybe so; or maybe they just got tired of being away from home, or the famine ended, or they went off somewhere far away; maybe they're still out there somewhere, all ready to come back again, soon as we've learned how to build cities as big and fine as the old ones. I don't know. But I'll tell you this: it's something that's been in my heart all these years, and I never knew what to make of it. You think about all the tales you hear, about great heroes and mighty Sons of the Achaeans, and the great kings of Sparta and Argos and Mycenae; and Hercules, too, and Perseus, and all the famous men we remember to this day. If what my own grandfather told me is true – and he'd got no reason to lie that I can see – then how can all those stories be true as well? How come they don't tell about these city-burners? And how could Agamemnon be a Son of the Achaeans when Mycenae was burned down and buried in the ashes before we ever came to live there? Hell, even if any of the stories are true, which I'm inclined to doubt, they must be stories about the old-city folks, not our people – and if that's right, how did we ever get to hear them, since most of those folks were killed, and the few that was left we drove out into the hills and made into wild men? You don't push a man off his land and at the same time ask him about what his great-great-grandfather did.'

So, my grandfather told me, that's the story that goes with this knife; he told me to believe it or not as I pleased, and I'm telling you the same thing. Me, I believe it, because I've been to the old city and dug and poked about, and seen where there's ashes and charred timbers, just like he said, and the bones of dead men; but no gold or silver or anything like that, which you'd expect to find in great palaces such as those people built. Hell, if you want I'll take you there and you can see for yourselves, though it's a powerful sad place. It's all still there, and what's in the earth can't lie.

So that's that (Glycus said); and when folks like you come here, telling me they're lost noblemen and by rights they're princes in their own country – well, I think of the old burned city and the wild men, and my heart tells me it doesn't matter what the crows eat who you were or who you should be, or who you reckon you might have been if things had gone different; doesn't matter much more who you will be, when you're dead and somebody remembers your name, because most of that's just tall tales and comfort. All that matters, I reckon, is who you are now, what you can do with your hands and what you carry round with you; which is why you're in here sharing the wine with me, and not out there in the dark with the old dead heroes and the goats.

CHAPTER TWELVE

'Actually,' the Phoenician interrupted, 'he was right.'

He realised that everybody was staring at him, as if he were a chariot race. 'What I mean is,' he went on, 'I went to Egypt once, a long time ago now, and while I was there the people I was doing business with took me to see the great temple – one of the great temples anyway, they have rather a lot of them scattered about the place. Anyway, on the walls of this temple were carved pictures of an amazing-looking battle actually fought on the decks of ships, just like your friend told you about. When I asked the people I was with what the picture was meant to be, they told me it showed the Great King of Egypt utterly defeating his enemies. Well, that didn't help much – all the carvings on all the walls in Egypt show the Great King defeating enemies, even when everybody knows for a fact that he lost that particular battle and ran home and hid under his bed for the next two years. But I asked them if they could tell me more and they said, Yes, it was all in the –' (here he used that word again, the one the Sons of the Achaeans didn't know) '– under the pictures. So I asked what it meant and they—'

'Excuse me,' Palamedes interrupted. 'Are we talking about scratched squiggles again?'

'That's right,' the Phoenician said.

'Well, you people understand squiggles; why did you have to ask what they meant?'

The Phoenician could feel a headache coming on. 'Different squiggles,' he explained. 'In Egypt they have an entirely different system of [that word again] which we can't understand, just as they can't make out ours.'

There was a moment of silence. Then somebody sniggered.

'Sorry if I'm being a bit slow here,' Palamedes said, 'but if not everybody can understand them, doesn't that defeat the whole object of the exercise? I thought the idea was that anybody looking at the squiggles would know—'

'Any *Phoenician*,' the Phoenician said with a sigh. 'Or, if they're Egyptian squiggles—'

'I see,' Palamedes went on. 'And those ones you were showing me earlier, they're Phoenician squiggles?'

'That's right.'

'Which only Phoenicians can understand?'

'Well, yes. But—'

'So even if we were to learn how to make the squiggles, like you said we should, only you Phoenicians would know what they meant?'

'In a sense, yes. However—'

'Assuming, of course, that there's enough Phoenicians who care about what happened long ago in Elis to bother with it.'

'I—'

'Or even enough of you who have the faintest idea where Elis is. Right, thanks for clearing that up for me. Do go on with what you were telling us.'

The Phoenician wasn't sure he wanted to now; but it'd have been rude to sulk. 'All I was saying was,' he continued, 'the Egyptians told me what the squiggles said, and it was an account of how this king had fought a battle against a huge army of savages from across the sea who'd been going around burning and looting all the great cities of Asia. So yes, what that old man told you was true; they must have existed, and it was the Egyptians who put a stop to it. And if that part of the story's true—'

'Doesn't follow the rest of it is,' someone interrupted. 'No offence, but what you saw on the stones, that could've been a lie, just as what the old man told Cratus and Cleander could've been a lie. Maybe it was the same lie, even, and both of them had got it from the same place.'

'Besides,' someone else put in, 'you're only going on what these Egyptians told you. Isn't it possible that they couldn't understand the squiggles and were telling you some old tale they heard from someone else who pretended he'd got it from his great-great-great-great-grandfather? You've no actual way of knowing, have you?'

'He's right,' Palamedes said. 'The Egyptians apparently say one thing. The Sons of the Achaeans tell it a different way. What makes you automatically assume that they've got it right and we've got it wrong?'

The Phoenician thought for a moment. 'Well,' he said, 'you're just going on what you remember being told, years and years later. The Egyptians told me the carvings were put up in the king's lifetime. Surely the carvings are more likely to be right, for that very reason.'

Cratus smiled. 'But you said yourself,' he pointed out, 'a lot of the king's victories and great deeds carved on the walls weren't true; and everybody knew this, I'm assuming because their grandfathers told them what they were told when they were kids. You see the point I'm making here: even the Egyptians have more faith in their memories than the squiggles, because they know the squiggles sometimes lie. Well, if they don't trust their own squiggles, why exactly should we?'

'But . . .' The Phoenician was beginning to wish he hadn't raised the subject in the first place. 'I only thought I'd mention it,' he said. 'I thought you'd be interested, that's all.'

Palamedes smiled at him. 'There's interesting,' he said, 'and there's telling us we aren't who we think we are and the people we think we're descended from never existed. If that's what your squiggles teach you, I think we'll make do with our memories, what's in our heads and hearts. Much more of this knowledge of yours and we won't know anything at all.'

'Anyway,' Cleander said, yawning and getting to his feet, 'I've been sat here long enough; I think I'll go and sit in the sun for a bit. I don't need to hear the next bit of the story,' he added, 'I know it, because I was there. Unless, of course, my memory's starting to play tricks.'

So there we were (Cratus said), just like my brother's told you. Somehow, we'd decided that the best way to get back to Elis was to go on to Corinth. A good idea at the time, as you might say.

The old man gave us more than enough food and wine to see us to Corinth; I have no idea why, unless for some reason he'd decided he liked us. Or maybe it was by way of compensation for making us listen to that damn fool story.

Now, I've met some travellers over the years; men who've been on a long journey, and real, genuine travellers. You can tell them apart quite easily. Put them down in the middle of some great and wonderful city they've never been to before. Your not-really-travellers will walk around all morning with their heads jammed right back, gawping at the arches and the gateways and the tall buildings; but you'll find your true travellers sitting in the shade somewhere, not particularly fussed about what they see or don't see, happier taking a rest while they can and talking to each other about home.

By the time we reached Corinth, we were real travellers. Shortly before we reached the city, we'd all started arguing about what we were going to do when we got back – what we were going to say to the king, whether we might possibly have recruited enough games-players already to be able to put on some kind of a show, whether any of the men who'd said they'd come would actually turn up. We were so busy arguing that we hardly noticed walking through the city gates or through the streets. In fact, we went straight through and out the other side, heading down to the harbour, without realising what we'd done.

'First things first,' Cleander told us, as we were standing on the dock looking at the sea. 'Let's find a ship we can hitch a ride on. When we've done that, we'll go and find Sarpedon's friend, see if he'll help us. Agreed?'

Apathy is the nurse of unanimity; we agreed, if only to make him shut up, and started touring round the dock, talking to anybody who looked as if he owned a ship or knew someone that did. Didn't take us long to realise that that wasn't the way it was done, at least not in Corinth. What we should have done, so we gathered, was hang about under the portico of the temple, or in the cool shade of the fig trees, looking like we didn't want to be disturbed. Eventually, a day or a month or six years later, someone would sit down next to us and happen to mention in passing that he was sailing to Elis but some bastard of a giver-and-receiver who'd promised to take space on his ship had gone and let him down at the last moment by dying. Of course, we wouldn't reply to that immediately; we'd change the subject and talk about something completely different for a while, then gradually work the conversation back to ships and spaces and the possibility that we might want to go to Elis at some stage in the next twelve months. That was the proper way to do it, the way Corinthians had been arranging these matters since the first fifty-oared galley was launched there. Anything else was unacceptable, verging on mortal insult.

After we'd been told to go away a couple of dozen times, we decided we could use a rest and a chance for our hearts to cool down; so we settled ourselves under a tree and shared out the last of Glycus' fairly drinkable wine. It was hot, we were tired and Glycus' wine was thick enough to glue planks together with; in other words, we were just about to drift off into sleep when we noticed someone standing over us.

'Excuse me asking,' he said, 'but I heard there were some men from Elis hanging round here. Have you seen them? Only, an old friend of mine is with them, and I'd hate to miss him.'

Dusa (who was better at waking up quickly than the rest of us) asked him what his friend's name was. Sarpedon, the man said, and his own name was Oxyxiphus.

At that, Sarpedon pushed his hat on to the back of his head so the man could see his face, grinned like an idiot and said, 'Hello, Oxyxiphus. We were just coming to look for you.'

'That's luck,' the man replied, grinning back. 'Saves us both a job. How are you, anyway?'

This Oxyxiphus – well, he looked like he might very well be Sarpedon's friend. They were both about the same age, both of them big and mean-looking with a few scars here and there on their faces and arms. If I was poetically inclined, I'd be tempted to say they were like a pair of old heirloom swords – a bit nicked and notched on the edges, polished a trifle thin and with all the sharp corners rounded, but still as sharp and keen as the day they left the forge. Luckily for you, I'm not.

To be honest with you, I couldn't have cared less at that moment if he'd looked like a corpse fished out of a river; the fact that he was alive and here and presumably willing to help us made him the most beautiful sight I could ever remember having seen in my entire life, the sunrise over the Taygetus mountains included. And his next words were lovelier than anything the Nine Muses ever warbled, with or without harp accompaniment.

'You people look flogged out,' he said. 'You'd better come home with me, have a bath and something to eat.'

I was just luxuriating in the glory of those words, letting their splendour wash over me like the water of a pure mountain spring, when dear brother Cleander chose to open his ugly mouth.

'We can't stop long,' he said, thereby moving swiftly to the top of my list of people I'd most like to feed to the crows. 'We've still got to find a ship, remember.'

'A ship,' Oxyxiphus repeated. 'So where are you headed?'

'Elis,' Sarpedon replied. 'Or anywhere near there, we're not too fussy. Would you happen to know of anything going that way?'

Oxyxiphus smiled. 'Well,' he said, 'there's my ship. It's due to sail for a trip round the Peloponnese the day after tomorrow. Would that be any use to you, or were you looking to sail earlier?'

'No,' I said, perhaps a little too loudly to be perfectly polite; but my heart told me this was a time for clarity rather than elegance of expression. 'The day after tomorrow will suit us just fine. Couldn't be better, in fact.'

'Well, I hope that's settled, then,' said that godlike man. 'I must say, this has turned out as well as anybody could have asked; pleasant company for a day or so, and the chance to do an old friend a good turn. What more could a man ask for?'

If that had been a genuine question, I could have given him a long tally of suggestions, beginning with food and including boots, clothes, a sturdy mule-cart and the head of Alastor buried in the ant-hill of my choice. Odd, how travel alters a man's priorities.

When we got to know Oxyxiphus a little better, a few minor character flaws did begin to emerge. For one thing, he was the noisiest eater I've ever met – I've heard quieter earthquakes – and for another, his attitude towards my sister would under other circumstances have offended me mightily, almost to the point of doing something about it. That's another perspective thing, though. When I was young, I had strong views about old men who pester pretty girls; didn't hold with it, thought it was wrong and shameful and to be discouraged wherever possible. It only goes to show how muddle-headed one tends to be in one's youth. Now that I'm an old man myself and have the benefit of a lifetime of wisdom and experience, I realise that it's the other way around: young girls are wasted on young men, who lack the maturity and understanding of the world that's so important in these matters. In those days, for example, what I looked for in a woman was beauty, wit, grace and charm. With the benefit of age, I now know that the ideal qualities in a woman are beauty, gullibility, poor eyesight, patience and a weak head for strong wine.

Fortunately, Dusa was too busy eating and drinking to notice the way Oxyxiphus was leering at her, and too preoccupied to pay any attention to his rather unsubtle lines; so that was all right. When not stuffing her face or combing her hair, she seemed to spend most of her time staring at Pentheus, his profile or the back of his neck (if he happened to look in her direction, she swung her head away so fast I was worried she'd wring her own neck). That troubled me far more than Oxyxiphus' wolfish grins; but what with the food and the comfort and the improbability of the door flying open and twenty armed men rushing at us, I wasn't really inclined to worry about that, or anything, very much.

'So you've come all the way from Elis,' Oxyxiphus said, when we'd eaten as much as we could fit in without displacing any organs, and were gently flaking out against the wall. 'That must have been some trip.'

Sarpedon grinned at him. 'You might say that,' he replied. 'We've certainly had one or two interesting moments.'

'I'll bet,' said our host. 'No offence, but you look like you have, anyway.'

'Ah,' Sarpedon said with a groan, 'I'm afraid you're not seeing us at our best. You see, we had a bad time in Argos and had to clear out in a hurry.

'Trouble?' Oxyxiphus said sympathetically. 'Easy to get into, in Argos. They're strange people there.'

'You can say that again. If you're in the mood I'll tell you about it; better you hear it from us than someone else, or you might end up thinking hard thoughts about us.'

Oxyxiphus lifted his head. 'I couldn't care less about anything you may have got up to in Argos,' he said. 'None of my business, whatever it was. But I'd like to hear the story, if you're minded to tell it.'

So Sarpedon told him, with due emphasis on the completely unexpected and unprovoked nature of the attack on Pentheus (who came out of it all rather well).

'Just like that?' Oxyxiphus said. 'No warning or anything?'

Sarpedon lifted his head. 'I suppose there must have been a reason,' he said. 'People don't just attack other people for no reason in the middle of a sacred truce. But they didn't honour us with their confidences in the matter, so we're completely mystified.'

'Though we can hazard a guess,' Cleander interrupted, slurring his words ever so slightly. 'After all, Pentheus here isn't short of enemies.'

I was probably the only person who noticed the way Oxyxiphus' face changed when Cleander mentioned Pentheus' name (Sarpedon had avoided saying it, as any sensible man would have done in a stranger's house). And even I didn't think much about it at the time.

'Really?' our host said. 'How unfortunate.' He was craning his neck now, to get a better look at our young freeloader. 'If it's not too rude of me to ask,' he said, looking Pentheus in the eye, 'have you been in these parts before?'

By now Pentheus had gathered there was maybe something wrong. 'No,' he replied. 'Never.'

'Though, oddly enough,' Cleander went on, 'Corinth is where those people originally came from. Isn't that right, Pentheus?'

Sarpedon stamped on his foot so hard we could all hear it, but it was too late by then. Oxyxiphus was half standing up, examining Pentheus with one eyebrow lifted.

'I knew a man with that name once,' he was saying. 'Or rather, I knew of him; never spoke to him, only saw him once. Years ago now, of course, and it's so hard to hold a face in one's memory. That said –' He peered again. 'You wouldn't happen to have family on Aegina, would you?'

'No,' Pentheus said.

Oxyxiphus nodded. 'Well, of course, that's right; not any more you don't. Going back a few years, though—'

I saw Sarpedon looking extremely edgy, and Dusa had gone as white as milk. Even Cleander was frowning slightly, as if starting to realise he may have said the wrong thing.

'Going back a few years,' Pentheus said, 'yes.'

Oxyxiphus dipped his chin slightly in acknowledgement, then shot out his hands round Pentheus' throat so quickly I hardly saw him do it. Pentheus sprang up out of his seat, but our host's hands on his shoulders pushed him back again.

'It's all right,' he said. 'You're a guest in my house, I'm not going to harm you. Not today, anyway. And probably not tonight. But if I find you anywhere inside my fences by sun-up tomorrow, then so help me you'll be going home to Aegina in a small bronze jar. Understood?'

'Now just a moment—' Sarpedon began. He didn't get any further.

'And as for you,' Oxyxiphus went on, giving his old comrade-in-arms a big eyeful of mustard, 'it breaks my heart to see what's become of you, going round the country with beggars and murderers. From a stranger it'd be bad enough; but you come in here, expecting me to help the man who killed my own sister's son—'

Strangely enough, what depressed me most of all about this turn of events – Cleander hasn't snuck back in, has he? Good, right. What depressed me most of all at that moment, more than the injustice of it all or even the rather desperate position we were back in, was the ugly possibility that Pentheus' prince-in-his-own-land story might turn out to be true after all. As you all know, I'd assumed from the start that he was lying blind; if I'd had to suffer proof that he really was a king's son escaping from a desperate blood-feud, I'd probably have broken down and cried my heart out, right there in front of everybody. But a moment's calm thought put paid to that; all that Oxyxiphus had confirmed was that Pentheus really did come from Aegina, and that at some stage he'd killed this man's nephew. Those facts could just as easily fit my wandering bandit theory, or any one of a dozen other disreputable and shameful versions of Pentheus' past. Once I'd realised that, I felt a whole lot better.

'I take it,' Sarpedon said quietly, once he had a chance to get a word in, 'that the offer of a ride home on your ship doesn't stand any more.'

It wasn't the cleverest thing to say right then. 'That's right,' Oxyxiphus said. 'Now, here's what I'm prepared to do. Since you used to be my friend, and I owe you a good turn for what you did for me back then, I'll let you all go, provided you're out of here by dawn tomorrow. What's more, I won't come after you, I won't tell the rest of my family you've been here, even. But if any of you so much as set foot in Corinth ever again – well, I'd advise against it. As a friend.'

Sarpedon looked at him, and sighed. 'I suppose I should thank you,' he said.

'No suppose about it. If it'd been anybody else—'

'Thank you for the food.' Sarpedon stood up, beckoned to us to follow. 'And thank you for the offer of a night's sleep, but we won't stay where we're not welcome. Cratus, Dusa, Cleander . . .' He looked round at Pentheus and scowled. 'Come on, you,' he added. 'We'll be going now.' He took a few steps towards the door. 'Just one thing,' he added. 'Out of interest only. Are there many good games-players here in Corinth these days?'

'Plenty,' Oxyxiphus replied. 'What do you want to know that for?'

Sarpedon lifted his head. 'Oh, no reason,' he said. 'Goodbye.'

So there we were again (Cratus continued); slung out of Argos, destitute and surrounded by enemies in Corinth, better off by full stomachs and thick heads but still in the same old rags we'd arrived in – unfortunately, we hadn't got as far as the new-clothes-for-old stage of traditional Corinthian hospitality by the time we were given our marching orders. Everything still as bad as ever it had been.

'And it's all your fault,' I couldn't resist pointing out to Pentheus as we traipsed back through the city towards the harbour – just in case he'd somehow missed that point himself. 'If it wasn't for you, we'd be lodging up at the palace right now, trading presents with King Bacchias and asking if he liked games-playing.'

'That's perfectly true,' Pentheus replied quietly. 'I never mean to pass around my bad luck, but it's catching, like the plague. I'm sorry. That's all I can say, really.'

I took a deep breath. 'Well, it's not going to help matters shouting at you,' I heard myself say, though it wasn't what was in my heart. 'But if you want to make it up to us, you'd better think of a way of getting us on board a ship before Oxyxiphus changes his mind.'

He looked at me. 'All right,' he said. 'Here's what we'll do.'

Of all the crazy, idiotic schemes I've ever had the bad luck to get involved with . . .

Picture in your mind the harbour at Corinth – yes, I know you've never been there, and take it from me, if you haven't been there you've got no chance of imagining what it's actually like. But do what we all do when someone tells a story: think of some place you do know that you reckon might be something like, and pretend to yourself that it's Corinth harbour.

There's a man called Callipous, sitting on a coil of rope beside his ship and thinking of very little. It's a warm day and he's been working hard, getting all his gear on board for a long, leisurely trip. He's made the run four or five times before, so he's no stranger to the sea and ships; and, like so many seafaring types whose lives are constantly in the hands of the gods, he's inclined to be just a little superstitious, a trait he unintentionally betrays by spitting in the fold of his cloak when a black dog trots past him on the quayside.

(You have no idea how long it took us to find a black dog; then we had to catch the wretched thing; then we had to persuade it to run along the quay past the various shipmasters who were sitting out there. Our diligence was rewarded, though, as you'll hear in a moment.)

A little later, just long enough for a man to eat an apple, a shadow falls across his face and he looks up to see a rather alarming-looking party standing over him; four men, and a girl holding a big, dusty jar. They look like vagrants, maybe highwaymen down on their luck. He doesn't like the look of them much.

'That your ship?' asks the oldest of the men, nodding sideways.

'That's right,' Callipous replies. 'And who might you be?'

The man doesn't reply; he turns aside, whispers a few words to the other men, and then something longer to the girl, who glances at Callipous, looking rather sad, and suppresses a shudder. Callipous is beginning to wonder what's going on.

'You planning to sail any time soon?' the older man asks him abruptly. He's very rude, that older man, but there's a sort of fierce intensity about his manner that gives Callipous the impression that it'd be wise to answer his questions.

'Tomorrow,' he replies. 'Depending on how the wind holds up.'

The older man gives him a perfunctory nod, and goes back into conference with his associates. Callipous can't hear what they're muttering without leaning forward and being obvious about it, but he can pick out the odd word, like 'omen' and 'unfortunate' and 'I still say we should tell him' (at which the older man lifts his head sharply and scowls hot mustard). Eventually, after their debate's apparently got quite heated, one of the younger men steps away from the rest, as if taking some unilateral action the others don't agree with, and comes over to where Callipous is sitting.

'Did I hear you say you were planning on sailing tomorrow?' he says, while the others glower frightfully at him.

'That's right,' says Callipous, who by now is distinctly rattled. 'What's all this about, anyway?'

The young man looks gravely at him. 'If I were you,' he says, 'I'd forget about it. Stay home. Find something else to do.'

'Why?'

'You don't want to know,' the young man says grimly. 'Just take my word for it; unload your gear, send your crew home, forget the whole thing. All right?'

Our friend is now very rattled indeed. 'It's not all right,' he says, 'not by a long bowshot. Who the hell are you people, anyway? And what's so damned interesting about my ship?'

At this, the older man laughs in a less than pleasant manner, while the girl looks away and stifles a sob. 'You're wasting your breath,' the older man says irritably. 'He won't listen. They never do.'

The young man shrugs and starts to turn away, but he's prevented by Callipous' hand on his shoulder. He turns round, looking angry.

'You'd better not do that again,' he says quietly. 'Ever.' Callipous immediately removes the offending hand, and apologises. 'Better,' the young man says. 'Look, I'm telling you for your own good: don't go out in that ship, understood?'

'No,' Callipous says wretchedly. 'Look, what's the problem? It's a good ship. We hauled her up at the start of the season and checked her over, there's nothing wrong with her that we could see. Have you spotted something we haven't, or what?'

The young man smiles sadly. 'Friend,' he says, 'what we've seen, you couldn't ever hope to see. And if you could, you really wouldn't want to.'

By now, Callipous is beside himself with apprehension; you can almost see his heart bobbing up and down, like it's trying to get out. 'Oh, come on,' he says, 'you can't just say something like that and walk away. What is all this?'

The older man steps forward, as if he's trying to stop his young friend from saying something he shouldn't. The other two men are looking very thoughtful indeed. The girl is starting to snuffle. 'I'm sorry,' the young man says, looking genuinely upset. 'I'd tell you if I could, but . . . Well, there's my advice. Take it or leave it.'

He starts to walk away, but Callipous darts in front of him, so the young man would have to shove him aside to get past.

'No,' he says. 'I'm sorry.'

'Tell me,' Callipous pleads. 'Please.'

You can see the struggle going on between the young man and

his heart; finally, his heart wins and he says, 'All right. But if you breathe a word of this—'

'No!' shouts the older man, grabbing his shoulder. The young man spins round and for a moment it looks like they're going to start fighting; then the older man slowly backs away.

'I promise,' Callipous says fervently. 'By the River. Honest.'

'All right.' The young man sighs; and he tells the wretched shipmaster that the young woman – apparently young woman – is in fact none other than the Titaness Pandora; and the jar she's carrying is, well, Pandora's jar. Callipous' jaw flops open as if someone had just cut the tendons, but he doesn't say anything, he just stares. Pandora, the young man continues, is trying to round up all the plagues and evils and horrible things she was stupid enough to let out of the jar all those years ago; it's taken her a hundred years just to snaffle one minor variant of plague, and the trouble is, every time she opens the jar to put something back, something else pops out again. Still, it's the job the gods have given her to do, and she's got to keep at it till it's done.

'That's awful,' Callipous mumbles.

'You can say that again,' the young man says. 'And if you ask me, it's even worse for us. You see, we're her mortal descendants; she's my great-great-great-great-grandmother, believe it or not, and it's up to us to spend our whole lives helping her. I mean, look at us; destitute, in rags, spending our whole lives trudging from place to place with no end to it in sight; and what did we do wrong? Nothing.'

Obviously Callipous agrees that it's a rotten shame. 'But what about my ship?' he says. 'What's my ship got to do with Pandora's jar?'

The young man gives him a very severe look. 'You want to know how your ship's involved in all this? All right. But first you've got to promise me, if I tell you, you'll do what I say.'

Callipous doesn't like that but he can't see any alternative. 'Go on,' he says.

'There's a singularly nasty and destructive plague nesting in your ship,' the young man says. 'Which is why the only thing you can possibly do is sail it a couple of hundred paces out to sea and set it on fire. No other way, I'm afraid.'

Callipous looks heartbroken – well, he would. That ship represents a substantial part of his wealth; to lose it, just like that – But on the other hand, a plague . . . 'Can't she just go on board and catch it?' he says. 'I thought you said that's what she does.'

The young man shakes his head. 'Too dangerous,' he replies. 'You see, if she drives it off the ship while you're in harbour, the horrible thing's quite liable to fly out over the town like a startled partridge, and then you'll have the deaths of every man, woman and child in Corinth on your conscience. I don't think you'd like that, somehow. On the other hand, if you get on that ship and sail it anywhere, you'll get the plague and die yourself. No, the only thing for it is to burn the ship, and just hope that'll kill the plague. It's a real long shot, but it might just work.'

Callipous is nearly in tears by this point. 'What about her?' he says. 'If she's a Titaness, like you said, the plague can't hurt her, surely.'

'Oh, she's all right,' the young man says, 'and so are we; it's an inherited immunity. But that's not going to do you any good, is it? Well, that's the whole story. Now you'd better do what you promised, and burn the ship. You ought to be all right taking it out into the middle of the harbour; usually the plague doesn't strike immediately. Depends on whether it's asleep or awake, of course.'

'I've got a better idea,' Callipous says, shivering. 'Why don't you take the ship and sink it? You'll be all right, you just said.'

The young man looks astonished. 'Us?' he says. 'What the hell makes you think we know anything about ships? Besides, you're the one who promised.'

'Please,' Callipous says desperately. 'After all, it's your plague. Surely it's up to you to deal with it.'

The young man bites his lip and his mouth twitches as he talks the idea over with his heart. 'Oh, all right,' he says eventually. 'I suppose it's up to us, we can't ask you to risk your life in our battle. I'll tell the others; though they really aren't going to like it.'

Then there's a long, seemingly acrimonious discussion between the young man and his companions; at the end of which the young man nods to Callipous – yes, they'll do it. He looks like he's just been saved from drowning.

'That's wonderful,' he says. 'Right, I'll just get my gear off the ship, and then she's all yours.'

'Oh no you don't,' the young man says. 'For all we know, the plague's already laid its eggs all over your cargo. No, that's got to go down to the bottom of the bay, just like the ship. Otherwise there'd be no point, and the deal's off.'

Callipous looks sad for a tiny splinter of a heartbeat; then his heart tells him, Bugger the cargo, your life's at stake here. 'You go ahead,' he says, 'do whatever you have to. Just get rid of the crow-struck thing.'

Which is how we came to acquire a ship of our very own.

I'd been sceptical when Pentheus told us he knew how to work a ship – comes of being an islander, he told us; pretty well everybody on Aegina knows about ships – but credit where it's due, he certainly knew his stuff. It was a pity, though, that he was such a bad shipmaster – he knew what had to be done and how to do it, he was just lousy at explaining. Since he was down the back end holding on to the steering stick – don't look at me like that, friend; you people may spend all your lives on boats and know the technical terms, but I don't, and I'm the one telling the story – since Pentheus was working the rudder (you see? I knew it really), he couldn't leave his post to show us how to do all the ropes and stuff; all he could do was shout at us until, by a process of elimination, we managed to do what he wanted.

It didn't help matters that we were all horribly seasick; apart from Pentheus, of course. If he'd had enough tact to fill a small acorn cup, he'd at least have pretended to groan and make a show of leaning over the side making horrible noises from time to time, instead of lounging about in the bows scowling at us as if we were children making a fuss over nothing.

'When he said there was an evil spirit on board this ship,' Dusa gasped, as she scoured the dregs out of an already empty stomach, 'I thought he was kidding.'

'You wait,' I replied, 'till the wind gets up. They do say that when there's a storm blowing, the movement of the ship can make some people a trifle queasy.'

'Shut up,' Dusa replied, reasonably enough; and just then, some unkind sea-monster grabbed hold of the ship from underneath and rocked it up and down, and I had other things on my mind than squabbling with my kid sister.

'You two,' bellowed Pentheus, 'I thought I told you to make those lines fast. Come on, or we'll lose the damned sail!'

I didn't reply – I wasn't capable of speech just then – but if I'd had the Gorgon's head handy at that moment, we'd have had a life-sized statue for a helmsman. The only consolation that I could see was that the rest of my family were suffering just as much, and in some cases rather more.

And that was only the first day.

We spent the night out at sea – there was some technical reason for this, to do with winds, currents, the attitude of the Pleiades and the fact that we couldn't find anywhere to put in before it got dark – and we spent it lying on our backs on the deck feeling very ill indeed, while Pentheus cheerfully informed us that next day we'd be putting in at Sicyon, which was traditionally hostile to Corinth and therefore likely to be reasonably safe. We'd make landfall, he predicted, just after sunrise. None of us believed him.

But, come sunrise – we'd been awake all night, so we didn't miss anything – we looked out over the left side of the ship and, sure enough, there was a city, exactly where Pentheus had predicted it would be. I'll confess, I felt a little bit guilty for having assumed that he couldn't possibly be right; everybody, they say, is good at something, and there was no reason to believe that navigation wasn't Pentheus' particular skill. We mumbled a few words of apology as he bossed us around, trying to get us to do all the complicated things that need to be done in order to get a boat into a harbour.

'This is better,' Dusa said, once we were on dry land again. 'I love the way it doesn't move about under your feet.'

'It's more or less as I remember it,' Sarpedon announced. 'It's a long time since I was here last, but nothing seems to have changed. Well,' he went on, after I'd asked him what was so unusual about that, 'on this trip I've learned not to make assumptions like that. Like, I'm not assuming that just because we've arrived safely, something horrible isn't going to happen to us.'

Pentheus frowned at him disapprovingly, then announced that we were going into the city to visit the princes; we might look like tramps, but the splendour of our gifts (Callipous' gifts, actually, but only we knew that) would soon convince them of our worth and true nobility, and then they'd probably give us some decent clothes and a good meal.

I couldn't remember having been at the staff meeting where we'd elected Pentheus as our leader; but it was a good suggestion, in spite of its origin, so I didn't object. Actually, I felt mildly confident. After all, we were going there as ordinary travellers; there was no reason why the subject of games-playing (which my heart had come to regard as the most dangerous and ill-omened topic under the sun) should possibly arise; which meant Pentheus was unlikely to get an opportunity to kill anybody in a terrible accident or offend any major local customs, and we might actually get out of Sicyon alive and with our ears still on our heads.

'The palace is up there,' Sarpedon said, 'just behind the side of the hill. We'll be able to see it as soon as we get to the top of this ridge.' He was quite right. Sicyon was larger than I'd expected from the few passing references I'd heard; the same size as Elis, maybe a little bigger or a little smaller – hard to tell when a city's spread out over the landscape, like honey on a handful of bread.

Somehow we felt a little bit diffident about marching up to the palace gate, something we wouldn't have given a second thought to not so long before. Understandable, I suppose; we were grubby and scruffy, and we'd just been thrown out of two major cities. These things tend to tarnish even the most brightly burnished heart. I think the gatekeeper shared our doubts about our suitability as guests of a great house; but Pentheus snarled him out of the way in best aristocratic style, and we marched past the gatekeeper without another word.

I suppose it was getting things right for a change that inspired the change in Pentheus' demeanour; instead of being wan and interestingly pathetic, he held his head up like a man who owns a herd of a thousand head, looked the princes straight in the eye and gave them just the right kind of cheerful, slightly offhand greeting that you'd expect from a man who was, to coin a phrase, a prince in his own country. As a result, the princes didn't seem to notice what we were wearing, or the dust in our hair; they called for food and water and tables, showed us to the seats of honour and sat quiet until we'd washed and eaten.

'Is this your first visit here?' asked the elder prince.

'For my brother and sister and myself, yes,' Cleander replied, wiping his hands on a napkin. 'My uncle's been here before, but that was quite a few years ago.'

'It was just after the war between Corinth and Nemea,' Sarpedon added. 'What would that be? Twenty years ago?'

The older prince smiled. 'That explains why I don't remember you,' he said. 'I'd only have been five, and my brother here wasn't even born then.'

'My name's Sarpedon,' Uncle replied. 'These are my nephews Cleander and Cratus, and my niece Eurymedusa. Our companion here is Pentheus.'

I was watching the princes closely out of the corner of my eye, but the name didn't seem to mean anything to them. So that was all right.

'I'm Oenophilus,' said the older prince, 'and my brother's called Hipposthenes.' He turned his head a little and gave Dusa a rather charming smile. 'It's a rare pleasure for us to get such a beautiful visitor,' he added. 'I hope you'll have time to stay a while, if your business elsewhere isn't too urgent.'

Big-brother instincts made me clench a little at that; and then I thought, Hang on, no; Prince of Sicyon's interested in my sister, best of luck to him. If he was seventy years old and never sober after sun-up, he'd still be an improvement on the competition. 'We'd be delighted,' I replied, before anybody else had the chance. 'We're in no particular hurry, after all, and what we've seen of your city so far has impressed us greatly.'

And stay we did; and very pleasant it was too, even after the relative novelty of good food, good company and nobody trying to kill us had worn off a little. In fact, we were feeling so relaxed and comfortable by the third day that one of us actually ventured to raise the dread subject of games-playing. What's more, it was me.

'That sounds fascinating,' said Prince Hipposthenes, after Cleander had given the standard speech. 'You know, Oenophilus, I think we ought to go. It'd be fun.'

'You go,' his brother replied indulgently, 'you're the games-player. Stands to reason,' he added, 'that someone called Strength of Horses should be a mad-keen charioteer. You are going to have chariot-races, aren't you?'

'Of course,' Cleander said. 'We're expecting quite a strong field; particularly if we can get Rhius of Aegeum to come. We'll be calling on him in a couple of days – well, we'll be virtually passing his door, so we thought—'

Hipposthenes looked puzzled. 'A couple of days?' he said. 'You'll be lucky, unless you've got all the winds tied up in a bag, like the man in the story. Or are you thinking of a different Aegeum?'

Cleander frowned. 'There is only one, isn't there? Aegeum, on the north coast of the Peloponnese, about two days' sail from here.'

The princes looked at each other. 'Excuse me if this sounds like a silly question,' said Oenophilus, 'but where exactly do you think you are?'

Cleander raised an eyebrow and smiled quizzically. 'Sicyon, of course,' he said.

'Oh.' Oenophilus pursed his lips. 'Well, actually, you're in Megara.'

'Megara?' Cleander looked as if someone had just dropped a chicken on his head. 'No, that can't be right, surely.'

'Well, we've lived here all our lives and we're pretty sure,' Hipposthenes replied.

In my heart, the mist cleared and I understood. Instead of taking ship from the northern harbour of Corinth and sailing north-west along the coast of the Peloponnese through the Corinthian Gulf, we'd sailed north-east from the eastern harbour, on the other side of the Isthmus, away from the Peloponnese and up the Saronic Gulf towards Athens; completely the opposite direction, in fact. Easy enough mistake to make, I suppose, provided the god's taken away your wits and you were an idiot to start with.

'Pentheus?' Cleander said.

'Not that it matters to us,' Hipposthenes continued smoothly. 'After all, we're us and you're you; the fact that you'd confused the place we live with somewhere else can't matter all that much, can it?'

'And we've really enjoyed having you as guests,' Oenophilus added. 'So if there's anything we can do to help get you back on the right course – food, wine, anything else you might need for your journey—'

'Especially since it turns out to be rather longer than you'd anticipated—'

(Which was an extremely valid point; instead of being eight days from Elis, we were – well, considerably more. We'd have to turn round, go back past Corinth, all round the southern Peloponnese – more or less the same way we'd come. It wasn't really the sort of thing we wanted to hear at that precise moment.)

I was looking at Pentheus, however; not because I was trying to kill him with a stare (if that technique had worked, he'd never have left Argos alive) but because he wasn't looking at all the way I'd have expected. Me, in his position, I'd be cringing with mortal embarrassment. Not Pentheus. He was looking – well, completely preoccupied.

'Megara,' he said.

'That's right, Megara,' Cleander repeated. 'And you promised us we were well on the way home. Of all the—'

'That's only a day and a half's sail away from—'

From Aegina; and the tiresome young fool had suddenly come over all thoughtful. I really didn't want to hear any more. Unfortunately, it wasn't up to me.

'From Athens?' prompted Hipposthenes. 'If you've never been to Athens, you really ought to consider a detour. For one thing, there's some really first-class games-players—'

'From Aegina,' Pentheus said. 'Where I come from. Only, I haven't been there in a long time.' He frowned, and I'll swear I could actually see the god standing over him, stuffing the idea into his mind so tightly that it's a wonder his head didn't burst. It was clearly an idea that would take some shifting. 'Oenophilus,' he said, in a strangely cold voice, 'did you say just now that you'd be prepared to help us out with anything we needed?'

No fool, the Prince of Megara; he could see trouble coming. 'Well, yes,' he said. 'Within reason, of course.'

'Oh, of course,' Pentheus replied. 'Look, if it's no trouble, I'd like to borrow an army.'

CHAPTER THIRTEEN

'I beg your pardon?' Oenophilus said.

'And some ships, of course,' Pentheus went on, 'to get the army over there. I don't know how many I'd need – it depends on the size of the army, doesn't it? – but we can work out the details later.'

'Excuse me,' Hipposthenes interrupted, 'but my heart is wondering if we've missed something. Why do you want an army? And what's this got to do with Aegina?'

'Ignore him, please,' Cleander said, his eyes as wide as wine-cups. 'He's been out in the sun without a hat; he'll be better soon, I promise, and then we'll be on our way.'

'Because,' Pentheus said, ignoring my brother completely, 'I'm the rightful Prince of Aegina, but I need an army to drive out the usurpers. Of course,' he added, 'I wouldn't expect you to help me for nothing.'

'You wouldn't,' Oenophilus murmured.

'Of course not. Once I'm restored to my throne, the traitors who supported the usurpers will have to be dealt with. Their estates and property are likely to amount to a substantial fortune.'

'Quite,' said Oenophilus. 'No offence, friend, but are you out of your mind? Even if you're who you say you are, what on earth makes you think we'd be interested in risking our men and resources on some crazy foreign adventure to help a stranger we've only known for a day or so?'

At which Pentheus smiled. 'Because it's the right thing to do,' he said. 'And because once you land and word gets around that you're bringing me home, the people will rush to help you, so the usurpers won't stand a chance.'

'You're sure about that, are you? I mean, you've been in touch with your countless supporters there for years, laying plans and making preparations?'

'No,' Pentheus replied.

'But you do have evidence to prove that the people of Aegina can't wait to have you back and get rid of these usurpers?'

'Well, no.'

'I see.' Oenophilus nodded gravely. 'So all you can offer us is unassailable proof that you really are who you say you are; some kind of tangible evidence that'd convince anybody, no matter how sceptical?'

'You have my word,' Pentheus said.

'Indeed.' The prince sighed. 'You want us to launch an entirely unprovoked attack on a powerful kingdom – by sea, which makes the whole thing about ten times as hard as a land attack would be – and risk death and destitution, on the strength of the word of honour of a man whose close friend and travelling companion claims is crazy in the head because of sunstroke. Tell me: if you were the Prince of Aegina –'

'I am the Prince of Aegina.'

'– And someone like you came to your house and put a proposition like that to you, what would you tell him? Really?'

Pentheus looked annoyed. 'At least let me tell you the story,' he said. 'That'll convince you, I'm sure.'

Oenophilus lifted his head. 'No offence,' he said, 'but I don't think I'll take you up on your kind offer. I'm sorry if I sound like I don't believe you. It's just that we had someone else come by here – what, six months ago? – and he said he was a prince in his own country and down on his luck, and we were terribly sympathetic and offered to help him with anything he needed. Turned out he was a stonemason's son from Athens on the run from the very angry father of a very pregnant daughter, not to mention being mixed up in some ghastly blood-feud. That experience made us uncommonly hard-hearted and cynical when it comes to exiled royalty; however worthy the cause, we simply don't want to know. And now, if you don't mind, we'd quite like to drop the subject and talk about something else, just in case we get angry with each other and spoil an agreeable friendship.'

Pentheus really did look heartbroken, as if he was a little boy and someone had trodden on his little clay chariot. He didn't say a word, just stood up and walked out of the hall. A moment later, Dusa swept out after him, having given me an entirely unwarranted eyeful of mustard.

'He'll be better soon,' Cleander said. 'I gather he got a bump on the head when he was young, and occasionally it makes him say strange things. When he comes round again, he doesn't even remember what he said. Entirely harmless, though.'

The princes gave my brother a much longer, harder look than ever they gave Pentheus; served him right, too. Then Hipposthenes started talking about the optimum size of chariot wheels.

After a distinctly uncomfortable evening, during the course of which neither Pentheus nor Dusa reappeared, we went to bed. After the princes had gone off to the upper room, Cleander heaved a great sigh and said he supposed we'd better clear out early next morning, since we obviously couldn't stay here any longer.

'I can't see what you're cribbing about,' Sarpedon put in. 'Sounded like a perfectly good idea to me. If I'd been those two, I'd have jumped at the chance.'

Neither of us could be bothered to reply to that.

'Do you think one of us should go and look for Dusa?' Cleander asked with a yawn, as he snuggled down on a thick pile of furs. 'I couldn't care less if Pentheus has jumped in the sea or been eaten by crows, but she is our sister.'

'The hell with her,' I replied. 'If she's dead now, she'll probably still be dead in the morning. If she's alive, I hope it rains.'

Unusually, Cleander didn't argue the point further; I think it had all been too much for him. He rolled over on to his side and fell asleep. I wasn't long in joining him, at that; stress and aggravation make me sleep soundly, rather than the opposite.

We were woken up not by the sparkle of pink dawn light glistening through the smoke-hole, but by the slamming back of bolts and the sound of loud voices. Gods, wondered my sleepy heart, now what've they gone and done? But when the princes came bustling into the hall, they didn't look angry or upset. Quite the reverse.

'Your friend,' said Hipposthenes briskly. 'The Prince of Aegina. Do you know where he is?'

The obvious explanation was that I was still asleep, and my dreams were being influenced by the huge chunk of Sicilian cheese I'd eaten the night before. For once, though, the obvious answer wasn't the right one.

The princes, it appeared, had had a dream; the same dream, even. Their eyes were sparkling when they told us about it; the dream had come and stood over them in the middle of the night, taking the form of a young and lovely woman, white as chalk from head to foot and with no clothes on. Her name, she told them, was Victory, and she'd come to tell them that if they went with Prince Pentheus to Aegina, not only would they drive out the usurpers quickly and with only nominal losses, they'd also acquire great wealth and imperishable glory. Then, in a sudden flash of light, she'd vanished and they'd woken up.

'So you see,' Oenophilus said, 'we've got to find the prince as soon as we possibly can, before he changes his mind. I'm afraid we were shamefully rude to him yesterday; we'd hate for him to go away and get help from somebody else.'

When I'd heard as much as I could take, I told them I'd go find Pentheus, and left the house. Actually, I did have a pretty shrewd idea of where I might find him; the previous day I'd noticed a fairly secluded spring welling out of the side of the hill, about two hundred paces from the house. Sure enough, there they both were. Dusa's hair was wet, and she was combing it while Pentheus sat on a rock gazing at her as if she was Odysseus' first sight of Ithaca.

'All right,' I demanded, 'how did you do it?'

Pentheus spun round and scowled at me. 'I don't know what you mean,' he said. Dusa, though, just lifted her head and turned to look at me.

'Flour,' she said.

'Flour?'

She nodded. 'Just ordinary flour, sprinkled generously over a coat of olive oil. I was afraid the oil would seep through and leave big ugly yellow patches, but it didn't. Of course, there wasn't much light for them to see by, only what was coming from the little lamp we smuggled in.'

I was curious. 'What about the flash of light at the end? That sounded like it was impressive.'

Dusa laughed. 'That was just Pentheus with a mirror – that ivory-backed one we found in the wooden box on board the ship. Knew it'd come in handy for something. Anyway, he flashed the mirror and then immediately pinched out the lamp. Pretty convincing effect, don't you think?'

'I don't know,' I said. 'I wasn't there, remember? But my opinion doesn't matter anyway; it's the princes you have to deal with.' I took a breath. 'Talking of whom—' I added.

'Well?' Pentheus said. 'Come on, time we weren't here.' He stood up. 'You aren't going to tell anyone, are you?'

'He wouldn't do anything like that,' Dusa said. 'Besides, if he goes to the princes and tries to make them believe that what they saw was just me all covered in flour, I don't think he'll succeed. And they might get quite upset, thinking he'd tried to make a fool out of them.'

I lifted my head. 'At least you were considerate enough not to tell me what you were thinking of doing before you did it,' I said. 'If I'd known, I'd have worried myself to death. But what god put such a crazy idea into your heart to begin with?'

Dusa giggled. 'It was that old story,' she said. 'You know, the illustrious ancestor who got slung out of his kingdom, and used the same trick to get back? That's why I thought it might work. After all, it worked back then.'

'Oh, so it was your idea, then?' I said angrily. 'Dusa, of all the idiotic—'

'It worked,' she repeated. 'Which means it wasn't idiotic at all. Quite inspired, in fact. Besides, I remember you and Cleander saying before we left that a variation on the scam might come in handy at some stage. You didn't think it was idiotic then.'

My heart wanted me to point out that we'd specifically agreed to use a more tactful approach to the basic principle. But, not wanting a mirror thrown at my head, I decided not to.

'Cheer up,' Pentheus said, coming over and slapping me painfully hard on the shoulder. 'We're going to go to war. Isn't that good news?'

'Just a moment,' the Phoenician said. 'Are you seriously asking me to believe that these two princes, Oenophilus and Hippo-whatever, these two *heads of state*, that they went from being completely against the idea of this war to all in favour of it, all because of a *dream*?'

There was a moment of silence, while the Sons of the Achaeans all looked at the Phoenician.

'Yes,' Palamedes said eventually.

'I'm sorry,' the Phoenician went on, sounding rather annoyed, 'but I can't see that, personally.'

'You can't?' Palamedes frowned at him, as if he'd just cast doubt on the existence of the colour green. 'How strange. Surely even in your country you recognise that dreams are sent by Zeus, or whatever it is you call him where you come from.'

'Not really, no,' the Phoenician said. 'Some of us believe that from time to time, what we see in our dreams may contain some kind of message from the gods. Usually, though, it's so obscure and downright tricksy that you're better off ignoring it completely, for fear of jumping to the wrong conclusion and doing exactly what the dream was warning you against.'

'I see,' Palamedes said, scratching the bridge of his nose. 'So if a dream came and stood over you and told you to do something—'

'I don't get that sort of dream very often,' the Phoenician interrupted. 'Usually it's really peculiar things, like I'm standing on the seashore watching myself sail away, or I'm making a speech in the market-place without any clothes on—'

'If a dream told you to do something,' Palamedes said, carefully ignoring the Phoenician's interruption, 'in clear, easy-to-understand terms, presumably you would do it, wouldn't you?'

'I doubt it,' the Phoenician said. 'That is, if my poor dead grandmother came and stood over me in my sleep and told me to shave off the left side of my beard and hop round the town square on one foot singing a drinking song, no, I don't suppose I would.'

Palamedes looked at him for a while, then shrugged. 'You're weird,' he said.

Later that morning (said Cratus), Pentheus told his story to the princes. I'll say this for him: he was consistent, almost word-perfect. Of course, he may well have told it many times before – more than likely, in fact, given his circumstances. Or maybe he just had an excellent memory, like I have.

Up till then I'd have described the two princes of Megara as level-headed, if not hard-headed. They certainly weren't hard-hearted. Maybe it was the thought of having missed out on a pretty girl who also loved racing chariots that brought tears to Hipposthenes' eyes, but I think the god put genuine pity in Oenophilus' heart. Only goes to show what you can achieve if you've got a way with words and a girlfriend who looks good in flour.

Talking of words, 'girlfriend' there was intended to convey its usual connotations; I don't know exactly what those two got up to after they rushed out of the hall the previous evening, but my guess is that anointing with oil and flour only came at the end. You can tell, can't you, by intercepting the eye contact, the sharp, almost instinctive glances back and forth. I don't know which I found more nauseating, the idea of the war or the prospect of Pentheus as a brother-in-law.

When I shared this sentiment with Cleander, though, his attitude amazed me. He wasn't pleased exactly; but my brother's always had this remarkable ability, when things are apparently at their lowest ebb, to adapt. He sort of gives himself a shake and changes his shape, like the Old Man of the Sea in the story; and next thing you know, he's transformed himself from a universal victim into an entirely different creature, ideally suited to take best advantage of the changed circumstances.

'Look at it another way,' he said. 'What do you reckon to the prospect of having the Prince of Aegina as a brother-in-law?'

'Not much,' I replied honestly.

'It's the only way I can see for Dusa to marry into a great house,' Cleander said. 'You know, things may not turn out so badly after all.'

Many famous men over the years have murdered their brothers. Quite a few of them, if the old tales are to be believed, have gone on to prosper and live long, happy lives. I could have been one of them, but for some reason the god prevented me, grabbing me by the hair and holding me back. So I didn't do anything. I just said, 'Well, so long as you're happy,' and walked away.

From Megara to Aegina is a day and a half, assuming the winds don't mess you about. The usual procedure is to stop roughly halfway at the group of poxy little islands whose name escapes me, but that's not a good idea if you want the element of surprise; fishermen from Aegina are likely to notice you, especially if you're coming with a fleet big enough to transport an army.

As to the size of that army; it turned out that Megara was a bigger place than I'd taken it to be. As well as the city and its western hinterland, the princes could call on people who owed them service from as far north as the mountains of Cithaeron (where their country has its border with Thebes) and as far east as the outlying farms of Eleusis, beyond which was Athenian territory. All told, Oenophilus reckoned, he ought to be able to put together an army of over six hundred men, enough to man twelve ships, not counting ours.

'Actually,' Cleander said, 'we haven't got a crew. Just us.'

Oenophilus frowned. 'Really?'

Cleander nodded. 'We lost the crew – well, they up and left us – in Corinth. Seems they liked it there and decided to stay.'

Remarkably, Oenophilus accepted this sorry excuse for an explanation at face value. 'Pity,' he said. 'But it doesn't matter; we can probably find enough people to man your ship as well, if we aren't too picky about who we ask along. Actually, there's quite a few of the better sort from the north who could use a ride; they're good people, but it's all a bit sparse and bleak up there in the mountains, they don't have a lot to spare, and ships are a rich man's toy, after all.'

Six hundred men. You can do the numbers yourselves; at least fifty chariots, two fighting men to a chariot, plus two grooms and a couple of men-at-arms. Quite a formidable army, in other words, especially if we did manage to get ashore before they knew we were coming. Once we were on land, the princes reckoned, we'd have the advantage even if they outnumbered us two to one. The Megarians, they said, had always been first-rate chariot-fighters, none better in the world, and over the years they'd had plenty of practice; when they weren't having to keep the Thebans from walking off with their cattle, they were scrapping with the Athenians (who they regarded as their traditional enemy, if only because Athenians talk funny and hate working for a living when they can steal) or dealing with bands of adventurers and no-goods slung out of Corinth for antisocial behaviour. Listening to Hipposthenes talking about his army – he was the battlefield commander, being more warlike and fun-loving than his brother – even I began to feel that we might have landed on our feet. I'm no expert and never have been, but we did have an expert with us, and while all these discussions were going on, I kept an eye on Uncle Sarpedon to see what his heart made of it all. And he looked impressed, no doubt about it.

'So what do you reckon?' I asked him, when I was able to get him alone for a few heartbeats. 'Are they as good as they think they are?'

Sarpedon stroked his beard. 'No,' he replied, 'but neither is anybody. If what young Hipposthenes has been telling us is even halfway true, though, I'd say that yes, they've got a first-class army: good fast chariots, experienced charioteers and fighters, most of them have fought together in the past – now that's important, you can put together a scratch army of the most talented individuals in the world and still end up with a ghastly mess, but men who know each other and each other's moves, that's an army. As against that, if you believe that Pentheus knows what he's talking about, we won't be facing more than forty enemy chariots, and I don't believe the Aeginetans are likely to be much of a match for these people; they're islanders, nobody bothers them, they won't have had the practice. In a straight fight, all things being equal, I can't see that there's likely to be a problem.'

I didn't want to talk to Pentheus; it's not a good idea to fall out irrevocably with a man who one day might well be the ruler of a large and rich island, as well as related to you by marriage. I was beginning to find Cleander more than usually insufferable as well. My guess is that after all the disappointments and failures of our journey so far, the thought that now (by virtue of fool's luck and truly rotten navigation) we'd stumbled into a positively heroic venture that looked like it had every chance of succeeding was too much for his feeble, optimistic little heart. The prospect of success and actually achieving something had made him drunk, and I've always found that it's no fun talking to someone when he's drunk and you're sober.

So I stayed away from him. And I definitely wasn't talking to Dusa, not after the flour stunt; and Sarpedon was getting all blood-thirsty and peculiar as the prospect of a good fight got nearer. That only left my heart to talk to, or the princes; and they were busy most of the time, counting jars and shouting at bowyers and fletchers and armourers and spear-polishers and shield-furnishers and potters and harness-makers and grooms and ropeweavers and charcoal-burners and carpenters and smiths and pretty well every-body who could do anything in Megara (none of whom were exactly thrilled about being dragged away from their farms at a busy time of year in order to make things for an unexpected war, on the vague understanding that there might be something in it for them in the middle to long term) – not to mention all the sitting around eating and drinking they had to do with all the mighty warriors who turned up at the palace door in answer to the heralds (that's one part of being a prince that'd never suit me, having to be polite to all those people, day after day . . .). In other words, they were busy, no time for idle chatter with someone who was at best peripheral to the success of the venture. So I kept out from under their feet, and resolved to go away and do something I've always been exceptionally good at: sulking.

But even that didn't make me feel a whole lot better (unusually); the essence of good sulking is feeling hard done by, and although I was that all right, my heart would insist on telling me that I was guilty of giving as many hard deeds as I was getting. After all, over the last month or so I'd been party to disrupting the Argive games, harbouring and protecting a man of blood, highway robbery, stealing a ship and plotting an entirely gratuitous invasion for the benefit of a fraudulent blasphemer. Added to which – and this was, for some reason, the chief accusation my heart brought against me – I'd cheerfully abandoned the job my king had entrusted me with, forgotten all about the problems we faced at home, and given up on the pursuit of games-players. Why the god chose to put guilt into my heart at a time like that, when surely I had every reason to count myself an innocent victim and not to blame for anything, I have no idea; the gods walk in clouds and mists, and their ways are obscure to mortals. Also, their sense of humour is rather different from ours, and not particularly nice.

The best way of dealing with guilt, of course, is to find something useful to do; and in the middle of the preparations for a war, there are so many things that need doing that anybody who wants to help can generally find an occupation. Now, when I was a boy, one of the things I used to love doing (though I didn't get many opportunities, since I wasn't supposed to do it) was hanging around the smithy helping the smith. Our smith was a small, cheerful man with a club foot; he wasn't much use on the land, partly because of his disfigurement but mostly because he just didn't like the work, so he spent as much time as he could in the smithy and left his brothers to get on with the farming. In consequence he wasn't very popular with them, and didn't have anybody to talk to, which in turn meant he was one of the few people around our place who had time to talk with a small, inquisitive boy.

The princes' smith was young for a man in his trade – he'd just taken over from his father, who had died unexpectedly of a fever – quite competent and extremely talkative, so much so that people with things to do tended to keep out of the smithy for fear of getting pinned down in a conversation and losing a day's work. That suited me fine, however, so I offered my services as an unskilled hammer-wielder, fetcher and carrier. Naturally, the order of the day was spear-blades, and arrowheads when we got bored and wanted a change. I would load the charcoal into the furnace and work the goatskin bellows, clean up the moulds, swing the hammer as directed, change the tempering bath when it got too filthy, scour and burnish the crap off the newly cast and forged pieces and generally do as I was told, while he did the clever stuff: gauging the alloy of the bronze, reading the heat by the colour, forming hard edges and folding sockets, quenching and tempering and grinding the contour of the cutting blade. He was an interesting man, and I wish now that I'd thought to ask his name.

'So you're here for the war?' he asked me, as we worked over a spearhead, me bashing with the hammer, him turning it in the tongs so the blows fell exactly where they were needed.

'Not me,' I replied. 'I'm one of the people who brought it here.'

'Ah.' He nodded. 'So you must be either Cratus or Cleander. And, since you've got nothing better to do than bash hot metal, I guess you must be Cratus. Welcome to Megara.'

'Thank you,' I said. 'I reckon I owe you an apology.'

He lifted his head. 'Doesn't bother me,' he replied. 'After all, nobody's asking me to go to war, thank the gods, all I've got to do is my job – and I'd rather be doing this than dragging round after the plough or busting up clods with the mattock; that's what the gods made brothers for.'

'Is that it?' I said. 'I've often wondered.'

'Oh yes,' he replied, 'but first you've got to know how to handle 'em right. They have to be broken to it, like horses. 'Course, it's different for you of the better sort, there's enough to go round when the old man dies and each of you gets a place of his own. Us poor buggers, we can't afford to split everything up and go our separate ways; that's why I learned the trade, that and my old man being the palace smith. Usually it works well enough; they get the stuff they want made for them, and we get jars of stuff sent down from the palace by way of saying thank you, though not as often as we'd like, of course. These two, they've got better memories than their father, but it's not something you can rely on when you're counting out the stores for the winter.'

I grinned. 'You get by, I reckon,' I said.

'Oh, I never said we didn't. And there's perks of the trade – like there's always a few bits and pieces of material left over when the job's done, but they don't have to know that.'

'I'll bear that in mind when I get home,' I said. 'Assuming I ever do get home, that is.'

He pulled a sympathetic face. 'My heart tells me you will,' he said. 'And if you don't – well, I expect Prince Pentheus won't forget you when he's handing out land and bronze on Aegina. Especially,' he added with a nasty grin, 'if you're his brother-in-law.'

I snarled at him and he laughed.

'So what do you make of this war, then?' I said, anxious to change the subject.

He shrugged. 'Nothing to do with me,' he replied. 'After all, whatever happens, the Aeginetans aren't likely to be coming over here or bothering me. If you noblemen want to bash each other around with dangerous weapons and you're prepared to do it somewhere else, the very best of luck to you.'

'Count me out,' I said. 'I think war's a rotten game, personally. I suppose I've got to take part, because my brother and my uncle will be involved and it'd look awful if I didn't join in. I don't want to, though.'

'Do me a favour,' he laughed. 'Think of all the immortal glory you're going to win. Isn't that all you noblemen think about, honour and prestige and living for ever?'

'The others might,' I said. 'Me, I'm less concerned about living for ever and more worried about living past the age of at least thirty. Is that so very wrong of me?'

He paused to get a better grip on the billet with the tongs. 'As a matter of fact,' he said, 'yes, it is. Means you aren't doing your job. It'd be the same as if the princes told me to make a dozen bronze axle-pins and I turned round and said, Sorry, I'm not in the mood. Now sure, they can't make me do it if I don't want to; but I do it, because I'm the son of a smith who's the son of a smith, and it's what I do. Same with any tradesman. I do it because I was born to do it; it's got its advantages and its disadvantages. Disadvantages are, I've got to stand here in the heat and work bloody hard, whether I like it or not. Advantages are, the princes make up to my family what they lose because I'm here and not ploughing or digging – which is also bloody hard work – and a bit more besides; and it makes me different, not just another man. I get respect. People listen to me.'

'Honour and prestige,' I said. 'It's all you smiths think about.'

'Ah,' he replied, 'but I don't figure on living for ever.'

'In a sense you do,' I told him. 'Like, for generations out of mind there's been a smith here, and it's been you, or your father, or his father, right back to the time when the Sons of the Achaeans first came here. When you're gone, it'll be your son, then your grandson, and so on for ever. Oh, the names might change, but the palace smith of Megara is immortal; far more so than any warrior, who'll only be remembered if he's lucky and it's convenient.'

He thought about that for a moment, then lifted his head. 'I can see the point you're trying to make,' he said, 'and it's clever enough, I suppose. But I don't agree with you. It's a better-sort-versus-ordinary-sort thing, if you ask me. A man like you looks at a man like me, all he sees is the job, the anvil or the plough or the spoke-shave or whatever. You see me, you see the palace smith. You don't see *me*. When I'm dead and gone, you'll look at my son and you'll see – guess what, the palace smith. I'll be lost for ever.'

'Maybe,' I said. 'But you're doing exactly the same thing. You say I should do my bit in the war because I'm of the better sort, it's my job and expected of me. You're looking at me and seeing my job, or my trade, or my position, just the same as I do when I look at you. And suppose by some miraculous chance I were to do some great deed or other, in war or playing games – I won't be remembered in song and story if I don't – well, it's the same thing, isn't it? People will hear about me and remember the deed, the little pip of heroism that stays behind after the apple's rotted away. I'll be cold ashes long since, but the deed may just live for ever. My deed, your trade; all the same, really.'

He smiled. 'I'll say this for you,' he said, 'you've got a way with words. Maybe you'll be remembered for all time as a clever bastard who could make any crowstruck thing sound right if you put your mind to it.'

'I'd settle for that,' I replied. 'Then at least they'd be remembering me, not what I said.'

It was the speed of it all that bewildered me most. One moment, it seemed to me, we were sitting in the hall and Cleander was saying, Don't mind him, he's crazy; the next, we were watching them load bits of chariot on to the ships.

There's definitely an art to taking chariots to bits and putting them back together again, and listening to our Phoenician friend here, with his scratches and marks that tell you things, puts me in mind of the worst problem of the lot: how to match up the right bits to the right chariot. It's all very well taking off the wheels and packing them carefully in straw, but what happens when you get to the other side and find you can't remember which wheels are supposed to go on which axles? A right fool you look sitting cross-legged in the sand trying to get a matched pair that'll run true while the enemy are thundering towards you on the skyline. Now, if you scratched or hammered some cute little mark on the wheels, and the same mark on the axles, you'd know which ones went with which, and it'd save an awful lot of fooling about.

But that's by the by; the traditional way to do it is by layers, with the wheels for Agesilaus' chariot on the bottom of the stack, then Protesilaus' wheels, then the next pair, then the next, and some poor fool has to try to remember the order they went down in. Meanwhile there's someone else who's in charge of remembering shafts, and yokes, and rails, and axle-pins, and finally the boxes themselves. It's all very well, I guess; but what happens if the man who's remembering the yoke-collars, say, gets swept overboard during a squall and drowns? You get to where you're going, and nobody's got a clue which collar goes on which shaft. Result: chaos.

Not, of course, that anything like that happened to us. No, we had as calm and smooth a ride as anybody could hope for. Even Dusa (who insisted on coming with us, 'to bind up wounds and be useful generally,' as if she'd ever been useful in all her sweet life) managed to keep her last meal down until we were well out of sight of the shore.

We left just before dawn—

'Sorry to interrupt again,' the Phoenician said, 'and I've got a feeling I'm going to regret asking this; but why exactly did you two go along on this invasion? It wasn't your fight, surely. And I'd got the impression you didn't even like Pentheus very much.'

Cratus nodded. 'That wasn't really anything to do with it,' he said. 'There were a number of reasons, really. First – what you might call the formal reason; we were the princes' guests, therefore temporarily part of their household, so it was just assumed we'd be going along with everybody else. To look at it another way, we'd have had every right to be frightfully upset if they hadn't invited us. Second – well, it's another conventional reason, but we Sons of the Achaeans of the better sort are supposed to like wars and fighting – it's what we're for, basically, it's what we train for, right from the day we're big enough to bash a tree-trunk with a little wooden sword. Now, conventional stuff like that explains why Cleander was ready to go; I had my own reasons as well. One, if Cleander and Sarpedon – and Dusa, of course – had all gone off to the wars, I'd have been left all on my own in Megara, which wouldn't have suited me at all. Two, I wanted to keep an eye on Dusa and Pentheus. And three – well, I suppose I had nothing better to do. The finding-games-players thing had more or less ground to a halt. My chances of getting home, realistically speaking, depended on the princes lending us a crew and supplies for our lovely stolen ship.' He paused, and let his face slide into a lopsided smile. 'And, gods help me, it was an adventure, a remarkable event, a chance to be remembered as part of a great deed of valour. I don't know,' he concluded, lifting his head. 'It never occurred to me not to go, is the simple answer. Will that do?'

We left just before dawn (Cratus went on) and were well past the poxy little islands by the time we had to drop anchor for the night; there was a chance we'd been seen, of course, but things seemed to be going our way – we didn't notice any fishing-boats, so there was at least a chance that no fishing-boats noticed us. It was a cool, still night and everybody else but me seemed to have no trouble at all getting to sleep. I wasn't so fortunate. Oh, I wasn't lying there quivering with fear, like a hare tangled up in a briar; I just couldn't sleep, is all.

But I must have dozed off eventually, because I had a dream. This dream came and stood over me, the way dreams do, and I saw it was a young woman, naked and white as milk from head to toe. To be precise, it was my sister.

'Dusa?' I said. 'For pity's sake. I told you, it wasn't very clever the first time.'

But the dream shook her head. 'I'm not your sister,' it said. 'I'm Victory; the real Victory. If you don't believe me, try to grab hold of my hand.'

I didn't, so I did; and of course, my hand passed straight through it, because there was nothing there.

'I'm sorry I doubted you,' I said, feeling rather silly. 'Only, you really do look just like my sister Dusa.'

The dream smiled. 'Actually,' it said, 'you've got that the wrong way round; Dusa looks like me. Can't you see the difference? Figure it out later, then, I haven't got the time to go through it for you step by step. I'm just here to tell you that when the foot-race begins, I'll be with you and all of you, even though you may find it hard to believe at the time. Remember: I'm usually where you least expect to find me, and nobody ever really recognises me at the time.'

It turned to go, but I called it back. 'Victory,' I said, 'can I ask you something?'

'You can ask,' it said.

'The other night,' I said, 'you didn't happen to visit the two princes, Oenophilus and whatsisname, Hipposomething?'

'As a matter of fact,' said the dream, 'I did. And before you ask, yes, I promised myself to them if they attacked Aegina. Shall I tell you something else, while I'm at it?'

'Please.'

It smiled. 'I don't always tell the truth.'

'Ah,' I said.

'Or at least, not the truth you're expecting me to tell,' said the dream. 'Some people hold that it's because we gods speak not for the moment but for all time. Or you could say it's because we like making fools out of you. Up to you which one you believe.'

Then it walked away, and as I was trying to call it back I woke up.

'Excuse me,' the Phoenician interrupted, 'I'm confused. When she said she didn't always tell the truth, who was she being?'

Cratus frowned. 'Sorry, I don't follow,' he said.

'I know, it's complicated. When the dream of Victory said she didn't always tell the truth, which one was she being? Victory, or a dream? Look, let me put it another way. Was she telling you that Victory sometimes tells lies, or that dreams sometimes tell lies, or what?'

'Oh, I see.' Cratus rubbed his chin. 'You know,' he said, 'I hadn't thought of it like that before. I'd always assumed that it meant dreams don't always tell the truth; but that could just have been me jumping to conclusions.'

The Phoenician nodded. 'That's the way I took it too,' he said, 'until I wondered if that was right after all. I mean, it's not my language, maybe I'd failed to grasp some fine nuance of word order or something.'

Cratus shrugged. 'Well,' he said, 'actually it could just as well have been the one as the other. For what it's worth, I assumed it was talking about dreams; and as a fall-back position, I assumed that if it wasn't that, it was my sister Dusa all covered in flour.'

'Thank you,' the Phoenician said. 'I understand now. I think.'

The next day (Cratus went on), we reached Aegina.

The first indication was the lookout up in the prow, yelling. Now, he'd been put there because he had amazingly keen eyesight, so it was a while before the rest of us could make out anything apart from waves and sky. But in due course we saw it too, a grey-brown hump sitting up out of the water. The shipmaster yelled to put on more speed, and the oarsmen quickened the pace – vitally important to waste no time, now that we were presumably visible to them. I stood by the mast and watched the hump get bigger and bigger;

hilly place, Aegina, I thought, as we crawled through the water, but then again, most islands were. The closer we got, the hillier it looked, until a rather disturbing thought occurred to me. What if Aegina was all hills, with no flat plain worth a damn? What if it sat up out of the sea and kept on going? Here we were, with fifty chariots and the best damned charioteers in the world, rapidly approaching a place where (by the looks of it) chariots were going to be absolutely useless.

Come off it, my heart told me. If Aegina wasn't suitable for chariot-fighting, Pentheus would have mentioned it. After all, he comes from Aegina.

I didn't bother to answer that, and my heart suddenly became unusually quiet.

CHAPTER FOURTEEN

'You should have warned us,' yelled Prince Hipposthenes. 'Look at it, for the gods' sakes, it's a bloody *mountain*. We can't use chariots on that.'

We were standing on the beach. Our ships, our twelve chariot-stuffed ships, holds full of wheels and fractious, cramped horses, were bobbing gently on the wine-dark sea, while We Officers held a rather fraught staff meeting.

'Can't you?' Pentheus said.

'Of course we bloody well can't,' Hipposthenes roared. 'We couldn't go above a slow ambling walk without tipping the bloody things over. Why the hell didn't you tell us it's like this?'

Before us, separated from us by a couple of hundred paces of flat, the gradient rose steeply and kept on going. Aegina, as far as we could see, was one big mountain, with a tiny skirt of sand.

'Maybe he didn't know,' Oenophilus said quietly. 'Maybe he's never been here before in his life.'

'I don't understand,' Pentheus was saying, in a wonderfully wounded tone of voice. 'My father had war-chariots; we had twenty-seven, all packed up and stored in a long barn. We never used them, of course, because we never had to fight any wars. But because he had them, I always assumed . . .'

It was a good recovery, one of the best I've heard in the course of a long lifetime of dealing with tale-tellers. It was good enough to deflect the suspicions of one prince, if not the wrath of the other.

'In any case,' Hipposthenes went on, 'we can't stay here. We'll just have to get back in the ships and go home.'

Another man – I have no idea what his name was, but I think he was the prince's chief shipmaster; anyway, he seemed to know a lot about boats – lifted his head. 'Not possible,' he said. 'Not today, anyway. We might get away tonight, if the wind changes, but my heart tells me it's not very likely. Besides, if you want to go back through that lot in the dark, *you* can steer the crowstruck ship.'

Hipposthenes' eyes opened wide, like a baby bird's mouth. 'We can't stay here,' he said. 'They'll cut us to ribbons, out in the open like this with no chariots.'

Oenophilus frowned. 'You really think so?' he said.

'This is infantry fighting. I'm a chariot fighter. I don't know spit about infantry fighting.'

'I do.'

We all looked round to see who'd spoken; well, I knew who it was, of course, it was Uncle Sarpedon. Needless to say.

'Do you really?' Hipposthenes snarled. 'Like our crown prince here knows all about his own kingdom.'

'No,' Sarpedon said calmly. 'I know about fighting on foot because I've done a lot of it. Very well too, though I say so myself.'

'Which is more than any of us have,' Oenophilus said.

Hipposthenes was getting more and more angry. 'But we've only got his word for it, dammit,' he said. 'We don't know if he's any good. We've never seen him in action.'

His brother grinned ruefully. 'You could say exactly the same about Hercules, but we take it on trust that he was a great warrior. I guess we have to do the same here. Come on,' he added, 'he can't be any worse at it than you and me.'

I think Hipposthenes tried to find some words to answer his brother with, but his heart was so full he couldn't manage to squeeze them past it; so he threw his arms in the air in a gesture of utter demoralisation, nodded and stomped away.

'I think that means he agrees,' Oenophilus said. 'All right, General – I'm sorry, I've forgotten your name.'

'Sarpedon.'

Oenophilus waved vaguely in the direction of the ships and the army. 'All yours,' he said. 'And the best of crowstruck luck to you.' Then he walked off to join his brother.

Sarpedon took a deep breath. 'All right,' he said. 'Cleander, Cratus, you're my adjutants.'

'What's an adjutant, Uncle?' I asked.

'You are. Follow me, and don't get in my way, understood?'

'What about me?' Pentheus said.

Sarpedon turned around, quite slowly, and looked at him for a moment, as if examining something long dead and pungent the dog had put in his slippers. 'You,' he said, 'stay the hell away from me. Is that clear?'

Pentheus nodded. 'And if you win,' he added, 'I'll make you my Grand Marshal of the Palace.'

I think Sarpedon would have broken his arms for him if he'd had time. Instead, he stomped off towards the ships, with Cleander and me tottering along behind him through the deep sand like a couple of young dogs chasing a chariot.

'Where's he got up to?' Cleander demanded.

Cratus looked round. 'There you are,' he said. 'I was beginning to wonder if you'd died in your sleep, out there in the sun.'

'You should be so lucky,' the blind man replied, as two of the young men helped him back to his seat. 'No, I did fall asleep, but not for very long. Have you reached the bit where the princes had the dream yet?'

'Ages ago,' Cratus replied. 'I was just about to start on the battle.'

'Really? You must have missed out lots. Never mind. You shut up for a while now, and let me tell them about the battle. You don't like battles, so you won't tell it properly.'

Cratus frowned. 'Depends on what you mean by "properly",' he replied.

'I know you,' his brother said. 'You'll just say that lots of people got killed and it was all terribly, terribly sad. You know what your trouble is, Cratus? You're more interested in telling people what you think about things than the actual story.'

'Well, at least I think about things, Cleander. Sometimes I even think about them before I do them. You really ought to try it some time.'

Don't mind us (Cleander said). We fight all the time, but that's just our way. That's the thing about brothers, you don't have to like them very much in order to love them.

Well, I'm assuming that he's told you all about Aegina not being suitable for chariot-fighting, and Sarpedon being asked to take command. Yes? Thought so. You can believe three quarters of what he's told you; the other quarter's probably fairly true, but not very true, if you see what I mean.

Anyway, I'll tell you all about the battle. We'd just about got ourselves sorted out and lined up when the enemy appeared. I guess they were as out of sorts as we were; at least we'd been expecting to fight some sort of battle, even if it wasn't the sort we'd thought it was going to be. I imagine that if you asked the enemy at their dinner the previous night what they thought they'd be doing the following morning, fighting a battle is probably the answer you'd have heard least. Islanders, you see; you get complacent living on an island, without neighbours constantly slipping across the border to steal cattle and work off high spirits.

So neither side was exactly at its best, I don't suppose. They must have wondered what the hell was going on – armed men disembarking on the beach, nobody even knowing who they are or what's upset them. What would you do in their position? Send a herald, of course; find out who you're dealing with, because once you know that you cut out the fear of the unknown, and things gradually start making sense. Otherwise, if you launch straight into a battle, you don't know who you're fighting – they could be pirates, or the best warriors in the world, for all you know they could be the invulnerable fighting men that jumped up out of the ground when King Cadmus sowed the dragon's teeth, against whom you don't have a chance.

So it was very sensible of Uncle Sarpedon to kill the herald.

Yes, I know, you're shocked. So was I. One moment there he was, some grave bald-headed old counsellor striding towards us with his white beard wagging in the breeze; next moment Uncle had given an order – he had to give it twice, actually – and the poor old fool was lying in the dust, with a javelinhead sticking a hand's span out from between his shoulders.

If it shocked us, you can imagine the effect it had on the enemy; such a thing was never heard of, killing a herald, so what kind of people were we? They were still standing there with their jaws dropped on to the rims of their shields when Sarpedon whirled his sword round his head (it's a wonder he didn't put someone's eye out) and yelled for us to charge. There was a tiny, tiny sliver of a moment when it was clear nobody wanted to, and then we charged. At least, we tucked our shields in close to our bodies so we wouldn't trip over them, took a deep breath and started to trot forward. I say trot; you ever tried running in ill-fitting greaves? Cratus and I, of course, we'd had to borrow armour from the princes; most of it was all right, but those greaves – I picked the best fit I could find but they were still a thumb's width too long, and every step I took they dug into my instep so hard that I wanted to scream. I don't suppose Achilles himself could have run far in those things.

So, with the greaves and the weight of all that kit, and me not being used to running in armour, I found the rest of the army was passing me by, and I was sort of sinking to the bottom, like dead yeast in a wine-jar. I'll admit, I wasn't too bothered about that. We had about four hundred paces to go – which is a long run if you're out of practice – and I wasn't really in a hurry. The enemy, I felt, was probably still going to be there when I arrived, even if I walked.

Of course, the fine straight line we'd made up when we started off became a ragged mess after we'd run a hundred paces; if they'd stood their ground and waited for us, like sensible human beings, we'd have been in trouble. But the god must have put Folly in their hearts; they threw their spears far too early, so that most of them pitched short (tends to happen a lot when you're nervous; waiting is the worst thing, you want to get on with the action, so the temptation is to sling your spear and get in close as soon as possible), and then drew and charged to meet us. Bad mistake on their part, because at sixty paces Uncle held up his arms for a dead stop; by the time they were thirty yards away we were stopped and more or less in line, and of course we hadn't thrown our spears yet. Well, our volley stopped them in their tracks. We didn't actually hit very many of them; if anything, most of us overpitched, and more men fell in the second and third ranks than the first. But we stopped them and frightened the life out of them; and then we charged for real, top speed (you don't mind a short sprint like that, even if your feet are all bloody and raw, if you think it's going to give you the edge), and smacked into them like a boxer's fist into the other man's jaw.

I think they'd have run if only they'd had a little bit more time. But there just wasn't enough room left for them to turn and get out of there, so the next thing I knew was the shock of my shield bashing into something, which turned out to be the shield of some Aeginetan. He was out of luck that day; I nearly muffed it, being scared and very uncomfortable because of my feet, but fortunately I'd had the manoeuvre drummed into me so often as a kid that it came as second nature. I pushed across his shield with mine until my rim slid off his rim, then I pulled back as hard as I could, a sort of hooking movement, and pulled his shield away from his body, leaving his armpit exposed. I don't know why the gods made us the way they did, but when they shaped us they left a very convenient way direct to the heart through the left armpit, and of course your armour doesn't cover it, or you wouldn't be able to move your arm. Now, when I was a boy and practising this routine, I'd always wondered if I'd have the strength in my forearm and shoulder actually to shove a sword through all that flesh and gristle, right into the heart. Take it from me, it's much easier than you'd think. I can't remember actually doing it, just this revolting shearing noise, and a sharp pain in the top joint of the first finger of my right hand, where it got trapped against the crossguard of the sword.

And that was that. He made a little grunting noise, like a happy pig, slid off my sword-blade and sort of folded up in a heap, like someone's discarded clothes. I didn't stop to check, but I'm pretty sure he was dead before he hit the ground. Poor bugger, my heart said to me, an hour ago he wouldn't even have known there was a war on. Only goes to show how suddenly things can happen, and how close we are to disaster all the time.

I've thought a lot about that encounter since; oddly enough, always in the context of games-playing. After all, fighting and competing against someone in a game are very nearly the same thing; you find yourself standing toe to toe with some other man, probably someone you've never seen before, and both of you are trying to achieve the same thing, to win – or not to lose (there's a difference, of course, but it's not relevant here). There's no malice in it, really, because the other man isn't a man, he's an opponent; all you know and all you care about him is that he's the obstacle you have to overcome – if you like, he's the great deed you have to accomplish if you want to win the prize. You don't stop to think, Is he a good man, is he the better man, which of us is more worthy to live or to win? Like I just said, he isn't human, he's a thing, an abstraction.

You speak our language pretty well, Phoenician; you've mastered the tricky way we can turn any group of words into a thing just by putting 'the' or 'a' in front of them – the-being-about-to-boil-a-cauldron-of-water, it's a thing, as real as the cauldron or the water or the fire, the way we say it. The words make it a thing, they scoop up an idea that has no shape or identity and give it – well, life, really. I reckon competition, in war or in the games, does that to your opponent. He becomes a thing, once you've put that word 'opponent' in front of him, and probably that's the way you'll always remember him; and as you grow older and the tales you tell of your youthful exploits get grander, that's the way he'll always be remembered, as a thing, an enemy, an opponent. And if you were to make scratches about him on one of your bits of wood, I suppose that's what he'll be for ever. Don't ask me what the significance of all this is, by the way; I'm just thinking aloud. It's a bad habit of mine. I guess it comes of being blind, at times you tend to think there's nobody else there.

So; I'd killed my opponent, and I looked up quickly to see what was going on.

The first thing I noticed was a rock, which came out of the air at me and dinged the side of my helmet before I could duck, smashing it to bits – it was one of those really old-fashioned cone-shaped jobs, leather core reinforced with rows and rows of boars' tusks (apparently it took the tusks from seventy boars to make just one helmet – why bother, for pity's sake?). You can tell the esteem in which I was held by the Princes of Megara by the way they issued me with a priceless family heirloom that wouldn't protect you against a sharp gust of wind, let alone violence.

So there I was in the middle of a battle, weak at the knees with no helmet, and a couple of large, well-armed Aeginetans coming towards me. It wasn't the happiest moment of my life, and properly speaking it should have been one of the last. But for some reason best known to himself the god decided to save me; he arranged for one of the princes' men to jump out between me and the two Aeginetans, and take them on. He was a good fighter, that man; he kept off one of them with his shield long enough to land a pretty smart blow on the other one's neck with his sword, then he turned on the survivor and feinted high, struck low, aiming to get behind the knee-joint and hamstring the bugger. But the Aeginetan saw through the feint – not at first, but he figured it out just in time, and instead of raising his shield further, he brought the rim down with a mighty crack across my man's knuckles. Of course, my preserver dropped his sword, but he was just in time to jump clear; then he made a grab for a spear sticking up out of the ground about a yard away from his hand. He nearly got there in time, but not quite; just as he was pulling the spear out, the Aeginetan got between his shield and the cheek-piece of his helmet and skewered him with a short thrust. Down my man went, but not before he'd whirled the spear up and stuck it in the other man's groin. There the Aeginetan was, completely out of it, with blood pouring down his legs. I don't suppose he even saw me. It took me two goes to cut his throat; the first attempt carved a horrible long gash but missed the vein completely.

(Now, you tell me this: why is it that the man who saved me, a better fighter than me and a braver man – why is it that nobody, not even me, knows his name? He was a hero, an achiever of mighty deeds, if ever there was one, but nobody other than me was watching, and I couldn't put a name to him. Makes you wonder, really.)

I looked round again. The field was clear ahead of me, but on either side I could see that things weren't going too well; we were being pushed back down the hill, I was already fifteen paces or so behind the lines and in danger of getting cut off, and there was a fresh wave of the enemy bundling down the hill towards us. I couldn't see anybody I knew, standing or on the ground. I certainly couldn't see any point in staying where I was. So I did the only sensible thing: I turned and ran for it.

You're not supposed to do that, of course, and if anybody had seen me do it, I'd have been in deep trouble. But nobody was watching, just as nobody was there to see the man whose name I don't know. Wouldn't have made the slightest bit of difference to me, of course, if the entire population of Elis had been lined up to see me scarpering, I'd have done it just the same. When your heart tells you to run or die, you run.

I'd have kept on running till I reached the ships, if I hadn't tripped over something and gone down on my nose. The something turned out to be a man called Ischophilus, a fairly important character around the princes' court. He was dead as a stone and his left hand had been cut off – I could see it lying a few yards away, still holding the handle of a shield. Anyway, I swore at him for getting in my way, but almost before I could get up, there were those bastard Aeginetans again, following up with a vengeance. I was in no position to do anything about them; no shield, no sword either, and I'd hurt my knee falling over the dead counsellor. Oh well, my heart said, the way they do when they think it's over; then the god put it into my mind to flop down again and sham dead until they'd gone away. Actually, it was too late to sham dead, but in the thick of a battle shamming horribly wounded does just as well, so I did that. Did it well, too, because the enemy just scampered past me, leaving me lying in the dirt.

When I reckoned it was safe to look up, I looked up. Nothing to be seen except a landscape with dead soldiers; so I picked myself up and tottered a step or so forward, until I realised I was standing on friend Ischophilus' sword. Well, he wouldn't be needing it where he'd gone, so I took it off him, also his helmet – a better fit than the boars'-teeth number, not to mention a bit more solid – and stood there, alone like a solitary tree on a bleak hillside, wondering what in buggery I should do next.

They were fighting like mad further down the slope. I watched them for a heartbeat or so; then the god put it into my heart that the really smart thing to do would be to walk away; not up the hill, because I wasn't really in the mood to try sacking Aegina on my lonesome; not down the hill, because there was a battle going on down there and I'm not that stupid; instead, walk away, parallel to the shore, and keep going until I'd got well past the end of the battle-lines, whereupon I could loop round and stroll back to the ships in relative comfort and peace.

It felt strange, very strange indeed; it was as if I was out for a walk with the sling and the dogs, and I happened to wander into the middle of someone else's battle. In this imaginary battle, there are two sides hammering the crap out of each other, but for some reason it's obvious that I'm not involved, so nobody takes any notice of me. I carry on with my stroll, walking round the battle like you'd walk round a patch of briars, fallen tree or other natural obstacle. You know, I suppose that sort of thing must happen from time to time; there's a battle, and some shepherd or drover walks round a bend in the road and finds himself unexpectedly in the middle of it. I wonder what they do, these accidental witnesses, who may not even know who the two opposing nations might be, let alone the names of the mighty men of valour.

I started to walk, and I kept on going, and for a long time no one bothered me, till my heart was beginning to believe I might actually get away with this blatant act of cheating. As if. Good luck, they say, is just the gods' way of telling you that really bad luck is on its way. In my case, the bad luck consisted of about a dozen Aeginetans running up the slope towards me – running away, let me add, from the battle, which was starting to go our way at last. Our good luck; my bad luck. I'd like to tell you that in spite of everything my heart rejoiced to see that our side was prevailing; but I can't, because I have a nasty habit of telling the truth.

A dozen Aeginetans, and me. Again, no question of there being a choice, or any doubt in my heart as to what to do. I took one look at them, said something vulgar, and ran back the way I'd just come, quick as I could.

Bad decision; because those dozen cowards weren't the only

Aeginetans to turn tail and run like deer. Another group of about twenty were coming up the slope on the other side of me. Meanwhile, doubtless shamed into action by the worthlessness of their comrades, yet another wave of armed men was scurrying down the hill from the city to join in the fighting. In other words, there was a triangle of converging hostile forces, with me in the middle, and the only way out that wasn't full of enemy spears was straight up in the air.

I'm not, unfortunately, a bird.

There are men, mighty men of valour, who'd have shrugged their mountainous shoulders, picked the smallest group of opponents and charged. Not me. Don't get me wrong, I didn't have such a low opinion of myself that I wouldn't have held still and slugged it out with one Aeginetan warrior, or maybe even two very short ones. Best part of fifty, though, that was a different matter. No; there comes a time in a man's life when he can't dodge and run any more. He's got to anchor his feet firmly to the bosom of his mother Earth, stand firm, listen to his dauntless heart and, at the proper moment, fling himself on his face in the dirt and grovel for mercy.

I was just about to do this when the dozen or so I'd run into first came up behind me. I was actually proposing to surrender to the twenty-odd in front of me, having underestimated the first party's speed, so they caught me by surprise and still standing. Oh well, I said to my heart, and turned round, hoping I'd get a chance to squeal 'No! Don't hurt me!' before it was too late.

There was an ugly great brute of an Aeginetan standing there staring at me. 'Well?' he said.

I was too bewildered to say anything. 'Well?' he repeated. 'What d'you want us to do?'

Still couldn't make any sense of it; and then the god put the meaning into my heart. This clown, seeing a lone figure running backwards and forwards behind the lines, and wearing a rather splendid bronze helmet with a big horsehair plume sticking out of the top, had taken me for some kind of officer on his own side. Made sense, I guess; after all, what kind of fool would be strutting backwards and forwards like a peacock, entirely surrounded by the enemy.

'Pull back,' I managed to say, somehow.

The man looked at me. 'You sure?' he said.

''Course I'm sure,' I snapped – you can sound terribly abrupt when you're just about to piss yourself with fear. 'You heard what I said. Jump to it. And you,' I added, because the other group was up with us now, 'you lot, go with them. Back to the city, quick as you like.'

The man dipped his head towards the reinforcements coming down the hill. 'What about them?' he asked.

'Tell 'em the same, from me,' I said. 'Get the hell out of here while you still can.'

And off they went; while I did a pretty passable imitation of a worried commander rushing back to the battle, even though well aware that he's unlikely to come back alive. I was so good, I nearly burst out crying at the tragedy and nobility of it all.

Remember what I said about good and bad luck? Think about it. My good fortune in being taken for an Aeginetan by the Aeginetans suddenly threw off its disguise and revealed itself to be bad luck as soon as I came up close to our victorious advancing troops, and I was taken for an Aeginetan by the Megarans. By one in particular, who slung a spear at me and hit me right in the midriff.

Now, that should have killed me very dead indeed; but I was back in a good luck phase by then. The spear hit me, to be precise, right on the belt-buckle; and whoever it was that made that particular belt for the princes' great-grandfather had obviously been given a big lump of bronze and instructions to use it all. To cut short, the spear hit me, went through about a thumb's width and lodged in the arms of the buckle. It also sent me staggering backwards, so that I fell over and bumped my head hard enough to put me to sleep for a while; so I guess I must have passed for dead, and managed to get ignored by whoever it was who had chucked the spear at me.

When I came round, and realised with as much surprise as joy that I still wasn't dead yet, the situation had changed yet again. In spite of my intervention, it seems, the Aeginetan reinforcements had come down and joined in the fighting, pushing our boys back yet again. This time, in fact, they'd shunted us all the way back to the sand, leaving me stranded behind the lines again. That, I guess, was the bad luck to follow the good luck I'd had with the buckle.

Oddly enough, though, I wasn't as panicked as I might have been, or ought to have been. I was, after all, an honorary Aeginetan – that is, it seemed as though they couldn't tell the difference between me and them. At that moment, the god put it into my mind that if I toddled slowly up the hill clutching my gut and looking sorry for myself (and I was; believe me, I was), maybe I could pass for an Aeginetan long enough to get away from the fighting and up into the hills for a day or so; after which time, assuming I hadn't bled to death, I might just be able to do what our friend Pentheus had evidently managed to do: steal a boat or hitch a ride, get off the island, maybe even – well, stranger things have happened – eventually get back home.

One thing for sure: dumb as the scheme may sound to you (and to me at the time), it looked a much better prospect than trying to rejoin my comrades in arms in the battle, who just then were taking a terrible beating from the enemy.

(Or at least, that's how it looked from where I was standing. Of course, I couldn't see more than one small area of the battlefield, and I wasn't entirely sure any more which of them were Us and which were Them. From a long way away, people on battlefields tend to look like people, which can be really confusing.)

So up the hill I went; and after a fairly steep climb I reached the city. It was smaller than I'd expected – listening to Pentheus' account of his adventures, I'd imagined something larger and rather more grand; but then, people always tend to remember the places where they grew up as being bigger than they actually are; even so, there were a lot of people milling about – some men with shields and weapons, older men mostly who I suppose were left behind as a last line of defence. There were other men shifting jars and loading stuff on to carts, and women and children helping them, or looking out anxiously in the direction of the beach. One old dear grabbed me by the arm as I walked up to the gate and asked me if I'd seen her son Theoclymenus. I said yes, he was fine (well, I guessed it was the easiest way to get rid of her) and walked away as quickly as I could without running.

My plan, if you could call it that, was to find somewhere dark and quiet where I could hide till just before dawn; then I'd set off up the hill along with all the shepherds and terrace-builders going off to work, get up into the mountains and keep out of sight there for a bit until things had calmed down a little and it was safer to sneak back down into the city in search of a ride home. First order of business, then, was something like a barn or a storage-tower; not a difficult thing to find, you'd have thought. But I was back in a bad-luck cloud; everywhere I looked, people were bundling their children and belongings up ladders into hay-lofts and hauling bundles and jars up the sides of the towers with ropes – wonderful thing, panic; if you could harness it somehow to do useful work, like oxen, you'd never have to bend your back again. The last place I could possibly hide, in other words, was in a barn.

And then the god put the thought in my mind: well, if everybody's hiding up in the barns and the towers, their houses are probably empty. Why not go and hide there?

The ideas the god puts in your mind are a bit like the water in lowland rivers – usually you can trust them, but not always. On this occasion, though, it seemed like he'd given me a good one. Now, I've always found that if you want to look inconspicuous, walk briskly as if you know where you're going; it's your furtive creepers who stand out like mud on a linen tunic. Trying to look like I owned the place, I walked up to the first house I came to and pushed the doors. They were open, and, sure enough, the house was empty. Wonderful, I said to my heart; now for somewhere to hide. I tried the inner room, but the door was locked. That left either the hall – far too open to hide in, even in a small house like this – or the upper room, which I didn't fancy either. Why not? Think about it. Yes, in the upper room you're reasonably well out of sight from people in the hall, but how are you going to get out again? To leave, you've either got to tiptoe through the hall, past the people sleeping on the benches, or else climb out of the top gallery window and shin down the front of the house, which is both conspicuous and dangerous. If you're in the inner room, though, provided you're quiet about it and you have appropriate tools (like a sword) it's generally no bother to dig your way out under the wall, like a burglar, and be gone without anybody knowing you were there until much later in the day.

I decided to compromise; I went up the ladder to the upper room, pulled back the rug on the floor and used my sword to prise up the floorboards directly above the inner room. Needless to say I snapped off the tip of the sword – even the best of blades isn't meant to be used as a pry-bar – but I got through in the end and dropped down into the room below, which was as dark as the inside of a bag. That was all right, but of course I was now facing a problem I hadn't considered, namely how to put back the planks I'd levered up, so as not to make it painfully obvious what I'd done. I promise you, I'd been sitting there for a long time, as long as it takes to plough all round the headland of a five-acre patch, when I followed up on the thin beam of light that shone through the hole I'd just made in the ceiling (the only light in the place) and realised that I'd been staring at the back end of the key, in the lock, all that time.

That solved that problem – all I had to do was unlock the door, nip up the ladder, put the boards back, job done – but of course it raised another one. If the key was inside the locked room . . .

Well, my heart told me, if you've been in here with whoever it is for this long, and they haven't tried to stab you or strangle you, chances are they're more afraid of you than you are of them. Maybe with good reason. In any event, the smart thing to do would be to leave, now, while you've got the chance . . .

But I didn't fancy that. As it was, I was sitting with my back to the curved rear wall of the house, where nobody could creep up behind me and bust me over the head. If I were to get up and cross the room to the door, I'd be losing that advantage.

Which left only one option: hold still, see who sneezes first.

That would probably have been all right if only I hadn't started to feel so damned sleepy. It's just the way it goes sometimes; you can't stay awake, even though you know you really must. You barricade the gates of your eyelids, but Sleep digs under the defences like a sapper undermining a city – she's a persistent enemy, Sleep, and very crafty. The more my heart told me, Stay awake, stay awake, the more I was aware of just how gritty and sore my eyes were. Come on, Sleep whispered, at least close your eyes; you can stay awake with your eyes closed, can't you, a big, strong man like you? And yes, I was very tired – it catches up with you, weariness, like the man you borrowed a hoe from the year before last, and it insists on getting its due – and it was pretty comfortable leaning up against that wall. I could feel my mind drifting away, like the boat you thought you'd tied up to the river-bank. Sleep sent me dreams disguised as wakefulness, the sort where you think you're just following some usual path of thought, but when you stop and look, it's pure nonsense, and, try as I might, I couldn't help but follow them . . .

I hate Sleep. People die in her. She's a pest, and I don't care who knows it.

What woke me up was the sound of the key in the lock; a scritchety graunching noise, the sort that tells you it's time to slap in some goose-grease if you don't want it to jam solid. Well, that told me all I needed to know – where this other person was and what he was doing; also a general area where his head might reasonably be expected to be. I'd already located a suitable weapon, something long and nicely balanced and made of wood; I took one step forward, raised it above my head and tripped over something.

The wooden thing, when the door opened and light streamed in through the doorway, turned out to be a yard-broom; and the something I'd tripped over was a small footstool. As for my unseen enemy, it was a small girl, about seven or eight years old, which put me in a hell of a spot. You see, I'd assumed for some reason that whoever was lurking in there with me was a man, someone it would be legitimate enough to kill in order to stop him raising the alarm. Now, a small child can raise an alarm better than anybody – it's odd, the way we lose the ability to make a huge amount of noise as we get older – but even I, a desperate pirate turned housebreaker, wasn't really prepared to go slaughtering children, not even if my life depended on it. An example of a rule which I think applies more often than you'd imagine: the superiority of the weak. I'd have killed a man, but I couldn't kill a child. A man slaps you round the face, you break his nose, but if a woman hits you, you don't hit back. We reckon that in this unfair world, the strong prevail over the weak, but isn't it sometimes just as unfair when it's the other way round? At that moment, I certainly thought so.

As I was scrambling up again, my heart thought of something else to worry me with: what if the kid got out and locked the door on me? If she then went and got help, they'd be on to me long before I could dig my way out under the wall. The essence, then, was to get out of there before the door closed. I jumped up, trod on that damned footstool again, and went down hard on my chin. I was still counting stars when I heard the lock graunch again. Wonderful, I told my heart, now look what you've made me do.

No time to waste; I had to start digging if I was going to stand a chance. For that I needed my sword – and of course I'd dropped it somewhere, and couldn't find the crowstruck thing anywhere. You feel such a fool, on your knees in a cluttered storeroom, scrabbling about in the dark looking for a sword. Well, I did find it – crawl with bare knees on a floor where there's something sharp lying, you'll find it all right, it's only a matter of time – and I started digging at once; only to find, after a couple of scoops, that I'd hit stone.

There comes a time when so many things have gone wrong, all you can do is sit back on your heels and grin. After all, if the gods have made it that patently obvious that they don't want you to escape, it seems not far short of blasphemy to keep trying.

Then my old friend the god put something else into my mind; I'd clean forgotten about the hole in the ceiling, the way through which I'd found my way into that crowstruck room in the first place. If I could climb back up through that – well, I'd be back in the upper room, which wasn't a place I particularly wanted to be, but it couldn't help but be an improvement on where I was. What I needed, of course, was something to stand on. I tried the footstool, cause of so many of my afflictions, but that wasn't tall enough. Eventually I found a jar and clambered up on to that. I felt the neck go crack under my feet as I hauled myself up through the hole, but so what? Not my jar. Besides, given the way that room had treated me, the more of its owner's property I could damage or spoil, the better.

Back up in the light and air, things didn't seem nearly so bad. Even the two choices that confronted me didn't seem like pathways to certain death, as they probably would've if I'd been thinking of them back down there in the dark. I could go down the ladder and out through the doors, or I could get out on to the platform above the doors and jump down. I was tempted by the relative ease of the first option, but my heart wouldn't hear of it. The way my heart saw it, as soon as I was down the ladder, the doors would fly open and the hall would be full of armed and angry Aeginetans who would chop me into little slices like a sausage; whereas if I followed the second option, even if they did burst in while I was still on the premises, all I had to do was wait till they were all inside, then drop down into the street and walk away, whistling a favourite tune.

Well, arguing with your heart is like arguing with your wife: just because you're in the right doesn't mean you stand a chance of winning. So, as carefully as I could, I slid open the double doors of the loft and poked my head out to see what was going on.

What I saw, down in the street below, was what I was most afraid of seeing: armed men and plenty of them, swarming through the city like ants in their nest. That told me that the battle was over, we'd lost, and the victorious enemy had come home. Not difficult to know what was likely to be in their hearts, after they'd just beaten off an unprovoked surprise attack; not much harder to figure out what their attitude was likely to be towards one of the enemy caught prowling about in someone's house.

I was just pulling my head back in, nice and slow, when one of those dreadful men down there lifted his head and was looking me straight in the eye. The good part about it was, it was Prince Hipposthenes.

'Hello,' he called out, 'we were wondering where you'd got to. Still alive, then?'

'Yes,' I replied.

'That's good, your brother's been worried sick, had us turning over corpses where you were last seen.'

'No,' I said, 'I'm alive all right.'

Hipposthenes nodded, making the plume on his helmet dip gracefully. 'You coming down from there?' he asked.

'In a moment,' I replied.

'All right. When you do, you can tell me what's been happening to you.'

I smiled; not my best smile ever, but as good as I could manage. 'Oh, nothing much,' I said.

Cratus, who'd been shifting about in his seat for some time, lifted his head and made a rude noise.

'You call that an account of the battle?' he said.

'Yes,' Cleander replied. 'At least, it's what happened to me in the battle. I'm not really qualified to talk about anything else, now am I?'

Cratus clicked his tongue. 'Absolutely right,' he said. 'And since, by your own admission, you spent most of the time either getting out of the way or hiding in somebody's storeroom, I put it to you, you're not the most reliable of witnesses.'

'All right,' Cleander said, 'but at least I'm telling it straight, like it happened. If it was up to you, I know you, you'd put in all this unnecessary and misleading stuff about what a bad thing war is and how dreadful it was, so many people getting killed. This is supposed to be a *happy* story, dammit.'

'Oh?' Cratus raised an eyebrow. 'Why?'

'Isn't that obvious?' Cleander shook his head. 'That's the whole point of telling stories about things that happened in the past, isn't it? To entertain, first of all – or nobody would want to listen – and secondly, to inspire, uplift, make people feel good about how things are and how they got that way. Depressing stuff, how pointless it all is – who needs to hear about that? It's all around us anyway, we don't want any more of it.'

Cratus shook his head. 'Amazing,' he said.

'Oh, it's all right for you,' Cleander replied angrily, 'you were born miserable and you'll die miserable, so miserable makes you happy. But the rest of us – normal people – we like to be able to look back on a past when things were better, people were better and braver – people need that. So tell me, Misery; if you take all that away from them, tell them that in fact the past was just as miserable as the present and people were just as mean and cowardly then as they are now – exactly what purpose does that serve?'

Before Cratus could reply (while he was still spluttering with rage, in fact), Palamedes held up his hands for silence. 'Seems to me,' he said, 'that you two aren't ever going to agree, so it's probably as well if we drop the subject while we're all still friends. Though I will say this,' he added, 'and then we won't mention it again. My heart agrees with Cleander; well, I think everybody would, if they stopped and thought about it. Remembering the past is a bit like saving things from a sinking ship or a burning house. You can't take everything with you, so you take the things that are worth keeping: valuable and precious things, or useful and essential things. You don't save junk or things that are worn out or broken; let them burn, they were no good anyway, they're best forgotten. Some memories just aren't worth anything – for instance, who cares what sort of hats they wore twenty generations ago, or what they used to thatch their houses with? Forget about that sort of thing, it's just clutter.

'And some memories are worse than that, they actually cause problems. For instance, if we remembered every war we'd fought and every city we'd fought against, we'd end up hating all our neighbours, pretty well every city on this side of the Peloponnese. We'd remember that in our great-great-great-grandfathers' time there was a dreadful battle against the Sicyonians, say, and a hundred of our best men were killed. So we'd hate the Sicyonians for ever – and who wants that? Next year it might be in our best interests to be friends with the Sicyonians and hate the Messenians (who were probably on our side back when we fought Sicyon all those years ago). Look, the point I'm trying to make is quite obvious, I'd have thought. The past is over and done with, we don't owe it anything; it's not like we've got a responsibility to tend it and guard it, like the temples of the gods. No, the past is like some fallen-down old building: either you leave it alone, because it doesn't concern you, or you pull out the well-cut blocks from the walls and use them to build your own barns and houses and walls. That's what the past is for, to be useful in the present. So,' Palamedes went on, 'to cut it short, I'm with Cleander here, and I think the way he told us about the battle, keeping it light and interesting and exciting and not dwelling too much on the bad aspects – I think he got it more or less right. And if you don't agree, Cratus—'

Cratus lifted his head. 'Of course I agree with the basic point you're making,' he said impatiently. 'I mean, you'd be a clown if you thought otherwise. All I was saying was, Cleander's not fit to tell you the story of the battle, because he wasn't actually there. I was.'

Palamedes sighed. 'All right,' he said. 'But keep it short, will you? I mean, now that we all know who won—'

CHAPTER FIFTEEN

We won the battle (Cratus said). And, contrary to what my dear brother's just told you, we won it rather easily – the only place we had any trouble, in fact, is down the end of the line where he was, or at least where he was when he wasn't off hiding in other people's houses. True enough, they gave us a bit of a hard time there – the few reinforcements who came down from the city all piled in there, and even managed to push us back a couple of times; but when the rest of us were through with our part of the battle, we came round them on all sides and sorted them out good and proper. We managed to surround them, in fact, and we killed or captured more of the enemy there than on any other part of the field, so you can say that the god gave us success there as well.

I was up the other end of the line, and we went through them like water through a cracked dam – first we opened a little gap in their front, when some of them just ran away before we even reached them, and then we pushed through the gap, and the rest of them did the sensible thing and went home before anybody else got hurt. It was the same elsewhere, though a few of them stuck it out and got killed for their trouble. Mostly they were Corinthians, or men who'd originally come over from Corinth about the time the old king was killed – yes, all that was true, apparently, what Pentheus had told us. But I'll tell you about that later.

As soon as we were sure we'd secured the field and there weren't any nasty surprises waiting for us – basically, when we'd cleared up the mess Cleander told you about – we headed on up to the city, expecting to find the gates shut. But they weren't. The Aeginetans, it turned out, had no intention whatsoever of letting themselves in for a siege; as far as the people in town were concerned – not the better sort, obviously, because they were all down the hill fighting – well, they didn't mind the Corinthians particularly but they sure as hell didn't like them enough to risk a siege for them, especially if they were all killed and dead in the battle anyway. Wouldn't have been any point, really. So they left the gates open, put their better stuff where it was more likely to be safe, and waited to see what happened.

Prince Hipposthenes and Uncle Sarpedon didn't take long to figure out how things stood; put simply, provided we didn't bother them, they weren't going to bother us. Good attitude, if you ask me. So the prince told his people, sorry, no looting today except for specified houses – where the Corinthians lived, and the better sort, who'd fought for them – and set off for the palace to see if anything needed to be done there. The essential thing was to find out if the Corinthian princes – the usurpers, if you like – were still in the palace, or if they'd been killed or captured in the battle, or if they were still loose somewhere. Turned out, luckily, that they were among the dead; they'd been killed quite early on, which was one of the reasons we walked through their supporters so easily.

At this point, Hipposthenes asked if anybody had seen Pentheus.

We found him too, eventually. He was right at the bottom of a pile of dead men, at the point where the resistance had been most fierce. By the looks of it, he'd been killed defending the ships when the enemy were threatening to get at them and set fire to them. Now, it's quite possible that he died there because he had no choice, if you see what I mean; he was with a bunch of men who were beaten back, overwhelmed and killed, and whether he died well, striving to be the best like the hero games-player he always made out he was (believed he was, for all I know), or whether he died badly, killed because he wasn't good or clever enough to defend himself, or even whether he died indifferently, stabbed in the neck by a man he hadn't even seen – well, that's something we'll never know, and I don't suppose it really matters. For my part, in spite of everything I may have said about him, I can see no point in saying he didn't die well, bravely, heroically, fighting ever in the forefront like a great warrior in a poem. Besides; we'd come all this way to put him on a throne, and now he'd got himself killed. We looked silly enough as it was without having our man prove to be a gutless wonder into the bargain.

Now here's an interesting thing, while we're on the subject. Naturally enough, one of the first things we asked when we were on speaking terms with the locals was, did they once have a Prince Pentheus who escaped when his family were killed, and was the rest of the story true? Turns out it was; even the stuff about the chariot-race that went wrong, and the king and his family being burned in their house. At that point, some accounts differed. At least two old men swore blind that they'd seen Pentheus' head on a pole over the city gate – it had been there for a month, they said, and there was no mistaking it. Other people said no, they couldn't remember a head on a pole, and they never heard that Pentheus was killed with the others. And then we found a couple of greybeards who were absolutely positive that all the royal family died in the fire, and when the bones were gathered up all the princes were accounted for. We put Pentheus' body on a trestle in the hall and asked people to take a look, tell us if that was the Pentheus they remembered or not; about a third of them said, Yes, that's him, a third said, No, definitely not him, and the remaining third said, Maybe it was, maybe it wasn't, they couldn't be sure. So whether Pentheus was *the* Pentheus, or just some kid who'd taken his name – well, that doesn't matter either. I knew a man who called himself Pentheus, who died fighting the enemy in a battle. I never liked him much, and when he died I must admit part of me was pleased, because it meant he wasn't going to marry my sister. But even I'm not so mean and vindictive that I'd deny his ghost a chance of life on the other side of the River; so, as far as I'm concerned, he was the rightful King of Aegina, and he died avenging his father and taking back his own.

There. Positive enough for you all? That's all right, then.

But I'm going to spoil it a little – sorry, but you'll just have to indulge me – by mentioning that my sister didn't take his death well. For some reason she'd been in love with him – anybody here know why women love the men they do? Thought not – and the thought that he might be killed in the battle hadn't crossed her mind until the news actually reached her. What made it worse for her was that none of this would have happened if she hadn't played that idiotic trick on the princes with the oil and the flour; so it was, in a sense, all her fault.

She dealt with it by crying a lot and keeping out of everybody's way. She didn't want to talk to me or Cleander or Sarpedon – when we tried to talk to her, she got hysterical and started screaming and hitting until we went away again, so that's what we did. She was like that for three days, and we let her get on with it. I don't know if that was the right thing to do or not, but it's what we did.

'All right,' said Prince Hipposthenes later that day, as we sat against the wall in the palace hall. 'What the hell do you suggest we do now?'

It was a valid question. We had no king to put on the throne, no reason to be there at all. We couldn't even reinstate the Corinthian mob, say, 'So sorry,' and leave, since we'd killed them all. If there were any Aeginetans of the better sort left, they weren't exactly lining up to offer their services as kings of Aegina. All in all, it was a mess.

Prince Oenophilus lifted his head. 'I don't know,' he replied. 'I don't suppose you'd fancy being king? We could say Pentheus named you as his heir—'

'Absolutely not,' Hipposthenes answered with a shudder. 'It's too hilly for chariots, I hate anything to do with the sea, and kings don't seem to live very long in these parts. Of course, if you want it—'

'No, thank you very much,' Oenophilus replied. 'All right, what about your sister? If we made out that she and Pentheus were actually married – we could tell people there's a kid on the way, I'm sure we could get a kid from somewhere – and then she could be regent, with a few of our people to advise her—'

'You lay off my sister,' I growled. 'Not that we don't appreciate the offer, mind,' I added, remembering that we needed these people if we wanted a ride home, 'but I think she's been through enough as it is. Getting involved in a game like the one you're suggesting – no, I don't think so.'

Oenophilus shrugged. 'Fair enough,' he said, 'I think the god who put that idea in my mind wasn't really trying to help. All right, has anybody else got any suggestions?'

There was silence for the time it takes to get an arrowhead to forging heat in a good furnace. Then Uncle Sarpedon looked up. 'I'll do it,' he said.

'Sorry?' said Prince Hipposthenes.

'I'll rule the kingdom,' Sarpedon said. 'As a loyal vassal of Megara, of course – I'm not letting you leave me here on my own. But provided you leave me some men for a garrison, and help me out with things generally, I'll hold the fort for you here. It's something I've always fancied doing, being a king.'

The silence that followed that was quite a bit murkier than the previous one.

'No offence,' Oenophilus said eventually, in the tone of voice you use when you know you're bound to offend someone, 'but I hadn't actually considered—'

Sarpedon grinned. 'If you're worried about how to make it all seem legitimate, that's easy,' he said. 'First, young Pentheus named me to the succession just before the battle. Second, his wife, my niece, has begged me with tears in her eyes to look after the kingdom until her unborn child comes of age. Third, lend me fifty men-at-arms and I'll have the heads of anybody likely to cause trouble up above the city gate before dawn tomorrow.' He shrugged. 'And besides,' he said, 'you really haven't got anybody else, have you? Unless you were figuring on installing one of your own people here, a Megaran – and any Megaran who volunteers, or even agrees to do the job, is someone I wouldn't put in charge of a toll-bridge, let alone a vassal state.'

Hipposthenes looked at him for a moment. 'You know,' he said, 'we could do worse.'

His brother looked startled. 'Could we?' he asked. 'It'd be like appointing a wolf as chief sheepdog.'

'Dogs are descended from wolves,' Sarpedon said with a grin. 'Didn't you know that?'

Oenophilus frowned, probably trying to figure out in his heart whether that last remark was exceptionally profound or completely beside the point. 'All right,' he said, 'supposing we did. What about stability? You'll excuse me saying this, you're not a young man any more—'

'You're as young as you feel,' Sarpedon interrupted. 'Or in my case, as young as the last man whose head I cut off. By that reckoning, I'm about twenty-six.'

Hipposthenes smiled. 'I think what my brother's trying to say is,' he said, 'he doesn't think you'd make a very good king. You'd be likely to be a bit – well, rough.'

'So?' Sarpedon shrugged. 'Do you care?'

'Well—' Oenophilus said.

'Do you care enough to leave your brother behind here, or someone else you value enough to trust?'

Oenophilus looked down at his feet. 'If you put it that way,' he said, 'no. But who's to say we need to install a king at all? Why not just let these people sort themselves out, elect a king of their own and go about their business?'

Sarpedon lifted his head. 'You can't mean that,' he said. 'You'd be a laughing stock. We all would. The Princes of Megara launch a mighty expedition, fight a desperate battle, win a glorious victory and then go home again? People will think you're mad.'

Oenophilus sighed. 'All right,' he said. 'But you're going to have to promise me, on your word of honour: do a good job, no unnecessary killing or stuff like that. If we're going to be associated with what happens here in any way—'

'Relax,' Sarpedon replied, with an easy gesture of both hands. 'And credit me with some sense. All I want out of this is to live in a nice house and have people flatter me rotten. I figure, since in spite of everything I've done in my life I'm not likely to be remembered as a fighter, the next best thing is being a good and wise king. It's not what I'd have chosen, but if it'll keep me off the Riverbank for a few generations, it'll do me.'

Hipposthenes studied Sarpedon's face for a while, then said,

'That really bothers you, doesn't it? Fear of being forgotten, I mean.'

'Of course it bothers me. Doesn't it bother you?'

Hipposthenes pursed his lips. 'A little,' he said. 'But then, I've still got plenty of time.'

'And I haven't,' Sarpedon said. 'So you see, this is just what I've been looking for. Now, you wouldn't deny an old man a chance at immortality, would you?'

And so – to my amazement and more than slight disgust – it was decided; Sarpedon would take over the throne of Aegina, as the heir nominated by Pentheus and also as the legal guardian of Pentheus' widow. To mark his accession, and mourn the loss of King Pentheus –

– I promise you; when the princes told us what they had in mind, I thought it must be a joke. Not a very funny one, but maybe (I thought) there were some subtleties of Megaran humour we hadn't mastered yet. When I realised they were serious, I nearly fell off my chair –

– Funeral games would be held, on a scale never before seen on Aegina, with competitors from as far afield as Megara, Athens and Elis—

'Elis?' I asked.

Oenophilus smiled sweetly at me. 'That's you,' he said.

'Me?'

Well, I was so utterly stunned I couldn't find any words; the god had emptied my heart and filled it with goose-feathers. So, in default of further objections, the motion was carried – it'd have been carried even if I'd objected like mad, since, after all, they were the princes. 'It'll help smooth over the transfer of power like nothing else,' Oenophilus assured me. 'And if we imply – nothing said out loud, of course, but it's easy enough to give an impression – if we imply that we regard these games as not just for Pentheus but for all the Aeginetans who were killed in the battle, regardless of which side they were on – well, it's the best way I can think of to give your uncle a good start and help the locals get on with their lives. After all,' he continued, looking at Cleander, 'someone once told me games are like war, except that wars create wounds and unsettle cities, games heal wounds and settle cities down. And I couldn't agree more.'

Cleander, the fool, nodded. 'And,' he added, 'it's the last serious chance we've got of recruiting games-players. Just think, if we can draw them here from Athens—'

Needn't have worried on that score. On the eastern side of the island, away from where we were, there was another small city; its people hadn't had much to do with either the rightful kings or the Corinthians, and tended to stay on their side of the mountain if they could, but they were keen enough to come over the rocks to play games, and what's more, they were good friends with a number of the better sort in Athens (which is only a day's sail away; they reckon that on a clear day you can see Attica from Aegina, but I couldn't be bothered to try this for myself). No; visitors from Athens weren't really at the forefront of my mind. The only foreign visitors I gave any thought to were Corinthians, who wouldn't be showing up to play games. Fortunately, they didn't materialise, whereas two shiploads of Athenians did, along with a party from Troezen (who must have hitched a ride on the backs of eagles to get there in time) and even a solitary Theban, who'd happened to be on the way to Aegina when we landed. All told, we had twenty-one games-players competing; four wrestlers, four boxers, six runners, five chariot-racers, four jumpers and three heavy wrestlers – yes, I know that's more than twenty-one, but some people took part in more than one event. If you want me to be more precise than that, hard luck.

Things went well. It was a warm day, not much wind, and the marshals (some of Hipposthenes' people who'd done this sort of thing before) were up well before dawn marking out, piling up stones, pacing out distances, raking the dirt, rooting out stones and tree-stumps. People started coming in about mid-morning, while Cleander and I were supervising the building of the funeral pyre. Being an island, Aegina isn't all that wonderfully off for gash wood, and the locals were muttering something about using another source of fuel – thatching reed, they suggested, or bean-helm or – I'm not kidding – dried cow-dung, which the smallholders burned on their fires in winter. Well, part of me could see how fitting it would be for Pentheus' ghost to be freed from its corporeal prison in an inferno of blazing cowshit; but there were appearances to consider, not to mention the smell. I borrowed a few men-at-arms from Uncle Sarpedon (he'd appropriated a dozen of the princes' Sardinian soldiers-of-fortune; evil as they come, didn't care what they did) and went foraging for damaged furniture in the houses of the dead Corinthians. By the time the Sardinians had finished enjoying themselves, there was enough damaged furniture to spit-roast an army, let alone one man.

Once we had the pyre built, and the platform for the marshals, and the stand for the chief mourners and guests of honour, it was after midday, cool enough to get on with the funeral and start the games. I'll say this for the Aeginetans, they know how to appreciate a good funeral. Cleander and I were the two front pallbearers, so I was in a good position to see the contented faces and nods of approval as we went through all the ordained palaver of grief, while the gaggle of old biddies we'd hired to be the Women in Mourning played an absolute blinder – shrieking, sobbing, thumping their temples with the heels of their hands, ripping out great bunches of hair, gouging their cheeks with their nails until the blood actually flowed; they couldn't have put on a better show, even though I don't suppose one in five of them had the slightest idea who they were supposed to be mourning for. Anyway, after they'd finished, one of Oenophilus' stewards took them back to the palace for a hearty feed and a jar or three of wine, which they'd thoroughly deserved.

We, of course – the princes, Cleander, Sarpedon and me – we were chief mourners and had to go through the whole business with long faces and sad frowns. Sarpedon managed some tears as he set the torch to the pyre – he told me later he'd got an onion crushed up in the palm of his left hand – and I did the best I could by looking down at the ground and dragging my feet as I walked. All things considered, it was a perfectly respectable display of grief, though ironically, the only person in the whole world who was sad because Pentheus was dead wasn't there; Dusa refused to come, and actually cracked Prince Oenophilus round the head with an earthenware plate when he tried to reason with her.

The cremation itself nearly went blue on us; we hadn't layered the pyre properly, and when it was just going nicely and the flames were getting presentably high, the whole thing started to shift alarmingly, threatening to topple over and dump burning logs into the crowd. The invaluable Sardinians saved the day, jumping up on to the pyre itself in their thick-soled boots and pushing it all back into shape with their spears, for which they got a splendid round of applause from the crowd. The singing of the hymn went perfectly – it's a real bitch getting the timing right so the hymn comes to an end just as the fire dies down. Sing too quickly, you finish early and have to stand around like overlooked figs on a tree; sing too slowly, and the fire's out before you've finished, and you have to hurry like mad through the last few verses. This time, though, we got it right. We were quietly pleased with ourselves; we'd put on a good show.

It was only afterwards, when we were raking through the ashes for the bones, that we realised the mistake we'd made. We couldn't find any bones. Not so much as a charred knuckle.

Prince Hipposthenes drew me aside and whispered, 'You did remember to bring the body.'

I looked at him. 'Me?' I said. 'I thought Oenophilus was seeing to that.'

The prince rolled his eyes. 'Bugger,' he said. 'I'll bet you the crowstruck thing's still back at the palace. How can anybody have a funeral and forget the damn body?'

I clicked my tongue. 'Can't be helped now,' I said. 'I don't suppose anyone's noticed. We'll just have to fish out some bits of twig that look like bones and bury them instead.'

So that's what we did; and it was a few blackened stumps of chair-leg and spear-shaft that got wrapped in fat, dowsed in wine and laid reverently to rest in a tasteful gold jar under a cairn of stones. Sure enough, when we got back to the palace that evening, Pentheus was where we'd left him; so while Sarpedon stood watch to make sure Dusa didn't see us, Hipposthenes and I wrapped him up in a torn sail and gave him to the Sardinians, who took a row-boat out into the bay when it was dark and chucked him over the side.

Back to the fun; after the interment we took off our white cloaks and put them under our chairs, and told the marshals to start the games. Sarpedon gave the order, and sat in the high seat where the king usually sits and hands out the prizes. Of course, the locals didn't know who he was, or who any of us were; don't suppose they cared all that much, either.

Here are my recollections of the boxing match, in which I personally took part. I was drawn against an Athenian, whose name is on the tip of my tongue. Before I'd even had a chance to take guard, he smacked me on the chin. That's all I can remember about the boxing match.

What about the other events? Let's see; the running race. An Athenian called Hipponicus was the clear favourite, with the other five considered to be pretty well matched. This Hipponicus certainly looked like he meant business while he was warming up – running on the spot, doing frog-hops, swinging his arms and doing that thing where you sprint forwards a few steps and then come to a screaming halt – and he looked even meaner and more determined waiting for the off, with the toes of his front foot curled into the little trench the marshals had scraped in the dirt to mark the start line, his arms outstretched as if he was getting ready to catch something, his head very slightly turned towards where the herald was standing – so the sound of the trumpet would reach his ear that much quicker, I guess. And he made a wonderful start, too; it was a pity his specially tailored runner's shorts came adrift, wound themselves round his knees and sent him down on his nose a few heartbeats later, because I'm sure he'd have won otherwise. I can't remember now who actually did win – it was one of the Megarans, but the name's gone. Isn't that crazy? I can remember who lost the race, but not who won it.

The jumping was quite exciting; one of the two games-players from Troezen made a fantastic jump, nearly ten paces, but was disqualified by the marshals because he landed left foot first, and so didn't make a clear two-footed mark in the dirt. He was quite calm about the decision, but his brother, the other Troezenian, got rather upset and waved his arms about a lot, even going so far as to chuck a jumping-weight at the herald. Fortunately he missed – they're heavy, those things – and the weight went ever such a long way before it landed, prompting the herald to say that it was a shame we weren't having a weight-throwing event at these games, or the Troezenian would've won it for sure. The winning jump, made by a Megaran called Timoleon, was a measly six and a half paces; a fine example of the best man not winning, though of course that's supposed to be impossible.

The chariot race was a non-event, really; not that I'd want to suggest collusion or fixing or anything, but the field as they came into the final straight looked like some sort of sacred procession, with Prince Hipposthenes way out in front and everybody else keeping a respectful distance. Since Hipposthenes had also donated the prize – a rather lovely tripod and cauldron with gryphon feet, the pick of his share of the plunder from the late king's personal storeroom – it all seemed rather pointless, but it kept the prince happy, and the crowd cheered like mad when he crossed the line. Once he was safely home, the remaining competitors put on a terrific spurt (maybe there hadn't been any directions about who was supposed to come second), and two chariots collided and got pretty comprehensively wrecked, so that the eventual second-place winner crossed the line on his bare axles and facing the wrong way, having lost his wheels, boom and horses in the pile-up. Third-place winner protested; but the marshals, after a long debate, declared the result valid. The second-place man was an Aeginetan, which I think had something to do with it; so long as he won, Hipposthenes didn't mind allowing a little glory to a local man, as a gesture of goodwill.

The orthodox wrestling was good, vulgar fun; an Aeginetan called Gonnadas won one heat, and met a Megaran by the name of Taxander for the final. The start of the bout was a somewhat tense moment up on the platform; if the Megaran killed or maimed the local boy, or if (even worse) he cheated, there was a chance that we could end up fighting our way back to the ships before nightfall. In the event, however, it was a thoroughly good-natured bout, more a test of strength than anything involving skill. After a few desultory holds, the two men decided between themselves to make it a matter of who could lift who off the ground first. Taxander may even have thrown the fight, I don't know; he looked a far more likely prospect for most of the time, then suddenly seemed to get tired and let Gonnadas pick him up like a jar of olives. Not to be outdone, Gonnadas chose to forgo the first prize (a silver-hilted sword with a bronze-studded scabbard and matching belt) and take the second prize instead – a young but not particularly special-looking slave girl, formerly the wife of one of the Corinthians, who was in fact, as we later discovered, Gonnadas' niece.

The last event was the heavy wrestling; and there we had a problem, namely only three competitors. That meant either giving one of them a bye straight to the final, which always looks bad, or finding someone to make up a fourth. Now, since two of the three games-players we did have were Megarans and the third was an Athenian, it made sense not to recruit an Aeginetan – we'd got this far without starting a riot, and heavy wrestling is probably the one event most likely to result in serious injury. Unfortunately, it's also a skilled business; you can't just pitch someone on to the floor and tell him to get on with it; against a trained opponent he won't last the time it takes to peel an apple. In the end, it turned out that the only man qualified to take part was Prince Oenophilus, who'd apparently been quite good at the game a few years before, when a back injury made him give it up.

Faced with a choice between getting thrown over someone's shoulder in a good cause and spoiling the show with a bye, Oenophilus finally agreed to do the decent thing, and allowed us to dowse him down with oil and dust, ready for the start. The ballot matched him against the Athenian – he'd had it fixed that way so as to spare himself the embarrassment of being beaten by one of his own people – and they squared off in the usual way. Before the bout started, Oenophilus had told us his plan was to dodge around just long enough to show he wasn't a complete novice, then give the Athenian a nice, clean opening for a quick, fairly gentle throw.

I think it would all have worked out just fine if the Athenian hadn't tried to bite the prince's nose off. For one thing, biting isn't really allowed, even in heavy wrestling; more to the point, Oenophilus had something of a vain streak in his nature – he'd apparently been very good-looking as a boy, with plenty of genuine admirers around his father's court, and although he'd inevitably lost the looks as he grew older, he was still self-absorbed enough to react badly to someone who'd just given him some ugly and permanent scars right where everybody couldn't help seeing them. So he lost his temper a little, which meant that he fought both vigorously and extremely badly, giving the Athenian no choice but to throw him around a bit, purely in self-defence. At one point he scored a quite obvious throw, but as soon as the marshal came up to announce the end of the bout he got an eyeful of concentrated majesty and, very wisely, backed off.

The Athenian saw that he was in a fix, and that the bout was going to continue until the prince won, rules or no rules, so he decided to accept the inevitable and make it as painless for himself as possible – you could see the thought being put into his heart, even from where I was sitting. So he opened his defence for a nice, conclusive throw that'd end the match and not break any bones; but the prince wasn't having that, he was downright angry by now, the way usually quiet and peaceful men get sometimes when they've had a lot to put up with and want to take it out on someone. So, instead of accepting the opening, he went for a rather more flamboyant throw, one which involved getting the other man over his shoulders and pitching him across the floor like a sack. Unfortunately he muffed the manoeuvre; and the Athenian, who was still expecting him to take the opening, dropped his own head down just as the prince's head was coming up. There was a crack they must have heard in Arcadia; the Athenian wobbled and nearly fell over backwards, while Oenophilus dropped to the ground with blood pouring from his forehead, where the Athenian's teeth had cut him. Luckily, the Athenian had the wit to fall over (otherwise he'd have won the bout, like it or not); he looked as if he was planning on staying there and conceding, but he wasn't given the chance. As soon as Oenophilus managed to get back on his feet, he charged over, grabbed the Athenian by the arm, dragged him upright and stabbed him right in the pit of the stomach with his outstretched fingers.

Now that's a neat, quick way to kill someone if you judge it right; but the prince didn't, and the Athenian, who was clearly terrified and afraid for his life, reacted on pure reflex and lashed out with his left hand, catching the prince a terrific blow on the side of the head. Oenophilus reeled away, roaring like a bull, grabbed a chair off the platform behind him and took a swing at the Athenian, who had no alternative but to step sideways or get mashed.

Either Oenophilus' brains were a bit shaken up by the punch, or he couldn't see properly because of all the blood in his eyes; whatever the reason, he staggered forward into the space where the Athenian now wasn't, tripped over one of the feet of the chair and fell heavily across it, catching the chair-arm in his mouth as he fell, with all his weight behind him. The effect was pretty catastrophic; a fractured jaw and well over half his teeth smashed like a row of pots. Even so he tried to get up and have another shot at the Athenian (who'd tried to run away, but was being held back by one of the Sardinians); after a valiant attempt to stand, however, Oenophilus wavered and slowly dropped on to the ground, out cold.

At first, Hipposthenes was as stunned as the rest of us. Fortunately he came round before anyone else; with a jerk of his head he gestured to the Sardinians to let the Athenian go, and sent some of his people to pick up his brother on a door and get him back to the palace as quickly as possible. Then, taking a deep breath, he stood up and announced that owing to the unfortunate accident (I liked that word, in the circumstances), the bout between his brother and whatever the Athenian was called was null and void, and the second pair would now wrestle for the match. Having said his piece, he hurried off after the door-bearers, leaving Sarpedon to finish off the games.

Gods know who won the match in the end; I don't think the competitors themselves were giving it their full attention. Nevertheless, Hipposthenes' prompt action saved the day as far as the public-relations exercise was concerned; the crowd stayed put and Sarpedon gave the prizes for first and second place; nobody mentioned third, for obvious reasons. It was only a boring old silver-gilt cup anyway, not the sort of thing you'd go out of your way to pick up if you saw it lying in the road.

Hipposthenes came back a moment or so after the prize-giving; he had an important job still to do, and family considerations have to come second when you're a prince. He stood up, raised his arms for silence and made the announcement we'd all been quietly dreading; all about Sarpedon, his various rights to the throne, and his immediate accession as King of Aegina.

Oddly enough, the melodrama with Prince Oenophilus probably helped; the crowd were still rather too shocked and bewildered by what they'd seen to take in what Hipposthenes was saying, and so it passed largely without a reaction of any kind. Hipposthenes produced a gold wreath, presumably recovered from the Corinthian king's store-room, and dunked it down on Uncle's head. A few of the Megarans dutifully cheered, while the Aeginetans looked casually on, as if none of this had anything to do with them. It was a low-key coronation all right, but in the circumstances low-key was probably as good a way to go as any. Nobody shouted or threw a stone, and a few moments later the crowd started to drift away, like a sea-mist when the sun comes out.

And that, friends, was how we overthrew the Corinthian dynasty on Aegina and replaced it with the Eleo-Megaran dynasty. One hell of a way to change the course of so many people's lives, if you ask me, but that's how it turned out; a combination of accidents, lies and mistakes, with a healthy pinch of human nature tossed in for seasoning. I suppose it worked out quite well for Uncle Sarpedon – he got something he apparently had always wanted, a kingdom of his own, though he died a couple of years later, of a bad cold. It won the Megarans a new vassal, which on balance must have been a good thing; certainly it changed the course of things in Megara, because shortly afterwards (so I've heard since) Hipposthenes became sole ruler following his brother's death in a fire – which was fairly convenient, by all accounts, since Oenophilus went a bit strange in the head after losing his teeth; he refused to let anybody see him, and threw the most alarming fits of bad temper during which he'd threaten people, even the better sort, and often get violent. Hipposthenes, so they say, turned out to be a good king – for all I know, he's king yet – so apparently it was all for the best. But he must have lost Aegina at some stage, because I have it on good authority that the Aeginetans are back running things themselves now, and making a very good job of it too, by all accounts.

As far as we were concerned, the Aegina business was a complete waste of time, if not a disaster. We'd lost two of our party – well, one of our party plus Pentheus, and opinions differed about whether that was good or bad. None of the games-players we approached showed any interest in games-with-nobody-dead; somehow the Aeginetans had got it into their minds that we Eleans were every bit as savage and undisciplined as Prince Oenophilus, the Megarans had had enough of us to last them a lifetime, and the offcomers, from Athens and Troezen, didn't stick around long enough for us to ask. Cleander half-heartedly suggested going to Athens ourselves, but even he conceded that it'd be a pointless exercise once news of what had happened on Aegina reached the city; we'd get the blame, just as the Argives had blamed us, and we'd be lucky to get out of there in one piece.

So I never got to visit the city of Theseus, which is reckoned to be the most beautiful place in the world, home of the wisest of men. Actually, I was relieved that we weren't going; I'd had enough of the quest for games-players, not to mention the games themselves, travel as a way of life, and (most of all) my brother and sister. All I wanted to do was talk Hipposthenes into lending us a crew for the ship we'd stolen from the Corinthian, and go straight home.

We got our crew – the prince made a good job of hiding it, but my heart knew he was only too glad to see the back of us, and I can't say I blame him – but I didn't get my straight ride home. That was Cleander's fault, needless to say – but we'll go into that later. Instead, we got a wonderful load of presents – well, Hipposthenes could afford to be generous, it wasn't exactly his stuff he was giving away; even so, he wasn't obliged to be quite so open-handed, so all credit to him. By the time all the furniture and tableware and textiles and bronze ingots and who knows what else were stowed aboard our ship, the hold was nearly full and we had trouble fitting in all the provisions we were going to need – so, from that point of view, the journey had been worthwhile, very much so. I suppose we should have felt rather more grateful than we did; I mean to say, we arrived in Megara destitute and starving, we departed rich and well-escorted, leaving our uncle behind as King of Aegina. But it was all so depressingly beside the point that – truthfully – we weren't all that bothered.

On balance, I'm glad there were no protracted farewells. When the wind got up and it was time for us to go, Sarpedon was busy eating and drinking with some of the higher-class Aeginetans and not to be disturbed, Hipposthenes was looking after his damaged brother, and nobody else seemed particularly interested. We trooped on board – Cleander busy talking sailing times and wind directions with the shipmaster, Dusa at her droopiest and least talkative, and me hoping for a keen wind all the way round the Peloponnese. At least the crew seemed cheerful enough; most of them were younger sons of Megaran smallholders, with a leavening of Aeginetan fishermen and regular sailors to add a touch of expertise, and they all appeared to be looking forward to visiting new places, seeing the cities of men and knowing their minds. Just like we'd been, in fact, a long while ago.

We'd been under sail half a day and were making good time, according to the shipmaster, when Cleander remembered to tell me about the detour.

'It's only a day or so out of our way,' he explained. 'And if we can recruit *him*, it'll make up for a lot of what we've lost. In fact, we could get quite a few games-players turning up of their own accord once they know *he's* coming.'

And for once, I couldn't have agreed more. Cleander had decided that we were going to stop off at Epidaurus and see if we couldn't enlist the greatest games-player of them all, Milon the wrestler.

'Assuming,' I said, 'he's still competing. He must be well into his forties by now.'

Cleander shook his head. 'Last I heard,' he said, 'he was still in the game, and if anything better than ever. And keen – he'll jump at the chance. You know, we might yet come out of this all right. My heart's got a good feeling about this.'

I couldn't help but agree. Everybody who was even remotely interested in games-playing knew about Milon of Epidaurus; how, when he was still little more than a boy, he pulled a full-grown ox out of a river, and wrestled a wild boar to the ground with his bare hands. The story of how he'd beaten the mighty Geraeon at the funeral games of the King of Aegeum was one of the spurs that got me into games-playing myself, for a while. He'd overthrown champions in Argos, Messene, Corinth, Athens, Arcadia, right across the Peloponnese and as far north as Thebes and Plataea. He'd been to Crete and Rhodes, and won famous bouts there. Some people even told a far-fetched tale about a match between Milon and Hercules, though that was clearly impossible, since Hercules died long before Milon was born. In any event; even if he'd only done half of what people claimed he'd done, he had to be the single most famous and prestigious games-player living, and I have to admit, I'd have taken a detour to meet him even if we hadn't been recruiting.

Epidaurus is a small, essentially poxy place, the sort of city you'd never go to unless you had business there. At first it struck us as odd that someone as remarkable as Milon could ever have come from such a place, until my heart pointed out that if you were a native of Epidaurus, you'd have a strong motivation for cultivating any art or skill that gave you the opportunity to spend a lot of time away from it. You want me to be specific? I'll be specific. The city wall was low, badly built and falling down in several places. One of the gates was off its hinges – in the unlikely event that anybody wasted their time attacking the place, the inhabitants would never be able to get the gates shut without rehanging them first. The streets were narrow and nearly empty, the houses were tiny and squashed together, the palace was no bigger than – well, my house, for one – and the palace orchard was little more than a courtyard with a couple of spindly old apple-trees hanging off their supports. Even the dogs were thin and languid, lacking the energy and enthusiasm to get up or bark when we strangers walked past. The only thing big or remarkable about Epidaurus that we saw was the palace dungheap, which looked as if it had been left to accumulate for several generations.

'This is the place, though,' Cleander said. 'Let's just hope he's at home, not away competing somewhere. Fools we'd look, coming all this way just to find we'd missed him.'

Dusa – you can tell how magical the name Milon was, Dusa had actually woken up out of her trance and come with us – shook her head. 'I think he's at home,' she said. 'Look.' She pointed to one of the outbuildings, which closer inspection revealed to be a trap-house; the door was half open, and inside we could see the back end of an old and rickety-looking chariot, with a sprung frame and tattered wickerwork in the left wall of the box. 'Don't suppose he's got another,' she said. 'He's home.'

So we walked up to the palace doors, which were slightly ajar, and called out. After a while, a small woman with a face like the last of the year-old apples strolled up and asked us what we wanted.

'We're here to see Prince Milon,' Cleander said.

The woman said nothing, just looked at us as if we were crazy.

'Prince Milon,' Cleander repeated. 'We're here to see him.'

Slowly, the woman smiled, revealing as comprehensive a lack of teeth as you'd ever hope to see (unless, of course, you were visiting the Princes of Megara). Then she shut the doors on us.

'Wonderful,' I said. 'Now what do we do?'

Dusa frowned. It was almost one of her old, look-out-here-I-go frowns, but filtered through a gauze of experience, the way you filter the oil from the mash. It upset me rather to see it. 'Leave this to me,' she said; so we did.

After a deep breath, Dusa picked up a stone and threw it, as hard as she could, at the door. A few heartbeats later, she picked up another stone; then another. Six or seven stones later, the door opened. This time, a man's head appeared.

'What do you want?' he asked.

Dusa put down the stone she was holding and gave him a brilliant smile. 'If it's all right,' she said, sweet as fresh honeycomb, 'we'd like to see Prince Milon.'

The man frowned, as if he couldn't understand. '*See* him?' he repeated.

'That's right,' Dusa said brightly. 'Is it a good time?'

'I suppose so,' the man replied. 'I mean, if you want me to take you to where he is, I can do that for you, sure.'

'That's wonderful,' Dusa said. 'Is he in the palace?'

The man lifted his head. 'Good gods, no. He's out round the back, in the courtyard.'

That figured; on a warm, sunny day he'd be out practising. If I'd thought, I'd have suggested we look there first.

'Splendid,' Dusa said. 'Right then, after you.'

The man came out, pulling the door to behind him. 'I'm Prince Dromus, by the way,' he said.

We replied that we were delighted to meet him, and added that we were from Elis, and we'd come all that way just to see Milon. Dromus thought about that for a moment, then shrugged.

'You're wrestlers too, then?' he asked.

'I am,' I said. 'At least, I was. But that's not the main reason we're here.'

'Oh,' Dromus replied. 'Well, anyway, here he is.'

We were standing on the edge of the threshing-floor; a wretched little thing, badly in need of fresh earth and a good tidy-up. 'Here we are,' Dromus repeated.

Dusa breathed in, then out, and widened her smile. 'Sorry,' she said, 'maybe I'm being a bit slow. Where exactly?'

'Here.'

'But I can't see Prince Milon,' Dusa objected, managing to keep her temper. 'Where is he?'

Dromus shrugged. 'More or less directly under where you're standing, actually,' he replied. 'At least, that's where the cairn of stones was, when I was a boy. My father had them shifted because they were blocking off access to the floor, we were having to take the carts right round the side . . .'

'You mean he's dead?' Cleander interrupted.

'Well, of course he's dead,' Dromus said. 'He's been dead for years. I thought you people wanted to see where his ashes are buried.'

'He can't be dead,' I broke in. 'Why, only last summer—'

Dromus grinned. 'Oh, I see,' he said. 'You're another one who's heard one of the old stories about him and not realised how long ago all that was. No, Milon died seven generations ago – in fact, he's my great-great-great-great-granduncle. He's been dead for – what, seven lots of thirty, that's over two hundred years.' He smiled. 'And you've come all this way thinking he's still alive. That's a pity.'

'You're joking,' said Dusa at last.

'No, I'm not,' Dromus said. 'You ask anybody in Epidaurus,

they'll tell you the same thing. After all, he's the only famous man we've ever had here, everybody knows about him. The thing is,' he went on, 'he's so famous that whenever people hear of a great feat of wrestling but don't know the wrestler's name, they tend to assume it must have been Milon. Odd, isn't it, the way people lose track of time. You just go on assuming that so-and-so's still alive, because you don't actually know when he was born or how old he is, and you've never heard the news of his death.'

'I see,' Cleander said. 'Even so—'

'In a way,' Dromus went on, tracing a pattern in the dust with his toe, 'it's a sign of immortality. Not just immortality – eternal youth, even. Although he's been dead so long, people keep him alive in their hearts. I think that's rather fine, don't you?'

So that was that. We said thank you nicely to Prince Dromus, but we weren't quick enough to avoid an invitation to eat and drink with him; so we had to sit still and listen to even more tales of the valour and prowess of the supreme Milon, about whom we no longer cared a damn.

'We could always pretend he's still alive,' Dusa suggested, as we walked back to the ship. 'I'll bet you more people believe he's still alive than think he's dead. So all we'd have to do is find a wrestler, someone about the right age—'

'What, two hundred odd? That's a tall order.'

'Shut up, Cratus. Someone about forty but still fit and strong, who's good at wrestling and knows enough about Milon to be able to pass for him—'

'No,' I said. 'Most certainly not. Not even if we pour oil all over him and sprinkle him with flour, like a slice of raw meat. I've had enough of that sort of thing to last me the rest of my life.'

Dusa suddenly went all dark again. 'What sort of thing?' she said softly.

Served me right, I suppose. 'Oh, you know,' I said awkwardly. 'Anyway, we aren't doing it, and that's that. For one thing, we haven't got a suitable wrestler.'

Dusa smiled. 'We could find one,' she said.

'Oh really? Where?'

'There,' she said, and pointed to the helmsman of our ship. 'He's the right age, and I bet he can wrestle. If not, you can teach him. We've got all the rest of the trip home, it'll help you pass the time.'

'No,' I said. 'Cleander, tell her; it's out of the question.'

The helmsman's name was Bias. He was a quick learner. In fact, I can still feel the place in my left shoulder from when he finally got the hang of the Flying Mare.

With hindsight, I think I preferred her when she was miserable.

CHAPTER SIXTEEN

'Let me just stop you there for a moment,' Palamedes said, 'while we get out the tables and fix dinner.'

Cratus nodded. 'Good idea,' he said. 'I don't know about all of you; all this talking's given me an appetite.' He smiled at the Phoenician. 'Talking and eating are what we Sons of the Achaeans do best,' he added, 'though we also make reasonable silverware.'

The Phoenician wasn't quite sure what to say to that. 'You live interesting lives,' he replied, 'considering your circumstances. In my country, we have far more, but do rather less.' He thought for a moment. 'Perhaps all the things we own tend to clutter our lives up rather, which means we don't have as much space in them as you do.'

Cratus frowned. 'Explain,' he said.

'It's quite simple, if I'm right,' the Phoenician said. 'In my country, for example, there's much more of a difference between the better sort and the rest of the people; we don't just have more land, we look different and do different things. Here, as far as I can tell, you all look more or less the same, do the same things – you don't leave all the field-work to serfs and hired hands, you turn out at ploughing and harvest and vintage, you hoe and prune and dig terraces—'

'Sometimes,' Cratus interrupted. 'But not all the time. If we want to, we can take off on a visit somewhere, or go to war, or spend a day or so sitting around eating and drinking, most times of the year. Your average smallholder can't do that, except at quiet times of the year.'

'True,' the Phoenician said. 'But where I come from, a man like you wouldn't want to do a day's work in the fields; in fact, he'd be mildly horrified if you suggested it. In a way, he hasn't got the same freedom as you have.'

'I don't follow,' Cratus said.

'Maybe I'm not putting it very well. Here, you have land and cattle and a few bits and pieces of clothing and – well, junk; sure, ordinary men have to work all the time, they haven't got any choice in the matter. But you can choose to work – or go visiting, or fight in a war. In my country, you wouldn't have that choice; you'd only do ordinary men's work if you'd fallen on hard times, become destitute, so you have to find ways to avoid ending up behind a plough or chasing goats down mountains. Fear of having to go to work makes you do things you might otherwise not want to do – me, for example, I travel all round the Sea giving and receiving presents, because I don't own enough land and livestock to support myself and my family in idleness. Damn it, even the kings of our cities can't really choose what they do. For example, they say that if the King of Egypt wants to piss, he has to go through a ceremony made up of six distinct stages and involving four noblemen and two priests – and if one of the proper officers happens not to be there, all the king can do is cross his legs and wait for him to come back. There's one city in Cilicia, apparently, where the king's only allowed to wipe his nose on a specific piece of purple rag – it's over two hundred years old, they say, and getting a bit frayed in places, and if it's in the wash or the Lord High Rag-Bearer's away visiting his mother, the king has to sit there all day with snot on his moustache, while everybody looks the other way. That's what I mean by a cluttered life.'

Cratus laughed. 'Rather extreme example, though,' he said.

'Maybe,' said the Phoenician. 'But it's the same for all of us, to a lesser degree. Take me, for instance. When I get home from this trip, I'll spend the first five days sorting out all the things I've brought back with me, storing them in my warehouse—'

'Warehouse?'

'Like a barn, but you store things in it, not jars of grain. Then I'll have to do the—' He used another unfamiliar word, which Cratus queried. 'Tallies,' he explained. 'It's all to do with the little scratches on wood we've been talking about. I'll have to make tallies of what I've brought home with me, including what I've given in exchange, where I've stored it, that sort of thing; then I'll have to go out giving-and-receiving, in order to turn all the copper ore and raw wool and oxhides and amber nuggets and who knows what else into something my family and I can actually eat, or wear, or put on the fire. By the time I've done all that, I could have sown a field of barley, cut it, threshed it, baked it and still have time to sit out in the street for an afternoon talking with my friends. Are you starting to see what I mean?'

'I think so,' Cratus replied, 'but I'm not sure I can understand how anybody can live like that. I mean, why bother? Is it just because you like having all the things you people have, or isn't there enough land for everybody, or what?'

The Phoenician shrugged. 'All sorts of reasons,' he said. 'For one thing, yes, there's a lot more of us than there are of you, so we're all squashed in tightly together. Then, when you've got that many people all around you all the time, for some reason things seem to matter more; you feel the need to have more and better things than the next man, just so you can show him who you are. It's our way of defining ourselves, I suppose; whereas you people seem to do that through deeds and actions – like your mighty warriors and famous games-players.'

'I think I see,' Cratus said, frowning. 'Like, if I was one of you and someone pointed me out in the street, you'd say, Oh yes, I know him, he owns fifty-six bales of raw fleeces and a hundred and twenty-eight bars of refined copper; and then your friend would know where to put me in the order of things, above someone with only forty-seven bales, but under someone with a hundred and two.'

'You've got the idea,' the Phoenician said. 'But here, they'd say, There goes so-and-so, who won a prize at such-and-such's games, or who killed such-and-such in the battle last year.' He frowned. 'I wonder why we always need to do that?'

'Same reason as games-players compete in games,' Cratus replied, 'or cities fight wars, or anybody does anything. The only way we can define ourselves is against other people. It's all a way of keeping score, knowing who we are, letting everybody else know who we are – or were, when we're dead and gone. Do your people sing long poems about great heroes who had lots and lots of possessions?'

The Phoenician shuddered. 'Perish the thought,' he said. 'No, we aren't as bothered as you are about being remembered after we die. After all, we have the scratches on wood and stone – though it's only really kings and princes who get remembered that way. The rest of us are just resigned to being forgotten. It doesn't worry us much.'

'What a strange attitude,' Cratus replied with a smile. 'So you're all quite happy at the thought of spending forever in the dark on the Riverbank?'

'Maybe,' the Phoenician replied. 'After all, I don't think it'll be all that different from what we do while we're alive.'

I think it's time my brother rested his voice (Cleander said, after the food had been cooked and eaten, and the tables cleared away). I'd hate for him to go hoarse and not be able to speak for a day or so; after all, the sound of his own voice is what he loves best of all, it'd kill him to be deprived of it for so long.

Now, I could tell you all about our journey home; we had a few adventures along the way, it's unavoidable if you spend any length of time on a ship. Things happen on ships, that's just how it is. But I won't, because if I start I'll have to finish, and to be honest with you, one sudden storm sounds pretty much like another, and you'll all be asleep by the time I get you to Cynuria. So we'll skip all that. If you feel the need, you can imagine choppy seas, sudden gusts of wind, people sliding about the ship and hauling on ropes; I don't suppose you'll be far from the truth.

We made landfall at Peneus-mouth eight days after we left Aegina. Believe me, the thought of being home again, within easy walking distance of Elis, was simply wonderful. I'd only started thinking about home after we passed the mouth of the Alpheus, which was the border of Elean territory back then, but once I'd started I couldn't get home out of my mind. Suddenly the ship seemed to be standing still in the water – actually, we had a good following breeze, we were making good time – and I nearly hopped over the side and swam ashore, figuring that I could run home faster than the ship could carry me. But my heart knew that I couldn't, so I stayed put and made do with staring at the shore, gauging our rate of progress by the landmarks I recognised. That last stretch, from the point and along the bay, seemed to take a whole year; I'll swear my beard grew an inch while I stood there leaning on the rail.

Well, we did get there eventually – but before we could grab our gear and race home, there was a slight problem: what to do about the ship. It was our ship – well, we'd stolen it, so it was ours – but the crew were all Megarans, and of course they wanted to go home just as much as we had. It was pretty clear that they weren't going to walk all that way. On the other hand, if they took the ship back to Megara – well, it might as well be at the bottom of the sea for all the good it'd do us. We nearly said, To the crows with it, and let them keep it; but a ship's just too large an item to say goodbye to in such a lordly fashion, so we had to figure something out, whether we liked it or not. You have no idea how frustrating it was, having to stand around arguing when we were so close to home; it was as if the adventure still had one claw stuck in us and couldn't quite bring itself to let us go.

In the end, they agreed to wait at the river mouth for three days, to give us time to find a crew of Eleans who'd sail with them back to Megara, then bring the ship home again. Bless their hearts, they were as good as their word – better, because as soon as we reached the city we forgot all about them, and it was only on the evening of the third day that we remembered, and had to go out recruiting in a hurry. But they stayed until the next morning (contrary winds, I think) and our people reached them in time. It was a whole year before we saw the ship again, and by that time we'd forgotten it even existed, so it came as a very pleasant surprise when it did show up. The following spring we traded it for a large orchard, some grazing land and a flock of sheep; all in all, we did well out of that ship, better than we deserved, when you think how we came by it.

If you laugh when I tell you this, I won't mind; it sounds crazy, I know.

All that time we'd been away, all the pain of wanting to be home – and when at last I saw Elis, squatting there in the middle distance like a dog sleeping on the midden, all I could see was just another small, unremarkable city, so like all the others we'd been to. It was so *small* – well, hardly surprising that it looked smaller than it had when I went away, because back then Elis had been the whole of my world, instead of one remote end of it.

I once heard someone say – can't remember when, where or who – that the more you get to know something, the smaller it gets. Like so many of these sayings that sound really profound and cute the first time you hear them, I'm not sure it actually means anything; if it does, it's something to do with the same effect that shrank Elis, like wool washed in overheated water, the day I came home. Needless to say, I'd learned more about Elis in a few months away from it than in all the years I'd lived there. It's like when you're in a strange town and you get lost, blundering about in narrow streets under the eaves of tall buildings. If you leave the town and walk up into the hills, you can look down on it from a distance and see it all laid out, like a plan scraped in the dust – but in order to see it that way, you can't be in it. You know – excuse me, this is my heart getting all thoughtful on me – I wonder if that's what we do when we tell stories about the past. Looking back, you see the shape of things that have happened to you, but you're outside, and also the distance blurs the detail; instead of known faces you see only the standard shapes and sizes of people, losing who they are in what they are.

Listen to me, bleating on like an old ram hung up in the thorns. Once we reached the city, of course, this crazy feeling went away, and it was like going outside in the sun after you've been lying inside the house with a fever for days on end. Everything I saw seemed sharp and clear, that wonderful combination of familiarity and freshness you only get when you come back to something you know.

Inside me my heart was urging me to go straight home to my wife and children (I'd hardly given them a moment's thought while we were away; now I was home, they filled my thoughts like stormwater flooding a ditch). I looked round to ask Cratus what he thought – go straight to the palace, or home first – but neither he nor Dusa were anywhere to be seen. Pretty obvious what his priorities were – though I don't seem to remember him mentioning his wife or his kids once while we were away. Ah, well. Maybe it's a natural thing, part of the way we divide up our lives into sections, the way a skilled cabinet-maker divides a jewellery-box into compartments with little thin sandalwood partitions.

The fact that Cratus had gone straight home somehow made me feel obliged to go and see King Leon at once, as if I had to make amends for his dereliction of duty. Silly, really; even a whole day wouldn't have made much odds. Or perhaps it was my heart, telling me that I wouldn't really have finished the mission and come home until I'd reported in and been given my discharge. If I'd had good news, of course, my attitude would probably have been quite different.

So I set off for the palace. I hadn't gone far when I saw a face I recognised – that's an understatement. A face that was squashed into my mind, like one of those wooden moulds they use for putting patterns on newly pressed cheeses. He saw me; he didn't try to get away, instead he headed straight for me.

'Cleander,' he said.

'Alastor,' I replied. 'You got home all right, then.'

He nodded. 'You too, by the looks of it. What about Cratus? And Sarpedon, and your sister?'

I wasn't sure I wanted to tell him; but the longer I talked to him in this reasonably calm and rational manner, the less likely it became that I'd pull my sword off my hip and stab him to death. 'Cratus is fine,' I said. 'Dusa, more or less. Sarpedon was fine the last time I saw him, a month or so ago. He's the King of Aegina now, in case you're interested.'

That shook him; but he rallied, like an experienced army after being charged. 'I'm really pleased,' he said. 'I know you've got no reason to believe me when I tell you this, but I was genuinely worried about you, all of you. I know we've been enemies, did dreadful things to each other while we were away; but that was there, not here. I'm hoping you can put all that out of your mind.'

I looked at him as if he had red-hot lava streaming out of his nose, but I didn't reply to what he'd said. Instead, I asked, 'What about Tachys?'

Alastor frowned. 'Bad news, I'm afraid – at least, I hope you'll take it as bad news, rather than being happy about it. He died.'

'Oh,' I said.

Alastor nodded. 'He caught a fever on the road between Sparta and Bassae. It came on him very suddenly, while we were out in the open; he woke up too ill to move, and by sundown he was dead. Nothing at all I could do.'

Poor Tachys, I thought; twice he'd picked the wrong side, and now he was dead. If we hadn't kidded him into coming with us, he'd never have blackened himself with the shame of betraying us, and he'd still be alive. I certainly didn't feel any pleasure, hearing he was dead; and at that moment at least, I couldn't really see any point in being angry with Alastor. That anger was part of the journey, part of being the someone else I'd left behind when I walked through the city gate, tethered outside like a pack-mule.

'Oh,' I said again.

'Anyway, you're safe,' Alastor went on. 'I've been calling round at your house every day to see if you'd got back – and that was wrong of me too, because it's made your wife worry. I'm sorry for that as well.'

I shrugged. 'Some god put it into your heart,' I replied. 'Don't upset yourself, there's no harm done.' I smiled, rather thinly. 'In any case,' I added, 'you've probably won, in which case the gods have shown us that you were in the right. And if I've won, I'll be happy enough to be magnanimous. Either way, I can't be bothered to fight you any more, now I'm home. As for Cratus,' I added, 'you'll have to make your own peace with him.'

Alastor nodded. 'I'll do that,' he said. 'Where is he? At home?'

'I expect so. Go and look, if you want. You might call in at my house on the way, tell them I'll be there shortly.'

He nodded again, and walked quickly away. What was all that

about? I asked my heart. Where did all that goodwill and forgiveness come from, right out of the dead ground? But my heart pretended it hadn't heard, and I let it go.

So I carried on to the palace, where the doorkeeper had to look twice before he recognised me.

'Come on,' I told him, 'you know me.'

He nodded, looking worried. 'We heard you were dead,' he said.

'Am I? That'd explain a lot. Now get out of my way, before I walk right through you.'

I do believe King Leon was genuinely pleased to see me; he shouted for tables and food and wine, shooed away whoever it was he'd been talking to, and virtually shoved me down into the seat next to him.

'Well,' he said, 'how did you get on? Any luck?'

A tiny part of me had been hoping that he'd given up on the idea of the games-with-nobody-dead, maybe even forgotten the reason why we'd all been away from court. I resolved to play for time. 'Would you like me to start at the beginning?' I asked.

He shook his head. 'No, save all that for later. Are they coming?'

My smile was as thin as the gold leaf on a locally made buckle. 'Some of them,' I replied. 'Probably.'

The hearts of kings can be very perceptive. 'Tell me the truth,' he said. 'You made a muck of it, didn't you?'

I nodded. 'It was bad luck, mostly,' I said. 'And it's not all bad. There's at least a dozen who said they'd come.'

His frown deepened. 'You've been all this time recruiting a dozen games-players?'

'We got side-tracked,' I admitted.

'Side-tracked.'

I nodded. 'Well, for one thing,' I said, 'we invaded Aegina.'

'You invaded Aegina.'

'Not just us – Cratus and me and Sarpedon. Actually, it was the Princes of Megara. All we did was talk them into it.'

'I see. Why?'

I took a deep breath. 'On behalf of a friend of ours. Well, not a friend exactly; not after he got us thrown out of Argos. Someone we met.'

'You got thrown out of Argos?'

Really, I wanted so much to lie to him. But lying to King Leon was never easy. 'For breaking up the Argive games,' I said.

'Right. And what are the Argive games?'

'Games they hold every year,' I told him.

'What, even if nobody's died?'

'That's right.'

'I see. And you broke them up.'

I nodded again. 'Actually, it wasn't us who did that, it was this friend of ours. Well, companion.'

'This stranger you happened to meet.'

'Yes.'

'And then,' Leon went on, 'after he'd broken up the Argive games, you helped him invade Aegina.'

'Yes.'

'You've been busy, haven't you?'

I tried to look him in the eyes, but I couldn't. 'It was a whole lot harder than I thought it would be,' I said. 'Just getting that far took a long time.'

'I can imagine,' Leon said. 'You went as far as Megara?'

'That's right.'

He thought for a moment. 'You must have made good time getting there and back,' he said.

'We had a ship on the way home.'

'I didn't know you owned a ship.'

'I don't. I mean, I didn't. It was a ship we stole in Corinth.'

'You stole a ship in Corinth.'

I nodded. 'We had to leave there quickly, you see.'

Leon closed his eyes for a moment. 'You were thrown out of Corinth, too.'

'Yes,' I told him. 'But it wasn't really our fault.'

'Let me guess,' Leon said. 'Your friend.'

'That's right.'

'I see. So, while I've been sitting here thinking you were out there trying to save my son, in fact you were stealing ships and getting expelled from cities and starting wars, on behalf of some stranger you met along the way.'

'Yes,' I said.

He shook his head and leaned back in his chair. 'Maybe I should have let you tell it from the beginning,' he said. 'Now tell me, honestly. These dozen games-players: are they going to turn up, or aren't they?'

'Some of them are bound to,' I replied.

He sighed. 'That's all right, then,' he said. 'Is there anything else you think I ought to know, or is that it?'

I thought for a moment. 'Tachys is dead,' I said.

'I see. Anything else?'

'Uncle Sarpedon's now the King of Aegina.'

'Really? I thought you invaded to help out this friend of yours.'

'Yes,' I said. 'But he got killed in the battle.'

King Leon smiled. 'You know,' he said, 'I can believe that, after what you've just told me. So that's what you've been up to, is it?'

'I suppose so,' I replied. 'But there's more to it than that, of course.'

He looked at me. 'You don't say. I'm amazed you found the time to do anything else.'

'It's not so much what we did,' I told him, 'as how we did it and why. If you'll just let me explain—'

He lifted his head. 'Later,' he said. 'Have you been home yet, or did you just come from your ship?'

'I haven't been home,' I told him.

'Then my heart tells me that'd be a good thing for you to do. It'll probably please your family, and it'll get you out of my sight for a while.'

So I went home.

It occurred to me, as I walked through the city, that maybe I could have expressed myself better when I reported to King Leon. But he'd asked me questions, and I'd told him the truth. I had given an accurate report, a true record. The thought depressed me.

Maybe because of that, I was feeling preoccupied and a little irritable when I reached the doors of my house; anyway, my temper wasn't improved when I found nobody waiting for me outside, and the doors closed. Clearly Alastor hadn't done me that one little favour I'd asked of him – typical, my heart told me, and serves you right for trusting him. I gave the doors a shove with my hand; they were barred on the inside. Odd, I thought.

But it was my house, I wasn't going to make a spectacle of myself by banging on my own front door and yelling. Better idea: I'd go for a walk, clear my head, calm down and come back a little later. So I strolled out to the edge of town, trying to make myself appreciate the familiar sights and sounds. I met a couple of acquaintances, who expressed surprise and a certain degree of pleasure at seeing me. I promised them a full account of my adventures once I'd settled in again. That made me feel a little better, and by the time I found myself back at my house I was rather more human.

The doors, though, were still closed. I couldn't make that out. Nothing for it, I decided, but to bash and yell after all.

I was at it a long time before the doors opened. It was my wife.

'Cleander,' she said.

I scowled. 'Oh, for pity's sake,' I said, 'is that any way to say hello, after I've been away so long?'

And then I caught a movement in her face. She wasn't actually looking at me; she was squinting over my shoulder. Why would anybody do that?

Unless . . .

I darted backwards and looked up at the upper-room balcony above my head. Sure enough, there was a man with one leg over the rail, about to climb down. To be precise, my second cousin Hegesilochus. Furthermore, he had his tunic on back to front and his cloak draped round his neck, for all the world as if he'd just dressed in a panic.

My wife squeaked and darted back inside the house, slamming the doors. Hegesilochus made the mistake of hesitating before clambering back over the rail; long enough for me to jump up, with a degree of suppleness and power that would have done credit to any games-player, and grab his ankle before it disappeared. Then I lifted my feet off the ground and pulled as hard as I could. As anticipated, Hegesilochus was dragged down over the rail and fell, almost but not quite on top of me. He landed on his hands and knees in a sort of crouch, his bum stuck up in the air – perfectly positioned to receive the spine-jarring kick I was all wound up to deliver. He howled, tried to scramble to his feet and fell over.

'Hello, cousin,' I said, and went to kick his head. But he was always a quick, slippery fellow, my cousin; he grabbed my foot with both hands and gave it a strong, sharp twist that made me scream with pain, before letting go and leaving me to drop to the dirt like an empty sack. By the time I pulled myself together, he was long gone.

Wonderful, I thought.

I got up slowly, gradually easing weight on to my very sore ankle, and hobbled across to the door. She'd barred it.

'Hey!' I shouted.

'Go away,' she replied. 'Don't hurt me. If you lay a finger on me, my brothers'll kill you.'

Now that was offensive; the thought of hitting her hadn't even crossed my mind. Shouting a lot, yes; maybe even kicking furniture and breaking crockery. But I'd never hit her in all the years we'd been married, and I wasn't proposing to start now.

'Don't be ridiculous,' I called back. 'And open the damned door.'

'No. You'll hit me.'

'Oh, for . . .' I was getting angry now. 'You want me to come back with an axe and bust the door down? Fine.'

She screamed, started yelling, 'Help! Help!' Which, needless to say, brought the neighbours out into the street. I felt an absolute idiot, and if I'd been able to move without hobbling I'd probably have retreated for pure shame. 'Open the *door*,' I roared, and the neighbours started to look uncomfortable. It was probably a tactical error on my part to draw my sword – all I was going to do was slide it between the doors, see if I could lever them apart, and all I'd have achieved, I'm sure, was a broken sword – but as soon as I had the thing out of the scabbard there were neighbours all over me, pulling the sword out of my hand and shoving me down into the dirt, on my knees.

'Grab hold of him,' someone behind me was saying. 'Madness has got him, you can see it in his eyes.'

'Told you no good would come of it,' someone else said, 'swanning off like that to foreign parts. Someone go and fetch his brother.'

'Why? Is he back yet? Here, Cleander, is your brother home too?'

I growled like a bear. 'Let go of me,' I said, 'or by the gods, I swear, I'll rip your arms off.'

'Definitely crazy,' someone else opined. 'We'd better tie him up and put him in the barn till he calms down.'

And they did, too, the bastards. Oh, a fine homecoming that was; up there with Agamemnon (hacked to death in his bath) and Ulysses, and all the other great wandering heroes you hear about in stories. Why is it, I wonder, when someone gets home from a long and dangerous journey, nobody's ever pleased to see him?

I wasn't in the barn for long. Shortly afterwards, Hegesilochus turned up with a bunch of his people to lay a formal complaint for assault and wounding – but at least they were kind enough to untie me, in return for a duly sworn ransom of fifteen yards of coloured cloth and a milch ewe.

'What happened to you?' Hegesilochus asked me, grinning, when I was free again.

'Don't ask,' I replied. 'And get out of my sight before I break your neck.'

He frowned. 'Are you threatening me?' he asked.

'Yes.'

'Thought so. All right,' he said, signalling to his men, 'tie him up again. You can forget about the ransom,' he added, as they did as they were told, 'I've changed my mind. You can damn well stay out here till you learn some manners.'

So they tied me up and went away. I wasn't alone for long, though; my wife came out to tell me she was going home to her father, taking the kids with her, and she'd be divorcing me as soon as she got there and could find the necessary witnesses.

'Fine,' I said. 'Now would you please undo these damned ropes?'

'Certainly not,' she said. 'You've gone crazy, you're dangerous. Everybody says so. You were coming after me with a sword.'

'No, I was just trying to – oh, forget it,' I said. 'Go away.'

After she'd gone, would you believe I actually fell asleep? Yes, hanging off the ropes, fast asleep. Well, it'd been a long, eventful day.

I don't know how long it was before I was prodded awake – by Alastor, who stood there looking very serious.

'Are you all right?' he said.

'Do I look all right?'

'No,' he replied. 'You've got a nasty cut on your forehead and a black eye.'

I scowled at him. 'It's all your fault,' I said.

'Me? I didn't do anything.'

'Exactly,' I told him. 'If you'd come round like I asked you to and warned my wife I was home, none of this would've happened. Where the hell did you get to?'

He lifted his head. 'I did come by earlier,' he said. 'I knocked on the door, but nobody answered, so I thought I'd come back later. Who tied you up, anyway?'

'None of your business,' I said. 'Look, just get these ropes loose and we'll call it all even between us, all right?'

'Sure,' he replied. 'You do mean that, don't you?'

'Of course I do. I swear by the River. Now untie the goddamn ropes.'

He didn't look happy, but he untied the ropes. 'Thank you,' I said. 'Now go away, please.'

He started to go away, then came back. 'Look,' he said, 'can I help you at all with anything? Only – I've got to say this, it strikes me as odd, a man comes home after several months away on a perilous mission and next thing you know, he's trussed up like a goat in his own barn.'

I looked at him. He really was trying to help.

'Thanks,' I said. 'I'll be all right. You go away.'

So off he went, and not long afterwards I followed him. The doors of my house were still shut, and the last thing I wanted to do was to make any more noise or fuss and have the neighbours round my ears again. So I decided to cut my losses and go to Cratus' house.

He wasn't pleased to see me. To be precise, he was in bed with his wife, having told the household to get lost, and was quite upset to find me banging on the door demanding to be let in. So I told him what had happened.

He didn't laugh. But he came close.

'Right,' he said, when I'd finished the story. 'And what do you want me to do about it?'

I frowned. 'For a start,' I said, 'give me a place to sleep for the night. Then—'

'I've got a better idea,' he interrupted. 'Why don't you go over to Sarpedon's place? After all, he won't be needing it. In fact, you could move in there till everything's sorted out – you'd be doing him a favour, looking after his stuff until we get it packed on the ship.'

My heart wasn't exactly filled with joy at the thought. But it was obvious enough that Cratus didn't want me in his house – fair enough, we'd been together for a long time without respite, which is bad enough for two brothers in the most harmonious of families – so it was either Sarpedon's place, or back home (Home home) and put up with Dusa . . .

'I'll do that,' I said. 'And in the morning, we'll get your people and my people and go and break down my door.'

He looked at me, and sighed. 'Well, that'll be something to look forward to. Goodnight.'

Then he closed the doors on me; so I traipsed over to Uncle's house, explained myself as best I could to his stone-faced household, and spent the night camped out among the dusty helmet-plumes and verdigrised sword-blades. Some homecoming.

News of my discomfiture was all round the city when we set off in the morning. Cratus called for me bright and early – 'Let's get this over with before there's anybody about,' he said gloomily, as soon as I opened the doors to him. He had an impressive number of men with him, including my people, all of whom were looking appropriately shamefaced and shifty, and thanks to our weight of numbers we didn't have any trouble with my dear neighbours. Of course, she'd barred the door from the inside and climbed down from the upper room on a borrowed ladder, so we did actually have to smash in the door, using a big log as a battering-ram – a damned shame, because my doors were solid oak, lovingly polished and fitted by me. I must have made a good job of them, because it took us a lot of time and effort to trash them.

We'd just finished when King Leon rolled up in his chariot,

escorted by a bunch of men at arms, to find out what all the commotion was in aid of. He was about the last person I wanted to see right then.

'You again,' he said. 'Still busy, I see.'

'It's a long story,' I told him.

He scowled. 'I don't like long stories,' he said; so I gave him a shortened version – my wife's left me, she locked me out before she went, so I had to bust the doors down to get in.

Leon nodded. 'Someone told me you were chasing her through the streets with an axe,' he said. 'I'm not surprised she left you. Also, I've had a complaint, assault with intent to degrade, from your cousin Hegesilochus.' He sighed. 'This sort of behaviour may have been all right where you've just come from,' he said, 'but we're quiet folks here in Elis. Knock it off, will you?'

I could have explained; but there are times when people just aren't in the mood to hear the whole truth. I promised I'd be good, and he went away again.

Cratus, on the other hand, was still there. 'Well,' he said, 'personally I can't think of any more ways for you to humiliate yourself, but I'm sure you can. I'll leave you to it.'

'Thank you,' I replied.

He waved a hand dismissively. 'Don't mention it,' he said. 'My pleasure. It almost made up for the last few months, watching your face when Leon appeared.'

Don't get me wrong. I love my brother, always have. You can tell how much I love him by the fact that, in spite of cracks like that, he's still alive.

Anyway; that was our homecoming, the end of our adventure in the wide world.

It didn't take long for things to get back to normal, as if our being away had been a wound, which healed over quickly and only left a small scar. Eventually I got to tell King Leon the whole story, from the day we left Elis to the moment he and his men rolled up outside my door; and once he'd heard it all he actually thanked me for everything I'd done, though it was more a never-mind-you-did-your-best kind of thank you than anything hopeful. My wife didn't divorce me after all; very magnanimously and in front of a large audience of her family she forgave me, after which it would have been churlish to ask her exactly what she and Hegesilochus had been up to, behind locked doors and in broad daylight. Likewise, my dear cousin abandoned his complaint against me, and I reciprocated the gesture of goodwill by not burning him to death in his house one dark night. For some time afterwards my neighbours tended to stare at me in alarm whenever I left the house, and scurry away whenever I came near; but you can't keep that sort of thing up for very long when you live in a city, and eventually they started trickling round to my doors, wanting to borrow hoes and whetstones and olive-presses and so forth, so it looks as if they found it in their hearts to forgive me, too.

Dusa was ominously quiet to begin with; she stayed indoors like a good little girl, spinning and mending and weaving, all the things she'd always maintained she hated most. That was peculiar, verging on scary, but I couldn't very well barge in, drag her away from the spinning-wheel and tell her to snap out of it. Then, quite suddenly, she announced that she was getting married. Furthermore, she was going to marry an entirely suitable, not to mention eligible lad, a distant cousin of ours on our mother's side, who'd been trailing along after her for years. Leucophron, his name was – a big, good-looking man with wide, bright teeth and broad shoulders, devoted to her, but – and this was why she'd never wanted anything to do with him before – about as intelligent as a small tree. I tried to figure it out, but I couldn't see it, unless she was somehow punishing herself – the oil-and-flour gag that led to Pentheus' death, I supposed, though she never mentioned it at all. It was only when I heard that this Leucophron was putting together a party to go and found a colony somewhere over the western sea – Italy or Sicily, some godforsaken place over in that direction – that I realised what she was up to. All she wanted was to get away – from Elis, from us, from the whole of the Peloponnese, and this was her best chance of doing it.

I didn't even try to talk her out of it; neither did Cratus, though he moaned to me about it until I begged him to stop. I guess she'd reached the point where she couldn't stand her life here any longer, and when someone's reached that point – well, Italy's better than the wrong side of the River, make no mistake about it. I could just see how well she would do as a colonist's wife; a woman's station in life is a good deal more flexible when you've got nothing at all except what you can carry in a ship, and nothing is firmly established.

They were married quite soon after that. We gave her a proper traditional wedding; led her through the streets by torchlight to her husband-to-be's house, lifted her over the threshold to avoid bad luck, sang the appropriate hymn, then went away. She didn't smile once; it was as if her mind was somewhere else, all the time. A month later they sailed for Italy, early one morning, without telling anybody, so I never got to say goodbye.

It was a long time before we heard news of the colony. Eventually a guest of ours mentioned that he'd spoken to a shipmaster who'd called there; everything was well, except that Leucophron the Founder had died from a poisoned cut during their first winter. His widow had immediately married again – one of the colonists, was all he could tell me – and she and her new husband were more or less running the place, insofar as anybody was. I got the impression that there were more important things to be done there than ruling and being ruled, such as clearing scrub, building terraces and fighting the locals. A few more reports, all in similar vein, trickled in from time to time; it was fourteen years later that I heard she'd died, nobody knew what of, leaving three sons and two daughters. Her eldest son, they told me, was now calling himself the King of Rhoma ('Stronghold'; that's what they finally decided to call the place) and wasn't making too bad a fist of things, all told. His name, according to the man who told me all this, was Pentheus.

So I had an uncle who was a king, and now (to the best of my knowledge) I've got a nephew who's a king too. I suppose that's not bad going, for a bunch of country boys. I can't help thinking, though, that my life has been a ship, blown off course by the fury of the winds, and I tend to consider Sarpedon and Dusa as having been washed overboard, while I stood by and did nothing. Silly, I know; but if I hadn't dreamed up the big idea, games-with-nobody-dead, and whisked them away from home and out into the perils of the world – well, they'd never have got to be kings and queens, and both of them would probably be dead now in any case. The idea that anything one does makes a difference is both misleading and dangerous, and I'm old enough now not to want a part of it any more. I should be dead too, by rights; five years ago I was desperately ill, I went blind and spent days lying on a bed coughing up blood. But I survived, and I have no idea why; maybe it was just to annoy Cratus, or get under the feet of my sons for a few years more, or maybe the gods have something for me to do that'll change the lives of everybody in Elis – I could be the one to open the gates to a besieging army, or intercede with the god to stop a devastating plague; or maybe the citizens of Rhoma will send a ship for me and I'll become their king, everybody else having died, and do something in the years left to me that'll save them from extinction or bring about their annihilation. Maybe I was left alive just to tell this story to someone who'll lay it to heart and go away and found their own games-with-nobody-dead, that'll be the wonder of the world and a great force for good or evil. Most likely not; most likely I'm still alive because I haven't died yet, just as I was on the day after I was born.

Anyway, that's the end of the story. I hope you liked it.

The Phoenician, who'd been starting to nod, sat up.

'Is that it?' he said. 'What about the games? Did any of them turn up in the end?'

Cleander smiled. 'Nice to know you're interested. That's the trouble with being blind, you can't see the expression on someone's face when you're telling him a story. Really, all you can do is talk to yourself and let other people eavesdrop. Of course, they drop hints now and then, like telling you to shut up, or pouring wine over your head.'

The Phoenician frowned. 'I can't believe you're really intending to stop there,' he said. 'Just when the story's starting to get – I mean, at the crowning moment.'

'You want to know what happened, then?'

'Well, of course.'

'Ah.' Cleander nodded. 'You want to hear about stirring deeds and great victories, stuff like that.'

'And whether the plan worked,' the Phoenician said. 'Whether the games were enough to make the people love Leon's feckless son. I mean, you can't have a story about people setting out to do a thing, and then not say whether they ever managed to do it or not.'

Cleander yawned. 'I suppose you're right,' he said. 'But tell me, which do you think is more important: the rise and fall of the Corinthian usurpers in Aegina, the founding and early kings of Rhoma, the vicissitudes of the kings of Elis, or who won the foot-race at the games-with-nobody-dead? Suppose you were alive – oh, five hundred years from now, and you were curious about how things came to be as they are. Suppose you could summon up a ghost from the past, a witness. What questions would you ask him?'

'I don't know,' the Phoenician replied. 'A lot would depend on what had happened in the meanwhile.'

'And of course,' Cleander went on, as if explaining something to a small child, 'you have no way of knowing what that might be.'

'True.'

'Obviously.' Cleander sounded like a man on the point of falling asleep. 'Aegina could be the most important place in the world, more important than Assyria. Maybe the overthrow of Pentheus' father was a turning point in the lives of all mankind, if Aegina goes on to build a mighty empire – in which case, you've heard the important part of the story, the bit that matters, and everything after it's just entertainment. Or maybe none of it matters at all.'

'Oh, come on,' Cratus interrupted. 'Now you're just fooling about with the poor fellow. Tell him about the games, and then we can all talk about something else, or go home.'

'Can't be bothered,' Cleander replied. 'You tell him, if you want. I think I'll go and sit outside for a while, get some air.'

'You mean some sleep,' Cratus said. 'You know your trouble? You're turning into an old man.'

Cleander lifted his head. 'That happened a long time ago,' he said.

CHAPTER SEVENTEEN

The games (Cratus said). Ah yes. Well.

We'd told everybody who'd listen that the games would be held at the time of the second full moon after the summer solstice, just after the rising of Orion, after threshing but before ploughing the fallow. It seemed to be the likeliest time of year, when there's not much work needing to be done on the land, but before winter sets in and makes getting about even harder than usual. Actually, we were thinking more of the Eleans who were going to come and watch than of the games-players themselves – what better way to spend the hottest, laziest part of the year than lying in the sun watching other people work up a sweat, we thought.

Harvest came and went with the rising of the Pleiades. It was a good year, so good that nobody had time to think about much else; because it was such a good harvest, with so much to get in, there weren't enough itinerant day-labourers to go round, which meant that we were working very long days, painfully aware that with every day that passed we were getting more and more behind. Tempers and patience got shorter as the work piled up, and nobody was in the mood to be fussed over something as remote and frivolous as games-playing. I certainly wasn't, and I was supposed to be one of the organisers.

Well, you know harvest. Every year, you can't imagine how you're possibly going to manage to get it all cut, shifted, threshed and stored; and every year you manage, just about. Every year, as soon as you figure you've finally got it under control and should be able to cope, either a freak wind batters down your standing corn and lets the crows in on the laid patches, or a neighbour breaks his leg and you have to help get his harvest in as well as your own; or there's a raid on the herds from across the border, or a fire, or some crowstruck thing that sets you off worrying all over again. Conversely, when the miracle's been achieved yet again, and you can stand in the doorway of your barn and count sealed jars until your eyes start to swim, you're so happy you'd agree to anything, and the whole world is your friend. Also, you've got a twelve-day thirst that won't loosen up for anything less than a full jar of the good stuff, blended with honey and spiced with nutmeg and cheese.

So, from that point of view it was a good time of year to hold games, assuming someone else had already made all the arrangements. Sadly, however, that wasn't quite the case as far as we were concerned. So instead of being able to take it easy and drink ourselves silly like normal human beings, Cleander and I suddenly found ourselves rushing about like sheep when there's a wolf in the pen, trying desperately to sort out things we should have addressed long before. I wouldn't have minded, but I was so tired after all those days with the sun on my neck, gliding a scythe and shouldering enormous great sheaves on the end of a pitchfork, that it was all I could do not to fall asleep standing up, like a horse, whenever I was out and supposedly on games business.

First priority was to find somewhere large enough to hold the damn games. Here Cleander dug his heels in and refused to be shifted; we were going to use the site he'd picked out (Dusa had seen it in a dream, if you remember), away south of the city beside the Alpheus river. It was no use pointing out that all the games-players we'd invited wouldn't know to go there, having been told the games were going to be in Elis proper. No problem, Cleander replied; when they can't find the games they'll ask in the city where everything's happening, and people will send them to the site. It's useless trying to argue with my brother when he's dead set on something. King Leon couldn't do it; I couldn't be bothered to try.

So we loaded up some mules and a cart with tools and set off for the place we'd found – seemed like a lifetime ago. It was still there; it hadn't been swallowed up in an earthquake, the river hadn't come roaring up and flooded it (actually, that part of the plain can flood like you wouldn't believe, just to the south and west of the spot Cleander had set his heart on; but we didn't know that then, of course).

First job was to clear a games-field in the middle, which meant cutting down a few trees, grubbing out their roots with crowbars and picks, levering out stones, filling holes, raking and levelling. Hard work on a hot day (and it was a hot summer that year) and the men we'd brought with us – well, they were the sort of people who tend to be available for that sort of work, the kind with absolutely nothing better to do. Their hearts weren't in it, let's say. In the end, it was generally quicker and easier to do the job ourselves than badger them into doing it, and they spent most of the time sitting in the shade of the cart, watching us like – well, like the audience at the games.

Once we'd done that, we set about making a stand, somewhere the distinguished guests – King Leon and his household, us, those of the better sort Leon wanted to keep his eye on – could get a good view from. For that we needed to raise an earth bank, firm it up, drive in some posts and build a platform, with a few raised tiers, like terraces on a hillside, for putting benches on. Digging the bank out was an awful chore, and of course we'd thoroughly underestimated the amount of timber we'd need, which meant dragging up the little hill to the north of the field, felling the lumber we needed out of the woods there, logging and planking it on site and then carting it back down the hill, with only our dozen or so mules and a few bits of rope. That part of it nearly killed us. I can clearly remember how completely exhausted I was one afternoon, after I'd spent the morning splitting a fat, knotty old pine into planks with nothing but a big hammer and some beaten-up old bronze wedges. Every time I whacked a wedge, the shock ran up my arms and made my teeth hurt, while the palms of my hands and the bases of my fingers were covered in squidgy white blisters. I'll give Cleander his due, though; he really worked hard, more so than me even. In fact, I don't know when I've seen a man go about a job with such cold determination, like he was at war with every billet of lumber, tool and length of rope. Scary, in a way.

We got the stand finished, more or less. It wasn't a thing of beauty; rough-hewn green timber, all adze-marks and botched joints, but at least it showed willing. All that remained was to pace and mark out the courses for the chariot and foot races, dig channels for the start lines and pile up stones for the finishes and turning-points for the chariots; job done.

'If nobody turns up,' Cleander said, as we stood and gazed at what we'd achieved, 'we're going to look such fools.'

'Relax,' I told him. 'They'll come. They said they were going to. Think how mad keen some of them were.' I sat down on the turning-point and stretched out my legs. 'The only thing that worries me is – well, there's two, actually. First, I want you to know that my heart really objects to this idea of having me pretend to be the famous Milon in the wrestling. Why can't Bias do it?

'Bias? Who the hell is Bias?'

'You remember. The helmsman of our ship—'

'Oh, him.' Cleander shook his head. 'No, hopeless, doesn't look a bit like him.'

I frowned. 'Milon's been dead two hundred years. How would you know what he looks like?'

Cleander pursed his lips. 'Well, I know for a fact he didn't look like that helmsman. For one thing, his eyes are too close together. Milon would never have looked like that. Milon was a *gentleman*.'

I couldn't be bothered to argue. 'Well, I'm not doing it,' I said. 'Find some other poor fool.'

'We'll see,' Cleander said. 'If we get enough real wrestlers, you can forget about it.'

'Thank you very much. Second, how are we going to fix things so that our young clown of a prince definitely wins the foot-race?'

Cleander frowned. 'We can't,' he replied. 'Games-players like the ones we've got coming, you can't bribe them or frighten them.

He'll just have to take his chances, do his best. If the god wants him to win . . .'

'He'll inspire our hearts with a foolproof way of cheating,' I interrupted, 'because as sure as winter, His Diminutive Majesty isn't going to stand a chance against some of the types we've come across. And if he loses – well, we'll have wasted our time, from start to finish.'

'Maybe.' Cleander sighed. 'Maybe not. The way I figure it, just seeing their prince out there, in the company of all those famous and exotic foreign games-players, the Eleans'll start looking at him in a new light, as someone they can feel proud of, worthy of their respect. That's what I'm banking on, anyway,' he continued, 'because you're right, that kid couldn't win a race if all the other runners had just been cut off at the knee.'

Nobody came.

Why they didn't come I still don't know, even after all these years. The second new moon waxed and waned; we took to posting men at the gates, to let us know as soon as a foreigner arrived; we posted men down at the field, in case they went straight there instead of coming to the city first (though how they'd have known to do that, we didn't even speculate). We ended up sending runners up and down the roads, looking for straying games-players who'd lost their way.

Nobody came.

At one stage, Leon decided it must be because Alastor and Prince Oeleus – you remember, the lad who stood to become king if our Prince Gormless failed to capture the hearts and minds of the people – because they'd been sending out their people to intercept the games-players and either beat them up on the road or lie to them, say the games had been cancelled or there was the plague or something; anyway, he'd convinced himself of this, so he had his men-at-arms bring them both in to the palace one morning just before dawn. They were both, understandably, scared stiff; and when Leon started yelling and cursing at them, they just acted dumb and frightened (because they were), which made Leon even more suspicious. He gave them the sort of working over you'd remember all your life – threatened to confiscate their property, exile them, have them strung up in front of the whole city; and the more they gabbled and jerked their heads about, the more convinced Leon was that they'd been up to all kinds of no good, and the louder and meaner he became. In the end he got himself so worked up that his son the prince, who'd been standing there in the background quietly dying of shame and embarrassment, stepped forward and told his father – in front of his two mortal enemies – to get a grip on himself and stop acting like the god had put Madness in his heart. That shook Leon up so much that he let Alastor and Oeleus go – and from that day on, though they carried on needling and scheming quietly in the background, they never tried anything that could possibly be proved against them, and kept out of the way of both King Leon and his son as much as possible.

Well, time was getting on; either the games had to go ahead or be cancelled, otherwise it'd just be ridiculous. Leon sent for us – not quite the men-at-arms-just-before-dawn approach, but not far off it – and asked us what we were planning to do about this mess we'd got him into.

'We've got to hold the games,' Cleander said. 'There'll be bloodshed otherwise, not to mention the harm it'll do.'

'All right,' Leon said, his voice ominously soft. 'And who do you propose is going to play these games, since you haven't managed to bring me one single, solitary foreigner?'

Annoying, that he'd chosen to focus on the one nagging little question we didn't have an answer to. 'We'll find someone,' Cleander said briskly. 'That's not a problem. We've got plenty of good games-players – right here in Elis, round and about.' He made a vague circular gesture with his hands, presumably intended to convey the infinite resources at our disposal. 'And you know,' he went on, 'when it comes right down to it, people don't really want to see foreigners doing well in games and stuff, they want to see the local boys doing well and winning the prizes. That's what it's all about, surely.'

Leon scowled mustard. 'And that's why you've been fluttering all round the Peloponnese all these months, is it; on purpose *not* to find foreigners who'll beat the shit out of the local talent.' He sighed and lifted his head. 'Too late to do anything about it now,' he said, 'we'll just have to struggle through as best we can, try to limit the damage you've done. When this is all over, though, I'm going to make you two regret the day you ever heard of games-playing. Understood?'

With that delightful prospect to look forward to, we set about finding games-players. Of course, by now we could do the patter as easily as an archer nocks an arrow, without thinking or looking; as for our friends and neighbours, it was a mixed response. For every one who couldn't see the point if there weren't going to be any famous offcomers to compete against, there were two who'd been put off by the thought that they didn't stand a chance against big names from Argos or Corinth, so by the time we were done, we had quantity. But no quality.

'Let's face it,' I told Cleander as we walked back from the southern border, where we'd been recruiting, 'the people who want to take part are precisely the people nobody's going to want to see. I don't care what you said to Leon; if we carry on like this, it's going to be a disaster. What we need are foreigners.'

Cleander looked at me as if I was being annoying on purpose. 'Fine,' he said. 'But we haven't got any, have we? Or haven't you been paying attention?'

I scowled at him; I wasn't in the mood. 'Then we'll just have to make some, won't we?'

He stopped and looked closely at me. 'You're not well, are you?' he said. 'Maybe what you need is a couple of days in a dark, locked barn, just to clear your head.'

'Don't be stupid. We've got to find some offcomers and pass them off as foreign games-players. After all, who the hell is going to know the difference around here?'

He was about to say something offensive, but hesitated. 'And where are you going to get these people from?' he asked.

I thought for a moment. 'A ship,' I said. 'I wish I'd thought of it earlier, we could have got the Megarans to come back. But there's bound to be a ship up at Peneus-mouth sooner or later; and where there's a ship, there's foreigners.'

I could see the thought seeping through into his heart, like blood showing through a tunic. 'We'd never get away with it,' he said. 'It'll be obvious they're not the better sort as soon as they walk on the field.'

'No it won't,' I replied. 'Foreigners, remember? All foreigners look alike to us.'

'You say that,' Cleander said uncertainly, 'but it's not going to work. A games-player looks like a games-player, a sailor looks like a sailor. You can't fool people like that.'

I frowned. 'We'll see,' I said. 'After all, it's not like we've got a choice. Tell you what: we'll scrub round all the other events, just have the foot-race. Then we can make out we've got a really fantastic field – Cleonymus of Athens, Menippus of Sicyon, Lydus of Thebes, Philonetor of Rhodes—'

Cleander stared at me. 'Who are all those people?' he asked.

'I don't know, I just made them up. But they'll do, won't they? After all, what we need is foreign games-players; a foreigner's someone who comes from far away, a games-player is a man who plays a game.'

Cleander shook his head. 'Not quite. A games-player is a *nobleman* who plays a game. You're suggesting we try to pass off a bunch of sailors as noblemen.'

I smiled. 'Relax,' I said. 'I'll say it again. Nobody will ever know. And besides,' I added, widening the grin a little, 'who knows, we might get lucky. Maybe all the sailors will turn out to be exiled noblemen – you know, the sort who are princes in their own country.'

There was indeed a ship at Peneus-mouth. And it did indeed contain a crew of foreigners. Extremely foreign foreigners. Not to put too fine a point on it, pirates.

Not particularly competent pirates, either. Apparently they'd set out from the south-eastern end of Sicily, so long ago they couldn't remember when, and managed to get so far off course that the first land they saw was the coast of Epirus (they'd been headed for Trapezus, a city in north-west Sicily, and had been wondering all the way across the open sea why it was taking them so long). Off

Epirus they sighted what looked like a nice fat ship, so they attacked; thanks to some fairly impressive heroics by a couple of their best fighting-men they managed to get away with their lives, but their intended victim chased them all the way from Corcyra to Leucas before breaking off to go after a likelier-looking victim –

('You mean,' I interrupted, 'you attacked another pirate ship?'

'Yes.'

'Ah. A *real* pirate ship.'

'Fuck off.'

'I see. Please, go on.')

– and all this excitement left them with a broken rudder, precious little in the way of food or water, and only the sketchiest notion of where they were. Fortunately, as they drifted down the coast they came across what looked like a small, defenceless fishing village . . .

It was a close thing in the end. At one point it looked as if they hadn't got a chance, but just when the fighting was at its fiercest they managed to grab a hostage or two and barricade themselves in a blacksmith's shop. After three days without food and only a jar of the foul, oily water the smith used for quenching hot metal in, the villagers let most of them go (they had to hand over their leader to be ceremonially hanged, drawn and quartered, but after what he'd put them through, they reckoned the villagers were just saving them a job) and they scuttled back to their ship as fast as they could go. A following wind got them out of there agreeably quickly, then scraped them against some submerged rocks and suddenly dropped, leaving them bailing frantically in order to stay afloat.

They were becalmed for two days and a night; then another freak gale picked them up and rammed them into Peneus-mouth, where they were (mostly) able to abandon ship before the storm piled it on to the rocks. Out of the fifty who left home, there were twelve survivors; and at the thought of doing something as safe and restful as impersonating foreign noblemen they nearly cried for joy. So that was all right.

We sat them round their fire and explained what they had to do, who they were meant to be, and so forth. At times it was hard going. Half of them weren't Sons of the Achaeans, or anything like us at all, though all of them could understand the language, just about; but there were two or three of them who simply couldn't pronounce the names we'd given them, so we had to think of different ones that were shorter and easier to say. There was one man – I think he may have been some kind of Phoenician, in fact – who couldn't even get his tongue round Melas son of Leucas of Argos; it came out something like Mewa son of Luha of Agwa, and we decided that he'd have to be Streuthes son of Chelidon, the famous deaf-and-dumb-from-birth games-player from Lemnos. But he was a big, tall, strong man, and when I asked some of his mates if he was any good at running, they replied that he'd made a pretty fair fist of it during the battle against the villagers, so probably yes.

So we had a dozen genuine foreigners, whom we'd transformed by the magic of a simple lie into Athenians, Argives, Spartans, Thebans, Corinthians, Cretans, islanders, even (a nice touch of my own) a Trojan prince in exile, directly descended from King Priam himself. The next step was to tell King Leon the good news, if possible without giving him cause to wonder how we'd suddenly managed to come up with the goods after so many months of failure.

'Easy,' Cleander said – he was getting the hang of this lying business by now. 'It's all our fault, naturally; we told them the third new moon after solstice, not the second; and then we forgot. Anyway, they're here now, so no harm done.'

As Cleander explained all this to the king, I'll admit I started to feel a bit worried about him. You see, it was almost as if he'd managed to convince himself that all the lies we'd made up were actually true. All that stuff about, Well, they're foreigners and they can run, so they're foreign runners – he'd taken it straight to heart, also the princes-in-their-own-country thing I'd said as a joke. Half the time, I think he actually believed it himself. Anyway, he made it sound so convincing that, for the first time since we got home, Leon actually seemed pleased with us. I only hoped we'd be able to keep it up long enough to see off these confounded games and send our piratical friends on their way. I wasn't bothered about us – Cleander and me. I'm a born liar, and Cleander had got himself fooled, so we were all right. No, what bothered me was our twelve prize specimens, who got over their pathetic gratitude at being rescued far too quickly for my liking and started throwing themselves into the parts we'd given them with just a scrape too much enthusiasm. Lithus the Corinthian, for example (can't remember his real name; couldn't say it if I could), soon got very boring indeed boasting about his games-playing exploits at this and that celebrated funeral, and as he got carried away, so he made more and more obvious mistakes. He'd won first prize at the funeral games of Pylades of Argos, he told us – but Pylades was the special friend of Orestes, Agamemnon's son, and must have died more than a hundred years ago. Luckily, he came across as a genuine Achaean games-player telling spurious tales of his own exploits, rather than a complete and utter fake – in a way, that made him all the more convincing. I didn't like it, though. It made me nervous. In fact, I was as jumpy as a hare at harvest time, whereas Cleander seemed to be completely relaxed and enjoying himself.

Sometimes I have this dream, where I'm a burglar and I wander into this completely deserted city; nobody in the streets, the houses all empty, everything so quiet it's enough to freeze your blood. The city is, of course, Elis, on the day of the games – but there weren't any break-ins in Elis that day. Even the burglars had gone off to watch the race.

They came on foot, in chariots, in carts, leading mules; they brought wine in little jars and bread and cheese in little baskets, sausages, cold meat wrapped in fat, figs, olives, garlic and honey; they came with their wives and their mothers and their children swaying astride their shoulders, faces I'd known all my life and faces I'd never seen before. They came with good humour and patience and hope, commodities that keep in the hot sun about as well as fresh milk. I haven't a clue how many of them there were; someone told me it was upwards of eight thousand, though I find that hard to believe. However many of them they were, it looked as if they were covering the plain like a rug thrown over a chair, or flies on a dead sheep – and the noise; well, imagine it, say five thousand people all chatting normally at the same time. It was a soft noise but deafening, like the hum of all the bees in the world, gathered together and dumped in one small place.

'This is very good,' King Leon murmured to me as we stared out over the crowd from our place on the platform. 'Or very bad, depending on how things go. One thing's for sure: if it fails, it won't be for apathy.'

I smiled wanly and didn't say anything. It's hard to talk when your tongue feels as if it's larger than your foot.

'It's just as well,' Leon continued, not looking at me, 'that all those foreigners showed up like they did. And isn't it odd, all of them turning out to be foot-racers.'

I nodded and made a respectful grunting noise.

'I'm just grateful,' Leon went on, 'that this show's been organised by people I can trust – do trust, implicitly. Otherwise I'd be sitting here thinking about how suddenly those games-players appeared from nowhere, and how wonderful it is that they're all taking part in the one event that absolutely had to happen. Not to mention,' he added, in exactly the same quiet, pleasant tone of voice, 'the really quite bizarre resemblance between the tall, thin Argive – what's his name? Alexicacus, that's it – and that cattle-thief we rounded up five or so years ago; you know, the one who managed to dig under the wall and escape, the night before we were due to string him up.'

'Really,' I squeaked. 'That's amazing.'

'I thought so,' Leon said. 'In fact, if I didn't know for certain that everything's straight and above board, because it's you two that's been organising everything, I'd be so worried I'd have to call the whole thing off, here and now, just in case it turned out that some *bastard* –' he spat the word in my ear '– some bastard was trying to make a fool out of me. Of course, all these people would be madder than hell when I got up to announce that the race'd been cancelled; but I'd tell them it was all right, I'd arrested the men responsible, and here they are.' He chuckled. 'You know,' he said, 'by the time this lot'd finished with them, you'd be lucky to find enough bits to fill a scent-bottle.'

I made a tiny tweeping noise at the back of my throat.

'But that's all beside the point,' Leon said. 'Thankfully. Call me squeamish if you like, but I never could stand the sight of a mob ripping someone to pieces with their bare hands. So depressing, don't you think, all that human nature in the raw? Phaedon,' he added.

'Sorry?' I managed to croak.

'The cattle-rustler who got away. I'm sure his name was Phaedon.'

For some odd reason, I found it hard to keep my attention from wandering during all the opening formalities – the sacrifice, the reading of the portents, the hymn, even Leon's speech to the crowd. Instead, my heart kept clogging up with rather horrible images of public disorder and violent death, even when I screwed my eyes so tightly shut I reckoned I'd pulled a cheek muscle.

I was sitting there brooding on such matters when Cleander poked me in the ribs with his elbow.

'Come on,' he hissed. 'We've got to go and start the race.'

I tell you, it seemed to take longer to walk from the platform to the middle than it had to cross the Peloponnese. I felt like every eye in the plain was watching me, waiting for me to betray my guilt by one false flick of an eyelid. In fact I don't suppose anybody noticed me at all. They were all gawping at the runners, who'd lined up and were standing with their toes in the groove, all shiny with fresh oil like a bunch of sardines. At least they seemed reasonably relaxed; and I was pleased to see that the prince, our boy, was at the end of the line-up where everybody could see him. That was, after all, the whole point of the exercise.

I was supposed to blow the trumpet for the start; but I couldn't, and I knew it, so I handed it to Cleander, who took it without saying a word. That meant my place was now at the finishing-line, where we'd piled up a little cairn of stones. It took even longer to walk the track than it had to get down there from the platform. I was an old man by the time I finally got there.

Typically, I was looking the other way when Cleander blew the horn. I turned round, and there in the distance – a hundred and ninety-two paces, or six hundred times the length of Hercules' foot, if you prefer – I saw the runners thundering up the track towards me.

You don't need me to tell you that we'd fixed the race. Fixed it? We'd rehearsed it five times, with Cleander playing the part of Prince Gormless; we'd trained those pirates like chariot horses, taught them exactly how they should run so as to lose without making it look obvious. We'd gone over it time and time again. It was the only foolproof part of the whole venture.

I'm telling you, though, we hadn't expected the prince to be quite such a classy runner. He tore away from the line like a hunting dog, kept his pace up, actually accelerated; but we'd planned it all on the basis that he was mediocre-competent at best. What I saw as I stood there gaping was the prince way out in front, the rest of the field panting along behind him trying to keep up. It looked awful, a clumsy fake, an obvious fix. If the rest of them had all fallen over at exactly the same moment, it could hardly have been any less convincing.

I guess even the prince felt embarrassed by the lead he'd built up by the halfway mark; I saw him glance back over his shoulder, notice the gap and slacken off the pace a little, as if he was giving them a chance to catch up. I groaned and looked away, oblivious to the noise of the crowd or the thumping of the runners' feet bouncing up through the ground at me –

– And then I heard the most terrific roar, and I looked round; there was one of our pirates, a Sicilian we'd decided to call Anax of Athens, tearing up the track at the prince's heels as if Cerberus himself was snapping at his heels. You never saw a man run like that; you wouldn't believe a man's body could put out so much effort, or endure such strain without tearing itself apart. It wasn't his arms and legs that were pushing him forward, it was purely an effort of will, of the mind refusing to accept the limitations of the body. And, as a result, he was gaining; the prince was aware of him and was piling the speed back on, but the gap was getting shorter and shorter – the question was, could he make up the ground in time to overtake and win, or had he left it too late to make his dash?

Well, of course he had, my heart told me; he's supposed to lose the damn race, he knows that if he wins, we'll cut him into slices and feed him to the tuna-fish. But looking at him, seeing that extraordinary effort, I couldn't accept what my heart was telling me. All the while, of course, the crowd were yelling themselves hoarse, cheering him on – our fake Athenian, you realise; they were howling and baying for the foreigner to win, this feckless fraud who couldn't even rob a ship right – and to my shame and disgust I realised that I was, too. But the prince was doing it now, running from the heart; and as the two of them closed in on me, with less than the length of a spear-shaft between them, it was the prince who looked to be pulling ahead, by no more than the breadth of a finger; whereupon my pirate suddenly found the god inside him, the one who held that last handful of strength and will, and surged up shoulder to shoulder with his man, so that if you'd been watching from the side you'd only have seen one runner, the nobleman and the scum of the earth combined, fused into a single figure in the moment of greatest pressure—

And then they were past me, down in the dirt and sprawling, gasping for breath like fish dying in the net. And – damn it – they'd gone by me so fast I hadn't seen them, I hadn't a clue which one of them had won the race.

It was so quiet, that moment, you could have heard a twig snap or a bird sing right on the other side of the plain.

Do something, you idiot, my heart screamed at me; so I did the only thing I could, in the circumstances. I took as deep a breath as I could hold without splitting open like a bullfrog, and yelled out the prince's name at the top of my voice.

Well, I don't know, do I? For all I know, he did win the race. And (for all I know) my friend the pirate was of royal blood, and a prince in his own country. But the race was a fix, our Prince Gormless had to win, that was why we were all there; it was why we'd crossed the Peloponnese, shed blood, fought a war. Tachys had died and Dusa had found and lost the man she loved, the Corinthian dynasty had been cleared out of Aegina and Uncle Sarpedon had become a king, all so that Leon's no-good son could win this race (the prince who was no good, the no-good who ran like a prince; merged together like molten copper in a crucible, at the crucial moment).

And besides, if I made the wrong decision, Leon was going to flay me alive.

It was, let's say, a popular decision; that is, the crowd screamed and yelled, the prince and the pirate helped each other up and grinned foolishly at each other on their way to the platform where

Leon was waiting to hand over the prizes. I assume somebody came third, but I can't remember anything about that.

And then it was over. People stood up, got their things together and went home. The pirates trooped off with Leon and Cleander for a celebration dinner at the palace, where Leon loaded them down with presents (over and above what they'd got from us) before saying fond farewells and getting the hell out of Elis, as they'd faithfully promised to do. (And they did; from start to finish, you couldn't fault them. Heroes, every one.)

I wandered over to the platform and nodded the pirate over to one side, where nobody could hear us over the racket.

'That was a good race,' I said.

He grinned feebly. 'I'm sorry,' he said. 'Don't know what came over me. I mean, I saw he was too far in front and it was looking silly, so I speeded up; and then the next thing I remember—'

I lifted my head. 'Did you win?' I asked him.

'Sorry?'

'Did you win?' I repeated. 'The race. Did you cross the line first, or did he?'

He thought for a moment, then lifted his head. 'Sorry,' he said, 'wasn't looking at the line. If you don't know, I guess nobody does.'

I smiled. 'Doesn't matter,' I replied.

So they all went away; except me. I stood there as the sun went down, gazing at where the race had been, and the crowd, and all. But what I saw was an empty stretch of flat ground, with nothing outside human memory to prove there'd been any excitement in that place beyond a few scratches in the dirt.

'Coroebus,' the Phoenician said.

'I beg your pardon?' Cratus replied.

'At the beginning,' said the Phoenician. 'You said, "This is the story of Coroebus." Which one was he?'

'What? Oh, the prince, Leon's son. Didn't I mention that?'

The Phoenician shook his head. 'And did it work? Did Coroebus get to be king after all?'

Cratus looked at Palamedes, who nodded. 'Oh, he got to be king all right, for about three years. Wasn't bad at it, either, in the event. But then he caught a bad chill and died, and Prince Oeleus took his place after all. My uncle,' Palamedes added, 'on my mother's side.'

The Phoenician looked at him. 'Oh,' he said. 'So,' he went on, 'it wasn't all a waste of time, then; or at least it was, because Coroebus died and Oen – I mean, your uncle became king. I'm not sure if that's a happy ending or a sad one, really.'

Palamedes smiled. 'I'm not even sure it's an ending,' he said. 'After all, human life isn't a race, where you cross a line and you know it's all over. There's all the stuff that went before, and all the stuff that's going to come after, you never know what was the actual race and what was just the preparations for it. As often as not, you can't even be sure what happened, or who it happened to, or anything. And a story's only worth repeating if it's a good story.'

The Phoenician thought for a moment. 'I suppose so,' he said. 'You know, if you people were to learn about making the scratches-on-waxed-board I was telling you about—'

Palamedes yawned. 'Oh, for pity's sake,' he said. 'Somebody give the man another drink quick, before he starts off all over again.'